continued...

Homeplace

BETH MASSIE

BERKLEY BOOKS, NEW YORK

THE BERKLEY PUBLISHING GROUP
Published by the Penguin Group
Penguin Group (USA) Inc.
375 Hudson Street, New York, New York 10014, USA
Penguin Group (Canada), 90 Eglinton Avenue East, Suite 700, Toronto, Ontario M4P 2Y3, Canada
(a division of Pearson Penguin Canada Inc.)
Penguin Books Ltd., 80 Strand, London WC2R 0RL, England
Penguin Group Ireland, 25 St. Stephen's Green, Dublin 2, Ireland (a division of Penguin Books Ltd.)
Penguin Group (Australia), 250 Camberwell Road, Camberwell, Victoria 3124, Australia
(a division of Pearson Australia Group Pty. Ltd.)
Penguin Books India Pvt. Ltd., 11 Community Centre, Panchsheel Park, New Delhi—110 017, India
Penguin Group (NZ), 67 Apollo Drive, Rosedale, North Shore 0745, Auckland, New Zealand
(a division of Pearson New Zealand Ltd.)
Penguin Books (South Africa) (Pty.) Ltd., 24 Sturdee Avenue, Rosebank, Johannesburg 2196,
South Africa

Penguin Books Ltd., Registered Offices: 80 Strand, London WC2R 0RL, England

This is a work of fiction. Names, characters, places, and incidents either are the product of the author's imagination or are used fictitiously, and any resemblance to actual persons, living or dead, business establishments, events, or locales is entirely coincidental.

HOMEPLACE

A Berkley Book / published by arrangement with the author

PRINTING HISTORY
Berkley edition / August 2007

Copyright © 2007 by Elizabeth Massie.
Interior text design by Laura K. Corless.

ISBN: 978-0-425-21689-7

BERKLEY®
Berkley Books are published by The Berkley Publishing Group,
a division of Penguin Group (USA) Inc.,
375 Hudson Street, New York, New York 10014.
BERKLEY® is a registered trademark of Penguin Group (USA) Inc.
The "B" design is a trademark belonging to Penguin Group (USA) Inc.

PRINTED IN THE UNITED STATES OF AMERICA

10 9 8 7 6 5 4 3 2 1

This book is dedicated to:

Waynesboro High School's Class of 1971,
for the memories and continued fun;
Ginjer Buchanan, for making this book possible;
Anya Rothman, the newest and sweetest
member of our Virginia family;
and Cortney Skinner, the most wonderful man in the world.

"Night, the mother of fear and mystery,
was coming upon me."

—H.G. Wells, *The War of the Worlds*.

"We are sons of yesterday, not of the morning.
The past is our mortal mother, no dead thing.
Our future constantly reflects her to the soul."

—George Meredith, *The Adventures of Harry Richmond*.

"Oh, haggard mind, groping darkly through the past...
seeking but a moment's rest among the long-forgotten
haunts of childhood, and the resorts of yesterday;
and dimly finding fear and horror everywhere!"

—Charles Dickens, *Martin Chuzzlewit*.

PROLOGUE

~

They waited until twilight to uncover the well.

It had been a long afternoon, hot with the kind of heat that comes in late August when rains and soft grasses have long given up the ghost, but spiny weeds and Japanese beetles have not. The driveway that led to the farmhouse was split open in several places, revealing bowels of dry red clay. Cars sat at various angles in front of the house on the weedy, rocky piece of field the grown-ups called the "yard." Each vehicle was reduced to the same rusty-orange by a heavy coating of Virginia dust.

The birthday dinner started at six-thirty, well past the time when the kids were ready to eat. The guests had arrived mid-afternoon, bearing casserole dishes; biscuit-filled baskets; fruit pies in aluminum pans; plastic coolers loaded down with sodas, lemonade, beer, and melting ice; and stories of how long it had taken to get to Homeplace, how hard it was to find the tree-shrouded entrance, and how fillings had almost popped loose on the rutted driveway. Several of the men hauled card tables from their cars and set them up in the yard, though by five p.m. they'd been refolded and reset inside the house. "Too damned hot and too damned buggy," muttered one of the men, not knowing some of the children were within earshot of his profanity, hiding under the front porch.

The kids found each other within minutes of their respective arrivals, and, after an obligatory attempt by the parents to make them go into the living room to acknowledge the shriveled old woman whose birthday they'd come to celebrate, had run outside and crawled up under the porch. They sat cross-legged in the summer-sticky shadows, close but not touching, batting flies from their faces and knocking ants off their knees, while the adults above them shifted about on the creaky porch, talking in monotones about the weather, illnesses, and how nice Ellen Alexander looked after all these years.

There were four kids. Joey was eleven, a loud-mouthed know-it-all with brown hair and a crooked nose. Nine-year-old Melissa was a silent, chubby blonde decked out in a pink halter top and a pair of green polyester shorts so tight she had to keep digging the fabric out of the crack of her rear end. Seven-year-old, auburn-haired Charlene bore a strong resemblance to her nine-year-old stepbrother, Ryan, with his thin frame, red hair, and brown eyes.

Charlene and Ryan had come to Nelson County with their mother, traveling south from their home in Washington DC. Charlene had been excited about going to a birthday party in the country, even for a ninety-year-old great-grandmother she'd never met. She'd imagined horses she could ride and goats she could pet. She'd pictured bales of hay to jump into and chickens to chase. She'd hoped her great-grandmother would give her chocolate sandwich cookies and they'd have a cookie-eating contest, like the grandmother on the television commercial. But Charlene's hopes had faded the minute the family station wagon had pulled into the "yard." There were no animals with the exception of a circle of buzzards over the forest to the back of the house. No barns, no bales of hay. And Charlene's image of a charming, white-haired, cookie-bearing woman died the moment she and Ryan stepped across the threshold of the farmhouse and stood in the shadowy hallway outside the living room door.

At first, Charlene didn't see the old woman near the win-

dow. The room was cluttered with odds and ends—a piano
and sofa, several chairs, a corner cabinet filled with lots of little dishes, a small table with an old-fashioned fan that swayed
back and forth with a soft grinding of gears. The woman
seemed to be part of the gray wall, a section of water-stained
paint, unmoving, almost colorless. When she shifted in her
rocking chair, she came into view. Charlene's heart caught in
her chest. She looked immediately at the floor. In that moment, Charlene had seen all she wanted to see. Knobby hands
latched to the armrests. Thin white hair lifting and falling like
cobwebs in the breeze of the rotary fan. A face swiveling toward the door, the sagging skin covered in brown spots. The
winking eyes were deep-set, rheumy.

"Hello, there, Grandmother Ellen," said Charlene's
mother. Her voice didn't sound like her normal voice. It was
pinched, the way it sounded when she tried to be polite to Je-
hovah's Witnesses who showed up uninvited at their house.
"Happy birthday. It's so good to see you." Then, "Go give
your great grandmother a hug." She pulled on Charlene's and
Ryan's arms simultaneously, moving them forward while she,
herself, stood in place.

Ryan obediently crossed the bare floor of the parlor to the
woman in the chair. From beneath her bangs, Charlene
watched her brother's sneakered feet go in slowly, then come
out faster. Charlene could smell the granny woman now, a
combination of soured milk and baby powder.

"Charlene? Honey?" said Mom.

Charlene didn't move.

"Charlene?" The voice was lower now. More insistent.

Charlene didn't move. A trickle of sweat cut the back of
her neck. In the wooden chair across the room, the old woman
tapped her dentures together, making a sound like little wet
seashells. She cleared her throat then coughed. Why didn't
she say anything? What was wrong with her?

Then the front door banged open. A man and woman came
in, brushing off dust and pulling on big, cheery smiles. Mom
turned, whipping Charlene and Ryan with her. "Oh, Ken,
Becky! Hey, great to see you made it!"

"Your mother couldn't make it?" asked the woman who was Becky.

Mom shook her head. "She broke her hip last week. Fell off a ladder changing a lightbulb in her bedroom."

"Ah. Too bad."

"Yes."

Mom's grip on Charlene's hand loosened. Charlene dipped back and away and scurried out through the screened door. Ryan followed.

There were daddy longlegs under the porch, dangling from the wood overhead, and there were mud dauber pipes on the lattice walls and cobwebs in the corners. The lumpy ground was pocked with holes the size of quarters. Joey claimed the holes were made by earthworms as big as snakes.

"Let me tell you," he said with a nod of certainty, "way out here in the country all sorts of stuff gets mutated. People. Animals. Bugs and worms."

Charlene tried to scramble to her feet but Ryan pulled her back down again. "It's just molehills, Charlene," Ryan said, staring hard at the crooked-nosed boy. "This kid doesn't know what he's talking about. I'm a Boy Scout and Boy Scouts know lots about animals. There aren't any mutated worms like that. Well, maybe in Africa."

Joey snapped up his hand like the school-crossing lady when kids tried to run into the road too soon. His face was war-streaked with the light that filtered through the narrow slats above. "You think I don't know what I'm talking about? I know a hell of a lot. How old are you, anyway?"

"Nine."

"I'm eleven. I'm two years older than you."

"So what?" said Ryan. "I know a guy lives down the street from us and he's forty-two. That's twenty-three years older than me. He still wears diapers and cries for his bottle."

"Nuh-uh."

"Yeah-huh."

"Nuh-uh."

"Yeah-huh."

Joey blew out a loud, sputtery breath, as if that proved his point. Melissa picked up a stick and put it in her mouth. Ryan rolled his eyes at Charlene.

In the dank beneath the porch, Charlene learned neither Melissa nor Joey was related to old Ellen Alexander. Joey's dad, a carpenter from the nearby town of Adams, had fixed the farmhouse stairs a couple years ago, though he had told his son he really didn't want to work on the Alexander house. "I think maybe it's 'cause the house smells like old lady," Joey explained. Melissa's mother and father had once rented part of the farmland to graze cattle. According to the chatter on the porch above, the other adults weren't related, either. One had fixed Ellen's truck back when she had a truck. Another had sold the old woman items at the Farm Bureau store in town. Two of them, Ken and Becky, were Charlene's mother's friends from Richmond, who came more as a favor than anything else. A couple others were next-farm neighbors.

"Why'd you come to the party?" Ryan asked Joey and Melissa. "You didn't have to. You aren't that old lady's grand-kids or anything." Melissa didn't know.

Joey puffed up and said, "My dad thinks she got money hidden in her house somewhere. Maybe in a safe or under her bed or stuffed in her freezer. So maybe if he's nice to her, she'll give him some of that money in her will."

Charlene slapped a mosquito from her cheek. "Your daddy tell you that?"

"Why else would we come to this stinky old place that smells like a stinky old lady?"

Charlene thought, *Why else?*

When the grown-ups at last went inside, the kids crawled out from under the porch to explore. Joey told them they needed a whacking stick to kill snakes that might come on them by surprise.

"You whack 'em with it," he explained as he handed each child a thin switch he'd snapped from an anemic bush by the house. "You break their backs and then they can't crawl any-more and they die."

"That's awful," said Charlene. She didn't like snakes but

the thought of one writhing for hours in the sun, trying its best to die, made her sad.

"That's not awful," said Joey. "It's what'll keep you from getting your little baby girl ankle bit. There's copperheads around here—rattlesnakes, too. You got to kill them before they kill you."

Ryan shrugged at Charlene, who said again, "It's still awful."

The kids meandered through the briars and the chicory, Joey and Melissa whipping the ground, Ryan dragging his stick behind him, Charlene carefully parting the grasses to watch for snake-sized worms. The first stop was the small cabin on the north side of the farmhouse. Its door was secured with a padlock encrusted with mud and rust. The windows were filthy. Charlene took her turn standing on a log to see in, but could make out nothing beyond her own warped reflection. She spit on the glass and rubbed it with her thumb, but that only made things worse. Joey said only babies spit on stuff.

Behind the farmhouse was a garden heavy with tomatoes, squash, and beans, some of which looked ready to pick and the rest rotting on the vines. Just beyond the garden was a lopsided pile of junk watched over by turbulent clouds of gnats. There was no official pathway to the pile, just a flattened lay of weeds where Ellen Alexander had trudged back and forth from the house, throwing things out—a dog-chewed chair, a dented TV tray, an old rusty grill, splintered lengths of wood riddled with nails, water-stained and molded bed pillows, plastic jugs, and cracked storage containers. The pile reminded Charlene of a piece of sculpture she'd seen once outside a Washington DC art museum, all angles and protrusions that made no sense.

"That old woman's crazy," said Joey, kicking at a rusted bucket. "All this shit dumped out here where black widow spiders and copperheads can hide."

"Hah!" giggled Melissa. "You said a bad word!"

"Crazy as shit," Joey said, pleased. "She could get somebody to haul this away, 'stead of making a mess like this. Nutty old bitch."

"Shut your big fat mouth," said Ryan.

Joey turned to Ryan. His lips drew up in a smirk. "She should be in a loony bin with chains and locks and bars."

"What's a loony bin?" asked Charlene.

"Shut your mouth, Joey," said Ryan.

"Don't you ever tell me to shut up," said Joey.

Charlene felt her fists draw up by her sides, though her insides trembled. "You're the stupid one! You're a big fat bully!"

Joey jammed his whipping stick under his arm and came up close to Charlene. He leaned down, almost touching his nose to hers. Charlene's heart picked up a fast and painful beat, but she didn't move.

The boy spoke slowly. His breath stunk like he hadn't brushed his teeth in a week. "I'll say whatever I want to, little girl. Don't ever talk bad to me, you hear? I'll take a whipping to you, break your back just like a snake."

Ryan grabbed Joey's shoulder and whirled the boy around so fast the stick flew from his hand. Joey stumbled over his feet but then popped up straight with a growl and slugged Ryan in the jaw. Ryan grunted and swung back. He missed. Joey drove a fist into Ryan's gut and Ryan crashed on his ass onto the bent TV tray, crumpling it further.

"Ow!" Ryan cried, clutching his stomach.

Melissa put her hands over her ears and squealed, "Mama! Mama!"

With that, Joey hopped back and waved his arms. "Hey, hey! I'm just kiddin' around! Just jokin', okay? We weren't really fightin'! We don't need mamas out here!"

Ryan wiped his face. It streaked, from either tears or sweat. He was breathing hard.

Joey lowered his voice. "Okay? I'm just goofin' is all. You call mamas out here and we'll have to go inside where that old woman is and sit there and listen to everybody talk about old-people stuff. You want that?"

"No," Charlene conceded.

"No," Ryan said as he stood on shaky legs and kicked the TV tray out of his way with a hollow thwack.

Melissa shook her head but kept her hands over her ears.

"But you can't hit anybody anymore," said Charlene. "You got to promise."

"No problem," said Joey. "This pile of junk is boring, anyway. Let's see what else is around here."

They circled the south side of the house, past a small, unlocked smokehouse that was empty but for some rags on the dirt floor and steel bars running the length of the ceiling. And then in the front yard, beside one of the station wagons, they found the well.

They would have missed it if it weren't for Charlene's stick steadily combing the weeds, back and forth, back and forth. The stick struck something solid in the tangle of dead vegetation. It was a large brick.

"Huh," said Charlene. She bent down and wriggled her fingers through the browned weeds and traced the brick. She tried to rock it back and forth, but it seemed glued to the ground.

"What you got?" asked Ryan.

"Brick."

"Brick, big deal," chided Joey. "Hey," he said, turning to Melissa. "You know you got a skull inside your head? A big old skull with eye sockets and everything?"

"No I don't," said Melissa.

"Yeah, you do."

The brick came free in Charlene's hand with a bit more tugging. The ground beneath it didn't feel like ground. It felt like a thin piece of crusted board.

"You're just trying to scare me," said Melissa. Her voice was quivery.

"Am I lying, Ryan? She's got a skull in her head. Hey, Ryan."

Ryan was on the ground now, next to Charlene, and had found another brick. He pounded the heel of his hands against it until it came free, then lifted it and tossed it aside. "What's this board under here?"

"I don't know," said Charlene. She found another brick near the first and wrangled it from the board. "Something."

Tracing the warped board, Charlene tried to yank it up from the ground. The heavy layer of growth and other obscured bricks held it down.

Joey stuck a piece of weed into his mouth. "Big deal, bricks. Watch your fingers or a snake'll get 'em. You think a whackin' stick's a dumb idea, but just you wait 'til you got a snake hanging off your thumb."

"Charlene!" The voice was sharp and clipped. Charlene spun about on her knees, catching one on a briar. She sucked air at the bite of pain.

"What?"

Her mother was on the front porch, her hands on her hips. Several other adults stood near her, shading their eyes.

"What?" Charlene repeated. She rubbed her knee and felt a spot of blood there.

"That's *ma'am*, Charlene."

"What? *Ma'am*."

"You kids stay away from that well. Come on now, go find somewhere else to play."

Well? There was a well under the board?

Charlene looked at Ryan. His face revealed the same sudden fascination that Charlene felt.

"I mean it!" called Mom. "Put those bricks back. Go find something else to do."

"Okay."

"Joey," said a woman in a pair of crop pants and a sleeveless shirt, waving a cigarette around like a wand. "You get away from there and stay away, you hear? We did *not* bring you all the way out here to get yourself hurt."

"Christ," Joey whispered.

"You hear me, Joey?"

"Yeah."

"You, too, Melissa," said a man in a white shirt and sunglasses.

"Okay, Daddy," said Melissa.

Charlene put one brick back, keeping her eye on her mom. That wasn't enough. She put a second brick back. Her mother seemed satisfied and turned with the rest of the adults to enter the house. Over her shoulder, Charlene's mother said, "Supper in a few minutes. Don't go far."

The kids didn't go far. They gathered inside the smokehouse, all urgent chatter and glances toward the door. Joey tried to take control. "When supper's over and the grown-ups aren't paying attention, I'll get the top off the well while you keep watch. I can do it quick since I'm bigger. Then you can all have a peek."

"No," said Ryan. "You, Charlene, and Melissa stay inside and sing for everybody. Something. Make it up. The grown-ups'll listen. They like kids singing. I'll get the top off the well and let you know what I find. It'll be a big secret except for us!"

"I want to get the top off," said Charlene. "I found it."

"You just found a brick," said Joey.

"Same thing."

"No, it isn't."

"Charlene, Ryan!" The voice cut through the smokehouse door. All the kids froze, as if they'd been discovered in their plans. "Time to eat!"

Charlene whispered to Joey, "Yes, it is."

Charlene begged her mother to let the kids eat on the front porch so they could watch for raccoons and skunks in the yard, though truth of the matter was that the idea of eating in the same room as the old woman had Charlene's stomach in knots. At first her mother hesitated, but Charlene's "please please please please?" worked, and so out through the screened door to the porch the table came, folded up under the arm of Joey's father, a rough-looking man with dark stained fingers. Charlene sat in her chair as Ryan brought her a paper plate from inside, loaded down with a scoop of beanie-weenies, some macaroni and cheese, fruit-filled Jell-O, and some barbecue chips. It wasn't brotherly love that did this; it was Charlene promising to give Ryan two dollars when they got home.

While the adults gabbed inside, first over supper and pie and then over birthday presents (Charlene's mom had wrapped up a pair of cinnamon-scented candles with little glass holders as well as a picture Charlene had drawn of the happy cows and chickens she'd hoped she'd find at Homeplace), the kids downed their dinner while trying to make the porch bounce up and down and seeing who could flick baked beans farthest into the yard. After the gifts came a white and blue birthday cake topped with two wax candles, one in the shape of a 9 and the other a 0. Charlene's mom cut the cake and brought pieces out to the kids first and then gave slices to the adults. Charlene could hear everyone oohing and ahhing at the cake, but heard not a word from the old woman in the living room. Charlene wondered if the great-grandmother could talk at all. Maybe she was so old her tongue had dried up and fallen out of her mouth.

Then Joey's dad said, "I brought some good stuff for anyone who wants a cup."

Charlene didn't know what good stuff was, but she wasn't going to go inside to find out. Joey picked up a glob of icing that had fallen off his piece of cake and flung it into Melissa's hair. Melissa squawked and pawed at the sticky mess while Joey said, "Hey, I was kiddin'! Now don't get all baby-actin' on me and call your mama."

The sky beyond the porch was darkening quickly, going ash silver then pewter gray. The trees on the far side of the yard grew together as their colors bled away. The house itself cast a huge and brief shadow across the weeds and the automobiles, as if a giant were rising up from behind, ready to swallow everything in its path. Tree frogs and cicadas awakened to chew the air with their raspy, nocturnal songs. Little blinking spots of light appeared over the yard, stitching erratic patterns among the cars.

Then Ryan leaned forward over his paper plate and said softly, "Let's open the well."

Charlene called through the door, "Mama, we're going to catch lightning bugs!"

Her mother called back, "Don't go far, honey. We'll need to leave soon."

The kids skittered off the porch.

Charlene was first to the well, though Joey tried to push

her out of the way. She plopped onto her knees and clawed a loose brick from the plywood board and tossed it aside. Melissa, Ryan, and Joey each took a corner and pounded the bricks free. Insects, invisible in the shadows, blew up and around Charlene's nose, making her sneeze and shake her head. She wondered about snake-sized worms. Did they come out at night? Did some live in the well? Was Ryan telling the truth that there was no such thing? In the oncoming night, impossible things seemed all the more possible.

"Got my side!" said Ryan in an urgent whisper. He pulled up on the weed-encrusted board and propped it on his knees so it wouldn't snap back down again. Joey had his side up next.

"Damn," Joey said. "It stinks in there."

"Shh!" said Charlene.

"But it does!"

"Shh!"

Charlene's side came up next, the rough edges of the plywood digging into her palms. From the void beneath the wood, she felt warm, wet tendrils of air crawl up and out around her fingers. Startled, she dropped the wood.

"Hey," said Ryan. "Pick that back up."

Charlene slowly lifted the wood again, keeping her fingers at the edge.

Melissa, panting and pouting, had her side up last. Ryan let Joey toss the board aside.

All four leaned over carefully and peered down into the lightless chasm.

"I think there's a flashlight in our car," said Joey. "Want me to go get it?"

"Yeah," said Ryan.

No, thought Charlene. *I don't want to see down in there.*

Joey skittered away as the other kids sat on their knees and stared into the maw. Ryan rhythmically, nervously snapped a stick into tiny pieces. *Twick-twick-twick.* There was no moon overhead; stars were just beginning to appear against the sky's navy backdrop. The air that rose up from the well was no longer warm, but a cold mist that smelled of mud, mildew, and sweet-sour decay. Beneath the chirping of night creatures and the sound of Ryan breaking the stick, Charlene could hear the pounding of her heart in her chest.

Twick-twick-twick.

Thump-thump-thump.

Melissa coughed. A grasshopper leapt onto Charlene's knee, causing her to start. She flicked it away. From inside the house, a man began to sing something in a loud, raspy voice. It sounded like Joey's dad. Maybe he was drunk. If he was, then it wouldn't be long before Charlene's mother hustled them away from Homeplace. Ryan picked up another stick to snap apart.

Twick-twick-twick-twick.

Joey was back, sliding into the grass like a player coming into home plate. He held up the flashlight like a trophy, and thumbed the switch. A beam immediately cut across the uneven sea of grasses.

"Okay," he said gleefully. "Here goes." He trained the flashlight's nose into the black hole.

Slowly, Charlene rose up on her knees to have a better look. Something with tiny wings hummed by her ear and she shook her head. Across the well, she could hear Joey panting. Back at the house, the singing continued, now accompanied by a woman's voice.

The well wasn't completely circular, as were the wells drawn in books of fairy tales and nursery rhymes. Instead, it was a lopsided oval, about three feet across and two feet wide, chopped from the earth not by a machine that carved tidy tunnels, but by old shovels and picks. The wall near the top of the well was wet and covered with a gray-green slime. It was made of some sort of brown stone, or what might have been stone long ago before earth had oozed out through the cracks to claim its rightful place again. Moist, black, stringy matter drifted back and forth against the wall, moving in a breeze or on its own. Charlene couldn't be certain which.

Melissa whined, "I wanna go in the house."

"Shhhh." Charlene's hands balled up against the ground.

"Shine it deeper," said Ryan.

Joey held his hand down into the well. He waved the flash-light back and forth. Light bounced off the damp walls. Stone-clinging centipedes scurried behind the algae and strands of black matter, seeking the eternal night that was their world.

"Deeper," said Ryan.

Joey scooted until his knees hung over the well's edge sev-eral inches. He leaned down even farther. Charlene squinted into the hole. The light carried at least twenty feet but then met with a black void that swallowed the light completely.

Ryan looked across the hole at Charlene. "Creepy," he said.

"Yeah."

"I think that's water down there. Smells like dead stuff."

Charlene felt a stinging inside her cheek and realized she'd bitten it. She shifted slightly, knocking several pebbles free from the well's lip. They fell into the hole, pattering softly against the wall. Charlene listened for the sound of them strik-ing water, but the sound didn't come.

"Wish I had a string," Joey said.

"Shhh," said Charlene.

"I could tie it to the flashlight and lower it even deeper."

"Yeah," said Ryan.

The inside of Charlene's cheek began to swell. She poked at it with her tongue. Melissa said, "Okay, we opened it. Let's put the top back now."

"Shut up."

"Really, it stinks. Let's put—"

And then a strangled wail erupted from the bowels of the well, parting the cold, putrid mist and rocketing upward to slap the children in their faces and knock them backward onto the ground. The sound was at once human and inhuman, a cry of pain and terror and furor. Joey's flashlight flew from his hand and tumbled end over end into the well. Charlene threw her hands over her eyes and screamed over the scream.

She screamed again.

Then there was silence. A silence like that of a barking dog that is suddenly shot dead.

And then, "Charlene? Get up."

It was her mother.

"Charlene, I said get up, it's time to go."

Charlene opened her eyes. The sky above was black streaked with thin bands of navy clouds. Her mother's face was in the center of the dark sky, as were Ryan's and Joey's.

Sitting up, Charlene saw that the well's cover was back in place. The other children were standing nearby, hands in pockets, looking sheepish. Except for Melissa, whose shorts were too tight, squeezing her pockets shut. She had her arms crossed over her round tummy.

"I see you tried to get that well cover off even when I said leave it alone," said Mom.

The look Ryan gave Charlene said, *Don't say a word.*

"It's time to go home. We'll talk about this later." Mom's voice was more tired than mad. "You and Ryan should go say good-bye to Grandmother Ellen, but she fell asleep in her chair."

Mom took hold of Charlene's and Ryan's hands and herded them to the car. Charlene glanced over at the well. The weeds were already rising back up around the warped plywood. Then she looked at the house, where a single light burned in the living room window and a motionless silhouette held place there. The other adults were clomping down the porch toward their own vehicles. Joey's dad and mother were arm in arm, still singing, some song Charlene didn't know. They seemed to be wobbling a bit.

Opening the car's back door, Mom tossed in the empty picnic basket and casserole dish.

Was I the only one who heard the scream?

Charlene tried to catch Ryan's attention as he trotted around the front of the car to get in the passenger's side, but he wouldn't look at her.

Mom touched Charlene on the shoulder and put on her happy voice again. "That was a nice visit, don't you think? And Grandmother Ellen really liked the picture you drew for her."

Charlene said nothing.

1

~

Charlene had eaten the worms before.

She remembered.

She remembered, and did not want to remember.

No...please no.

Her first realization was that she was a child again, with thin arms and scabby knees, and that she was being held down in darkness. The hands that held her were invisible. There were whispers above and around her, speaking in unintelligible hisses that bore into her ears like chittering termites. Saliva washed her mouth with a taste of brine, a dreaded expectation of what was to come.

Her second realization was the reason they were holding her down.

No, wait! I don't want to! Don't make me!

"Shhhh," something in the blackness whispered. "Shhh-hhh."

There were soft giggles. A single hand moved across Charlene's body, insistent and firm. Her skin prickled with its own, traitorous sense of pleasure even as her mind railed in horror.

Get up now, and get away!

"Shhhh."

And then the darkness directly above her parted like an ebony velvet curtain, revealing the face of the witch. It was bone white and dry, the eyes eager orange coals, the lips crusted and yellowed, the hair long, oily, and dark red. Charlene's body went rigid in obeisance to the gaze. Her brain, enraged, screamed silently into the blackness around her.

Get away! Leave me alone!

"Now, shhh, now," hissed the witch. She winked both her eyes. Her breath was putrid; the lips parted to reveal browned stubs of teeth. "Now, my dearest, my darling."

Dangling from a long clump of the witch's oily hair was a row of glistening earthworms. Charlene's gut spasmed; her mouth opened on its own accord, widening as the worms coiled, stretched, and then dropped onto her tongue, one by one. She tasted their earth-rich, blood-heavy taste. The witch smiled.

"Eat, my darling."

The worms lengthened, reaching from the back of Charlene's mouth, down her esophagus, and into the pit of her stomach. Cold bodies probed the moist, intimate spaces—insistent, determined. She heaved, trying not to taste them, not to feel them, but the witch and the hands stroked her, whispering, "My, my such a fuss. This is for your own good, my dearest. Swallow now. There are more where these came from."

Charlene swallowed. The worms throbbed and curled against the lining of her stomach, content for the moment.

The witch's smile widened, and she turned her face to the side to present another greasy strand of hair, another cluster of worms for Charlene's open mouth.

Tears, furious, submissive, filled Charlene's eyes and followed the line of her cheek to her neck.

Stop!

The witch leaned down and brushed Charlene's forehead with her foul lips. The worms likewise reached down, their damp, obscene mouths lowering to kiss Charlene's own.

She awoke, screaming.

Her fingers flew to her mouth to make sure there were no worms crawling there.

No no no!

There were no worms.

Nothing. Nothing. Thank God.

Charlene swallowed, and there was nothing but her own spit. Panting, gasping, Charlene swiped her forearm along her eyes. Her breasts were covered with sweat; her teeth were set against each other as if biting through bone.

Damn it.

The bedroom was still and shadowed. Somewhere outside the world of the room, somewhere in the apartment below, a television was playing a late-night movie. Some kind of chase scene or fight scene—heavy bass, sirens, muffled shouts.

Charlene rolled over and looked at the alarm clock. She'd knocked it around with a dream-flailing arm. Her cat, Reginald, who usually slept on the bed until the alarm rang, was gone, likely hiding underneath the sofa in the living room. The shade on the tiny blue-based lamp was at a tilt.

She cleared her throat and whispered, "Stupid, stupid dream."

She had dreamed of the worms before. It had been a long time, but it was no less terrifying. Clawing a tangle of auburn hair from her forehead, Charlene turned the clock back around: 2:43 A.M. She counted along with the sweeping second hand for a full minute, easing her breathing. The hairs on her arms were still at attention, and she rubbed them, hard, scrubbing away the evidence of her ridiculous fear.

Of the pathetic, cartoonish, hideous dream.

Oh, she knew a little something about dreams, their supposed meanings, symbolism, collective unconscious, blah blah blah, yada yada yada. In her spare time, between teaching watercolor technique and art appreciation at Powhatan Community College, she had taken a Jungian class on the meanings of dreams.

Dreams are voices of the deepest self, little compensatory messages meant to teach the dreamer about herself.

Himself. Itself. Whatever.

She believed the theory to a point. Some revelations made a sort of sense, while others flew in the face of what she would accept. In recording her dreams as a required activity for the class, she'd discovered that she had broken her engagement to Kevin two years earlier because she had felt she had little to offer, she feared she would never be the artist she wanted to be and didn't want to burden the man, and she didn't truly love him in the first place. Other dreams, however, suggested that she did want a relationship. This had come as a surprise, because she'd thought she was happy to be totally independent. But maybe, she'd rationalized, the subconscious desire for a new lover was more a yearning for financial help than for a soul mate. In that light, yes, perhaps the dreams did offer a little insight. Yet another rash of dreams had shown her that when faced with a display of her artwork, the rush of adrenaline that threw her into a productive frenzy was not so much pure unbridled creativity as it was cold and desperate fear of failure. This rang true without even having to study the visionary tea leaves very much.

But then the damned worm dream came tonight.

She had dreamed it before. Several times as a child, once in high school, and again while a sophomore in college. But not since then. In the ensuing nine years the dream had been forgotten.

Yet it had come again. If there was a compensatory message in this one, it had taken its sweet time in remembering that it had forgotten to get the message across to Charlene.

She sat and drew her knees against her face. Her T-shirt had ridden up to her hips; her knees were bristly with three days' stubble and the hairs prickled her chin. "Stupid ass dream."

She slipped to the floor and padded down the hallway and into the living room. She dropped to the sofa, dug the remote control from between the cushions, and clicked the power button. After a pop and sputter, the old television hummed into life. Channel 38 was showing a rerun of *Law & Order*. Charlene pulled her feet up under her and drew one of the throw pillows to her stomach.

On the screen, McCoy and Carmichael were realizing that an Ivy League student had killed his mentor for forcing him to continue with his schooling. Charlene pushed the mute button. After a good fifteen seconds, closed-captioning picked up the dialogue slack.

"Mr. Anderson, why did you and the accused go to the victim's apartment on the night of the murder?" Jack McCoy asked silently. "It certainly wasn't for a late-night tutoring session."

The young witness looked nervously at the defendant and mouthed, "We went to pick up some books for a research paper."

Out in the hallway Charlene could see the suitcases she had packed, suitcases waiting to be put into her silver Cruiser in a few hours. There were three of them, a clunky red set given to her by her mother on her twelfth birthday. Scuffed red fabric, wobbly wheels—a large, a medium, and a small. They all had plastic tags reading "Charlene Myers, 482-B Sandbridge Lane, Norfolk, Virginia."

Three suitcases were going with her. So were three heavy-duty garbage bags with blankets, sets of terry sheets, a pillow, a hairdryer, one frying pan, one saucepan, a melamine plate and teacup, a handful of mismatched flatware, a pack of paper towels, a pack of toilet paper, and her small radio/CD player. Then there was her large black leather portfolio containing her sketchpads, watercolor paper, box of pencils, brushes, and paints, a secondhand collapsible wooden easel, a laptop, and an inkjet printer.

Back on the television, there was a close-up of Jack McCoy, his caterpillar eyebrows up to his hairline at some lie from the stand. He sneered in the direction of the witness. The closed caption read, "And do you, Mr. Anderson, really think a jury is so ignorant as to believe you had no idea your roommate was on the edge of sanity, when you saw him kill a dog with his bare hands?"

Charlene let out a breath she realized she'd been holding and closed her eyes. The beginning of the dream strode determinedly across the black field of vision. An old house. A porch swing. She opened her eyes again. Jack McCoy was sitting down and casting a disparaging look at the judge. Carmichael crossed her arms and shook her head.

Reginald hopped onto the sofa. Charlene put her cheek on his gray, satiny back. He arched up into the touch then lowered himself to the cushion, his shoulder against Charlene's thigh.

"You'd love a dream about eating worms, would you?" Charlene said. "Worms, flies, cockroaches. All that tasty stuff?"

Reginald tucked his front legs beneath him and began to purr.

Charlene looked back at the suitcases in the hallway. She didn't much like old things, yet most of what she owned now was old. Old suitcases. Old sweatshirts loose at the neck. Old socks thin at the toes and heels.

The old farm in Nelson County.

Fuck old stuff. Old emotional baggage. Old doubts. Old dreams.

Like the old worm dream. Charlene rubbed her eyebrows and shook her head.

The worm dream always began on the front porch of a huge, old house. Charlene was sitting on the swing, her feet dangling toward but not touching the rough-planked floor. The swing's chains groaned like metal bones. Somewhere beyond the porch, dry autumn leaves rattled in a breeze. She was not afraid, not at that moment. The place was familiar, comfortable. She thought if she were able to put her feet on the floor she could push hard; she could make the swing go up and back really high. That would be fun. Really high she could go, up and over all the way, and run the bottoms of her shoes across the ceiling of the porch. She could leave sneaker prints up there, and everyone would wonder how she'd done it. They would wonder if she knew how to fly.

She gripped the wooden sides of the swing and inched her body down so the toes of her shoes could take purchase on the narrow, painted wooden slats that were the porch floor. There, one toe down. A little more scooting and the second touched the wood.

Suddenly straps flew up out of the sides of the swing, leather straps flicking to life with the lightning speed of constrictor snakes, looping around her chest and waist and lashing her to the swing's back. Her feet jerked from the floor, her sneakers flew from her feet. She attempted to wriggle free, but the straps were secure, bolting her tightly.

The swing began to move slowly. *Clack, clack, clack.* Like a car in a carnival spook house ride, it traveled the length of the porch, and then turned to face the outer wall of the old house. A black, gaping chasm appeared in the wall.

"Let me off!" Charlene cried, but the cry on the air was nothing but a faint gurgle.

The swing shuddered, hesitated, and then rushed forward through the ragged opening and into the darkness, clacking rapidly and rhythmically like the rusted gears of some ancient machinery.

Clack-clack-clack-clack-clack.

Charlene's stomach pitched with the motion. She closed her eyes but her eyelids were transparent and she had no choice but to look.

The bowels of the house were a tangle of empty, lopsided loony-tunes rooms off a long, zigzagging hallway. The ceiling was low, wet, and rippled like a skin sack filled with maggots. The floor was covered in a thick liquid, a slimy brown mud that slopped upward in waves, reaching for Charlene's feet. Charlene could not pull her feet away.

The swing clacked and shook, careening down the hall on its invisible track between rooms, pausing before some of the open doorways. Each stop was quick and abrupt before the swing yanked forward and away again, and Charlene had no time to make sense of the fleeting images inside the rooms. But she did not have to. She could smell the dead things, the dying things there. She could hear the agonized whispers in the air, in the walls.

The swing reached the end of the hall and turned sharply to the left, snapping Charlene's neck painfully. There were stairs running up along the wall, carpeted with red, delineated by a banister of woven black wood. Flakes of skin-textured wallpaper peeled from the wall in sheets; behind the paper rips Charlene saw rivulets of blood zigzagging in odd, cryptic patterns. The swing tilted backward, slamming Charlene's head against the slats, and climbed the steps.

Click-click-click-click-click.

"Don't go up there. I know what's up there!" Charlene tried to cry.

The swing reached the top of the steps, leveled out, then rattled toward the front of the house in the flickering light of ancient brass sconces. The swing stopped in front of a door. The door to the witch's bedroom. The door was closed. The doorknob was rusted.

Charlene knew before the door opened that the witch was inside. She wanted to scream it away, but there was no scream to be had, only a knot in her throat so thick she could not swallow. The door clattered in its frame and then swung open. The swing clacked into the room.

On a sagging bed sat the witch, a hideous female with long, greasy hair. Her face was thin and white, her eyes red hollows. Candles burned on a bedside table. The witch grinned, reached out her bony hands, and effortlessly lifted Charlene from the swing. She put Charlene on the bed beside her. Charlene could not roll away. Her body seemed determined to please the witch and remained obediently in place. Her heart was the only dissenter, pounding against the cage of ribs.

The witch leaned over and blew out the candles. For a moment there was nothing but perfect darkness, perfect silence. Disembodied hands slithered into place along every inch of her body to hold and stroke her. The witch's face appeared above Charlene, smiling in approval. Then she tipped her head, smiled a pus-yellowed smile, and positioned a strand of her hair over Charlene's mouth. Hanging from the hair were earthworms. The witch lowered the worms to Charlene's lips. Charlene was forced to eat.

"Jesus, let it go!" snarled Charlene, dropping her hands from her face and grabbing up the remote control. "Don't play it over. It's stupid, it's worthless, it's a ridiculous dream." She jabbed the mute button. Executive A.D.A. Jack McCoy's voice cut through the den. He was making an appeal to the judge, having been slammed with the overruling of an objection.

"Your Honor, to borrow a phrase from an old detective show of many years ago, we need 'just the facts, ma'am!' And we're getting very little of those here today!"

Reginald rolled over onto his side. The pink tip of his tongue stuck out between his teeth, making him look like he was a couple days' dead. The cat was going to be highly insulted come noon. By then he would have realized that he'd been left in the care of one of Charlene's fellow faculty members, Mary Jane Ferguson. Reginald was not going with Charlene. Maybe it was a bit of self-flagellation, a bit of extra red-hot coals heaped upon her own head, Charlene's decision to leave the cat with her friend, though she told herself that Reginald was an apartment feline, a city kitty, not a country cat. He would have hated Charlene had she hauled him to the Virginia wilds. Regardless, she knew she would miss the warm, rumbling body when the cold nights came.

Charlene would be driving to the foothills of the Blue Ridge Mountains. Nelson County. She was taking her mother's old gift of three suitcases to her mother's most recent gift, a 127-acre mountainside farm called Homeplace, inherited when her mother had died back in March. It was mid-September. Charlene planned on staying at Homeplace through the first of the year and into late spring. She had no idea of the condition of the land and the house. She had decided to go and face it however it was, sight unseen. If she'd taken Mary Jane's suggestion to drive to Nelson County one weekend to check it out, she might have changed her mind, like a person who is preparing to jump into a lake but first toe-tests the water to find it chillingly cold and so turns back. And Charlene wasn't in a position to turn back. She would use her time there wisely. She would regain her nerve and would paint with renewed passion. She would start the new watercolor collection that would earn a spot in next summer's lineup of solo shows in Norfolk and would put her back into the realm of "respectable artists."

"Yep, that's what I'm going to do," she said to herself, to

Reginald, and to Jack McCoy. "Once I have my new paintings complete, I'm going to sell the farm to some country-fried dude so he can graze his cattle or sheep or goats or park junked cars or raise pot or whatever the hell it is farmers use land for these days. If it's in fair enough condition to bring in a couple hundred thousand dollars, I'll pay off any leftover bills, buy a small house back here by the Elizabeth River, and open up my first real in-home studio. And I'll start my life for real."

Reginald's face drew up in a near-smile and then relaxed. He agreed with her. Or he was having a gas attack.

Mary Jane had tried to get Charlene to sell the farm right away, as soon as it had come into her possession, but Charlene had imagined the farm as a retreat, a place to regain herself and her artwork. She needed that desperately, if only for a matter of months. Knowing she could make some money off it when she was done gave her a sense of impending relief.

She'd had precious little of that in the last few years— money and peace of mind. "Just the facts, ma'am," as Jack had said. Her salary from the community college paid the rent, the electric, and the food. An occasional sale of original pieces, mainly lighthouses and seashells—which she'd grown to hate but which tourists and locals seemed to want—helped with the car insurance and basic cable. But there was often not enough for gasoline. For long distance calls or vet bills. Never enough to rent movies or go on a vacation.

Her mother, had she been alive, would have demanded, "Take a second job, Charlene. You come from strong stock, people who never let life get the best of them. You could wait tables. Do you know how many places at the beach need seasonal and sometimes year-round help?"

But Charlene just couldn't do it. Her weekends, her nights, were reserved for painting. She needed time to paint. If she gave that up, then what was the point? If she had no time to paint, then why was she born to be a painter?

Even though she'd not really painted in almost a year, save the damnable seashells and lighthouses.

Running away to the old farm seemed like the only option

left. She had quit her job at the community college a week earlier. She had a partial paycheck due her by the end of the month. She'd sold her bedroom set, television, sofa, and recliner to the landlord for a grand total of $825. And last and but absolutely not least, she had written to the Commonwealth of Virginia about cashing in her retirement. That should bring in another $4,000 or so. With this cash scraped together, she could pay off her Visa card and have a little something left over. Country living had to be cheaper than city living.

It all made practical, creative sense. Starting over where she would not be known or disturbed, where she could be free to create and dream. Where she could make one last attempt to become the artist she was supposed to be.

At least it all made perfect and practical sense in the light of day.

But in the darkness of two A.M., clutching a throw pillow and staring at a late night cop show rerun, it seemed terrifyingly desperate.

2

~

Andrew Marshall leaned his elbows on his desk, scratched the three-day old stubble on his cheek, and let out a breath he'd just realized he'd been holding. The story was going nowhere. He needed a cup of coffee. He needed a nap. One or the other. Maybe a beer and something to eat at the café and screw the coffee and nap.

Beyond the desk and the computer, out the grit-speckled, second-story window of his den, he could see a portion of Route 782—Main Street—as it passed through the small town of Adams. From this vantage point atop a rise in the town's center, several of the town's economic mainstays were visible: the Shop 'n' Save, Randy's Hardware, the corner of Marlie's Pet Parlor, The Styling Corner, and the empty, weed-strewn lot where Blue Ridge Bar and Grill had burned and then been razed three months earlier. Several ornamental pear trees, planted along Main Street by the Adams Historical Society—consisting in its entirety of two of the town's lifelong wealthier residents, Mrs. Denise DeBoer and Mrs. Udenia Caldwell—were just beginning to change red from green. Occasional gusts of wind brought on muted explosions of sunlight and shimmering leaves.

Andrew reached over his desk and clawed the window open with his fingertips, letting in the mixed scents of damp earth, wood smoke, and exhaust. He inhaled through his mouth, held it, let it out. It had been over a year since he'd quit smoking; a good move, but the wood smoke and the faint fumes of farm machinery often brought back the craving.

Beneath his desk there was a slow shifting and a raspy grunt. Rex, the aging black lab-shepherd mix, rescued seven years earlier from the Boston SPCA, thumped Andrew's leg with his foot as he jockeyed for a more comfortable position. The tail twapped the floor twice then went still. Andrew rubbed his bare feet over the dog's smooth back and the dog sighed a soft, canine sigh. Rex was a good old dog, a fine friend, a companion through thick and thin. Eleven years old, muzzle and whiskers gone white, a slight limp from a car accident eighteen months earlier, there was no better friend than the sometimes snoring, sometimes drooly, sometimes smelly dog.

Andrew put a mug filled with pens atop a stack of papers to keep them from blowing off the desk in the breeze and then turned his attention back to the computer monitor. On the screen were the first four paragraphs of "Chapter 2: Murder at the Port." So far, protagonist Detective Hugh Chase had been called out to check on three bodies found crammed in a single bathroom of a ferryboat at the Port of Boston, each neatly folded with knees drawn up and arms lashed around them. Hugh and his partner, Deborah Alamong, were arguing yet again about what the motive was for such a hideous crime and the fact that Hugh hadn't said anything to Deb about the long, passionate night they'd spent at her apartment the weekend before.

The book completely and totally sucked so far.

"Shit," said Andrew. He highlighted the entire text of chapter 2 and reached for the delete button. He hesitated. Then he unhighlighted it all, pressed save, pushed back from the desk, and left the den for the bedroom. He plopped down on the unmade bed, reached for the socks he'd tossed there earlier that morning, and dragged them onto his feet. "I've got to start it over again," he said to himself. Rex trotted into the room and sat on the braided rug beside the bed. Andrew repeated himself, "I have to dump what I've done and start fresh. Why does everything sound so good in my head but sucks so terribly on the screen? Is this what all writers have to suffer through?"

Rex's tail wagged. He had no idea.

"Well." Andrew shoved on his shoes, tied them, and then grabbed his khaki jacket from his bedpost. As he stood, his knee cramped, and he held for a moment until the pain subsided a little. Left leg, just like Rex's. Lasting injury from the same car, same wreck. Then, he made his way downstairs and out the front door.

The chipped concrete walk angled down the well-trimmed yard toward a wrought iron fence and an appropriately ornate Victorian gate that never quite stayed shut due to the shifting of the earth over the past one hundred years. Rex followed happily after his owner, hoping, most likely, to accompany him to the café. But as doggy brains don't often remember what they don't want to remember, Rex forgot yet again that without his leash he wasn't going anywhere. Andrew slipped through the gate, pushed it shut behind him, and adjusted the chain he'd installed over the closest fence spike. Rex immediately began to whimper.

"Not this time, buddy," said Andrew. He scratched the dog's wizened muzzle through the gate. "I'm counting on you to guard the house. Bark at 'em, bite 'em, whatever it takes."

It wasn't okay with Rex, and he just whined louder.

Andrew took the steep cement steps that connected his property to the sidewalk along Main Street. At the bottom he stopped and considered going back for his cane. Damned leg. It was burning now with a long-familiar fire. Sometimes it gave him no grief at all, and he could take the stairs two at a time or stroll through town with ease. Most days, however, it acted like the appendage of an old dude, not an otherwise healthy thirty-four-year-old, at times shooting hot spears to his thigh and down to his calf, at other times wrapping the knee in a dull ache. There was nothing to do, really, except pop a handful of ibuprofen or just try to ignore it until it eased up.

He shoved his hands into the pockets of his jacket and headed for the Fox's Den, favoring his right leg slightly. It was nearing five o'clock, after all; almost suppertime. No one would have to know he'd done virtually nothing worthwhile all afternoon, that while most of the male citizens of Adams and the surrounding county were harvesting pumpkins or vaccinating livestock or repairing small engines or selling hardware and gasoline, he'd been staring at a computer screen trying to make fictional detectives come alive over three dead bodies.

Writing a detective novel had been a goal of his for years, though his work pace in Boston had been insane, most often fifty to sixty hours a week, and his social life a flurry, so the time had never presented itself. Now, however, with work relegated to the morning hours and no friends to speak of, he had his time. He'd begun his book, and begun it again several times. Writing was more of a struggle than he'd imagined it could be.

Nobody in Adams knew he was an aspiring author, and he wasn't about to say anything. A few months earlier, when the town's librarian mailed out fliers announcing that a best-selling novelist was going to be visiting a little bookstore in nearby Lovingston to talk about the political direction of the country, the reactions around town were pretty much one of two things: "Who cares what some man who makes up stories for a living has to say about politics?" and "Never heard of the guy."

Not that all Adams citizens were illiterate or under-literate. There was evidence that a good number of them read books, because the wobbly rack of paperback novels at the grocery store was constantly in flux with its sales of romances, westerns, and mysteries. Hell, Denise DeBoer and Udenia Caldwell—poets, the both—traveled once a month to Charlottesville to attend meetings of that city's chapter of the Virginia Writers Club. But still, Andrew could only imagine the look on some of the faces if they discovered that their expatriate New England lawyer was not just doing their wills and settling their property disputes from his home office before lunch, but during his afternoons was trying to create a thriller in hopes it might someday find a spot on the lopsided wire rack in the grocery store.

"Ho, Mr. Marshall!"

Andrew looked up to see Yule Lemons at the corner of Main and Maple, unusually large hands dangling at his sides and a shit-eating grin on his face. The man wasn't a bad sort— gregarious, a little too loud and a whole lot opinionated, smelling more often than not as if he'd been hosed down with diesel fuel. He was only a few years older than Andrew but had a face that showed at least a decade more of hard living. His teeth were bunched together in the front as if a rubber band had drawn them up, and his hair was short, greasy, and usually, as was the case today, topped with a grimy Randy's Hardware ball cap.

"Hey there, Yule," Andrew called. "So what's got you smiling this time? Beat Herm Johnson at pool for another hundred bucks? Get a good deal on some new tires?"

"Nah. But the mother-in-law's gone for a week," Yule said, nodding and flexing his huge fingers cheerfully. "So is the wife, both of 'em off to Atlanta. Left this morning on a Greyhound. You know what that means?"

"It means they left on a bus?"

"Ha, that's a joke," said Yule. "What it means is that I'm goin' fishin' for two whole days on the Tye with not having to come home, not having to take a shower, not having to answer to nobody. Just me, my cousin Howard, my boat, a couple bedrolls, a bucket of bait, a cooler full of beer. Leavin' to-morrow morning early to catch them browns and smallmouths in their sleep. Hell, hook 'em before they even know what's what. Watch 'em yawning on the line! We catch enough, you come to a fish fry over my place?"

"Sure. Give me a call if it pans out."

"Pans out!" Yule chortled. "Good one. Fish fryin' in a pan, pans out. Ha!" He burped into his hand then sniffed the palm.

"Now Yule, don't get in trouble camping on someone's land without permission. As good a lawyer as I am, even I might have trouble convincing a judge you couldn't just go home to sleep."

"I hear ya, Mr. Marshall. We'll be careful."

"And Yule," Andrew said, "if you don't start calling me Andrew I'm going to sue you for all you're worth. I've lived in Adams since a year ago August. This formality has got to stop."

The two men crossed the street side by side, Andrew concentrating to keep his limp to a minimum, Yule swinging his arms wide and long like a gorilla on parade.

"Got to call you mister," said Yule. "You're more a mister than a Andrew."

"What does that mean?"

"Well, sir, you got that funny accent from up north and I don't hear it goin' even after all this time. You don't know much about engines or huntin'. You don't even have no work boots, just them shiny shoes you wear when you're in your office or them tie-up suede things you got on now. That all makes for a mister in my book."

"You aren't being fair. I bought an old truck the week I moved down here. Doesn't that count for something?"

Yule shook his head.

"So if I lose my Boston accent, learn to repair a lawnmower, kill a deer, and trade my shoes for work boots, you'll call me Andrew?"

Yule and Andrew reached the sidewalk. Yule turned to face the lawyer. "Could be. But could be not. You're a lawyer. Teachers, doctors, preachers, lawyers, they's always misters to me. Home trainin', you know."

"No, not really."

"No home trainin' where you grew up?"

"Not about misters, no."

"Huh, well," said Yule. "I'll give you a call should we have that fry."

"Good deal. And good luck. Don't come back until your boat is ready to sink under the weight of all those fish."

Andrew and Yule parted ways, Yule heading toward Randy's Hardware and Andrew heading for the Fox's Den café. Along the way he nodded at the people in the window of the Laundromat and the doorway of Main Street Antiques. For the most part Adams's citizens were friendly, but Andrew still didn't feel a member of the community. He had wanted to when he'd moved south, but it just wasn't happening. Sure, Yule invited Andrew to a picnic on occasion, Eugene Derry tried to get him to come to Sunday School at the Baptist Church every so often (which he avoided with numerous excuses, stopping short of telling him he didn't believe in anything much beyond the here and now, the tangible and the seeable), and the ladies of the Historical Society had encouraged him to attend their sporadic events in the small office on Hewitt Road. Some of the wealthier residents in this part of the county, old and new Virginia money, had made a point of motoring into Adams to introduce themselves and let him know that even though he was not "from here," they considered him an equal. He'd attended several fancy dinners and parties at their vineyards and thoroughbred farms. But he had yet to reciprocate. No, Andrew didn't feel a part because he wasn't letting himself become a part. He wasn't ready to develop any real friendships yet. It might be a long time before he could even consider it.

It was tragedy that had driven him from a beautiful Boston townhouse and an enviable job at a respected law firm. A tragedy that left his young wife dead. A tragedy he could have prevented but had not.

Because I wanted her hurt. I was furious at her.

"Shut up," he said to himself as he reached the glassed front door of the Fox's Den. "Don't go there now. Enough of that." He tightened his jaw and pulled the door open.

There were two waitresses at the Fox's Den, Sallie Gibson and Dawn Reed. Sallie, just out of high school, was an angst-ridden Goth wannabe, all black clothes, black hair, and various nose and ear piercings, stuck in a small town and champing at the bit to get out and away. She had an on-again, off-again crush on Andrew, which translated to him becoming her father confessor for everything from how much she hated her mother to her suggestion that now that she was eighteen, they should go to the beach for a weekend. Andrew smiled at her when appropriate, nodded, shook his head, and furrowed his brow. He listened as she poured his coffee and then stood with the pot on one hip and a fist on the other, grinding her jaw and narrowing her navy-lined eyes. Other times she'd slip into the booth seat across from him, and when Dawn would call for her to get back to work she'd say, "I'm talking with my lawyer, okay? There's some kind of privilege with that, if you didn't know."

Dawn, on the other hand, was an even-tempered woman in her mid-fifties with a round face and cheerful outlook on life. She was one of Adams's readers, who enjoyed everything from novels to classic short fiction to political satire to the weekly county newspaper's obituaries. She always had a witty comment or intriguing tidbit to share with her customers.

On deck today for Andrew's booth was Sallie, looking particularly glum. She handed Andrew the wrinkled menu, poured the cup of coffee he always ordered, and said, "Well, Steve dumped me. Are you happy?"

"Why would I be happy?"

Sallie made a loud sound of exasperation—part sigh, part cough. "You said he didn't sound all that interested in me, if you care to remember. You said he sounded like somebody who would dump me if I didn't do what he wanted me to do."

Of course, Andrew had never said that. He knew better than to give advice to impressionable young girls. Though he couldn't remember specifically, the conversation had most likely gone thus:

Sallie: "I don't think Steve is all that interested in me anymore."

Andrew: "Maybe not."

Sallie: "I get the feeling he would dump me if I didn't do what he wanted or did something he didn't like."

Andrew: "You could be right."

Sallie: "That sucks, don't you think?"

Andrew: "It could suck, yeah."

Andrew picked up his mug of coffee and wrapped his fingers around the warm porcelain. He would have liked to put it on his aching knee. "I'm sorry, Sallie," he said with a sympathetic smile. "It's hard to know how a relationship will turn out. That's part of being human, unfortunately."

"So, how does that advice help me?"

"I don't know if it will."

"Thanks for nothing."

Andrew took a short sip. The taste was bitter and made his tongue curl. He reached for a little cup of half-and-half Sallie had dropped onto the table, peeled up the lid, and dumped it into the mug. Then he emptied a small packet of sugar into the mix.

Sallie glanced over her shoulder then back at Andrew. Her expression changed from frustration to mild seduction. She cocked her head to the side, a curl of night-black hair clutching her throat.

"You know all about relationships, don't you?" she said. "You must of had lots of girlfriends before coming down here to Hicksville. Did you break their hearts like Steve broke mine?"

I broke my own heart. Not sure hers was breakable.

"Actually, Sallie, I'm really hungry. I'd like to order now."

"Yeah, okay, whatever," said Sallie with a roll of her eyes. "What do you want?"

Andrew ordered a country ham sandwich, side salad, and fries. The sandwich was salty and hot, the salad greens a little limp, and the fries seasoned a bit too heavily with garlic salt. As Andrew ate, he tried to put his head back into Boston, back at the dock, back at the ferry where three bound bodies had been found inside a small, unisex bathroom. Hugh Chase was slipping on his latex gloves while Deb Alamong continued to harangue him about him being an insensitive shit and ignoring their "night of passion." She leaned over and whispered so the Crime Scene crew couldn't hear her. "Do you ever think about anybody except yourself? Can you at least clear that up for me?"

Hugh felt bad for Deb's hurt feelings and pissed at himself for being insensitive, but felt worse for the dead people in the restroom. He said, "Not now, Deb. This isn't the time or place."

"Will there ever be the time or place?"

"Deb, we've got work to do."

A flash of silver outside the café window caught Andrew's attention. It was one of those little PT Cruisers, designed to look like a retro 1940s vehicle. The car slowed and stopped at the stoplight. Andrew didn't recognize the Cruiser and didn't recognize the driver. She looked to be in her late twenties, with reddish brown hair held back by a green hair band, and a pair of dark glasses obscuring her eyes. Her driver's side window was down, and her arm hung out, tapping the outside of the door to some tune from her radio or player. There was an unfolded map up against her steering wheel.

Sightseer, Andrew guessed, though there really wasn't much to see in Adams. Autumn leaves weren't in full color until late October. That was when handfuls of tourists stumbled upon the town on their way to the Blue Ridge Parkway or to Wintergreen Resort, armed with cameras, hiking gear, and money. Outside the month of October, a stranger in town was most likely someone who was lost.

Yet this young woman didn't look lost. She seemed to be looking for something. Some place.

The light turned green. The little silver car hesitated, and then pulled away.

Andrew rubbed his stubbly chin and looked down at his nearly finished sandwich. Susan's car hadn't been a Cruiser, but it had been silver. A silver Toyota Highlander Hybrid. "A cute set of wheels" is what his wife had called it when she selected it off the lot at the Cambridge dealership. It was a second-anniversary gift from her husband.

"It's about time he bought me something besides crappy little odds and ends like dishes and dogs," she had joked with the salesman with a toss of her head. "He holds on to a dollar like he was holding on to a life preserver. You'd think he was some kind of desperate blue-collar worker, some kind of starving day laborer, the way he behaves with money. But he's a rising star in the legal world. He's a big name, going to be a bigger one soon. Aren't you, Andrew?"

Andrew had given her a smile that he'd hoped had looked genuine, and then gone back to signing the final papers.

Maybe, he thought, this would calm her down and make her happy, at least for a little while.

"Marry in haste, repent in leisure," his good friend Tom had told him.

Damn, Tom, why were you always the smart one?

But Andrew had loved Susan, had wanted to keep on loving her. He was elated when they had exchanged their wedding vows on Tom's yacht on the Charles River. She was beautiful and bright, twenty-two, daughter of his firm's senior partner. She had a sharp sense of humor, an incredible touch in bed, and the most beautiful eyes he'd ever seen. There was also an underlying sadness in Susan, an unspoken desperation that he felt he could ease by loving her enough. He'd encouraged her to pursue what she'd claimed was her passion, her desire to go back to college to study architecture.

But he never knew how well one person could hide a true identity. A lawyer who worked with clients who often bullshitted their ways though life, Andrew was nevertheless caught completely off guard with his wife. Sweet and tender one moment, within months Susan had evolved into a complaining, demanding bitch on overdrive. Tom had warned Andrew that she was looking for an easy life, easy money, all she'd expected from her wealthy father. That any sadness she had exuded was just her pining for more, more, more.

"Can't you see the manipulation?" Tom had said the night of the bachelor party. He'd taken Andrew aside, out to the porch where moths batted themselves against the light globe. He'd put his hand on Andrew's shoulder and pleaded. "Listen to me, I know what I'm talking about. You only dated Susan, what, eight weeks before you gave her the ring? You don't know her, but I know her type."

"Shut up," Andrew had said, his fingers crushing around his glass of whiskey.

Tom didn't shut up. "My mother was like that, like Susan. She could hold it together for a long time if she thought there was something in it for her, something just out of her reach. But once she had what she wanted, there was no need to expend any more energy on playing nice. It's not too late, my friend. An engagement ring is not a wedding ring."

Andrew was furious, insulted, and hurt. He threw his glass down, shattering it at Tom's feet. It was all Andrew could do to keep from punching his best friend. "I can't believe you are asking me to give up something that means so much to me, and to her," he said. "What the hell's wrong with you? Are you jealous? She loves me, you asshole. And I love her. If you're going to speak ill of her, it might be best if you just left this party. And we can find another location for the ceremony."

Tom had let out a long breath. Then he apologized and said no more.

But Tom had been right. It had been a charade, after all. A cold, calculated, perfectly performed charade. She'd gotten what she wanted and no longer had to hold it together. The real Susan had come shining through within a matter of months, with her whining and nitpicking. Nothing was ever fast enough, good enough, stylish enough, expensive enough.

The day they bought the car had been rainy and windy, March at its nastiest. Susan had snatched the keys from the salesman and trotted out through the rain to her new vehicle, her short brown hair caught up beneath the collar of her long gray raincoat, her expensive leather purse and unopened umbrella slapping her side. "Come *on*, Andrew," she called. "Don't get drenched! You'll ruin the upholstery."

By the time Andrew had tossed down a towel for Rex in the backseat and ushered the dog in out of the rain, and had climbed into the passenger seat, Susan already had the engine and the radio on. She was thumbing the dial to catch blips of countless songs. "This player will hold up to ten CDs," she said, more to herself than to her husband. "I can go for hundreds of miles without having to change anything."

"I'm glad you like it."

"Of course I *like* it," said Susan with a toss of her head. Tiny raindrops flew. "I wouldn't have picked this if I didn't *like* it." Then she sniffed the air, wrinkled her nose, and cut a glance into the backseat. "Oh, God. Why do we have to take that dog along with us? It's stinking up the car, Andrew!"

"It's not a good idea to leave Rex in the SUV while we're gone. Somebody might try to take him."

"We're not going to be gone long. I'm just taking it for a maiden trip, a few minutes, tops. And if someone took it, it wouldn't be that great of a loss, really."

"I know you hate the dog, Susan, but I'm not going to leave him alone in..."

"Fine!" Susan said. With that, she slammed the gearshift into position and hauled ass out of the lot. In the back, Rex scrambled to stay on the seat.

"I'll buy you a can of air freshener," Andrew said, but Susan didn't reply.

She drove the speed limit for the first few miles, but once they hit the Mass Turnpike, she pushed the vehicle up to eighty-five. In spite of the rain-slicked tarmac, she darted in and out between cars, sometimes so close Andrew could see the furious or frightened faces of the other drivers.

"How about slowing it down just a bit," said Andrew.

"You always want to tell me what to do!" she snapped.

"I don't always tell you what to do."

The car zipped up beside a truck, and then left it behind, a foggy smudge in the rearview. Susan giggled. It sounded forced, defiant. "This is great!"

"Slow down, we're going to hit something." Andrew's pulse had picked up and his breathing had shallowed drastically.

"You don't trust me, you never have!"

"Susan, slow the fuck down!"

"It's my car! I can drive it however I want!"

"Fine, Susan," Andrew said, suddenly and surprisingly not caring, so sick and tired of her attitude, her whining, her constant demanding. Let them run off the road, let them total the car. "Fine," he said. "Do whatever you want. And you smash this thing into something and kill yourself and me, just who do you think they'll blame? It won't be the guy in the passenger's seat."

"You asshole!" Susan slowed the car down to eighty, then seventy-five. Her fingers were tight around the steering wheel, and he could hear her angry breaths coming in gasps. It sounded as if she were beginning to cry. She looked over at her husband. Her eyes were pinched. "You happy now? You son of a bitch, you..."

And then she lost control. The car skidded and spun across the lanes and into a commercial bus, crushing the car, the edge of the bus, and blowing the airbags from the front and side. The car then ricocheted into a guardrail and slid to a stop with a shard of metal through the driver's door. Neither Andrew nor Susan saw the frantic gathering of onlookers in the rain or the bright red flashing lights from the emergency vehicles, because Andrew was knocked unconscious and Susan was dead. Rex, thrown to the floor in the back, survived with a broken leg.

I was furious. I was devastated that she didn't love me, that she only loved herself. I wanted her hurt. But I didn't want her dead.

"Need anything else?" Sallie was back at his booth, chewing a wad of gum that reflected brightly at the front of her mouth.

"The check."

On the sidewalk across the street from the café, Yule was gabbing with Rick Evans, a county deputy. Rick, a man in his early sixties with a white crew cut and a potbelly, was a fisherman, as well. From the animated motions Yule was making with his paper bag from the hardware store, Rick was being invited to join the wifeless, mother-in-lawless Tye River fishing expedition. Yule probably knew that having a deputy along for the ride would make camping anywhere on anybody's land a little easier.

Andrew took one last bite of salad and pushed the plates away. He thought he'd call Tom later, see what was up in the great white north of Massachusetts. Maybe he'd invite Tom down to Adams in a couple weeks for a short getaway. He had plenty of room in the house. He could give a dinner and invite some of the locals, to get that growing social obligation off his shoulders. He wasn't much of a cook, but he could probably hire Dawn to help him out. He could throw a few autumn leaves in a couple vases, stick one on the front hall sideboard and another on the dining room table, and call them decorations. It would be great to see his best friend again after all this time. And it was about time he tried to fit in to his new community beyond just morning legal appointments and occasional, passing conversation on the streets or in the café.

"And it's time to get back to work," he said to himself. He'd let Hugh and Deb wait long enough. They had a crime to solve.

3

~

The Cruiser stopped next to the dented mailbox beside the dirt road. Charlene drew her lower lip in between her teeth, clamped down, and then let it out. Sun filtered through the branches and the heavy, green and gold foliage of the roadside trees, making her realize yet again how filthy her windshield was. The Pepsi in her drink holder had spilled when she'd hit a pothole about a half-mile back. Her lap was sticky with drying soda.

The mailbox's painted letters were chipped black. ALEXANDER. Generous spatters of bird poop across the name made it look like ALE AND from a distance, but up close it was clear enough. Charlene had found Homeplace.

She'd made it to the tiny town of Adams in Nelson County a little over three hours after leaving Norfolk. According to the map she'd picked up at a roadside fruit stand, Adams was easy to find—up Route 56 then west on 840 for another three miles. Couldn't miss it. But, of course, she could miss it because the freaking map had a typo. Charlene had flagged down a hump-backed man on a blue tractor, who gave her a long-winded set of directions that included descriptions of the families whose houses, cattle farms, and orchards she would pass before getting to town. She backtracked and found the turn she had missed, Route 804 instead of 840. The Alexander Homeplace would be on a tiny byway, Route 782, Craig Road, approximately three miles on the other side of Adams, slammed up against the Tye River and the rise of the Blue Ridge Mountains. And it was, though the byway was more of a foot trail by the time it got to Homeplace, growing more narrow with each quarter mile and reducing itself to clay and rock by the time it reached the Alexander mailbox.

The place was right. She recognized it, even though five minutes earlier she would have sworn she had absolutely no recollection of the old homestead. It wasn't the mailbox she knew, but the way the dirt driveway left the road and made an immediate and severe downward dip, disappearing within tangles of blackberry bushes, cedars, honeysuckle, and wild cherry.

"I remember this," Charlene said to the streaky windshield. "I remember Mom saying how she hated this driveway, how it cost her a fortune in wheel alignments. I can see why."

Clearly no one had been hired to excavate the drive in the last many years. Great-grandmother Ellen Alexander was the last person to live on the farm, and she had died sixteen years earlier. The property had been passed on to Ellen's only daughter, Charlene's grandmother Sissy, who, at seventy-four, was already living in a Richmond nursing home with severe arthritis. Sissy would have lived at the nursing home longer if it weren't for the antics of an angry child who had come to visit his own aged relative and had thrown his game player down the hall in a fit of rage, striking Sissy on the head as she sat in her wheelchair. Charlene's mother, Patricia, took ownership of the farm, but had no desire to leave DC for Nelson County. Then, last winter, Patricia was diagnosed with cancer of her lymphatic system and was dead in two months. Ryan, Charlene's stepbrother, did not inherit the land or even a portion. The wills of the Alexander family, each in turn, stipulated that the property would always remain in the hands of blood relatives. Ryan knew this, and when Patricia died, he did not challenge the claim. It could have been kindness, respect for tradition, generosity. It could also have been that he and his wife, Dede, were more than comfortably wealthy up in Silver Spring, Maryland, and they had no interest in dealing with farmland of questionable condition or value.

And the driveway had ruts a good eighteen inches deep.

Oh, this is just marvelous.

Charlene steered her car onto the dirt drive. She scooted up as far as she could to watch the ground ahead of her, to keep from disemboweling the vehicle before she even made it to the house. She aimed for the left side, which looked a bit less furrowed than the right or center, and for several tenths of a mile eased down through the trees, between rain-carved embankments and across a rickety plank bridge that forded a shallow stream. Once over the stream, the driveway headed upward. A moment later, the trees parted and the drive crossed a weedy, rocky yard and petered out in front of the house.

Oh, my God, I do remember the house.

She got out and stretched her shoulders. A cool September breeze cut across the yard and stirred her hair. She plucked at the damp soda spot on her jeans and then looked back at the house.

It didn't look much like the house of her dreams; that was the only saving grace.

"Oh, jeez," she said, looking around as if there might be someone else there to agree with her. "This place is the shits."

It was two whole stories of the shits, splintery wooden siding atop a rugged stone foundation, with white paint faded to a mottled, molded gray and a roof covered with rusted tin shingles. Vines and spiny shrubs clung to the sides, the front porch railings, and the stone chimneys on the north and south sides. The corners of the porch steps looked like bears had chewed on them. The porch floorboards were warped and a few were missing. There was no porch swing, which was a good thing. The first-floor window on the left had a screen hanging at a tilt. The right window had no screen at all, and a zigzagged crack traced the glass from bottom to top. The windows above the porch bore the tattered remnants of brown shutters, and inside, torn shades hung like victims of war.

Set off in the weeds to the left of the house stood a smoke-house with a missing door. Near the smokehouse, surrounded by thistles and covered with rain-bleached plywood and bricks, was the well.

The well. Oh, yeah, I remember the well.

She recalled other children, but not their names, playing with her near that well, then finding the bricks and taking them off. They'd all come to Ellen Alexander's birthday party. Charlene had been seven, or maybe eight, at the time. She remembered expecting balloons, music, and laughter. But the whole day was oppressive and uncomfortable. The kids had been bored out of their skulls, trying to find something to do. When they'd found the bricks, the grown-ups had told them to get away from there.

But later the kids had poked around the well again. Charlene remembered that besides herself and Ryan, there was a boy and a girl. The boy had been bossy. She didn't remember the girl much. They'd taken the wood off the well so they could look down inside. It had been nighttime, or almost nighttime. There had been lots of bugs, and she thought someone had a flashlight.

Then there had been a scream from deep inside the well. It was a child's scream, high pitched and agonized, spiraling up the wet stone wall and knocking Charlene backward...

Certainly I only fell backward, there was nothing to knock me, there was nothing in that well...

...into the grass.

Charlene had thought, *Maybe no one screamed in the well, maybe it was only me screaming at nothing and now I look like a baby.*

The adults never found out the children had peeked down the well.

She shut the car door, rubbed her eyes beneath her sunglasses, and crossed through the thigh-high weeds and dead Queen Anne's lace to the well. She stared down at the bleached plywood cover. One edge of the wood was so curled that Charlene imagined little furry field animals had probably run underneath, fallen in, and drowned. She'd get a brand new board

soon, so more creatures wouldn't drop to their deaths. She patted the board with her foot and then waded back to the car.

Electric wires ran from the house to a pole by the edge of
the trees. Charlene had called the power company several
weeks back to make sure the place had at some point in time
been wired for electricity ("Yes," they said, "back in 1946.")
and to see if she could have the service reconnected ("Well,"
they said, "we'll try."). To the right of the house and behind it
slightly was a small cabin. Charlene guessed it had been the
family's original house, used before the larger one was built
in the late 1700s.

Charlene dug her cell phone out of her purse. Two bars
were showing. Maybe there was enough power to make a call.
She needed to make a call. It would be good to call someone,
to touch base, to reconnect with civilization, if just for a few
minutes.

But there wasn't anyone to call. Mary Jane was in class.
Ryan was at work and never took social calls while at the office. Charlene didn't much like Ryan's wife, Dede. Charlene's
mother was dead. Reginald was at Mary Jane's place but
couldn't pick up.

Charlene slid back onto the driver's seat, pressed her forehead against the steering wheel, and cried. Then she wiped
her face hard, opened the car trunk, and hauled out the first of
the old, red suitcases.

4

~

places smell like what they are—Italian restaurants, ...tations, hospitals, stables. Homeplace smelled like the two-hundred-year-old building it was, a house whose last occupant had been an old lady who died in her rocking chair at age ninety-six, dentures still in her head, cup of whiskey-laced tea on the nightstand. According to Charlene's mother, Patricia, Ellen had caned to the chair from the kitchen, carrying the teacup, only to sit down, take a sip, and never get up again. She was found nine days later, after a snowstorm and after the mailman noticed she wasn't getting her catalogs, her skin blue and stretched and her insides popping with gases.

It had been a long while since Ellen Alexander had died, yet the walls and floor held the faint but sweet stench of her life and death. There were also the scents of musty magazines and urine-soaked mouse turds, both of which were strewn in healthy measure across the foyer and otherwise empty living room.

Charlene wrestled two suitcases over the threshold and into the foyer. Immediately, the hairs on her arms stood up against the chill. She dropped the cases and stared down the hall. It seemed slightly tilted, with walls covered in fading and peeling peony-patterned wallpaper. At the end of the hall was the open doorway leading to the kitchen.

To the left were a filthy window and a dust-encrusted staircase that wandered up into the second-floor shadows. To the right was the living room. As Charlene watched, a matted mouse skittered across the piles of magazines and disappeared into a crack beside the fireplace. Then she looked back at the stairs. Two other mice sat side by side on the sixth step, daring her to challenge them.

"I wonder if somebody in Adams would hire to clean for a week?" Charlene asked the mice. They stared at her, noses oddly still for vermin. "My retirement cashes out in a few weeks. What would a maid charge out here in the country, six dollars an hour? Seven? They don't expect as much as city maids, right? What the hell is minimun wage these days, anyway?"

The mice didn't give a shit. One tipped its head, the light reflecting on its eyes and making them look like tiny, silvered beads. Charlene clapped her hands. Challenged, they vanished through a hole in the step.

Mice had never bothered her much; she liked most animals, in fact. She had gone to summer camp several years as a Junior and Cadette Girl Scout, and was always getting in trouble with the counselors for making pets of the voles, chipmunks, and field mice that gathered in her wash bucket. Most wild creatures with fur were cute, angry opossums not withstanding. But as an adult, Charlene didn't care to share her house with them. Reginald might have been a good addition to this place, after all, though Charlene doubted he'd know prey if it nipped him in the nose. He was a kibbles kitty, through and through.

"I'll be fine, I can clean this. It's not *that* bad." Her voice echoed down the hallway and died in the kitchen. She drew her jacket more tightly around her body. It was then she noticed there were no baseboards in the hall, no radiators in the living room. She'd seen no oil tank outside against the house. The place had electricity; she had assumed that meant the place also had some sort of updated heating system. "Oh, come on now, this is ridiculous. Grandmother Ellen had to have some kind of heat in this place. It's going to get damn cold as winter comes on. Don't tell me she only used wood in the fireplace. I'll be in a shitload of trouble if I have to chop and haul wood the next nine months." She took a deep breath. "Slow down now. One step at a time. I refuse to be stymied by an old house."

Charlene nodded as if she were talking to someone else, then felt stupid for nodding, then felt stupid for feeling stupid. Who cared if she nodded, or shouted, or even took a piss off the front porch? This was her house, as bad a shape as it was in, and she could do whatever she wanted.

"Maybe living here alone I'll turn into one of those whacked-out women whose equally whacked-out paintings demand millions. Now that'd be cool."

Something thumped hard and heavy at the top of the stairs. Charlene stumbled backward over a suitcase, righted herself, and stared up into the darkness, bug-eyed, heart pounding.

What the hell . . . ?

Was someone up there? An escaped mental patient? A murderer?

Oh, shit shit shit!

Charlene fled to her car and locked the door. She sat for twenty minutes, clutching her tire iron, watching the door to the house, staring at the cracked, shaded windows on the second floor, debating whether to call 911 and end up looking stupid because an old ladder had given way upstairs. Her heart eased. The sweat on her palms dried.

Old houses settle, was her conclusion. *Old houses make odd noises all the time.*

She went back inside, carrying the other suitcase and her leather portfolio, leaving the front door open in case she might need to make another hasty retreat. The wind had picked up, gusting into the foyer and stirring the papers on the floor. The mice clearly didn't care for wind; none were in sight.

Flicking the foyer light switch, Charlene was relieved to discover that the power company had come through. The single bulb glowed with soft, dismissive light. Then she walked to the kitchen.

The kitchen was long and narrow, with a bricked-up fire-place and warped linoleum flooring. Against the left wall was a poorly constructed bathroom cubicle with a filthy bathtub and a toilet that rocked like a coin-operated hobbyhorse. The kitchen itself contained a battered enamel sink with a hand pump instead of a faucet *(A hand pump? What kind of water comes out of a hand pump?)*, a dead refrigerator—the kind her mother used to call an "icebox"—and grimy, contact paper–covered wooden shelving that clung to the wall with varying degrees of success. Charlene yanked open the icebox door. Inside were empty wire shelves and dark brown spatter-ings on the sides and bottom. It smelled faintly of soured milk.

All over the floor were more crumbling newspapers and magazines, glued in place with mouse poop. The kitchen win-dows looked out on a screened back porch on which a small pile of age-bleached firewood was stacked. A door with blis-tering yellow paint opened to the porch.

There isn't a discarded condom or beer can in the place. Why isn't this a hangout for local teens? It's perfect for par-tying. There's space, shelter, and it's far away from everything and everybody. Are they all that law-abiding out here in the wilderness of Virginia?

She returned to the front of the house and took the stairs, staying close to the wall, remembering from various horror movies that if a step were going to cave in, it would cave in at the middle. Grit stuck to the bottoms of her shoes, making them tick softly on the wood. Her hand trailed the wall, and then was caught by something small and hard.

Jerking her hand back, she saw what had snagged her. A nail head. There were nails on the wall, following the grade of the stairs. Charlene guessed that portraits had hung there at some point in time. When Ellen died, someone had taken them away. Maybe Grandma Sissy, or Charlene's mother? Maybe some third or fourth cousins Charlene didn't know about, though she doubted that. Charlene's mother was an only child, as had been her own mother, so the family line was pretty slim. Maybe the pictures had been auctioned off with

the other junk, or stolen. But what did they look like, those old
dead people in those long-lost paintings? Charlene squinted,
trying to recall the face of Ellen Alexander as she'd sat in the
living room in her chair. But she couldn't remember—it was
just a face, a chilling yet fuzzy blur. All the photos in albums
she'd enjoyed looking at as a child had been of her father's
family from Illinois and Ohio. Aunts and uncles and cousins,
of all ages but all of similar shapes and sizes—tall, thin, with
pale skin and dark hair. Charlene could spot a member of the
Myers family in a lineup, easily.

However, her mother's family, the Alexanders, were elusive.

And as gone as the pictures from the wall.

Upstairs was a dark hallway covered in heavy burgundy
wallpaper. Off the hall were three bedrooms, two at the front
of the house and one at the rear, their doors standing open,
pouring puddles of tainted light onto the hall floor. All were
empty except for dust, dirt, magazines, mouse flecks, and
some two-by-fours and planks that might at one time have
been shelving. Charlene stood in each room for a few minutes, trying to picture her ancestors there—reading, talking,
playing, arguing—but feeling nothing but a powerful sense of
disconnection.

Charlene walked back to the top of the stairs and then
glanced at the wall immediately across from the stairs. There
should have been a fourth room there, considering the small
size of the only bedroom at the rear of the house. Cautiously,
Charlene felt along the wallpaper, and her fingers discovered
a lumpy line that suggested a door.

*There is a room behind the wallpaper. Could the thump
have come from inside there?*

She put her right hand to her chest and pressed against the
sudden, heavy pounding of her heart.

*Stop it. It was nothing. It was a piece of wood falling, it
was a floorboard adjusting. It was something blowing and
banging through a broken back window. Don't make yourself
crazy. Okay?*

"Okay."

But why is it boarded up?
"To conserve heat."
Then why not the others?
"Shut up, Charlene."

She clawed into the brittle paper, tearing away what turned out to be seven layers of wallpaper in all, and letting the dusty strips flutter to the floor. There was indeed a door behind the paper, with strips of wood nailed across it near the top, center, and bottom. It was additionally secured with several latches and locks. The once-white paint was blistered and the door-knob was tarnished with many years of sweaty hands. Charlene touched the wood; it was painfully cold. She peeked into the keyhole and saw only darkness.

"There's nothing in there," she said. "It's just a creaky, crappy old house. With a major emphasis on crappy." She sighed, more deeply than she thought she would. Then she collected a couple two-by-fours from a front bedroom and leaned them against the door to the locked room. Just in case something inside tried to come out. Whatever or whoever would knock the wood down and she would hear it before it could get her.

You're such an idiot.

She trudged downstairs and sat on top of the largest suit-case in the foyer. She had known there wouldn't be furniture at Homeplace, but had hoped there would be. She knew the place would be filthy, but had hoped it would be manageable. She knew the place would be chilly, but had hoped she would only need to turn a thermostat to warm it up.

"You artists are dreamers of the worst kind," she said. She went outside, locked the front door, and turned the car around in the yard. In town, she would pick up cleaning supplies and a space heater.

"I hope they have cheap..." she began, but then out of the corner of her eye, she saw someone standing at the well... *FUCK!!!*... and she slammed on the brake and stared. Iced blood raced along the back of her hands and her arms.

Shit shit shit...!

There was no one there, only the waving thistles and

Queen Anne's lace and the shadows from the trees across the yard, thrumming the ground silently with translucent gray fingers.

After taking a couple minutes to pull her heart back into her chest, Charlene steered the reluctant Cruiser down the driveway to the road, and turned its nose toward Adams.

5

Yule Lemons manned the outboard as his cousin Howard Bryan, dressed in camouflage and a pair of thigh-high boots, sat on his bench at the front of the boat and cracked open a can of beer with the nub of his thumb. The river in early autumn was not as turbulent as it was in the spring, when winter snows, melted from the Blue Ridge, came rushing down various streams and creeks to create the Tye. The water was covered in a skim of leaves, sticks, and grasses wrenched loose from up-river, and it sparkled with near white, early-morning daylight.

The men had put in at quarter after five that morning at a brush-hidden spot behind the county's water treatment plant. Yule's younger brother, Danny, had driven the men to the spot in his truck, hauling the fourteen-foot boat and trailer behind, and then helped them take it to the river's edge. Danny had wanted to go, too, as he had his own twelve-footer, but he worked at the Farm Bureau Co-op over in Nellysford, and couldn't get the days off.

"They'll fire my ass I ask for any more time," Danny had said forlornly as he watched Yule and Howard toss their junk into the boat. "Got no more vacation, or more unpaid leave, neither. Used them up when I got sick in June."

"You weren't sick in June," said Yule. "You were hung over for a week after your birthday party."

"Same thing. Ain't fair you two can get away."

"Carpenters' helpers got seasonal work," said Howard as he tugged his Virginia Cavaliers cap down tight on his head, sideways, with the bill sticking out to the right. He looked like a duck with a broken neck. "I ain't got nothin' to do 'til middle of October."

"Auto World told me 'Go on and have fun,'" said Yule. "That's cause they can depend on me. I don't go off gettin' drunk and not showing up the next day. Or the next. Or the next."

Danny gave Yule a middle finger. Then he studied Howard. "What, you think you're a rapper with that hat like that?"

Howard felt his hat. "No. I'm...I'm just doing this to keep my ear from burnin'. Later on, I'll turn it the other way to cover the other ear."

Danny grinned. "Okay, well. Now you catch a bunch-a big ones, you hear? I'll bring some charcoal to the fry."

Howard sat on the front seat, his legs straddling two coolers, one of scratched blue plastic, the other of bulky white Styrofoam. The blue cooler was loaded down with a twelve-pack of beer, a pound and a half of ground beef, a drooling mustard squirter, a baggie of shaved onions, and a couple plastic containers of night crawlers, corn, and hellgrammites. The Styrofoam cooler held two bags of ice. Beneath Howard's seat was a plastic grocery bag bulging with beef jerky, lighter fluid, chips, pretzels, hamburger buns, and the men's fishing licenses tucked in a manila envelope. In the small triangular space at the front of the boat were two well-worn sleeping bags, rolled up tightly and bound with red bungee cords. On the floor, slid against the sides with the oars, were two well-used fishing rods.

In the back sat Yule, hand on the outboard stick. His hardware store cap was pushed back on his head and there was a cigarette clamped between his teeth. He didn't really smoke much; he wasn't like one of those guys who had to have a pack or two a day. Smoking wasn't a habit; he didn't even like it so much, but it was a special little extra he did when he went fishing. There was something about plugging your mouth with a white roll of tobacco, catching the tip with a lighter, and then letting the smoke trail behind you down the river. Back when Yule was a little kid, there used to be a Marlboro Man, riding his horse across a desert in the setting sun, shaking his fist at God and convention. Fishing with a pack of cigs in his shirt pocket made Yule feel wild and handsome like the Marlboro Man.

They puttered upriver a couple miles, past thick clots of forest and occasional patches of field where sleepy cows with snotty noses watched them with disinterest from behind wire fences. A couple kayakers heading south—youngsters, college kids, looked like—raised their oars as they passed Yule and Howard. The men nodded in response.

Yule's favorite fishing spot was an indentation along the riverside, where the water was especially deep. Yule cranked the outboard around and steered the boat over. Howard, who had been in some sort of silent, river-induced trance, started and cleared his throat noisily. "Let's get to it."

Yule chose worms. Howard chose corn. They fished off opposite sides of the boat, Howard singing bits and pieces of "Lucille" as Yule reminded him again and again that fish hated his singing and he best shut up. Howard would shut up but then forget he was supposed to shut up and start singing again. By ten A.M., the Styrofoam cooler held two smallmouths (Yule's) and one brown (Howard's).

"Not much here today," Yule said as he flipped the blue cooler open with the toe of his boot and then leaned in to pull out a beer. His pole was draped across his lap, the line still dragging the water.

"Pollution's got 'em," said Howard, his mouth filled with chips.

"Don't know about that."

"It's true. Happenin' all around the state. Up the Shenandoah they got heavy fish kills. Says the fish got spots on 'em that look just like burns."

"Shenandoah ain't the Tye. I think our problem is that

these fish prefer to hear a little Waylon over Kenny, or maybe a little real music over your squawking." Yule popped the beer tab, pulled a piece of hair out of his mouth, and tipped the can back. The cold liquid filled his mouth and coursed down his throat. Damn, it was good.

"Could be pollution," Howard pressed. He wiped salt from his lips with his thumb nub. He'd had two nice thumbs until a few years back when he'd caught one in the tailgate of Yule's truck as Yule was driving off. Yule took half the thumb with him and it wasn't until he stopped for gas and a drink at a 7-Eleven up the road that he saw the piece of his cousin stuck in the gate. He'd crammed the thumb bit into his cup of cherry Slurpee and drove back home as fast as he could. Then he'd taken Howard to the doctor in Charlottesville, but it didn't do any good. The thumb was too well mashed to reattach.

"Ain't pollution," said Yule. "So just shut up. You see any burns on those fish we pulled in? They ain't got three eyes or two heads, do they? I think they's all just gone somewhere else this time. We got to go find 'em."

"Where?"

"Head upriver a bit more. Where the fish don't hear so good."

"What?"

"Never mind."

Yule laid his pole in the bottom of the boat. Howard followed suit. The boat rocked gently as Howard reached out and pulled a large branch out of the way. A quick tug on the cord and the outboard was back in commission, grinding at the gasoline, spitting out a small cloud of gray. The boat moved out into the center of the river, dodging sharp rock tips and a drifting log.

"Let's make it up past Tannen Bridge," said Yule. "There's another good spot there, where Colley Creek joins the river. We could fish some, maybe even set up a camp there where the land makes the V. Don't think nobody'll come snoopin' around to mess with us. Lots of trees. We keep our fire low we'll be all right."

"All right," said Howard.

"Should we cook what we caught today or use the burger?"

"Burger. If we eat the fish we might not have nothing to take home tomorrow night for the fry."

"You got a lot of confidence in our fishin' ability, don't you?"

"Can't count your trouts before they hatch."

"You do know that trout don't know camouflage from a hole in the wall."

"What?"

"Hey, that one ear's gettin' sunburned."

"Shit." Howard turned his ball cap so the bill was poking out the other side.

The river bent northeast, then west, then north. The sun was higher now, and the men slipped on their sunglasses against the glare off the water. Yule finished his latest cigarette and flicked the butt into the water.

"There's your pollution right there," said Howard.

"Shut up, Howard."

And then Yule slowed the outboard motor and stared off to the right.

"Damn, that place gives me the creeps."

Howard looked where Yule was looking. On a rocky cliff that rose about twenty feet from the edge of the river was the brick husk of a huge and long-abandoned textile mill. Numerous spots in the walls had crumbled into lopsided piles of scab-colored clay dust. Large chunks of metal were scattered about, pieces that at one time might have been machinery. The wooden doors were shredded beneath their iron straps and hung at odd angles. Saplings, vines, and scrub pines embraced the structure with such force that the building seemed to be gasping for breath. Any glass that had been in the windows was long since blown out, and the dark holes that remained seemed to stare out at the river with mute fury.

"Never been in there," said Howard. His voice sounded chilled.

"Shit, no, why would you? I haven't, neither."

"Alexander Mill."

"Yeah."

"It's haunted."

"Yeah, everybody knows it's haunted, Howard, that mill and all the Alexander land it sits on. Who ain't heard that? But I'm way too old to believe in ghosts. Ghosts is for sissies and diaper babies."

"Then why'd you never go in there?"

Yule tugged his cigarette pack from his shirt pocket, tapped out a smoke, crammed it into his mouth. It didn't taste as good as the last one, but he lit it, anyway. "I never went in there 'cause there's rotten floorboards and shit that'll swallow you whole."

"How you know that, you never been in?"

"Shut up, Howard."

And then something in one of the dark, empty window holes caught Yule's attention. His stomach drew into an instant knot. "Shit," he said.

"Shit what?"

"I seen a light in there."

"No, you didn't. Did you?"

It had been a small light, just a few seconds of pointed brightness, and then it was gone. In one of the many lower windows where there should be no light at all.

"Maybe it was deer eyes."

"No, Howard, it wasn't deer eyes. Deer eyes got to glow off of something. This was its own glow. It was...it wasn't deer eyes."

"Let's go see, then. We ain't diaper babies no more. Come on."

Yule took a long drag and held the smoke in, deep. He dangled the cigarette over the water and flicked off the ash, which caught on a pin oak leaf and drifted away. "No. We got fishin' to do."

"We got what we want to do to do," said Howard. "Rick ain't along to stop us from snoopin' about. Just a couple minutes. Let's go up in there and see what that light was all about."

"No."

"Bet it's kids. Stuff like that is always kids. Maybe smoking dope. Maybe you saw their lighter light up. We could scare the crap out of them, you think?"

"Kids don't go there. When we were kids we didn't go there."

"Kids is different these days."

Yule flicked his cig away and turned the outboard engine to high; the boat lurched forward, making Howard flop forward then catch himself on the boat sides. "Hey!"

Through clenched teeth, "What?"

"I want to go in there."

"No, you don't."

"Screw this, Yule. Turn the boat around. Get over there to the side. I want to go in and see what's up."

"No."

"I said get it over there, now!"

"No."

"You ain't the boss of me, you fucker."

"Now you're sounding like a kid, Howard."

"I mean it, you ain't in charge of this trip. I paid half the food, half the bait, half the fuel. I just want a couple minutes."

Yule turned the engine down a bit. The boat slowed. "But why?"

"I don't know. Just because. Ain't you never wanted to do something other people won't do?"

Yule considered this. "Sometimes. But not this time."

"Hey, we go in there, we can say for sure it ain't haunted. Once and for all."

"It ain't haunted, Howard. Once and for all."

"I'm fucking thirty-eight years old. I can do what I want to do."

Yule spun the outboard around and the boat veered off toward shore. "Okay, then. Have it your way. Go in there. Get snake bit. Get spider bit. See if there's a teenager in there with pot. You think a teenager won't also have a gun? A knife? Go in there, Cousin. Don't let me stop you."

"Good."

"Good."

The boat reached the edge of the river, upstream a bit from

the mill, where tall grasses grew and mud had collected over a shallow pit of stone. Howard hopped out of the boat into the water, pulled the nose around, and tied it to the sagging branch of a redbud tree. Then he scrambled up the embankment. "Why don't you come with me? A quick look around."

"No," said Yule. He felt an odd knot in his throat. It hurt to swallow against it. He wished Howard would stop being such an asshole and get back in the boat. "You go on, be the boss of you."

Howard shook the water from his fishing boots, pulled the seam of his camouflage pants out of his crotch, and hiked off triumphantly toward the old mill. Yule wanted to call him back, to try to convince him one last time that going into that building wasn't a good idea, that he'd seen a light and he sensed there was nothing good inside there. But damn it, Howard was such a child when it came to things. He was always trying to prove he was smarter, braver, stronger, better than other people, when in fact he was average, or maybe just a tad below average. (Yule remembered Howard's mother bitching after her son's eighth grade year-end report suggested he wasn't college material, that he'd be better off taking courses at the Tech Center than signing up for the more academically geared sciences, languages, and maths. Of course, the school had been right. Howard never did much above a C or D in most of his classes, yet having someone attempt to steer him in the direction he eventually steered himself was, to Howard's mother, the insult to top all insults. Howard retained that "you can't tell me nothing" attitude into his adulthood, for all the good it did him.)

At the back of the boat, Yule lit another cigarette. This one tasted nasty, like dirty laundry. He crushed it out on the seat beside him and then looked up to watch his cousin stroll along the flattened stretch of land that led to the mill. Howard laughed aloud and jabbed his thumb nub in Yule's direction.

"Come on, do this with me!"

"No. And make it quick."

"Shut up." Howard reached the thick brush against the nearest brick wall and wrangled himself through, his arms out and parting the branches like a stumbling Frankenstein. From the vantage of the river, he was dwarfed against the building. Like Dorothy, preparing to enter the Emerald City, although this was no sweet fairy tale castle.

A dragonfly hummed over the boat and Yule let his eyes follow its erratic movements—back, forth, up, down—as if trying to determine who had intruded into its space. It lit atop the Styrofoam cooler and probed the knotty white surface with its legs. Yule reached out slowly with one finger, sure it would fly away before he could touch its delicate stained-glass wings. The creature turned toward him, kaleidoscopic eyes considering him for a moment, then it rose like a tiny helicopter and darted off across the river.

Yule looked back at the old mill. Howard had made it inside, somehow. The empty black window holes watched Yule. Taunted him. Cold fingers of dread crawled up his spine and tightened his scalp.

Jesus. Let's get out of here.

He started to tap another cigarette from his pack but threw the pack down on the floor of the boat. *Come on come on, Howard.*

There was no sign of movement inside the gigantic building. Howard didn't poke his head from one of the windows to wave.

What if he's caught his foot in a floorboard? Well, then he would call for me.

But what if he's been stabbed?

"Howard!" Yule shouted. "You okay in there?"

Nothing.

Shit. "Howard! You okay in there?"

A faint voice, from deep inside the building, "Yeah, I'm okay!"

Good. Good.

Yule leaned toward the cooler for another beer, but stopped and said aloud, "No, we'll need those later." Then toward the mill he shouted, "Hurry up, man! Beer's getting impatient!"

No answer.

Yule rubbed a rash of sudden sweat from his neck. *Fuck this.*

"Howard, that's long enough! Get your scrawny, camouflage-wearin', rapper-hatted ass out here now!"

No answer.

And then something burst from one of the lower window-holes, a ball of fire blowing through the black maw and into the daylight, a man-sized sun leaping to the ground, stagger-ing through the weeds to the rocky cliff, clawing with ap-pendages for purchase but then losing its footing and dropping like a stone against stone, striking the curve of the cliff and then the edge of the river and rolling into the leaf-mottled water.

Steam rose where the ball of fire had struck. There was a struggle, a frantic churning of the water, and then a charred, blackened arm reached upward, clutching toward the sky in tortured supplication.

"Howard!"

Yule leapt from the boat, turning it over as he went, spilling coolers and poles and sleeping bags, and forced him-self through the waist-deep water at the river's edge. His teeth bore down into his tongue but he didn't feel it. Blood pooled in his mouth but he didn't taste it.

"Howard!"

He lost his footing on slippery river bottom rocks and went down, face first. He came up spitting and coughing. "Howard!"

There was a soft groan from the scorched body.

Yule reached his cousin, whose arm had dropped back down and who was floating with his face up, his eyes open.

"Oh, my God, Howard!" He reached out but then pulled back.

Howard's flesh was alternately black and red, with small pieces breaking free and drifting away like flakes of goldfish food. His nose was gone. His skull showed through the cooked skin of his forehead. His upper lip was burned off but his lower lip remained.

"Sweet Jesus, Howard!"

Howard opened his mouth and at first only air came out, hissing, like steam escaping a teakettle. Then he whispered, "Wasn't nobody."

Furious, terrified tears filled Yule's eyes. He slid his arms around his cousin's chest as gently as he could. He could still feel the heat radiating outward. "Don't talk! Shhh, shhh! I gotta get you to the hospital!"

"Wasn't...nobody. Wasssssn't...kids," managed Howard. The "s's" hissed with the absence of the upper lip.

"Shut up, you stupid idiot!" Yule screamed. He couldn't look at the open eyes. "Just hold still! Fuck it, I don't have a cell phone! Why the hell didn't you or me ever get a damned cell phone? Hold still, I'm gonna get you in the boat. Okay? Okay?"

"Yuuuullle..."

Yule could hear the pure and perfect agony in the voice. "We're gonna find out who did this! We're gonna get them!"

"Wasssssn't...nobody...wassss ghostssss..."

"Shut up, Howard!"

And then Howard began to tremble violently, as if his body had just realized what had been done to it. His teeth clacked together, and through clenched jaws he began to wail, an unearthly, whistling, hellish sound.

"Don't die, man! No, don't you fucking dare!"

Howard kicked and writhed, fighting the pain, the moment, and the realization that he had been killed. Yule tried to hold his cousin more tightly, but that made the man howl louder. Yule let go.

Howard's body went under, and then popped back up again. He kicked and thrashed. Yule stood back and watched, unable to move.

And then Howard went still.

Yule's heart twisted in his chest. His jaw fell open and he coughed, gagged, and then wretched into the water, spitting bile and vomit and what felt like his soul.

Dear Heavenly God!

But it didn't seem as if God was listening at that moment.

So Yule was alone to flip the boat and haul his dead cousin up and over into it, trying his best not to let his burned clothes or flesh fall away. He was alone to steer the boat back downriver to their putting-in spot, to pull the boat up and out of the

water and to walk the mile and a quarter into Adams to find a
phone. Alone to tell Rick Evans that Howard's body was back
in the boat, up near the water treatment plant. That after a couple too many beers, he'd gotten stupid and had fallen face first
into the campfire while Yule was gathering more firewood.

Alone to return to his trailer, with his wife and mother-in-
law off on their little Greyhound jaunt, all by himself to face
the oncoming night and the terror that the memory of
Howard's open eyes brought on. Alone to decide as he gazed
at the sliver moon off his redwood deck that it was indeed a
campfire that had killed Howard. Because nobody in their
right mind would try to catch or punish a ghost. That dead
things were best left dead.

6

~

Charlene returned to Homeplace at ten thirty in the morning, having chickened out and spent the night in a room in the town's only motel, with its unique and catchy moniker, "Adams Motel." The Cruiser was filled with cleaning supplies from the Dollar General store—a broom, a wet mop, several plastic buckets, rags, and various liquid products that might chew through years and layers of scum and rodent turds. She had stared for a good fifteen minutes at her choice of mouse traps. The store offered an array—snap-their-necks traps, stick-to-glue traps, and some stainless "humane live" traps. *Could I kill mice?* she had pondered, staring at the display. Little warm, furry things with cute little toes and white tummies, distant relatives, perhaps, of those she'd doted on as a Girl Scout? But could she spend the next seven months catching and letting them go only to have them come back into the house through one of the small holes in the foundation and poop in her kitchen, under her bed, on her paints and papers? She went for the snap-their-necks traps, eight of them. She could only hope they would die immediately and not stare at her with blame in their eyes as they lay caught beneath the wires.

Next she'd stopped at Randy's Hardware and picked up a sleeping bag, a box of lightbulbs, batteries, a hot plate, a manual can opener, a hammer and nails, and a box of canned foods—peas, carrots, corn, deviled ham, and Lite Spam. An attractive, sandy-haired man in his mid-thirties, leaning on a cane and dressed in jeans and a khaki jacket, was in line in front of her, buying tulip and daffodil bulbs. When done, he stepped aside and watched as her selections were rung up. He held the store door open for her, and said as she passed with her wire cart, "You're new to Adams?"

"Ah, yeah." She hit the button on her key chain to beep open the Cruiser doors. She maneuvered the cart behind the car, popped the hatch, then pulled the boxes and bags out of the cart and placed them on the tarp she'd laid out in the back.

"I'm Andrew Marshall," the man continued, sticking the bag of flower bulbs beneath his arm and shifting his weight against the cane. She wondered if he'd sprained his ankle or broken his foot. "I'm the lone lawyer in town."

"Are you going to serve me with something?"

"What? Oh, no," he said with a chuckle. "Just introducing myself."

"That's good. Well, it's nice to meet you." She slammed the hatch, hesitated, and then held out her hand. He shook it warmly, firmly.

He asked, "I'm guessing you are the new owner of Ale And. Am I right?"

"Excuse me?"

Andrew Marshall grinned, rubbed his short growth of beard, and said, "That's what the mailbox looks like from a distance, anyway. Sounds like a pub that wants to offer more but can't quite decide what that should be."

"Ah."

"Ah or ha?" said Andrew, eyebrows up.

"Ha, ha," said Charlene. How did he know who she was and where she lived? That was disconcerting. She didn't want people sneaking up on her like that.

"Hey, sorry if I'm being intrusive," Andrew said, raising one hand apologetically. "There are so few new people in the area, and word gets around. I heard this morning at the Exxon station that someone was moving into the old Alexander place. I was just trying to put two and two together. Sorry if I'm wrong. Or if I'm being irritating. Or both."

"No, that's fine. I mean that's not irritating. And yes, I'm at the old Alexander place."

"I'm a newcomer to town, as well," said Andrew. "Relatively speaking. Been here a year, down from Boston. It's a peaceful place. Quieter than Boston, anyway."

"That's good," said Charlene. "Peaceful is good. Quiet is good." *You sound like a moron. He's going to think something's wrong with you.*

"Well, then," said Andrew. "Nice to meet you."

"You, too," said Charlene. She hopped into the Cruiser and steered out of the hardware store parking lot. It wasn't wise to talk to strangers, she'd heard time and time again, though she'd also heard that a stranger was a friend you didn't yet know. Okay, then she wasn't into making friends. Not now. Maybe not for a long time. And that was fine. She had plenty of things to do that didn't require friends.

But he really was a nice-looking guy, and he had a wonderful handshake.

Charlene looked in her rearview and watched Andrew watching her leave.

*O*ne *room at a time,* she told herself as she eased the Cruiser back down the rutted driveway. *The living room first.* She would sleep there, paint there, and eat there. She would grow there, and evolve there. She didn't need the rest of the house. *Well, the living room and the kitchen.*

"This is good. This will be good."

And then she pulled into the yard, she looked at the house, and her heart sank once more.

But the work of the day was all-consuming, and she was surprised to catch herself humming random tunes as she trash-bagged the aging magazines and newspapers, shoved grit out the front door and off the porch with her new broom, scrubbed the living room and foyer windows with ammonia, and filled the bucket with cold water from the hand pump.

Thank you JESUS, the hand pump works and the water looks potable.

Then she started on the living room floor on her hands and knees with a scrub brush. On the floor near the fireplace, the radio was tuned to FM WBAM, "The Piedmont's Premiere Station, Featuring the Finest Virginia-Based Artists," offering up songs from Calf Mountain Jam, Wanda and the White Boys, Blues Soup, and Don't Look Back. At first Charlene whipped the dial back and forth, trying to find something else, but WBAM was the only clear station out this far, and so WBAM it was. Having listened to little beyond her Tim Janis, Secret Garden, Jim Brickman, classical ensembles, and movie soundtrack CDs over the past year or so, she found the musical change of pace enjoyable. She scrubbed to the rhythm of the songs until her shoulders hurt, and it felt good.

After a lunch of a Spam sandwich and green tea, heated on her very own hot plate in her very own teakettle, she sat on her sleeping bag on the clean floor and scribbled a list of things she would accomplish in the next few days:

1. Clean the kitchen floor.
2. Clean the toilet and the tub.
3. Set up easel by the living room window.
4. Check out the property on foot.

She drew a line through "the" and over it wrote "my."

4. Check out my property on foot.

Homeplace was large, and Charlene wasn't sure exactly where the boundaries were, except that one bordered the Tye River to the west. Her family had owned a textile mill in the mid-nineteenth century, producing cotton fabric along the Tye River fall line. But other than that, she didn't have a clue and she didn't have a map. Surely there would be some sort of fencing to delineate the rest of her land from her neighbors'.

By three thirty in the afternoon, Charlene's enthusiasm for cleaning was gone. It wouldn't be dark for another few hours. She slung her camera strap over her neck, slipped on her jacket, boots, and leather gloves, and went through the kitchen and out the screened porch to face her world.

Surrounding the yard on all sides was forest populated with oaks, sycamores, elms, maples, and cedars. Behind the house to the southwest the forest rose into the aqua foothills and then the ash-blue mountains. Charlene stood in the backyard, took a long deep breath, and sighed. The place was a cluttered mess. She eased around a pile of discarded odds and ends, stacks of old planks, a slimy compost pile, a scraggly plot that had once been a garden, and then on across the yard. She snatched up a large stick when she realized there were certainly copperheads and possibly timber rattlesnakes in Nelson County. She swung the stick back and forth along the ground in front of her, smacking the weeds as she walked. Where had she heard about whacking sticks? Maybe it had been at Girl Scout camp. She didn't really want to kill anything, just scare it away.

When she reached the edge of the backyard she spotted a trail laced with vines and layered with pine silt, leading into the woods. She took the path. She struck the ground with her stick—whack, whack, whack—and trudged along, feeling quite free and surprisingly pleased, tracing up and down small knolls, hopping over logs and broken branches. She'd not done anything outdoors since she and Mary Jane had hiked the Dismal Swamp, and that was months ago. But it felt good, being outdoors. On her land. She tossed her head and picked up her pace.

This is good. I'll be fine. I'm going to do fine here. I'm rugged stock. Mom was right. I can make it.

She grinned. Then she chuckled. Then she laughed as hard as she could, and listened to the echo somewhere up the trail. "I can make it!" she shouted.

The path took a sharp right, and there, just off the trail, were the ruins of five small huts. None had roofs or doors; only one had all four stone walls still in place, though they were degrading at the top, crumbling and caving in toward the center. Each had clusters of twisted trees growing from their centers. Charlene stared at the huts, trying to imagine who had lived there. And then she knew.

My family owned slaves.

She took several steps closer, snapping twigs beneath her feet.

Oh, my God, that's right. I haven't thought about that for years. Mom mentioned it when I was a kid. We were in our kitchen when she told us, I think, or the family room, eating Christmas cookies. Dad was saying how he'd marched for Civil Rights in Alabama in the sixties, and then Mom said off-handedly, "My family owned slaves, you know." She said no more but there it was. A dark family secret.

And here they were, or what was left of them, of their lives. Five ancient hovels set away from the main house, destroyed in equal measure by nature and human forgetfulness. A rusted, encrusted iron pot lay on its side in the weeds. Charlene wondered what had been cooked in that pot, who had served the food, and who had eaten it. She felt like a voyeur, standing there amid broken saplings and grasses, staring at the remnants of—how many lives? What had they felt, living here in the woods and the shadows, tucked away as if to be kept out of sight and out of mind of those who lived in the big house? What had their day-to-day been? Did they grow crops, cut wood, tend children? Did they secretly plan to escape? Did they have family members sold off to other farms? Charlene felt a twist in her heart, wondering what the answers to those questions might be. She snapped photos from various angles, forming the basis for a new and poignant composition in watercolor.

"This could be the first of my new series of paintings," she said to a small lizard in the pot. "Things from my past. Things from the past of others that tie into my past. A personal, historical, yet universal collection. That could be powerful. That could be good."

A squirrel raced up a tree next to one of the huts' foundations, chased by another squirrel. They reached the top and vanished into the foliage, their fight—or their lovemaking—causing the branches to shudder and shake. Several orange leaves fell to the ground, looking like large copper snowflakes. Charlene reached out and caught another. It was damp and slick and covered with tiny black spots. She held it to her nose and inhaled. It smelled of life and death, earth and sky, beginnings and endings. She tossed it away and moved on.

The path curved north then west again, the ground sloping downward then leveling off. Trees bowed over the pathway; wind whistled through the dense growth around her. Birds squealed, unseen, from brush piles.

She sensed the river before she saw it. The temperature dropped and she could smell the water. Gaps between tree trunks and fanning branches revealed slices of sparkling white. Charlene pulled her hood up over her head. She picked her footsteps more carefully, as the ground had grown wet and slippery. Then she was out of the trees and standing by the water.

The river was wide, fast, and patterned with currents of foaming, rushing wet. Across the water was more forest, with mountains rising behind. A flat, mangy-grassed, two-yard-wide stretch traveled along Charlene's side of the river in both directions as far as she could see.

I bet this is where the train tracks used to be. A train would have to have carried cotton to our family's mill and then the cotton cloth away to some major trading center, like Richmond, maybe, or Roanoke. I guess this section of the tracks was torn up when the mill stopped producing.

She followed the barren train line south, tapping the ground with her stick. No snakes leaped out of the way, but clouds of gnats swirled up before her, and she covered her nose. Several went into her ear; she dug at them with her finger. The river angled abruptly to the left. Around the bend was the mill.

Charlene stopped and stared. "Whoa."

It stood on a stone embankment by the river—a three-story, city-block-long behemoth of brick and broken windows.

Waves of kudzu, poison ivy, warped saplings, and Virginia creeper embraced the brick walls. Arched double doors were sealed with massive locks, though the doors looked to be at a tilt. The train trail ran up to the archway.

The train ran through the center of the mill. In one end and out the other. I can't imagine how noisy, how dirty it was when the whole thing was running full steam. I can't imagine how many employees they had to have to keep this thing up and running. No, not employees. They must have used the slaves.

Smaller doors along the front of the building had obviously served the workers. Enormous brick smokestacks rose from the sides of the building. What had once been large turbines lay in bits and pieces, caught and rotting in the rocks and the back-swirling current of the river's edge.

Charlene lifted her camera, thinking that if she had five or six million dollars, she could have this place renovated and rebuilt into one kick-ass artists' commune.

"That would be fantastic. Put in a scenic drive along the river out to the main road. Patch up the holes in the walls, put on a new roof, add northern exposure windows, and skylights. Partition it into huge studios with hardwood floors, a café, a large communal gallery. It could be the toast of Nelson County, the new creative Mecca for Virginia—hell, the East Coast."

She smiled with the whole idea of it all, stepped closer, and took a picture. A baby rabbit dashed out of the grass in front of her. She flinched, then took another step.

"Artists would have to compete to be a part. They'd have to impress me, instead of me always trying to impress them. I'd be the crowned head of the art community. I'd decide if their work was worthy or if it was a pile of senseless crap. That would be great, wouldn't it?"

Of course, there was no one to answer.

Charlene let out a breath. "That's what I thought."

Click. Another photo.

She could hear it then—a soft, rhythmic pounding from the building. She clutched the camera to her chin and tilted her head. "What's that?"

At first she thought it was the pounding of her own heart,

as soft as it was. She had exerted more energy in her hike than she'd done in a while, and she was breathing just a bit heavier than usual, but still...

The sound persisted, a little louder now, a dull and insistent thumping...

Is that coming from inside the mill?

...sounding much like machines inside the mill.

No, of course not, that's ridiculous...

Machines that should have long since died running on their own.

That's impossible.

She let go of her camera; it fell to the length of its strap and thwacked against her stomach. She stepped backward several feet, squinting at the old building and its pocked and mottled façade, listening but not wanting to listen. Sweat popped out on her shoulders and adrenaline shot through her arms. She swallowed, and her throat was dry.

Pound, clack, whir. The muffled sounds of ancient wheels and straps spinning and clacking.

"Be quiet," she whispered aloud. A scattering of birds flew out from a niche between broken bricks in the mill's massive north wall.

And now with the pounding came a whining sound, distant yet clear, a metal screeching like that of a train as it lurched to life on steel tracks. The ground began to tremble slightly.

Shit, oh shit!

Her hand went over her mouth and into her fingers she screamed, "Shut up, shut up!"

The sounds stopped.

For a moment the ground continued to shiver beneath her feet in repercussion of the pounding machines...

...no, it's only the repercussions of my own muscles, acting like the idiots they are.

...deep inside the mill.

It was me, it was my own nervousness, my own imagination. Pull yourself together, girl, or you'll scare yourself from your own land before you have a chance to even make yourself at home.

She stood, blowing easy breaths through her teeth, staring at the long-dead mill. Then she climbed through the thorns and vines to take more photos, gathering images at a closer distance now, capturing the glistening chips of sunlight on the broken window glass, the towering black chimneys against the clouds, the fractured line of mortar between bricks where a mummified moth's cocoon was wedged.

What amazing paintings these will make!

She checked her watch. It was already 5:24. It would be dark in just over an hour. She repacked her camera and re-traced her steps along the river to the path through the woods. Her feet were beginning to sting. Pine silt and grit had sifted inside both boots and socks, and chewed at her soles and toes. Her cheeks and neck, she realized, were popping with insect bites. Flying ants buzzed her ears and landed in her hair. She clawed them out and walked faster.

The path was colder now, the shadows thicker; the trees seemed more oppressive and the brush closer against the sides than before. Thorns snagged at her jeans. Her breath hung before her in small frosted clouds.

A striped snake slid onto the path in front of her and stopped, considering her with its flickering tongue. "Scoot!" Charlene shouted at the snake, then snapped a broken branch from a dogwood and hurled it at the creature. It drew back, then slithered into the path-side brush.

Note to self: Don't go off and leave your whacking stick by the river next time.

"I'll figure this country living out soon enough. I'll learn the ins and outs of being a hick." She said it aloud, to hear herself so she would know everything would be all right. She was just a babe in the woods today, but in a couple weeks she would be the Amazon empress of the forest, identifying edible bushes, charming the creatures, hell, swinging through the trees on wild grapevines, why not?

"Yeah, baby, that's me, Mama Amazon, Empress of the Woods!"

She hiked the dips and hills as fading daylight grew blue on the pathway. She could still see; it was amazing how little

light one needed to keep from tumbling over logs or running
off track, but a flashlight would be a good idea next time.
Night birds were already taking their cues from the setting
sun, and whistled shrilly from unseen perches. The path took
an easy left and then went down again. She looked up at the
sky through the forest tangle and saw a single, first star.

She looked back down at the path. And stopped short.

There was a small, white cross hammered into the center
of the path.

Where did that come from? That wasn't there before.

It was a foot and a half tall, tied with twine and tipping
slightly to the right, as if pointing to something off the path.

Did I walk past this and not see it?

No. It wasn't there.

"It had to have been," she said, pulling the cuffs of her
sleeves down over her chilly hands. "I was looking elsewhere
and walked right by."

A new wind cut up the path, causing the white cross to nod
slightly.

*But how could I have missed it? I'd have tripped over it or
whacked it with my snake stick.*

Charlene tossed her head then felt silly for doing it. "I just
didn't see it. I'm not the most aware human to ever walk the
Earth. Anybody can tell you that."

The cross bobbed again, pointing to an obscured fork in
the path.

Charlene hadn't noticed the deviation when she'd hiked
out; it was narrow and veered off at a sharp angle, where it
disappeared in dense vegetation. Where did it go? A quick
side trip to check it out would be all right, just a few minutes
up and then back. It was her land; she could do that.

But I can't be long. It's getting dark quickly.

The growing night shadows across the white cross made it
look as though it were bathed in translucent black blood.

*One hundred fifty steps forward, one hundred fifty steps
back. That should be all right. I can't get lost retracing my
steps that way.*

She moved onto the smaller path, hesitated, and then

walked on. The low-hanging branches over the path were riddled with spiders' webs, and Charlene put her arms in front of her to keep them off her face. This path was rockier, its dips sharper. Night came on in a rush, sucking away the last of the early evening light, leaving her with just the faint moon glow.

"...one twenty-three, one twenty-four, one twenty-five..."

Just stop here, Charlene. This is far enough. Turn back. Go home, get warm—well, as warm as possible. She dug her cuffed fingers into the bites on her face and started to turn back.

Then she saw the spot of light.

At first she thought she'd neared someone's campfire. Who dared to camp on her land without permission? Screw that!

But are you still on your land?

She eased closer, stepping as quietly as she could, her face scrunched up as if that would help her be silent. It was not a campfire but a lantern, sitting atop a flat, upright rock. Leaning against the rock was a downed tree trunk, heavy and black.

No, not leaning against a rock—it was a tombstone.

Sticks cracked beneath Charlene's feet and she froze, wondering what might be out there, listening. The dark tree trunk pulled away from the tombstone and stood slowly and with effort. It was then Charlene could see its eyes. They were huge, and in the lantern light, deep red.

7

The old woman's name was Maude Boise. She lived on the
land adjoining Homeplace, and had considered it her job
ever since Ellen Alexander died to keep up the small Alexander graveyard.

She sat on a tombstone with her plastic scrub bucket at her
feet. Charlene sat on another stone, holding her camera, wanting
to capture this odd, lantern-lit moment but afraid the woman
would protest. Around them on the ground, amid the trees, were
the headstones of dead Alexanders and what appeared to have
been the family slaves. Weather had cracked some of the headstones and had worn others down to barely legible tablets. Mildred Alexander, 1874–1927. Ellen Alexander, 1895–1992. Posey
Alexander, 1839–1891. Julia Alexander, 1855–1894. Sarah
Alexander, 1822–1848. Ginny, died 1864. Rose, died 1861. Nel,
died 1833. Manama, died 1846. Charlene's mother, Patricia, had
buried Grandmother Sissy in Richmond, near where she had
died, and then Patricia herself was buried in a small public cemetery in D.C. Patricia had told Charlene and Ryan that she had
never lived at Homeplace and felt no connection there, and so
preferred to "spend eternity" where she had been married and
raised her children and had her happiest memories.

Maude's breathing was at last slowed; she'd been startled badly by Charlene's appearance in the woods and had coughed and patted at her chest for several long minutes to pull herself back together. Charlene had been a little more than startled, as well, but didn't have the heart to tell the old woman that she'd looked like a dead tree with red eyes. She listened as the woman tried to explain the reason for her trespassing.

"I'd no idea somebody was movin' out here to the Homeplace," said Maude. "If I had, I'd've introduced myself proper. I didn't mean to give you a start, or to get one myself." She chuckled, shook her head. "Ask anybody lives round here and they'll tell you I know my manners." In the pool of lantern light, Charlene guessed that Maude was in her eighties. She was short, thick, with a pleasant yet time-creased face. Beneath the fabric of her blue checked blouse, two ancient breasts hung almost to her waist like sacked oranges. She wore a skirt just short enough to reveal she didn't shave her lower legs, and dirty tennis shoes with rolled-down socks. "I'd've brung you one of my fresh baked chess pies had I known. But I didn't know. I was just doin' my weekly tendin' of the stones. Nobody been on this land for years and years, and it's the least I could do to care for these poor souls' restin' places."

Charlene said, "I appreciate that," although she wasn't sure she appreciated it at all. She didn't want someone traipsing over once a week to scrub lichens from grave markers that belonged to her.

"I live yonder," said Maude, nodding back over her shoulder. "My property's Willow Vale. It borders yours to the southwest. My family's like yours. We've owned our land round about two centuries. None of us goes far in our wanderin's, now do we? Here I am. Here you are. We don't let no developers get holda what's ours, no ma'am." The woman smiled a brief but lovely smile, one that caught Charlene off guard. What a painting she would make, this old woman on a tombstone, with only the light of a lantern revealing her features.

"Excuse me, but may I take your photo?" Charlene began. "I'm a painter, you see, and..."

"Two hundred years we lived by your family, both rooted deep," said Maude, tapping the bucket with one filthy sneaker. "But that might be the only thing your family and mine have in common."

Charlene removed the lens cap from the camera. "What do you mean by that?" *Maybe they manufactured moonshine while we manufactured cotton cloth?*

Maude leaned from her tombstone, close enough to Charlene for her to smell cheese and onions on the old woman's breath. "Oh, I don't care to talk about that. It's all I can do to get my old self over here once a week for the dead."

"You don't like it here at Homeplace?"

The old woman's bushy brows drew together and she looked at the ground. "To be honest, I don't."

"Why's that?"

"Don't care to discuss it, if it's all the same to you, Miss Alexander."

"It's Charlene Myers, Miss Boise," said Charlene.

"Shouldn't that be Alexander?"

"My family's Alexander. My mother's family. My father's family is Myers."

"Myers a family in Nelson County?"

"Northern Virginia. My real father, I never knew him. I think it was a passing thing with Mom, a fling, if you know what I mean. But Mom married Derrick Myers when I was two, so he was always the man I thought of as my father."

"You an only child?"

"I have a stepbrother, Ryan. He's in Northern Virginia, too."

"That's nice." Maude slapped a bug from her nose. "A child alone can be lonely, Miss Myers."

"Yes. And please call me Charlene."

"If you call me Maude."

"Sure." Charlene looked at Maude through the lens, snapped a photo. "Listen, are you the one who put that white cross in the center of the path? I found it on my way back from the river and it directed me here."

"Cross? Oh, there's crosses all about. They's been there long time, put there to let the family find this lil' graveyard from any direction."

Okay, it was there, I just didn't see it. That's what I thought.

Charlene snapped another photo. Maude didn't say anything, just waited until the snapping was done.

"You do know something of my family, don't you?" said Charlene. "I'd love to talk to you about them sometime. My mother never bored me as a child with tales of my ancestors, not that I would have cared much. You know kids. Now, I wish I'd been bored, even a little bit. I'm really curious about a lot of things. I'm sure there are tons of stories. Such as the fact that all the women kept their maiden name. I think that's really rather feminist for a bunch of women back in the old days. Don't you think so?"

"Maybe so."

"I'm sure you can tell me some things I don't know."

Maude's shoulder hitched, a shrug.

"Do you know why my mom's family held on to this land for so long?" Charlene lowered her camera. "The mill is long gone, in total disrepair for what looks like a hundred years at least. The Alexanders must have farmed something at some point, being out this far, but much of the land is forest and the rest is pretty rocky. This place is out in the middle of nowhere, no offense. It can't be very valuable. You said we don't give in to developers, but honestly, I'm surprised one of us didn't just go ahead and sell it to somebody, anybody, who might have thought they could do something with it. A Girl Scout camp or a hunting lodge?"

Maude touched her chin and considered this. Then she said, "The Alexanders have always been scared to sell the land."

Scared?

"Considering what might happen if they did," Maude added.

This was hardly the answer Charlene expected. She blinked. "What do you mean, scared to sell the land?"

Maude only shrugged.

"Well," said Charlene, straightening her shoulders, "whatever you might believe was their reason for hanging on to the property, my plans are to stay here until spring, and then sell it and move back to the beach. I appreciate the fact that it's my family's history, and I plan on doing paintings in respect of that history, but it's not something I care to pay taxes on." She laughed lightly, hoping to sound more carefree about the whole thing than she was now feeling.

"So you say?" said Maude, her pale eyes widening. But she said no more about it. She then slipped her wash bucket over her arm and offered to walk Charlene home with the lantern.

"But if you don't like being here, on this land...?" Charlene began.

"Oh, 'tisn't too bad when there's some nice company along. But hear me, Charlene. Don't be wanderin' around too much. You might stumble on things that won't do you no good at all."

"Such as?"

Maude just shook her head.

They took yet another path that left the graveyard from the rear, and within five minutes they emerged into the yard beside the old house.

From the front porch Charlene bid the old woman goodbye, feeling oddly bothered to see her leave, thinking that if nothing else, an acquaintance nearby would be a good thing.

"Do you want a ride home? I can drive you," Charlene asked as Maude thumped across the yard toward the forest. Maude kept walking, but called back, "I knows a shortcut."

"Do you have a phone?"

Maude stopped then, and turned about with her hands on her hips. Her smile was good-natured. "I may be old but I ain't old-fashioned. 'Course I got a phone. Got me a television, too. Even running water, can you believe it, a ole biddy like me?"

"Oh, okay. Good," said Charlene. "I don't have a land line but I have a cell." They traded numbers. Then Maude disappeared into the night, her dirty white sneakers the last thing visible, winking up and down. Charlene went inside and locked the door.

"I wonder what my family thought would happen to them if they sold this land?" she asked her shadow on the foyer floor.

Charlene pulled down the dry-rotted window shades in the living room, turned on the electric space heater, and curled up with her sleeping bag and pillow on the floor. She gazed at the glowing heater, then across the hall to the foot of the stairs. She thought of the room at the top, locked, boarded up. The room where she'd thought she'd heard something crash.

I wonder why the Alexanders were afraid to sell.

She realized that she had balled up one of the blankets and was petting it as if it were Reginald. She tossed the blanket aside.

Then she grabbed for it and pulled it back again.

From somewhere beyond the living room, beyond the house, out past the forest where the Tye River flowed and the old mill sat like a crippled old man, she thought she could hear a rhythmic pounding start up, hold steady, and then fade after a long number of minutes and disappear beneath the hammering of her own pulse.

She slept at last, and the sleep was empty of sound, empty of dreams.

8

~

Hugh Chase stood on the walk outside the station house, facing up the street into the sleet-riddled Boston wind. The ice slammed into and around him, angry fistfuls of winter, and he welcomed it. Let it chew him awhile. Let the city take out her anger on him. He deserved it, he deserved it all.

The murder victims in the ferry had been identified, but their murder hadn't even begun to be solved. Two weeks had passed. And as any detective worth his weight in ink and report paper knew, if there weren't any major leads or discoveries within forty-eight hours of the crime, it became less and less likely to be solved.

It had snowed several hours ago, huge, sloppy flakes that were filthy before they even hit the streets. For a short while it had looked like the city might be in for a blizzard, but then the snow had changed to frozen rain and so it remained. The air smelled of cold metal and exhaust. Rivulets coursed down Hugh's face and into the upturned collar of his brown leather jacket. He wore no hat, and his hair was plastered to his scalp. His hands were bare, chapped and cracking, one shoved into a coat pocket, the other exposed and clutching a slip of paper with an address on it.

"This isn't half bad," Andrew said, then focused back on the screen.

He was done for the day, but not really done. He had agreed to meet Deb at the address she'd handed him, a little private Italian club on the North End. They were going to talk.

How he hated the thought of that talk.

She was beautiful and smart. She had more insight and more instinct for her work than most detectives rolled together. When she'd first come to Hugh's district, most of the male employees had noticed her. How could they not? She was tall and lean, with shoulder-length blonde hair, searing green eyes, and a biting wit. Deb could exchange barb for barb and leave most of the guys either laughing or scratching their heads.

Hugh, of course, had been likewise intrigued with the young detective, and pleased when she'd been assigned as his partner. But he'd been in the business for fifteen years. He wasn't going to let desire get in his way. He knew his good friend at the courthouse, District Attorney Tom Inglis, was right when he said, "You watch your step, friend. I can see it in your eyes, even though you..."

Andrew lifted his fingers from the keys. The friend couldn't be called Tom.

He knew up front that his friend at the courthouse, District Attorney George Inglis, was right when he said, "You watch your step, my friend. I can see it in your eyes, even though you are denying it. You have a thing for that girl."

Hugh had laughed it off. George was a good old fart who had something to say about everything. Much as Hugh liked him, George's opinions could get on his nerves.

But then Hugh had found himself with Deb after hours, following a particularly difficult and tense day tracking a serial rapist, and they had touched hands briefly as they each reached for the car door. They turned almost instinctively, embraced tightly, and Deb had whispered earnestly in his ear, "I've wanted you ever since we met. You have anywhere you got to be for the next couple of hours?"

Andrew slammed up from his chair and walked back and forth in his den, staring at the computer screen. Rex, beneath the desk, stuck his head out to watch.

Damn it all, that was what Susan said to me in the parking deck beneath my law office. Same damn thing. "I've wanted you ever since we met."

He and Susan had encountered each other several times when she'd come to visit her father at the firm. They'd exchanged glances, a few friendly words, and he suspected there was something brewing in himself and in her. And then, in the parking deck, she'd made her intentions clear.

They said writers should write what they know. But it didn't need to be all that personal, did it?

Shit.

The phone rang. Andrew glanced at the clock on the wall. It was 9:26, almost time for his first client of the morning. He glanced at the phone on the desk. The caller ID read, "Yule Lemons."

That's odd. He's never called me before. I thought he was out on his grand, wifeless fishing trip.

Andrew snatched up the receiver after the third ring, before the voice mail could kick in.

"Hey Yule, what's up?"

There was a silence on the phone, then, "Hey, Mr. Marshall."

"Yes?"

"You hear 'bout Howard?" The voice was pinched.

"Howard?" *Howard, oh, right, Yule's cousin.* "No, what about Howard?"

"He got burned up yesterday. Burned to death."

"Oh, Jesus, Yule." This wasn't what Andrew had expected. "I'm so sorry. How'd it happen?"

"We was...he was drinking. A lot of beer, that's Howard on a fishin' or huntin' trip. He fell in the campfire and couldn't get out. I wasn't there when it happened. I was getting firewood."

"That's terrible. What can I do to help?"

"Well, you see, Howard's got a will needs readin'. He

didn't have no wife, no kids, and I doubt he left anything to his daddy, though maybe he did, who can say? I thought a lawyer would have to take care of it. The will, I mean."

"That's a good idea, yes." *Yule, I'm so sorry, man. I know you guys were best buddies.*

There was a heavy sigh on the other end of the line. "It was awful. He looked...he looked bad. Really bad, all burned like that. I never seen a burned-up man before."

"I can't imagine."

"Rick says there's nothing to worry about, that I wasn't at fault, that nobody's to blame but Howard hisself. But do you think Howard's daddy could sue me? Could he say I shouldn't have let Howard...fall in the fire like that?"

"Anybody can sue anybody for anything."

"That's what I was afraid of."

"You think he'd do that?"

"Not so much for whatever's in Howard's will, 'cause Lord knows that can't be much. Maybe some plywood and a couple screwdrivers. But what if he thinks I was at fault? That I coulda stopped it from happening? Something like that?"

"Well," said Andrew. He heard a knock on his front door. His first appointment had arrived. He took the phone out in the hall and down the stairs. Rex lumbered after, making soft umph sounds with each step. "Tell you what, Yule. Just make sure Howard's daddy knows about the reading of the will. I'll set up a time and call you back on that. But you be here, be calm, be respectful, and more than likely everything will be all right. I know how to ease people through things. If it looks like it could get nasty, I'll be happy to smooth the waters as best I can."

A moment of silence on the phone. Andrew tugged open the front door to let in sunlight and Daisy, who was there to have Andrew look over the rental agreement she'd written up for the apartment in her attic she wanted to lease. Daisy Donovan, a seventyish woman with puffy gray hair and large tortoiseshell glasses, came in quietly, clutching a white cardboard box to her chest.

Then Yule said, "Okay, then. Call me back with a time."

"Will do, Yule."

The phone went dead. Andrew let out a breath, pressed the end button to cut the connection.

"So, Mr. Marshall," said Daisy. "How are you this morning?"

Andrew said, "Fine," though he wasn't fine, because the image of a young man burning up atop a campfire like a pig in a barbecue pit stuck in his mind like a thorn. He put the phone down on the front hall table. "And how are you?"

"I've been better." This was Daisy. Sweet as pie but miserable as a toad on a hot city street. "I brought you some cookies. I hope you like coconut cookies."

"Coconut cookies are wonderful, thank you so much." He took the white cardboard box and led Daisy into his downstairs office. Rex tapped after, his in-need-of-a-trim nails clacking on the hardwood floor, but Andrew closed the dark paneled door before the dog could get through. Dog allergies were part of Daisy's myriad troubles.

"So." Andrew sat behind his wide oak desk and nodded for Daisy to take a seat on the cushioned chair across from him. He pushed a pile of folders out of his way and linked his hands on top of the desk. "You want to rent your attic."

Daisy nodded and pulled a piece of paper from her purse. As she flattened it and passed it across the broad surface of the desk, Andrew glanced out the office window and caught sight of Rick's dented patrol car cruising down Main Street, slowly, as if there really wasn't much to watch for and nothing much to do save stir up a few fallen leaves on the road. Since Andrew had moved to Adams there'd been a few battery cases between drunks at Frankie's, the bar at the edge of town. There'd been a couple domestic disputes resulting in some bruised husbands and one wife with a broken arm. There was the break-in at Adams Elementary School, which turned out to be two students who wanted to pee on their teacher's desk but were caught by the custodian before they'd had a chance to whiz. But there'd been not a single burglary or rape. Not a single murder. The only deaths in and around Adams had been from illness, old age, or accident.

"Mr. Marshall? Is everything all right?"

What a bizarre accident that killed Yule's cousin. Andrew's mind revealed a quick film clip—Howard throwing an empty can of beer into the bushes, leaning over to stoke the fire, no, light a cigar, leaning over too far, chuckling and wobbling, then crashing into the flames and the coal. Too drunk to know how to get himself out. Going up like a torch. Ghastly.

"Mr. Marshall?"

"Yes, Daisy, everything's fine. Shall we get started on this?"

9

~

It felt good to spread the first dabbings of watercolor on the paper, to step back, and realize she was painting again. The sun pooled bright in the living room, revealing floating clouds of dust she'd missed while cleaning the day before. Warm autumn air eased through the open window. The radio by the fireplace belted out tune after tune of heartache and patriotism. Next to the radio, their cords tumbling across the floor to separate outlets in the walls, were Charlene's laptop and printer. Clipped to the easel were several printouts of the photos she had taken the day before at the mill. Unfortunately, all the shots at the cemetery were too dark to be of any use, so she'd deleted them off the card.

"This will be my first creation in my new digs," she said with satisfaction. She wasn't sure exactly which angle of the mill she'd paint, but she'd slapped on some blue dots of sky, and that was, at least, a start. It would come to her if she just relaxed into it.

An hour later, she was still staring at the same dots of blue. She had made herself a cup of green tea, had sipped most of it down, but was still unable to make the next stroke.

Damn.

She pulled her hair back into a ponytail with an old rubber band then picked up the paintbrush. She put it down.

"Double damn," she said. She went into the hallway to stare out the open door. A fly blew in and out. A stray leaf pattered in over the threshold and rolled against her foot. She kicked it off.

Out the window at the bottom of the stairs Charlene could see the smokehouse. Its door had come loose and lay on the ground next to the building. A large crow sat on the roof. Charlene had been in there, once. She and Ryan, and those other kids who'd come to the birthday party. They'd hidden in there for some reason. So they wouldn't have to come inside the house? Maybe.

There was a creak up the steps, and a muffled thump. Charlene whipped about, grabbing hold of the banister, and glared up into the darkness there. Her heart skipped a beat, and another. The hairs on her arms stood up against the fabric of her sweatshirt. She waited, holding her breath, listening. Cold air drifted down the steps.

"What *is* that?" she said aloud.

Of course, there was no answer.

"Well, I'll do something about it!"

No answer.

She went out to the car to retrieve the tarp, and then, with hammer and nails, climbed the stairs to the second floor. The wood she had put there was still leaning against the door. The planks that had been nailed there long ago were still secured. *What did you expect? You're being silly.*

Reaching out with a trembling hand, she felt the door. It was cool to the touch, as would be expected. Then she took hold of the plank across the middle of the door and pulled. It didn't budge. She stuck the claw of the hammer beneath one of the brackets holding the wood in place, and drew down with all her might. It did not give way, even a hair's breadth.

Just as well, she thought. *If I open this room, then I'll lose even more heat when I have to start using the fireplace.*

She put her eye to the keyhole, and still there was nothing but blackness.

And if I leave it shut, nothing in there can get out.

"Would you stop that?"

Climbing on a wooden box from a front bedroom, Charlene nailed the tarp across the ceiling and down both sides of the top of the stairs, sealing the upstairs off as best she could with the silver plastic.

"That's good. That will help."

Help with what?

"With drafts. With losing heat. With minimizing sounds I don't need to hear."

Charlene retreated to the kitchen to make use of the rocking, hard water–stained toilet. Halfway through, she nearly jumped up thinking, *I wonder if snakes can get up in these pipes?* But nothing bit her on the ass, nothing hissed down in the watery depths. She flushed quickly and then dropped the lid over the bowl.

Arms crossed, she stood in the middle of the kitchen, staring at the icebox. She had no more money except for a twenty spot in her wallet and some loose nickels and quarters in the bottom of her purse. Her credit card had been cut in half two months ago, a good move it seemed at the time. She could not buy a new refrigerator. What was she hoping for, coming out here—that not only would there be furniture but a working fridge? She could live off canned foods, but every so often it would be nice to have chilled veggies or fresh fish.

"Good grief, Charlie Brown."

Out through the back porch she went, stepping over several chunks of firewood that had rolled out of place, and pushing through the door with its torn screen. The air was fresh and cool. She took a long, deep breath, turning toward the house to get the full effect of the late-morning sun on her face.

She hadn't really studied the back of the house until now. The screened porch looked rattier from the outside than it did from the inside, with numerous dents and rips. The wooden siding on the house was split severely in numerous places, suggesting to Charlene that there would need to be an expensive re-siding soon, before some of the pieces just up and fell off. The windows upstairs were without screens.

Then she noticed that the room across from the stairs had no rear window.

Moving around the house, she checked to see if there was a window on the side, but no, nothing. Not even the outline of a window that had been bricked in or covered over. The room in which she thought she'd heard the thumping seemed to have been built without windows at all.

Why would someone want a room with no windows? So no one could see in? So no one could see out?

"Damn weird people," she said, the side of her mouth wrinkling. "Am I really related to them?"

A groundhog lumbered out from beneath the smokehouse and trotted past Charlene into the backyard. It stopped beside the junk pile, lifted its little black nose, and sniffed at the air. Then, having caught the scent of a human on a shifting breeze, it turned and galloped away across the stretch of grass and into a dark hole beneath the little cabin.

I wonder what's in that cabin?

Charlene walked over. Strange little building, up on stubby stone legs, sitting alone and apart like a forgotten pet. There was a stone chimney, but it had folded in on itself and now fingers of dry grass poked from its ruins, evidence of the birds that had laid claim. The roof's shingles looked as if they'd been hand-split; the walls were chinked with clay.

The door did not have a lock, but there was a heavy wooden latch on the outside that could be slid into a bracket beside it, thus sealing it shut.

From the outside? What the hell good is that? Doors are supposed to lock from the inside.

Charlene slid the latch back and shoved the door open. She stepped into the dim and the chill, leaving the door open.

There was one room, with water-stained floorboards. There were single windows on two of the walls and a fireplace on the third. Along the fourth wall, a set of rail-less steps led up to an attic trapdoor.

Dead leaves spun in the center of the floor in a tiny whirlwind. The interior wall of the fireplace was caked with fragments of wasps' nests. Swallows had built homes in the low rafters, and they were none too pleased with the intrusion. In a flurry of wings they flew across the room and up the fireplace. Feathers and dust spun in their wake.

Charlene stood against the windowsill and looked through the warped window glass at the main house. It was no more than fifty feet away, yet through the window it seemed to be far from the cabin. The yard appeared to be stretched and distorted like a Dali landscape. Looking at it made Charlene feel lightheaded and nauseous.

She shut her eyes, squeezed them tightly, and then looked back. The distortion was gone. *That's good. The last thing I need right now is to get sick.*

It was then she noticed the marks on the windowsill. Dug deep and evenly spaced. They were hash marks, counting off something. All across the bottom sill they marched—*five, ten, fifteen, twenty, twenty-five.* They traveled up the side of the window, around the top, and down again. *One hundred, one hundred five, one hundred ten, one hundred fifteen.* She stepped back from the window. There were small hash marks on all four walls, the floor, and the steps. She had seen the marks when she first entered, but hadn't realized what they were, assuming in passing they were just cracks in the wood.

But these were done by human hands. Some of the marks were smaller, others larger. It looked as though they were made by different people. There seemed a desperation in the marks. So who was it, or who were they, those people of the past who were compelled to cut countless slashes in the walls, floors, and windowsills inside the cabin?

She thought again of the latch outside on the door. Someone, or more than one someone, had been locked in this place.

Oh, man, that's creepy. Why would someone be locked up in here?

She stood at the bottom of the steps and gazed up at the trapdoor. No brave mice on these steps, just more hash marks, dust, and loose nails. The trapdoor had a latch and a padlock.

Along with the mice and old newspapers, why didn't I inherit all the keys for this place?

The wind picked up outside, blowing against the open door

and banging it, hard, on the exterior wall. Bits of weeds and small sticks flew in around Charlene's feet. Her ponytail whipped across her shoulder.

She touched the marks on the wall by the stairs. Instead of portraits that could be removed or destroyed, these marks remained here in the cabin. Had slaves been locked here as punishment? If so, what had they done that was considered wrong? She moved up the steps, tracing the marks with her fingers. Then she spied something different from the hash marks, on the wall at the top of the steps. Small letters carved into the wood, spelling something that was difficult to decipher in the shadow. They grew more visible with each step upward, until she could read:

"The Children's House."

The children's house? Was this a playhouse, then?

A black widow spider came out of a hole on the step ahead of her. It stretched its long, needle legs to their full length then strode confidently along the shaded lip of the step to the side of the stair, where it paused and prepared to lower itself to the cabin floor.

Charlene took off her shoe and crushed it. She shivered.

On the top step she touched the carving. *The Children's House.* What children had stayed here, had played here? Not Charlene or Ryan on their visit long ago, not the vague, other children who were there that day. They'd messed around the well. They'd played under the front porch.

But they'd never come into this, the Children's House. She thought they had tried, but either it was locked or they'd been told to get away.

Charlene grabbed the lock on the trapdoor and tugged. Rust flaked off, tinting her hands the color of dried blood. She twisted it and pulled harder. There could be some great shit in the attic of the Children's House. Antique toys? Old school books? Maybe some old furniture? Artifacts she could photograph for references, then paint and sell and have enough money to get a bed and maybe even a refrigerator. She spit on the residue on her hand, wiped it on her jeans, then tugged the lock again.

A sudden gust of frigid air flew up and around Charlene. An invisible hand slapped her soundly, forcefully across the face. She stumbled, lost her footing, and crashed to the bottom of the stairs.

The world cracked and went black.

10

~

The world opened again slowly. Charlene was on the floor against the cabin door, one leg beneath her, warm blood trickling from a cut on her forehead. Her skull hurt, her right hand hurt. She grabbed for the bottom step with her left and eased into a sitting position. *Even my ass hurts!* Gingerly, she probed her forehead and found a small gash. Then she looked at her right hand.

"Ah, Jesus."

There was a chunk of wood driven into the meat of the palm, a good half-inch thick and two inches long. Charlene sucked air and turned the hand away so she didn't have to see it. Then she looked again. It was hideous, all bulging and ragged, but not bleeding. Yet. Carefully, yet shivering, she pinched the end of the wood, counted to three, *no four, no five, six, seven, eight, just pull it out!* and yanked.

"Ahh!" The hand flared hot, but little blood came out with the wood. There was a flap of skin and muscle, and a small spec of black splinter remaining deep inside. Charlene winced at the pain and at two thoughts: *I have no health insurance anymore* and *I hope to God I can clean this well enough so I don't get an infection.*

"And how the hell did I fall down the steps?"

She looked up at the trapdoor and the lock. Something had struck her face.

It felt like somebody slapped me!

She held her face with one good hand and one ruined hand and stared, eyes wide, up the steps.

Ghosts of the children who had played in this cabin. They don't want you in their hiding place. They hate you because you want to sell Homeplace.

"Oh, just shut *up*, Charlene. You start believing everything your imagination throws your way, it won't be art they take out of here, it'll be you, wrapped up in fucking canvas and foaming at the mouth."

The words sounded concrete, but her body continued to tremble.

She had slapped herself, that was all. When she'd jerked on the lock, her hand had slipped off and struck her own face. It had happened so fast, it didn't register.

Of course that's it.

Limping across the yard to the house, Charlene held her damaged hand close to her chest. Nothing grosser than the idea of loose flesh flapping in the breeze, getting caught on the tip of some thorny shoot. Inside, she pumped cold water onto the wound, rubbed liquid soap in it—this hurt the most and she groaned as loud as she wanted, because there was no one there to chastise her for acting the baby—then rinsed it out. She found three large Band-Aids in the first aid kit in her purse and pulled them on as tightly as she could, hoping it would do in lieu of stitches.

As she zipped her purse and dropped it on the floor beside the easel in the living room, she heard her cell phone beep on the mantel. There was a message. Someone had called, had gotten through even though reception was only three bars inside the house.

Someone misses me.

The number on recall was Ryan's. He'd called at 11:05, twenty minutes earlier. She sat on her sleeping bag and punched redial. Then she peeled back a Band-Aid and stared at the dark spot in her hand. When she got up her courage, she would dig at it with a needle. Right now the rest of her body ached enough as it was. Inflicting intentional torture could wait a day.

A click. "Charlene?"

"Yep."

"Hey little sister! Are you really down there in the wilderness?" She could hear his sympathetic smile through the line.

Damn, it's good hearing your voice. She felt tears well in her eyes, and was surprised at the flush of emotion. "Wasn't sure I'd find it, but I made it."

"I got your letter about you moving to Homeplace just yesterday. I couldn't believe it. You blow off your art teaching job for what?"

"You wouldn't understand."

"Try me."

"You're a computer geek. I'm a painter. We think differently. We live differently."

"Not that differently. I know you. Jeez, is this some throwback hippie thing? Have you gotten into that Earth Mother, Mother Goddess, grow-your-own-herbs-and-raise-your-own-mushrooms lifestyle?"

"See, Ryan, that's exactly what..."

"Never mind, never mind." She could hear his good humor, and it warmed her heart. "But, Charlene." Here it came. "To drop everything and move out to there? I remember that place. I remember that birthday party there when we were kids. And if I remember right, the house was old and falling apart."

"It's still old and falling apart."

"Is there any power?"

"Yep. Toilet flushes, too, though it rocks at about a seven-point-three on the Richter."

"Home sweet home." His voice was patient but baffled. She had not handled letting him know as well as she might have, she knew that. Two days before leaving Norfolk, she had drafted a letter and mailed it to him, explaining briefly that she had quit her work at the community college and was moving to Homeplace to paint. That was pretty much it. She knew he would try to fill in the blanks, and wasn't particularly keen on helping him with that task. Maybe what he guessed would be better than the truth.

"Are you having money trouble?" asked Ryan.

"Well.." *If I admit it, he will offer me money. If he offers me money, I'll take it. I want to do this on my own. I want to free myself up from obligations to other people.* "What do you mean by 'money trouble'?"

"Charlene, can you pay your bills or not?"

"Damn, Brother, but you're nosy."

"I can float you a loan if you need it, you know that."

"I know that." *I can't ask for anything now.*

"Would a couple hundred help? You don't have to pay me back for a while—after you sell some of those paintings you plan on painting out there in nowhere land."

How about a couple thousand? "Yes. That would help."

There was a soft chuckle, and Charlene felt her throat tighten. Her stepbrother was such a good guy.

"Okay, if you actually have a mailing address I'll..."

Charlene said, "Wait, did you hear that?" There had been a soft whisper on the line. It had sounded as if someone had spoken her name.

"What?"

"Is there someone there with you?"

"No."

"I thought I heard someone, whispering."

"Maybe it's an interference. A party line kind of thing. You're out in the boondocks, remember."

"True. I'm just a little jittery, is all."

"But you're okay?"

"Yes."

"And so you plan on living there until spring? The winter there can be really bad. What kind of heat do you have?"

"I have heat, Ryan."

"I hear you." He paused, then, "What's your mailing address?"

"It's 238 Craig Road, Adams. Zip 22890."

"All right, then, this afternoon I'll send you..."

"Now I *know* you heard that," said Charlene, the hairs on her neck standing up. It had been the whisper again. Again, it sounded like someone far away, someone deep in a well or cave, calling Charlene's name.

"Heard what?"

"The woman's voice."

"No, I didn't. But I think you should get your cell service checked."

"Okay." *I can't afford to get anything checked.*

"Love you."

"You, too."

She snapped the phone shut, put it back on the mantel, and plugged it into the recharger. She wiped her mouth, finding it dry as sandpaper. She sipped her tea, stood at the easel, and forced her mind to her work. A beautiful composition this would be, sky, forest, and a brick hulk, representational of mankind still holding its own after all these years.

Surely the voice had only been interference.

Maybe I should call Ryan back and tell him to come visit.

She picked up a brush and her palette, dipped the brush tip in the jar of water on the easel's tray, and poised it over the paints. The mill's brick was not truly red, but the color of dog-wood autumn, the smokestacks almost a pure black, the weeds in which the building stood a wonderful array of Payne's grays, raw umbers, cobalt greens, Indian yellows. Such a difference from her seashells and lighthouses. This would be her first real painting in years.

I could clean out one of the upper bedrooms, tell him to bring a folding cot. I'll even encourage him to bring Dede along, even though she's such a snit. We could have fun. Play board games. Have a bonfire in the backyard and burn up some of that old scrap wood.

She squiggled the brush tip in the raw umber. "I'll paint my first Alexander mill weed," she said. But the brush wouldn't move toward the paper. She leaned her body, but the brush held in place in the air, in her hand.

"You just don't want to paint a weed yet. Your mind says rough out the mill first."

*Ryan could bring his CD player. We could listen to some-
thing besides WBAM. I have a handful of CDs at the bottom
of my little suitcase. I'd love to hear those again.*

She forced the brush to a spot higher on the paper, but
couldn't make the first stroke. The splinter in her hand stung
slightly.

"Come on." She tried to move her arm toward the paper. It
would not move. The splinter burned hotter now.

"Blast!" She flung the paintbrush across the living room at
the wall, where it bounced and fell to the floor, leaving splats
of raw umber.

Out on the front porch, she crossed her arms and looked at
the Cruiser. She was alone, and she was lonely. How long did
it take to get used to a new place? Would she ever? Why didn't
she bring Reginald? He would have been fine. Hell, he might
have loved it here, all these mice.

She climbed into the Cruiser and headed down the drive. A
little visit with a neighbor might help. A little time away
would be refreshing. She steered carefully down the drive,
then turned southwest on Route 782, heading for Maude's
place.

11

~

The Boise place was easy to find. The mailbox was bright yellow and lettered with blue vinyl letters. BOISE, WILLOW VALE, RURAL ROUTE 2, BOX 266—226 CRAIG ROAD. The driveway was as narrow as Charlene's, but the trees were trimmed back and ruts were patched with gravel. The same stream flowed across the front of the Boise land, but the bridge was wider and sported a railing on either side. The two-story house, sitting on a knoll in a clearing, was not as large as the one at Homeplace, but was certainly in better repair. Shingles had new coats of green paint and the open front porch appeared to have been rebuilt recently out of knotty pine. On the porch were Adirondack chairs, a small table, and a potted palm.

As Charlene knocked on the frame of the screened door, she realized she should have brought something. A moment later, Maude's weatherworn face appeared at the door, squinting. "Hello, yes? Oh, my goodness, it's you. Charlene Alexander, isn't it?"

"Yes, Maude, well, Charlene Myers. I just thought I'd stop by and say hello."

"That's sweet," said the old lady. She stepped outside, sporting a wide smile that revealed chipped, uneven teeth. She wiped her hands on the dishtowel stuck in the waistband of her flowered skirt. "I was ready to take me a rest, and a visit an' a rest together is so much nicer. Here," she said, motioning to the chairs, "have a sit-down. I'll get Dennis to bring us some lunch. You ain't had lunch yet, have you?"

"Yes," Charlene lied. She wasn't sure if she could trust lunch with Maude. The woman looked like a fatback and souse kind of gal.

"A snack, then?" said Maude. "I ain't had lunch, but I'm old and got the right to spoil my appetite now and then."

Charlene settled into one of the chairs and leaned back against the smooth wood. It was very comfortable. *I need one of these chairs for my own porch. After the fridge, I mean, and the bed. And the new toilet and bathtub.*

"Who's Dennis?" she asked. "I thought you lived alone."

"No, I wouldn't want to live alone out here in the country. I've got my boy, Dennis. There's plenty to do in the country for more'n one person. I'm sure you're findin' that out." Maude called through the door, "Dennis! Get out some of that limeade and some them muffins what I baked last night!"

Maude eased herself into the chair next to Charlene, groaned, and slipped off her dirty sneakers. Her pink socks were perfectly clean up to where the shoes ended and the cuffs were coated with grit and dust.

"Good to sit," said Maude. "Why God give us butts."

"I should have brought you something," said Charlene. *Like you have anything to bring. A can of Spam?* "I don't really cook or bake, but I do paint. I think I mentioned that to you last night. It's why I was out with my camera. I'm starting a new collection of paintings of the area. Perhaps I could give you a small original when it's done? Of the river or the mountain skyline? Those are two things we share."

"Honey," said the old woman, her eyes crinkling kindly. "A pitchur you done would be a treasure."

They sat silently for a moment. Then the door clapped open and a middle-aged man came out holding a ceramic platter. "Here, muffins and cookies. We were low on ice, but you forgot to fill the trays again." He glared at Charlene.

Immediately she knew she did not like Dennis Boise. He was average height, with a sagging belly tucked inside a plain blue shirt. He sported a poorly trimmed mustache, dyed and thinning black hair, and twitchy eyes. His smugness was palpable, and she felt like sticking her tongue out at him but was able, with a clenching of jaw, to resist.

"Dennis, this is our new neighbor, Charlene Alexander. She's moved into the old Homeplace next door."

"Hello," said Charlene, refusing to even lean up to offer her hand. He didn't look as if he expected her to, or that he wanted her to.

"Nice to meet you," he said, his voice as oily as his hair. "Though I can't imagine anyone in their right mind moving into that piece of trash house. What are you trying to do, prove something to somebody?"

Charlene's mouth dropped open. *Who the fuck do you think you are?*

Then Maude said, "Dennis, don't. Charlene's not trying to prove anything. Why, she's a painter! A real artist! Aren't you, dear?"

There was so much she wanted to say, but what she did say was, "Yes. And I am not trying to prove anything, Dennis. I don't need to prove anything. Are you?"

One of Dennis's eyebrows hitched up, then down. He put the tray on the table and handed a drink to his mother. He let Charlene get her own. She tasted one of the muffins—blueberry with almonds. It was almost good enough to forget Dennis and just be friends with his mother.

"You like it?" asked the old woman.

"Mmm."

Dennis went back inside. Maude and Charlene sipped and chewed. Then Charlene put her tumbler on the table. "I'm really glad to meet you again in the light of day. Our meeting last night was strange, don't you think, there in the cemetery?"

"People meet when they's supposed to, I believe. We met when we did, where we did. S'fate."

"You believe in fate?"

Maude swallowed her bite. Her wrinkled face wrinkled more as she considered the question. "Why, 'course I do. Fate, God, same thing. Don't you?"

"I don't know."

Maude picked muffin from between her front teeth. "You're still young."

"I suppose," said Charlene. Then, "My mother died not long ago—I guess you might have heard that. I inherited Homeplace, even though Mom seemed to have no use for it. It's empty. No furniture, no family keepsakes. There used to be portraits above the main stairs, but they're gone. Like I said last night, I know virtually nothing about the Alexanders."

Maude quit picking at her teeth.

"I have no photos, no journals or diaries."

"I see."

"I want to paint the history of my family. Not the people so much, but the things around Homeplace. I think my new collection will be powerful. But in order to do the paintings justice, I need to know more about my ancestors. You seem to have information that could be helpful. But last night you didn't seem very willing to share. I thought maybe it was because we didn't know each other yet. But now, hey, we've just shared some great muffins. Is that bonding enough so you can fill me in?" She raised her brows, hoping to draw Maude out of herself.

Maude let out a long, audible breath. "When I was five, my brother shot hisself in the head."

"Oh, I'm really sorry." *And that has to do with my family how?*

"My parents told me he got killed in a huntin' accident."

Charlene waited.

"That was a good thing to tell a five-year-old, that it was an accident. How could I handle my brother shot hisself over some girl he thought loved him?"

"But what does that…?"

"You ain't ready to hear the history of your family's what I's sayin'. Would be too hard to handle, too hard to take in."

Anger flushed Charlene's neck. She pushed, keeping her voice as even as possible. "I appreciate your concern, Maude. But I'm twenty-nine, not five. I want to know anything you know."

Maude took another bite of muffin and chewed in silence.

"Please?"

Then Maude leaned from her chair and shouted through the screen door, "Dennis! You getting out to them punkins? I wanna make a pie this evenin'."

Dennis didn't call back.

"An' check on Polly. See she ain't just starin' at the television. She could be doin' something, maybe foldin' that pile of towels if she can manage it. She needs to be movin' around. Good for her circulation."

"Polly?"

"My granddaughter. Not Dennis's child, he ain't never married, but my son Walter's child. Walter left Polly with me when he divorced his wife. He's in the army, eighteen years. Overseas now, Middle East."

"I see."

"But she's not right."

"What?"

"Sweet child, turned twenty-two last week. Got nerve damage, though. Can't really walk much without help. Hard to understand her when she talks. Cord was around her neck when she was born, cut off some air. Smart, I know she is, but other people can't always see that."

"Oh."

"Polly's a sweetheart, but Dennis, there's my gem. Bless his heart, he's lived with me his whole life. Such a help he's been with everything. Garden, house, Polly."

"That's very nice, Maude. I'm glad he's been here for you. But do you think you could tell me something about my own family?"

The woman bowed her head, and when she lifted it again, Charlene knew a story was coming. And with the way the old woman's eyes were drawn at the edges, she suspected it wouldn't be good.

"You had a great-great-great-great-grandma, Phoebe Black Alexander."

"Okay, yes. I mean, I didn't know, but go on."

"From Ireland, come over to Virginia all by herself, I dunno, 'bout 1808, 1809. She was a slight woman, her hair about your color. They say her eyes never stayed the same color, though. They'd go blue to green to ash gray."

"Like hazel."

"Like magic."

"Okay."

"She was a witch."

Charlene almost laughed at the absurdity, but the expression on Maude's face prevented it. The woman's cheeks pulsed in and out. Her fingers latched on to each other like anxious snakes.

"A witch of the worst kind," the woman said. "Came in sheep's clothin', joined the church where the Alexanders went to preachin', but she weren't no Christian. She flirted with William Alexander 'til he fell in love and married her. That was his downfall. Phoebe's power took over the entire household, that same house you've made up your mind to live in. The woman hadn' a speck o' kindness or love. She bore children, thirteen in all, but when they angered her, she killed them. Not even quick, merciful deaths. She locked those boys and girls up first in a little cabin, for days and days and days, starved them, beat them. Then she bound them with baling twine and threw them down the well. She left the cover off the well for a few days so the other children and the slaves could hear their hideous cries of fear and sufferin'."

The backs of Charlene's hands went cold.

"Her husband didn' challenge her, 'cause she would spell anyone who offended her. She got the textile mill built by the river for to make money, lots of it. Managed the mill herself, too. Used the Alexander slaves to do the work along with some she hired from neighboring farms."

"Your family's slaves?"

"No, we was Quakers. Didn' have no slaves. But that

dreadful mill ran day and night, churning out cloth with the cotton that come in from the Tidewater plantations. Cotton'd come in on the trains, cloth'd go out on the trains. Them machines never stopped clankin' and whackin' and thumpin' and spinnin'. Slaves got killed in there. Fell into the carding machines and got chewed up, or had their necks broke in them big leather belts. Phoebe used their blood to grease the wheels and just kept on goin'."

"Wait, hold on. These have to be urban legends."

"What?"

"Stories hatched in someone's twisted mind and passed down all these years."

"They's true all right. People around here give the place wide berth. They know it's true."

"Impossible."

"It's as true as that cut on your hand. How'd you get that, anyway?"

"It was an accident. I fell down some stairs."

"What stairs?"

"The cabin stairs."

"Weren't no accident, I'll bet on it."

"Of course it was…"

"Honey, Homeplace is still filled with Phoebe's spirit. I feel it even as I go into the cemetery to take care them graves, so I go with a prayer and with God's good grace. I even laid out a ring and star of stones around the graves to keep me safe while I's inside there."

"You laid out a hex? You have to be kidding me."

"You felt Phoebe's spirit already."

"I haven't felt a thing. No disrespect, Maude, but this is make-believe. And even if it were true, which it isn't, then why would my relative's spirit come after me? I'm the only living Alexander."

"You told me you're gonna sell Homeplace."

Charlene picked up her tumbler. It was empty except for ice. She put it down. The splinter in her hand had started to sting. "Yes, I am."

"Phoebe swore the land would stay in her family's control. She swore to take revenge on anyone who challenged that."

Charlene picked up the glass again and downed the melting ice. A lump stuck in her throat, but she said nothing as it slowly melted away.

12

~

Witches, she thought as she lay on her sleeping bag. *That old woman's been scared all these years, living on land next to a place she thinks is haunted by the spirit of a hazel-eyed witch.*

Charlene was dressed only in her underwear and T-shirt, as the night had turned surprisingly warm and sticky. The window was open just enough to let in a thin sheet of air along with the noisy peeping of tree frogs and cricking of insects. Charlene drew a blanket around her. It was warm inside, yes, but a blanket was a good thing, a safe thing.

You baby.

The overhead light was still on. She had no idea how high her electricity bill would be, but tonight she didn't care. There were absolutely no such thing as witches or the ghosts of witches, but an overhead light made it all the more certain that they did not exist. The shade was drawn most of the way down. The wood was still against the door of the locked room upstairs. In the walls, she could hear the nocturnal business of mice.

She had tried to paint on her return from Maude's, had picked up her brush and driven the bristles hard against the

Bristol board. All she was able to accomplish were some random streaks and splotches. Frustrated and tense, she decided a bath might calm her down. She quickly scoured the tub of all loose debris and then filled it with water from the hand pump. She heated two pans over her hot plate and added that to the cold, making for a barely tolerable room temperature. Bathing, she realized, would be a bitch come winter, but who would be there to smell her, anyway?

After drying off and dressing, she had walked to the end of her driveway and checked her mail. There was none. Back at the house she cooked a meal of Hormel chili and wrote a letter to Mary Jane to ask how Reginald was holding up, hoping Mary Jane would write back and ask how Charlene was holding up. Along with everything else, having no e-mail was going to be a bitch. She thought she had a stamp in her purse, but there were none. Tomorrow she would drive into Adams and get more. She had no idea where the post office was, if the town even had one, but surely the grocery store carried stamps.

Lying on her back on her sleeping bag, Charlene watched a small spider crawl back and forth across the ceiling. It was not sleek and black, but a brown, dusty creature, going somewhere, having some agenda Charlene couldn't know. Charlene counted how long it took for the spider to get from one crack in the ceiling to the next.

Sleep finally came in spite of the spider and the overhead light. Sometime deep in that light-filled night she awakened to the sound of soft banging upstairs, but when fully awake she heard nothing. She snatched up her blanket in spite of the heat, wrapped it around her legs, told herself there had been no noise, and drifted back down into dreams of sweat and little substance.

The following morning was filled with odds and ends—scrubbing the kitchen floor, scouring the toilet and jamming wood chips beneath the base so it didn't rock, and rearranging the pile of junk outside so it took up less space. In the pile she found a rusted set of tools—a hammer, wrench, and box of assorted nails. These could come in handy. She put them on one of the shelves in the kitchen. At eleven she took a break and returned to the easel in the living room.

The paper glowered at her, demanding something fill it besides the few streaks and spots she'd put there the day before. She wet the brush, raked it over the dried paint on the palette, and swiped a long, red streak across the center. Only a faint, pinkish streak appeared. The paint wasn't wet enough. She dunked the brush, wiggled it around the paint until the top appeared slightly runny, then angled her hand in preparation for a vigorous sweep on the paper.

Her right hand flared with sudden, hot pain, and she dropped the brush. She massaged the hand, noticing that the spot with the splinter was bright red and puffy. *When did that happen? It was okay five minutes ago when I hauled that heavy-ass tub inside.*

She picked up the brush again, clenched it defiantly in her throbbing right hand, and walked around the easel, staring at the contraption from the front, the back, feeling stymied, angry. Back in Norfolk, insecurity and lack of acclaim drained her of her passion. Here, what, the same insecurity and a fucking splinter in her hand would do equal damage?

There was a knock on the front door. The brush flew from her hand again.

What is this, a Laurel and Hardy routine? Calm down!

She peeked out the living room window. "Oh, just great," she said, then went into the hall and unlocked the door, wondering in that brief moment before she was in view of her visitor what she looked like, if she looked okay or like scraggly white trash.

Andrew Marshall was smiling and holding an aluminum tray covered with some sort of round baked things.

"Ah..." Charlene began. "Hello."

"Hi," said Andrew. "Andrew Marshall. We met at Randy's Hardware. I hope I didn't catch you at a bad time?"

"Why, do I look bad?" She hadn't meant to say it, only think it.

"Oh, no. You look fine." He shifted the tray of round brown whatevers from one hand to the other. He was a little taller than she'd remembered from their first meeting. His brown eyes were crinkled at the edges and his short beard looked as though he'd combed it. "I thought I'd do the Welcome Wagon routine, bring a little something you might like."

"That's a big tradition in these parts, isn't it, bringing stuff?"

Andrew looked down at the tray, then back at Charlene. "I suppose. People brought me food when I moved to Adams. So I thought, you know, pay it forward."

"Oh. Yes." Charlene didn't want to invite him in, but knew there was some social response required on her part. He seemed harmless enough, but that was never a guarantee. "Those look...good." She nodded at the tray.

Andrew blew air through his teeth. "Well, I don't know about that. This was my wife's cookie recipe." *(Wife, okay, now at least I know that much.)* "She was a pretty good cook for the most part." *(Was? Okay, he's no longer married.)* "I'm still learning my way around the kitchen. These are sugar cookies in case you can't quite tell. I think I let them cook a bit too long, but I tasted one and it wasn't too bad. I mixed in some coconut cookies someone else gave me, for good measure. In case you found mine to be really nasty you could at least eat those." He paused, looking hopeful.

"Do you want to come in a moment?"

Andrew said, "Sure." She stepped back and he moved past her into the front hall. "This is an amazing old house. When was it built?"

"Late 1700s. I'm not sure the exact date."

"Really? There's a lot of potential here."

Charlene stuck her hands in her pockets and shifted from one foot to the other. "Potential and actuality are separated by a shitload of work."

"Oh, hey, wow, you're a painter." Andrew was staring at her easel.

"Oh, that, well, yes..."

"What is it? I mean what's it going to be?"

"The ruins of a mill that my family owned and operated. It's along the Tye River. It'll be the first painting of a new series of paintings, things I find around my place." *Too much information, Charlene. You don't know him.*

"I love art." He smiled. "You know, most lawyers are big on art."

"Really?"

He shrugged. "I don't know. It's something to say. I just wanted to remind you I was gainfully employed and not some ne'er-do-well who just bakes crappy cookies and drops in on people unannounced."

Charlene couldn't help but grin. He seemed like a really nice guy.

Andrew grinned, too. "Maybe someday I'll collect your works. I have lots of room in my place."

"If I can ever get some work done."

"Oh." Andrew grimaced. "I did intrude."

"I didn't mean it that way. You're not intruding. I've just been struggling, trying to get something started. I seem to be having artist's block."

"That sounds painful."

"It is. Constipation of the imagination."

"Well, I just wanted to bring you these." He handed the tray to Charlene. "And to let you know if you need anything, I've learned to be fairly handy around my own place back in town. I can't repair a lawnmower engine but I can wield a hammer and nails, level, and sander, stuff like that. I could lend a hand if..." He trailed. He was looking at the paintbrush on the other side of the floor and the trail of red paint it had left. Charlene saw a flicker of compassionate humor cross his face. "I can do repairs. I've even learned some electricians' tricks and taught myself some plumbing out of desperation."

"I'm sure that's really helpful." *I wonder if he's dating somebody.*

She wrote his phone number on the paper on the easel. He jotted hers in his PDA.

"Good luck with the mill piece," said Andrew. He went outside to his vehicle, an old pickup truck. He might have money, but he was practical. Charlene liked that. She could relate. Well, she would have been able to relate if she already had the money and then had chosen to be practical. As he walked, Charlene noted that Andrew still had a slight limp, but it could have been the irregular lay of the yard.

"Thanks, I'm sure I'll get back in the artistic flow soon!" Charlene called from the front porch. "And thanks for the cookies. I'm sure they're good."

"Be honest if they aren't," said Andrew through the truck's window. "I can handle the truth." He started the engine.

"Hey, wait." Charlene trotted down several of the front porch steps. "You have any stamps?"

Andrew leaned his head out the window. "What?"

"Stamps?"

"No, but the grocery store sells them. Want to ride along?"

13

~~

The grocery store did sell stamps. Andrew picked up a few items while Charlene got a book of first classers from the cluttered customer service desk and then considered the freshly made sandwiches in a glass-fronted cabinet by the checkout lanes. She was hungry. It was lunchtime. But she didn't have any extra money. The retirement cash-out needed to come, and come quickly.

She waited for Andrew at the front door, standing to the side and out of the way of cart-wielding mamas and papas. After a few minutes, Andrew met her there with his paper bag of groceries and said, "Have you had lunch?"

He took her to a café in the center of town called the Fox's Den. It was a homey little nook with booths and several kitchen-style tables in the middle of the floor. They sat by the front window, through which they could watch the comings and goings along Main Street. Women wrangling toddlers or dogs or both along the sidewalk. Teenagers hanging around a parking meter across the street. Cars, trucks passing by.

Aren't those kids supposed to be in school? Charlene mused. *Wait, it's Saturday. I'm already losing track of days. Sheesh.*

"The food here's pretty decent," said Andrew. He sat directly across from Charlene. She had her legs apart so she wouldn't bump his, though she knew she wouldn't mind if he bumped her. "I eat here most of the time. I'm not much of a cook. Well, except for my exquisite cookies."

Charlene smiled. "I'm sure they're fine. I'll have one this afternoon. It will probably be the fuel and inspiration I need for my new painting."

"I guess we'll wait and see how much of an inspiration they turn out to be." He grinned. She grinned back.

Andrew ordered chicken fried steak. Charlene ordered a crabcake sandwich and a Pepsi. What she really wanted was the rib-eye steak, but this was lunch, he was paying or so she hoped, and she didn't want to come across as either too hungry or too greedy. And, if it turned out this was Dutch treat, she had at least enough cash to cover the sandwich and soft drink.

In Andrew's truck it had been too noisy to talk. The engine whined and the toolbox in the truck bed rattled like an old machine gun. Here in the Fox's Den, however, the instrumental music was low and the other patrons talked in civil tones. Between bites, Charlene discovered Andrew was a contract lawyer. His wife had died in an automobile accident a year and a half earlier. Beautiful lady, he described her. After her death, Andrew decided he needed a change of pace, and so sold his Boston townhouse and moved south.

Charlene readjusted her napkin in her lap. "Why on earth here? What'd you do, toss a dart at a map?"

"I actually had an ancestor from Nelson County, way back when, so I saw this as a chance to get back to where I started. Or where they started. Something like that."

"No kidding? We have something in common, then. Besides noses and fingers, that kind of thing."

Andrew waved over the young waitress and asked her to refill his coffee cup and Charlene's Pepsi. The girl, maybe a high school senior, wore a nametag that read SALLIE. Sallie poured the coffee and snatched up Charlene's nearly empty red plastic cup then spun on her toe as if she was pissed about something. Charlene hoped the waitress being pissed didn't translate into spitting in Charlene's drink.

"My great-great-grandfather James Pinkerton was from here. An itinerate Methodist minister in the 1880s. That's as far back as I know. His two sons grew up here but then moved to Detroit to get jobs in car manufacturing."

Sallie brought the red plastic cup back and put it on the table in front of Charlene. It looked okay. No viscous fluid drifting amid the ice and soda. She took a sip as Sallie wandered away.

"To make a long story short, when..." He hesitated, brows furrowing. "When my wife died, I knew I needed to start all over. Start over somewhere completely different. I just... well, that's what I needed. I guess I could have chosen Detroit, but this seemed the more appealing choice at the time."

"That's what I had to do, too. Get away."

"I thought, why not try out the good old, magnolia-scented south for once, down among the cotton fields and the Spanish moss. Didn't find any of that, but anyway...Thought I'd find the county where James used to live. See what these people are like."

"And what are they like?"

Andrew tapped the tabletop and glanced out at the street. "You've got your haves and your have-nots, and those in between, like most places. They're friendly for the most part. Respectful of a person's privacy."

"What do you do for fun around Adams?"

"Good question."

He sounds a little lonely. Seems we've got that in common, as well. "Do you live in the house where the Pinkertons lived?"

"No." Andrew put his finger on top of his spoon and spun it. It clattered softly against the Formica top, twirling like a little helicopter blade. "That place was torn down years ago, according to the records in the Adams Historical Society. But I was lucky to nab a Victorian in fairly decent shape for a fairly decent price. There's even a small apple orchard in the backyard. Fourteen trees that still bear fruit. I still do law work, but it's not like it was back home. Nothing high pressure, no multi-million-dollar deals on my plate anymore. Some contract work, some other simple stuff—deeds, divorces, that kind of thing—during the mornings. Some is pro bono, if it's a cause that I feel is important but which wouldn't otherwise get a fair legal shake. My law office is in my house, so it couldn't be more convenient. In the afternoons I work on, well, other things."

"You don't, like, kill people in the afternoons?"

Andrew laughed out loud. It was a very pleasant sound. "No, not that I can remember, anyway." Charlene reached for an extra napkin the same time Andrew did. Their fingers brushed each other.

"You going to sell apples on the sideline?" Charlene asked. "You could have one of those hand carts, push it around town. Get a monkey with a cup. That could be a lot of fun, make some extra spending cash."

"Unfortunately, monkeys aren't easy to come by in Nelson County."

"Okay, no monkey. You could do a little song and dance yourself to attract customers." *Oh, wait, I saw him limping. That was a crappy thing to say!* "Oh, listen, I..."

"Hey," Andrew interrupted, unfazed. "If you want some of the apples, there are still quite a few that haven't dropped yet. Most don't have worms. Feel free to come by."

"Thanks. I might take you up on that sometime."

"Don't wait too long."

"Okay."

"But what about you, now?" Andrew pushed his plate forward slightly and folded his arms on the table. "You've hardly had time to talk. You're another out-of-towner transplanted to this Virginia wilderness. How'd that happen?"

She gave him the homogenized version of her recent life— the inheritance, the move to paint—leaving out her dire financial straits and worthless attempts to capture something on paper. She tried to make herself sound like an intentional minimalist, a back-to-basics Thoreau with a paintbrush. But then she surprised herself by saying, "In addition to all this, I've come to find out that I have a bizarre family history that I knew nothing about. According to a woman named Maude Boise, that is. Do you know Maude?"

"I've heard of her, but haven't met her. Some people in town have mentioned that she has a son who lives with her? Some kind of hard-ass guy who only comes into town when he has to and never has a good word for anyone."

"That would be Dennis. Seems pretty unpleasant. Actually, downright rude. Maude also has a granddaughter I didn't meet. Maude's sweet, but she has this odd belief that one of my ancestors was...oh, Jesus, I hate to even say it."

"You hate to even say what?" Andrew leaned forward with a conspiratorial grin. "Don't leave me hanging like this."

"She says one of my ancestors was a self-proclaimed witch."

"Really? Wow." His eyes widened slightly, looking a bit bemused, a bit intrigued.

"Yeah, really. And wow."

"I get the feeling you don't believe she was a witch."

"No, not hardly."

"You finished there?" Andrew nodded at Charlene's almost-empty plate. "Want some dessert? They have some pretty good choices here."

Are you paying? "Well..."

"This is all on me, by the way."

"Sure. Thanks a lot."

After German chocolate cake, Andrew drove Charlene back to Homeplace. His truck was a master on the rutted driveway, straddling the pits like a tightrope walker. They crossed the flat bridge and pulled up into the yard. With Andrew in the truck next to her, the place didn't seem quite so looming or unwelcoming.

"Thanks for everything," she said as he cut the motor. "The trip into town, the lunch. The company."

Andrew put his elbow on the steering wheel. "I enjoyed it, too. It's nice to chat with someone about more than just deeds and child custody issues. Maybe we'll see each other again?"

"Maybe. I need to get some of those apples."

"And I hope you don't mind my being personal..."

Oh, shit, now what?

"...but I think you might want to get your hand checked. That splinter looks small, but it does seem irritated. If I'm being too nosy, tell me to take a hike, jump in a lake, whatever terminology you'd prefer."

"Fuck off?"

He laughed. "Tell me to fuck off."

"You don't have to fuck off," said Charlene. "I do appreciate the concern."

He turned slightly toward her. She turned toward him, her hand on the door handle. There was a sudden, surprising rush of unbidden expectation. Her chest flushed.

"Thanks for the lunch," said Charlene. Her voice was softer, unintentionally so. It sounded strange in her ears. "Did I already thank you?"

"Yes," he said, then leaned over, hesitantly, but clearly hopeful. Charlene did the same, tipping her face upward and kissing his lips briefly. She could smell his warmth, his gentleness, a faint scent of sandalwood soap. A spiraling energy moved from her mouth to her chest, causing her to inhale deeply, her heartbeat to quicken, and her nipples to harden against the fabric of her bra.

"Oh," she gasped, and sat back.

Andrew blinked and looked at her. "Oh, jeez. Was that all right?"

The energy continued to move to the pit of her stomach and to the delicate place between her legs, where it stirred and caused her spine to arch. *Oh, my God, I'm horny! Wow, I haven't felt that in a long time! What the hell?*

She let her breath out and touched her neck. "Yes, it was very much all right."

Then Andrew said, "Look at the deer."

Between the smokehouse and the well stood a white-tailed doe with a long neck and huge eyes. She stopped her grazing as Charlene and Andrew watched through Andrew's window. The dead grasses in her mouth dangled nearly to the ground.

"She's beautiful," said Charlene.

The deer walked slowly toward the truck, then angled toward the house and passed several feet in front of the truck's hood. She never took her gaze from the humans. Charlene could see her steamy breath, which seemed odd, because the air outside was still rather warm.

"I think she's afraid if she looks away, we might do something stupid, like shoot her," said Charlene.

"I know a few good ol' boys in Adams who would be aiming their shotguns at this very moment."

The doe moved steadily, lifting her legs one at a time in graceful arches, stretching them out, planting them down. *A ballerina should have such elegance,* Charlene thought. The deer circled around the truck and stopped a good forty feet away, her body facing the truck, the grass still dangling from her lips. Her flanks quivered, shaking off insects.

Charlene thought, *I wish I had my camera with me. This would make a great—*

The deer charged. Head down, nostrils flaring, she raced toward the passenger's door.

"Oh, shit!" screamed Charlene, and she scooted to the middle of the bench seat. Her hands flew over her ears. The deer slammed into the truck with enough force to cause it to rock sideways off its right tires. The passenger door folded inward, the window glass cracked. The doe's head lifted just enough for Charlene to see its face before it dropped out of sight. The eyes were scarlet and popping, the tongue lolling and spewing blood, bitten nearly in half by the impact. The deer fell away. The truck crashed back down onto all four tires.

"What happened? Why did it do that?"

Andrew gasped. "I don't know. Maybe...maybe it felt challenged."

"How? We weren't getting out of the truck. We weren't moving at all!"

Andrew put an arm protectively around Charlene's shoulder, but she shook it off. "I don't know," he repeated. "I've never seen anything like that. Let's have a look." Andrew popped his door.

"I don't want to look."

"It might still be alive. Here, scoot out my side."

I don't want to see it!

Andrew went around the truck. Through the cracked window he said, "It's dead. Neck's broken. Strangest thing. So sad, too."

Charlene got out of the truck and joined Andrew, though it took a few long seconds to get up her courage to look at the deer. When she did, her stomach clenched. Its head was twisted completely backward, and blood oozed from its nostrils, its destroyed and exposed tongue, and the sockets of its once shining eyes.

Turning from the dead animal, Charlene hurried up the porch steps, unlocked the door, and went inside. She didn't shut the door, hoping that Andrew might come in, too. But he just called from the yard, "I'll take care of this mess."

"I'll help you with the cost of replacing the truck door," she called back. *And just how will you do that?*

"That's all right. It was an accident."

Charlene went into the living room and sat on the sleeping bag. She wrapped her arms around herself and stared at the floor. Outside was thumping and banging. A few minutes later, Andrew's truck engine roared and she could hear it drop into gear. She went to the window in time to see the truck's dusty trail. The grass where the deer had fallen was coated in dark, sticky red. In the back of the truck, something heavy bounced up and down beneath a blue tarp.

Charlene took her paintbrush, coated it with blue, and tried to force a streak of Tye River across the paper. The splinter in her right hand screamed with pain when the brush neared the paper. Furious, she broke the brush in half. Then she tore the sheet of paper from its clamps and threw it to the floor.

14

~

Things had been going surprisingly well until that damned bonko Bambi decided to commit suicide against the side of his truck. What the hell was that? It cut short the afternoon and left Andrew feeling a little awkward over his time with Charlene.

But it had been nice to that point. Very nice. That he had moved to kiss her surprised him. That she had moved to reciprocate had both surprised and pleased him. Yet there was a fragile thread there, a spider's web of connection that could just as easily break apart as become stronger. Charlene seemed shy, a bit hesitant to open up. He had noticed that when they'd first met at Randy's Hardware. He understood that hesitation perfectly, being in the throes of self-imposed emotional isolation himself since moving to Adams. The tenuous sense of kinship he felt for her had, for some reason, compelled him to bake a batch of overdone "welcome to the neighborhood" cookies that morning, to stick some of Daisy's much better ones into the mix, and to drive them out to her place.

He was glad he did. He'd opened a door. Not for a girl-friend or lover necessarily, but at least for a friend. And then the damned deer had decided to play bighorn sheep with his truck and had lost.

Andrew took the doe to the county dump, where he was told they didn't have the facilities to render the carcass and he'd have to either burn or bury it. Andrew drove back into town, thinking he'd just have to pay someone to bury it. While at the stoplight he saw Yule waving to him from in front of the hardware store, and he rolled his window down to hear what the man was saying.

"Mr. Marshall! Hey! What you got there?"

Andrew pulled into the hardware store parking lot and Yule trotted up to the truck. Andrew climbed out to join him. Yule lifted the canvas and whistled low. "Check that out, will you? You been huntin'? Don't you know deer huntin' season ain't until November? Well, 'less you use a bow an' arrow, then you can start in October."

"I didn't go hunting. Do you think I killed a deer by breaking its neck?"

Yule shrugged. "I don't know how guys from Boston hunt."

"It killed itself."

"You mean you hit it with your truck."

"I mean it ran itself into my truck. While my truck was parked and I was just sitting there."

"How 'bout that."

"I said more than 'how 'bout that' when the deer hit. Scared the shit out of me." *Almost literally. I've had my share of vehicle accidents. I don't need any more. Ever.*

"Just ran into your truck? Was something chasing it?"

"No. It was just chewing grass like a normal deer and then got it into its mind that, I don't know, that it really hated me. Or hated my truck."

Yule glanced at the passenger door, then tried it, finding it stuck tight. "Yeah, that's a mess."

"Expensive mess."

"What you gonna do with that doe?"

"Pay somebody to bury it."

"Huh."

"Could you possibly do it, Yule? Do you have time, or do you know of someplace? I'd like to get it done before it gets dark today. I can't leave it in the truck. It'll start to go bad."

"How long ago this thing die?"

Andrew checked his wristwatch. "It's almost three now. It's been about an hour and a half."

"It's still good, then," said Yule. "You drive me to my house. I got a big freezer there. I could get this chopped up and in there before my wife and mother-in-law get home. They'll be thrilled with the meat. Free food's a good thing. Well, maybe not to you."

"Free food is a good thing."

"Yeah, okay." Yule let out a long sigh. "Having that will let them know I didn't just do nothin' while they were gone. I didn't just take off and fart around and do nothin'. Even though, well. I think it'll help..." His voice went very low, almost inaudible. "Maybe it'll make them feel better about..."

"Sure," said Andrew. He put his hand on Yule's shoulder, pleased at his sudden ability to reach out to the other man. "You can have it. I'll even help you cut it up for your freezer. Even though I might be a tenderfooted northerner, I do own a chainsaw."

"You want to cut up a deer with a chainsaw?"

"Or we could use your tools, Yule. But I'll only help if you stop calling me Mr. Marshall."

"Yes, sir, Andy," said Yule. "But you know what that means? It means we's friends now, not just acquaintances."

"I guess that is what that means," said Andrew. He nodded, more to himself than to Yule. *A friend. How about that. That wasn't so hard.* "And don't forget that will-reading we got set up for Monday morning. Ten A.M. sharp. If you're the only one that can make it, that's fine. I'll have copies for anyone who needs it."

"Service is tomorrow afternoon. Mountain View Baptist. Know where that is?"

"Oh." Andrew hated funerals. But maybe as Yule's friend, he needed to make the effort. "I'm sure I can find it."

As he opened the driver's door to let Yule slide through to

the passenger's side, Yule asked, "Where'd this happen, anyway? The deer smackin' into your truck?"

"I was with Charlene Myers out at her place. She was on the passenger's side. Good thing there wasn't more damage than there actually was."

Yule put his foot into the truck, looked over his shoulder at Andrew. "Who's Charlene Myers?"

"New lady, nice, moved into the house out near the end of Craig Road, the place people call Homeplace."

Yule blanched. He let go of the doorframe and moved back a step from the truck. "Homeplace?"

"Yes. What's wrong?"

Yule rubbed his chin vigorously. "I don't like that place. Most people around Adams and the county don't like that place."

"Why not?"

In the shadow of his ball cap, Andrew could see the struggle in Yule's eyes. "It's not a good place to be."

"How so?"

"Just isn't." The tightness in his voice requested Andrew to let it drop. But Andrew couldn't.

"Something bad happen there?"

Yule looked away, out across the parking lot to the road, then back again. He let out a noisy breath. "Yeah."

"What?"

"Oh, just stuff, Mr. Marshall. Andy. When kids grow up here they know not to go on that land. They know to stay far away."

"Come on, Yule. You and I aren't kids. What's up with Homeplace?"

"Nobody talks about it much, nobody brings it up much. It's out there by itself in the country, no need to have anything to do with it. Kids suspect ghosts, witches, something like that. Grown-ups just say stay away."

"Witches?" Andrew almost laughed but swallowed it back. "Really?"

"There are enough good places in Nelson County, why mess with the bad?"

"So you'd be saying Charlene is messing with the bad, living there?"

"I'm saying she probably ain't too smart living there."

This wasn't going anywhere. He wasn't going to convince Yule that some vague, country-fried childhood stories were ridiculous. But he had to get rid of the deer. So he said, "Well, the deer wasn't exactly on Charlene's land. It happened on the road, near her driveway. I'd stopped to adjust the radio, and wham. There it came, smack into the side." *Liar, liar, pants on fire.*

Yule took off his ball cap, scratched his head, and considered this. "You tellin' me what's right? It weren't really on her land?"

"No, just off it."

"Truthin'?"

"Truthin'."

Yule brightened. "Well, all right, then. Let's take this deer over my place before the flies find it. And we can cut a good steak or two off for you, if you want."

"You have a good recipe for venison?"

"Recipe? Ha! What you mean, recipe? You toss it on the grill is what you do. Rub it down with salt, pour a little beer on it, let it get almost black…"

Like my cookies. I can do that.

"…and there you go. Think you can remember that?" Yule climbed into the truck and moved over to the dented door. Andrew got in and pulled his door shut with his hand on the open window.

"Oh," he said, "I'm betting I can."

15

~

The next few days were long and tedious. Charlene imagined herself like the doe, trying to look strong and confident, but filled with enough confusion to wonder what it would be like not to have to feel anything anymore.

She discovered a bent scythe in the rubbish pile out back, and spent the hours whacking weeds down in the front yard near the house and then collecting rocks in a dented wheelbarrow she found in the smokehouse and removing them, small load by small load, to the edge of the forest. Her arms ached, her shoulders stung, and her face was sunburned, but at least, she told herself, she was accomplishing something. She sure as hell wasn't having any luck painting. The splinter in her hand stung off and on. She tried, twice, to dig it out with a needle, but it was too deep and she just ended up bleeding, then crying. Her mind kept going back to the dead deer with the blood-red eyes and twisted neck. Maybe Maude was right. Maybe there was major bad mojo at this place.

Of course that was ridiculous and she knew it. She'd been where she was before; she knew it well. It wasn't bad mojo. It was depression.

Sunday afternoon she drove to Maude's house to visit. She

took a gift of late-season wildflowers—Queen Anne's lace, chicory, black-eyed Susans—since she felt it wasn't polite to stop by without something after Maude had shared her tea and muffins. It was an impromptu idea, the visit, and a stupid one in retrospect, because Maude was taking a nap, and Dennis, who answered the door, wouldn't wake his mother to see her guest.

"What's that?" he said from behind the screened front door, nodding abruptly at the jarful of flowers.

"They're called flowers."

"I know flowers. What the hell you bring 'em over here for? We got more of them weeds than we know what to do with. I chop that stuff down, burn it to get it out of the way."

"I brought them for your mother." *Asshole.* "I think they are pretty. I'm sure she would think so, too."

"Well, I ain't waking her up to see a bunch of weeds. She's an old lady. Needs her sleep." Dennis lifted his chin defiantly. It was all Charlene could do to keep from whacking the jar of flowers into that pompous chin.

A pretty young girl's face appeared over Dennis's shoulder in the doorway. "Den-dis?" she said, the word softly slurred.

"Get out of here, Polly."

"H-h-hooo?" asked the girl. She stepped closer. Charlene could see she was very unsteady on her feet, moving as though one leg were shorter than another, or her back were broken. One shaky hand came up and caught Dennis on his arm. Dennis shook it off. The girl stumbled and caught the edge of the door.

Polly. Yes. This is Maude's granddaughter.

"Hi, Polly," said Charlene, leaning over to speak around Dennis. "My name is Charlene Myers. I'm your new neighbor. I live next door at Homeplace. It's nice to meet you."

Polly's head jerked up and back, and she smiled. Dennis spun about and said, "Polly, go! Now!" As he turned, Charlene could see Polly's twisted body. And she saw that the young woman was very pregnant.

Oh, my God, who the hell did that to her? Did Dennis rape his own niece? Is he that foul?

"She's going to have a baby?" Charlene asked as Polly moved back into the house.

"Girls do that all the time," said Dennis. "Din' your mama teach you about birds and bees?"

"Is she...married?" *Don't push it, Charlene. He might just slit your throat.*

Dennis's eyes flashed. "You made enough noise as it is. My mother needs her sleep. You got to leave."

"You'll give Maude the flowers?"

"Hell," said Dennis. He paused, then opened the door and snatched the jar from Charlene's hands. Charlene went to her car. As she opened the door, she could hear Dennis toss the jar of flowers on the porch, shattering it. She didn't look back.

16

~

Monday evening Andrew had called to see how she was. She told him she was all right, though she really wasn't. She was depleted, exhausted. Andrew was respectful enough to believe her, and she found that disappointing. He said they should get together sometime soon and she said sure but didn't offer anything more than that, and he didn't press it. She hung up, feeling all the more lonely.

Tuesday evening it started raining, hard. The little stream swelled quickly, flooding the plank bridge by morning. She had to wait until afternoon, when the rain had finally eased, to drive up for the mail. She clenched the steering wheel as hard as she could, commanding the car to make it up the slippery slope to the main road. It slid a few times, but she was able to back it into rocky places for purchase, and then ease forward again. She floored it the last ten feet and the Cruiser rattled up onto Craig Road.

Under the rainbow canopy of her umbrella, she tiptoed through the puddles to the mailbox. At least a piece of junk mail, she hoped, to keep her in mind that she was still a person with an identity. The worst was an empty box.

Inside the rusted box was her retirement check: $3,845.27.

Oh, my God, yes yes yes!

There was also a cute "Hi There, Prairie Dog, How Are Your New Digs?" card from Mary Jane and a letter from Ryan. Mary Jane included a photo of Reginald curled on her sofa, which brought a sudden surge of tears, missing her pet, jealous that he'd so readily adopted Mary Jane as his surrogate mom. Ryan sent a money order for five hundred dollars along with a note telling her he admired her courage and determination *(Ryan, if you really knew the truth)*, that she should embrace her passion and make him proud come spring when she presented her new works to the world.

She drove straight into Adams, dripping, sloshing, and barely able to contain her joy at the new and unfamiliar sense of financial relief. She opened a checking account at the Planters Bank, deposited her checks, and wrote out a final payment of $2,813.28 to her flesh-eating credit card company.

Now what, now what? Whoo hoo!

The town of Adams was at her disposal. She imagined running into Andrew and treating him to lunch at the Fox's Den, buying him two chicken fried steaks if he wanted them. She'd have the rib eye. The rain was not an irritant anymore. Charlene turned on the car radio and listened as the music and her windshield wipers found sync and then lost it again.

At Sieber Appliances on the east side of town she ordered an inexpensive refrigerator and a stove for a total of $627, hesitating for a moment because she had not checked all the kitchen outlets to see if they worked, but then deciding they worked. They had to work. So there. The man at the counter said they would deliver the items by five o'clock that afternoon. At Barrie's Bedding and Antiques, a rather dingy and uninviting store a few miles south of town, she pondered the wisdom of buying a cheap mattress set. But with just two thousand dollars left from the check and the sale of her furniture back in Norfolk, and months to go before finishing *(you haven't even started)* her new series of paintings, she figured she could live with the sleeping bag.

Her last stop was Randy's Hardware, where she bought malted milk balls and a bolt cutter. She didn't see

Andrew, but hoped he might come jogging in from the rain to get more flower bulbs. She would thank him properly for taking care of that poor, pathetic doe. Maybe they would sit in his truck together and talk a bit. Maybe he would follow her home and they could visit. She could apologize for sounding like a whipped puppy when they last spoke on the phone. She could make up for it in the living room. On the sleeping bag.

At home.

"Home. I'm thinking of it as home now. That's really odd, but it's a nice odd."

17

~

There was something on the front porch of her home.

The rain had stopped by the time she reached her yard. The heavy clouds held in the sky, refusing to let the sun through, ready to pick up with a downpour at any time. Charlene parked near the porch, where she'd whacked the weeds down, and dug the house keys from her purse. She glanced through the foggy windshield and saw something on the porch near the door. She wiped the misty glass and squinted. Some old paper, blown in on the rainy winds? She didn't think so. A package delivered by UPS? No, she never mail ordered anymore.

With her umbrella under her arm and a Randy's Hardware bag at her chest, Charlene trotted through the soaked grass and up the porch steps.

Five dead rabbits lay against the front screen door. Charlene's pulse picked up. Her breath locked in her lungs. *What the hell is this?*

The little pink tongues lolled between tiny bucked teeth. The small furry heads were cocked at impossible angles. Charlene put the bag down and cautiously reached for one of the rabbits. It was a cottontail; all five were, with silky gray-brown fur and white puffed tails. Blood matted the fur around the eyes and mouth. She touched the rabbit's back; it was still warm. *Jesus.* Slowly, she picked it up. The head flopped. Its neck was broken.

"What did you guys do?" she asked the dead rabbits. "Break your necks on my front door? Why?"

And then the rabbit in her hands screamed and wriggled violently. It dropped to the porch and went still once more. Charlene screamed, too, but no one in the wilds of Nelson County could hear it.

18

~~

When she was sure they were all dead, Charlene gathered the rabbits up in her bath towel then took them to the backyard and burned them.

The rabbits were possessed. To break their necks on my door like that, they had to be possessed. The deer, too.

Stop thinking like that. Charlene shook her head to clear the thoughts. She picked up a stick and flung it onto the crackling pyre composed of rabbits, scrub brush, and a few logs from the back porch. Ash and sparks burst from the flames and flew into the air.

Maude said Charlene's family was never to sell this place. What if something here at Homeplace really was angry that she didn't plan on keeping the land?

Damn, would you just stop this? If someone else were here to bounce those thoughts off, like Ryan, Mary Jane . . . or Andrew . . . then you would see how silly they sound.

Beside her on the ground were three buckets of water, ready in case the flame was blown from the bald patch of earth into the weeds. But there was no wind and it did not spread. She stood, arms crossed against the chilling air and her own trembling. After ten minutes she doused the flames and left the blackened, skeletal remains to the elements or to wild scavengers.

By five o'clock the appliances had not arrived. Charlene called to ask what the holdup was but only got a busy signal. *Come on! Who has busy signals these days? Don't they have call waiting? Or at least a second line? What's with these guys?*

By five thirty, still nothing. She tried to call again, but their answering machine picked up, "Sieber Appliances closes at five P.M. Please call us again during our regular business hours between..." Charlene jabbed the end button on the cell.

Damn it! I want my appliances.

She picked up her camera, flashlight, and bolt cutter, and tromped to the Children's House, casting a sidelong glance at the flattened, charred pile of rabbits and wood, getting another shiver from the idea of what they had done on her porch and what she had done to their little bodies. But back to the task at hand. She might have knocked herself out last time she was in the cabin, but that wouldn't happen again. She would get into the attic. She would take pictures. If she couldn't paint the mill yet, she would paint something else. She would paint the mysteries of the cabin's attic. Artists had to press on through the mire if they were to get anything done. Neither this place nor worries about it would control her or hold her back. Besides, she now had a bolt cutter.

It took several good, hard squeezes with her knee braced on the handle to slice through the old padlock on the trapdoor at the top of the steps. Once the lock was dislodged, Charlene pushed the trapdoor open and crawled into the blackness.

The flashlight cut a pale ribbon across the cluttered attic floor. The roof was too low for Charlene to stand, so she crawled forward through the thick dust, praying that black widows would hide from the light. She discovered a scattering of old medicine bottles with water-stained and illegible labels, rotting leather children's high top shoes, and empty, mildewed haversacks. She sneezed and her eyes stung.

I should have bought a paper mask for this.

She reached a small straw-stuffed mattress, covered with

scraps of what must have been clothing at one time. She trained the light along the length of the mattress. Mice had chewed chunks out of it, leaving huge sores from which the brittle guts protruded. Putting the flashlight down, Charlene carefully reached beneath the mattress and turned it over. It struck the floor with a soft *thud*, sending more dust into the air. Charlene covered her nose and mouth until it settled. She picked up the flashlight. There, in the center of the ticking, was a large, brown stain.

It was blood.

What happened here?

A tingle ran down her back and across her shoulders. She sat back on her heels, gathered her camera up, and took a number of flash photos of the mattress. Then, bracing the flashlight between her knees, she snapped photos of the items near her, catching the bottles and the shoes, the leather bags, an old shotgun, a mildewed saddle and rusting stirrups. The flashlight loosened and fell from her knees to the floor with a clack. Charlene aimed the camera where there was no light at all, and continued to snap photos.

The flashlight suddenly snapped off. Charlene spun about on her knees and felt for it but came up short. It clicked on again, throwing its beam across the jagged mounds of litter in the attic.

Then, on its own, it began to roll.

Slowly, like a child's toy with a wind-up spring, it moved forward across the uneven floor, thumping up and over the thumb switch with each revolution. There was no sound in that attic, not the creaking of boards or the shifting of winds outside against the roof, only the slow, rhythmic *thack-thack-thack* of the flashlight as it propelled itself along. Charlene stared at the light, unable to move toward it or away from it, held in place by terrified revulsion.

Thack-thack-thack-thack. The flashlight inched its way purposefully across the attic floor, over papers and shredded socks, books and string.

Then it ran into the base of what looked like a big box. The flashlight's glow grew dim then, as if rolling had drained the life from it. But the puddle of illumination it cast allowed Charlene to see that it had indeed struck an old trunk with a canvas cover and scratched metal corners.

She crawled hesitantly toward it, refusing at first to touch the flashlight but then holding her breath and snatching it up. It did not burn her. It did not come alive in her hand and try to bite her or to leap away. *The floor must be at a tilt. It was gravity that pulled it along.*

It's mojo, Charlene. The floor is flat.

She unlatched the rusty buckles with her thumb and pushed the lid up. More dust and years' worth of stink lifted from the trunk. Charlene shone the flashlight about, revealing piles of more old newspapers and magazines. Removing the top tray and putting it aside, she peered at the contents in the bottom.

There were baby mittens and christening gowns, browned with age and eaten through by silverfish. Tarnished silver teething rings lay amid lace collars and hand-crocheted bibs. There were loose sheets of paper, tattered on the edges, written on in fading pencil by a child's hand. A small leather journal, still intact and stitched with thin lacing, was tucked in one corner. Charlene pulled it out, wiped the cover with her sleeve, and opened it. The first page was inscribed in ink: "To God. From Opal Alexander. 1821." Beneath the heading was, "Be quiet. Don't Tell."

There was a thump on the roof directly over Charlene's head, and she flinched and cried out, nearly dropping the journal and the flashlight. But then more thumps came, with increasing speed and rhythm, and she realized it had begun to rain. As carefully as she could, she backed to the open trapdoor with the journal in her hand and the flashlight in her teeth and eased out onto the steps.

She raced across the yard through the downpour, and, once on the porch, stripped from her shoes and wet jeans. As she shook the jeans to make sure there were no spiders in them and draped them over the firewood pile to dry, she glanced out at the spot where the bonfire had been.

The rabbit skeletons were not there. There was only the charred spot where the fire had been.

Those scavengers are quick about their business. I wonder what picked them up? A fox? Maybe a skunk? They'll eat about anything.

It didn't matter. They were gone.

She tugged off her socks and padded down the hall to the living room. On the sleeping bag she wiped rain from her face with a bath towel and pulled the journal from her shirt.

"To God. From Opal Alexander. 1821."

Opal must have been one of Phoebe's daughters.

Thunder rumbled outside the house. Charlene pulled the rubber band free from her hair and ran her fingers through the strands, untangling a few rain-matted clumps. More thunder. The room darkened. She got up to turn on the overhead light. It blinked but went on. Rain blew across the front porch and batted the closed window.

I hope the electricity hangs in there.

She flipped through the journal, trying not to break the fragile edges. The first three-quarters of the book were filled with writing. The last quarter of the pages were blank. Each entry was brief, and inscribed with a large, juvenile, but careful cursive.

The first page: "May 14, 1821. I was caught. I didn't mean to but I broke it. I am in here until I am forgiven, if I am forgiven. God forgive me."

Another page, deeper in the book: "June 23, 1821. I am sorry I am sorry. I am sorry. I will say it until I am believed. So many days counted on the walls. I am sorry."

Poor child. What was she sorry for? What had she broken? Although she had no idea of the age or face of this child, she imagined herself in the girl's situation. Frightened. Alone.

How sad.

She turned a number of pages. She stopped on July 2. The handwriting was particularly unsteady. "July 2, 1821. Help me Jesus. Help me God. Help me or I shall die! Save me from the hands!"

The hands. What hands?

A chill clutched at Charlene's shoulders. Were the dreaded hands Phoebe's hands? Did this little girl truly fear for her life? Were the stories Maude told based on truth, that the woman called Phoebe Alexander was a witch in the way she hurt and terrified her children? That the Children's House was not one for play but for banishment and punishment?

"Did Phoebe threaten to kill Opal?" Charlene whispered to the walls.

Charlene's hands trembled madly, making it difficult to turn another page. The next entry was so garbled that it was almost impossible to trace one letter to the next, as they traveled not on a straight line but up and down.

"Ju...ly 3, 1821. My...ey...es...are...g...one...T... he h...a...nds ar...e coming for me...soon soo...n...no no no Ple...as....e God...no no no...I don't wan...t... to...g... o...."

Sickened, Charlene threw the journal toward the fireplace. It smacked the sooty wall beside the hearth and fell open on the floor. She could see the tiny scrawls of horror..."The hands...are coming for...me!" She got up, kicked the book shut, and then slid it under her suitcase. She didn't know exactly why she did that, except that the book terrified her. She had no idea what had happened to the little girl *(Yes, you do. Her mother blinded her and threw her down that ghastly well, God rest her terrified little soul!)* and didn't want to dwell on it. The mere presence of the book was too disturbing. Maybe it would be best to burn it like she had the rabbits.

But it's a piece of your family, Charlene. You wanted to find something.

Snatching up the journal, she took it to the kitchen and put it into the icebox. It would be safe in there. *You'll be safe with it there.*

She returned to her easel, her hands balled into fists, her stomach twisted in knots. "Paintin' time," she said, belting out the words like Big Sam in *Gone With the Wind*, loud and strong to belie her dread. "Paintin' time, Miz Scarlett. Now get your Southern ass in gear."

She opened her water jar. Her thumb slipped through the palette and held it at the proper angle near her hip. Her brush swiped back and forth against the hardened hues, mixing together the colors of early fall and cool shadows.

"Just do it," she hissed at the brush, and raised it to the paper. Her hand was instantly cut through with a hot, stabbing pain at the point of the tiny splinter. She growled and then put the brush in her left hand. The smarting in the right subsided immediately.

"Like I'm going to paint anything with my left hand. I can barely unlock the car with it." She put the brush to the paper. Instantly, as if on its own accord, the hand moved lightly and easily, creating unfamiliar vegetation along the lower quarter of the paper.

What... ?

She didn't recognize the lacy, overlapping leaves, but she stood still and let the work emerge. One plant by one plant they appeared, the hues vibrant and shimmering. Charlene held her breath, afraid that by moving she would break whatever spell had her back on track...

What is this? I've never painted this plant...

...and she would find herself right back where she had been, unable to paint a single worthwhile stroke.

The brush moved from paper to paints to water to paper to paints to water. Charlene watched, silently, detached, carried along.

And then the plants were complete. Deep in color and dotted with specs of yellow light, they filled the bottom of the paper. Charlene stared at the lifelike renderings, feeling the sway in the leaves and the pulse of the forest floor...

Wait. I do recognize that plant. When I was a Girl Scout we learned wildflowers. I learned wild geranium, arrowroot, May apple, all sorts of stuff. This plant is bloodroot.

Suddenly, she felt odd, woozy. She shook her head and blinked, hard.

She dipped the brush—*no, the brush dipped itself*—back into the water jar, rinsed off the greens and yellows, and then collected a blend of oranges and corals. The brush moved to the center of the paper. She watched as it made a slow, curving downward stroke. Then several other strokes beside it, with slight angles out and back. Charlene's eyes blurred and she couldn't refocus. But she didn't care. She was painting.

Maybe this was how impressionists did it. Maybe they went into trances and painted even as the world around them seemed to shrink and disappear, even as the floor beneath them seemed to rock back and forth, ever so slightly.

I'm dizzy. I don't feel so good...

The brush gathered more paint, dark browns this time. Smaller strokes, oval in shape, leaving tiny white slices to either side of the brown. Nausea gathered at the base of her throat.

I'm dizzy oh shit I need to sit down...

The brush made tiny detailed impressions in the oval, bringing black to the center and then working small black slashes beneath it.

That's an eye.

Charlene's vision refocused.

A human eye.

She pulled the brush back from the paper with conscious effort and dropped it to the tray.

She had painted the side of a face, an ear and a patch of sunburned skin. And staring at her from the flesh on the paper, watching her with near-black, perfect concentration was the eye.

It winked at her.

Charlene flipped the paper around against the backboard, then stood with her fists to her chest, her heart thundering against her ribs, staring at the spot on the blank paper back where the eye had been.

The cell phone rang.

I painted an eye!

It rang again.

It winked at me! Oh, my God!

The phone rang a third time, a fourth. Charlene hurried to the mantel and snapped the phone open. It was Ryan.

"Hi there, Sis. How's it going?"

Charlene looked at the living room window. A few loose maple leaves were plastered there on the glass. Thunder pounded in the distance; the storm was moving away. "There's a storm...it's almost gone...I can't see that any trees were damaged out front." She didn't want to talk to Ryan. She didn't want to talk to anyone. It was too hard to gather her thoughts. Her head was fuzzy, her vision uneven. She wanted to be alone.

Alone with that eye?

"Yeah, I saw you on the Weather Channel. Nelson and neighboring counties. Scattered thunderstorms through eight P.M., mid-fifties, clearing tomorrow. See, I'm keeping an eye on you, Sis. Ha ha."

Charlene looked at the easel. She could feel the eye watching her, even through the backboard.

"Charlene? You sure you're okay?"

"Yeah... yeah."

"You sound scared."

"What did you say?" As she watched the backboard, the visible top edge of the paper rippled as if in a breeze.

"I said you sound scared. Are you okay there by yourself, Charlene?"

"There's nothing..." The paper's edge rippled again, harder, peeling up off the backboard and then settling down again. Charlene's heart lurched.

Stop it, I don't want to see that eye...!

"I was wondering if you got the check I mailed? It should have gotten to you today. I wish it could have been more, but I hope it will help some."

"The... what...? Yes, I got it."

"That's good. Charlene? Are you still there?"

The paper blew up and off the easel, spun in the air, and landed face up on the floor near Charlene's foot. The dark eye gazed up at Charlene.

Charlene cried, "I don't want to see that fucking eye!" She kicked the paper over with her bare feet. She stomped on it and pulled it in opposite directions, tearing it into chunks. She could hear Ryan shouting, "What eye? Hey, what's going on there?"

Charlene scooted the paper pieces into the fireplace. She tossed Ryan onto the mantel, then lit a long camping match and set the paper chunks on fire. The dented fireplace screen was shoved over the hearth so the paper couldn't drift back into the room. She bared her teeth at the burning pieces, feeling at once terrified and triumphant.

"Charlene!" came the tinny voice on the mantel.

She picked up the phone. Her mouth was dry. "It's the damn picture I painted. It had an eye, and..." *Don't tell him, he shouldn't know. It will be bad if he finds out.*

Why will it be bad?

"Charlene, hold it! What is wrong? I'm worried about you!"

Don't tell him, Charlene!

She counted her heartbeats. One, two, three, four, five, six, seven, eight, nine, ten, eleven. Then, "Don't worry... about me... I'm all right. I just got a little startled. Something I painted surprised me, that's all. Don't worry... please."

"I do worry. I'm going to come down there and check on you."

"There's no need to. I'm okay."

He can't come.

Why can't he come?

It would be dangerous! He'll get hurt!

Why? What is happening here?

"I don't think you're okay, Charlene. You sound kind of messed up. You're not doing some kind of drug, are you?"

"Drug? No, no drugs. Of course not."

"I want to see you face-to-face, to make sure you're all right."

The fire peaked in the fireplace. The paper curled inward, black and crisp. Then it died down as quickly as it had flared, leaving carbon crumbs behind the screen. It was gone. Good.

Good.

"Do you hear me?" insisted Ryan.

"I hear you."

"I mean it. I want to see you."

Whose eye was that? "Ryan, listen to me. I'm fine." *Why did it wink?* "Haven't you ever jumped at shadows?" *It wasn't a shadow, it was an eye.*

"I'm still going to come visit you. All right? Not quite sure when, but as soon as I can get out from under some of this work. Next week, maybe? You're my sister..."

Your stepsister.

"...and I care."

"I know you do. But please don't come."

"Charlene."

"Ryan, I'm all right. Don't come."

"But I'm..."

"Please. I have to do this on my own. I've made my bed and I have to get used to it."

What bed, Charlene? Don't you mean a sleeping bag on a hard living room floor?

"Well, all right, but I still feel wary about you being there alone," said Ryan.

"I don't want you to come here just yet."

"I hear you. But some other time, and not too long from now, okay? Now why don't you brew yourself some tea, go out to a movie, watch a goofy television show..."

I have no television. And there are no movies to go watch. But there is something watching me.

"...get some fresh air. Just relax. You're an Earth Mother hippie now, right? Do some yoga or meditate on something."

"Okay."

And then Ryan was gone.

Charlene went to the hall and faced the front door, putting her fingers on the old wood, feeling the chill seeping through. Her head was hot and her hands were ice cold. The back of her throat was raw, as if she'd swallowed a cup of ground glass.

Suddenly, up the stairs, there was a crash. Charlene whirled about, crying out. The tarp across the top of the steps flapped outward, like a hand reaching for her, billowing high, revealing for the briefest second the boarded-up door in the shadows, then settling back down. *Something's in that room up there! What is in that room?*

She crushed her hands over her ears and screamed, "Stop it! Please please stop it!"

She listened. She waited. There were no more noises. Slowly, she lowered her hands.

There was silence upstairs.

Wind. It was just wind. Wind knocking an old house sense-less. Wind blowing down the hall from one of the bedroom windows.

"That's all. That's all it can be." Her voice quivered.

She turned again to the front door, and tugged it open. *Oh, God, fresh air. Ryan was right. That feels good.* The storm was gone, leaving flattened weeds and scattered twigs in its wake. The night was heavy, weighing the air down with sounds of cicadas and crickets and other frantic creatures of the night. She stepped onto the wet porch. One bare foot came down on wood, the other on something that felt like a slippery beanbag. She lifted her foot immediately, then stepped back over the foyer to flick on the porch light.

There, in a tidy and hideous pile, were the burned rabbits, eyes melted away, bones contorted, little white teeth protruding from blackened jaws. The leg of one dead bunny twitched, slightly.

Charlene pulled herself back inside, slammed the door, and twisted the key in the lock. She braced her cheek against the wood. *Oh God oh God the spirit of the witch put them there to threaten me!*

"No, a fucking fox dragged them up here! It wanted to eat them out of the rain!"

A fox wouldn't drag dead rabbits to a front porch and lay them in a neat pile. They don't do stuff like that.

"I don't know shit about foxes! Maybe foxes do!"

But maybe they don't.

She listened through the door, half expecting to hear only the wind ebbing and flowing through the porch, half expecting to hear the chatter of little dead rabbits' teeth.

19

~

The phone rang four times before he was able to answer. He dropped the novel he was reading and reached across the arm of the sofa to pick up the receiver. He cleared his throat before he spoke. "Hello?"

"Andrew, hi."

For the briefest moment it sounded like Constance, Susan's sister. He shifted the phone from one ear to the other as his mind raced. *Constance? What could she want? She hates me. She blames me for Susan's death.*

"Yes?"

"I hope I'm not calling too late." It wasn't Constance. Thank God. It was... "This is Charlene."

"Sure, yes, of course. Charlene. Hey. How are you?" Andrew rubbed the bridge of his nose and cleared his throat again.

"Am I calling too late?"

The digital clock on the television read 10:57. "Ah, no. Not at all." He hadn't heard from her since they'd spoken briefly on Monday. He'd come to the conclusion she had no real interest in staying in touch. He was glad to hear from her. Except that she sounded... stressed? "What's up?"

There was a pause, and then, "Oh, just more issues with the house. The electricity has gone off."

"Yeah?"

"The rainstorm was pretty hard."

"Must have been harder out there than here in town. It was just a nice easy rain here. Good for the flower bulbs I put in. Washed off my truck, too—saves me ten dollars at the car wash. I swear this town attracts dust like New York City attracts wannabe actors."

"Well, it's done a job on me. No lights. Can't use the hot plate, and the batteries on my radio are low."

"You don't have a stove?"

"Nope. Guess I hadn't mentioned that when we had lunch the other day. No stove. No heat, either, except for what I decide to burn in the fireplace."

"Wow. I didn't realize that."

"Yeah. Little Miss Pioneer, here."

What does she really want? "Do you need a place to crash tonight?"

"Maybe. I was thinking that, yeah." A pause. "If you don't mind."

"Of course I don't mind. Do you know how to get to my place? Do you want me to come get you?"

"If you just give me directions?"

"Come back into town. Craig Road becomes Main Street, you know that."

"Yep."

"I'm easy to find—762 Main Street. The white Victorian on the hill with the wrought iron gate. Next door to the little green house with the black shutters."

"Where should I park?"

"You'll be fine leaving your car on Main. I have a small driveway off Pine Avenue into my back yard, but there's only room for two vehicles. My truck and car fill it pretty tightly."

"Okay. That sounds good."

"Are you all right, Charlene?"

"You're the second person to ask me that today. I'm okay, really." Her voice was even yet tense.

"Okay. See you soon?"

"Twenty minutes."

"I'll leave the porch light on."

"Thanks." Charlene hung up. Andrew placed the phone down on the end table next to the lamp. He picked up the novel, a fast-paced thriller that blew his feeble efforts out of the water, and opened it to the piece of torn newspaper he used for a bookmark. Then he shut it again. He was suddenly uncomfortable with the idea of her being there. They'd had a good time Saturday, yes, but then things got weird with the deer, and then she sounded cool on the phone Monday. After that, nothing for two days. Not that they were a couple in any sense of the word. They didn't really even know each other beyond a couple fun hours spent talking over sandwiches, and a single tentative kiss. He'd had a lot of single dates when he was at the University and during his first few years at the firm. Nice women, most of them, engaging, bright, but some for whom he'd forgotten names, some faces. None with whom he felt any connection. It was all part of that twenties game of romance. He had no doubt most of the women had forgotten him, too. But for some reason, he'd held out a few minutes of hope that Charlene Myers might be more than a one-date girl. He didn't think the attraction had anything to do with the old rebound mythos. People didn't rebound from someone who was killed in an automobile accident. Only from people whom they dumped or who dumped them.

Susan had emotionally dumped you at the altar, Andrew.

Andrew pulled himself up from the sofa, and, leaning heavily on his cane, wandered barefoot into the front hall to unlock the door. His knee was offering its usual dose of late-evening pain, though he'd taken pills an hour earlier.

He caught a glimpse of himself in the mirror over the sideboard. "Yeah, that's how you should open the door, standing there in your boxers and ratty Red Sox T-shirt. Make a real good impression. She'll wonder what you have in mind."

Rex, who had awakened from his dog bed in the living room, limped into the hall to join his best friend. He wagged his tail and stared at the door as if they were going out. "Nope, not now," said Andrew. "But let's see if I can get the two of us looking a little more presentable before company arrives. Think I should shave?" He ran his fingers across the short beard. "No? I agree. I look casual, don't you think?"

Rex's tail wagged harder.

Upstairs, Andrew slipped on jeans, a clean sweatshirt, and fresh socks. He combed his hair and brushed his teeth, then found a blue bandana in his underwear drawer and tied it around Rex's neck. "First impressions," he said to the dog. Then they went back downstairs.

It was 11:09. He sat back on the sofa, picked up the novel, read one sentence, then put the book back down again. Rex, his eyebrows twitching with expectation, stared out the living room to the front door.

"Should I make popcorn?"

Rex glanced at Andrew, then back at the door.

"Maybe I should build a fire in the fireplace?"

Rex wagged his tail.

"You think her call is a ruse so she can come over here and jump my bones?"

Rex let out a long, silent sigh then lay down with one paw over Andrew's socked foot.

"I take that for a no."

Rex farted, then rolled over onto his side and smiled, eyes closed.

20

~

Charlene sat in the Cruiser in front of the Fox's Den, watching the clock on her dashboard, making sure it was at least twenty minutes before she started up the car and drove to Andrew's house. Downtown Adams on a weekend night was depressingly dead. Streetlights blazed and a few neon signs glowed from storefronts, casting their sputtering, iridescent colors onto the wet slick of the rain-covered street.

She clutched the steering wheel, the key in the ignition, and turned to auxiliary so she could listen to WBAM on the radio, turned low. An occasional car whooshed by, headlights leading the way, going anywhere other than downtown. But that was it. It was so different from Norfolk, from her old neighborhood, where regardless of the time of night, time of year, or weather conditions, teens would cluster to smoke and talk trash, couples would meander up and down the sidewalks, and cars were a steady parade.

I should just go back to Norfolk. Ask Mary Jane if I can move in with her for a bit. Beg for my job back. It hasn't been very long. They may not have even officially replaced me yet. They probably only have a sub still, a temp, manning my podium.

A stray cat trotted down the wet street, keeping to the side and darting in and out between the occasional parked cars. It neared the Cruiser, hesitated, then raised its back and snarled. Then it raced across the street to the other side, where it continued on its way.

"That would be Reginald if I went back."

Two minutes to go. The music on the radio gave way to news. Nothing of interest.

She'd left the house as soon as she'd discovered the rabbits back on the porch, snatching up her purse, her jacket, and her phone, and running out the back door and around the side yard to the car. She'd imagined the burned rabbits flying across the yard to attack her, but as she crammed the key in the ignition and jammed on the gas, she saw nothing move up on the porch. No stirring of hideous burned bodies, no dreadful nightmarish creatures clicking up on brittle legs, scurrying across the wooden slats and down the steps in her direction.

Driving into town she had the music up as loud as the radio would go to drown out her thoughts. She wasn't sure exactly what she was going to do, except that she needed to be out of the house. Once she passed into Adams and saw the Fox's Den, she had an idea. She pulled over, turned the radio down, and dialed Andrew. One part of her hoped he would answer. The other hoped he would not.

But he did, and he had said she could come over.

Time was up. Twenty-one minutes. She turned the car on and drove up Main Street to the white Victorian on the hill.

21

~

"Hey."

"Hi, there. Come on in."

Andrew stepped back to let Charlene into the foyer as Rex, in his sporty blue bandana, did his "I don't know this person who is this person who is this person?" doggy dance.

"Let me take your coat," Andrew offered. Charlene nodded and slipped out of her jacket. Andrew put it on the mahogany coat tree by the living room doorway.

"It's really good to see you again," he said, though she didn't look particularly good. Her hair was tangled, her over-sized blouse wrinkled and paint-spattered, and her face was pale and drawn.

"Is it really?" she asked without looking him in the eye.

Odd comment. But not totally unexpected. What could he say he knew of her, her moods, her real personality? Nothing.

Then she shook her head, glanced at him, and her expression softened a little. "I'm sorry, that was rude. It's been... quite a night, to put it mildly. And you're really nice to let me drop in on you like this. I just couldn't stay there tonight."

"No problem. Nobody wants to be without power." Damn, this was awkward, as if they'd actually done the deed and now were face-to-face afterward, not sure what to say. "Do you have things? I can show you your room."

"I, ah," Charlene began. She looked suddenly embarrassed. "I didn't bring things with me."

"No change of clothes? Toiletries?" *None of your business, Andrew.*

"I was in a hurry." Charlene glanced around the foyer, up the wide carpeted stairway, into the living room and then the dark paneled office across the hall. "Great place. Nice dog."

Rex, who understood the word dog, wagged his tail, hard.

"Thanks," said Andrew. *She doesn't so much look frustrated, but... scared. That's it, she looks frightened.*

"Come on to the kitchen. You want some wine? Coffee? Tea?"

Charlene's eyebrows drew together, as if she suddenly wanted to cry, but then she held up her chin and said, "Yes. Yes. Or yes." She tried a smile.

Andrew led Charlene and Rex down the hall, through the large dining room, and then to the kitchen. Charlene said nothing about the cane. He wondered if she even noticed.

The kitchen was a small yet cheerful nook, with a hardwood floor, oak cabinets, sunny yellow curtains, granite countertops, and a red and chrome vintage 1950s table and chairs that had reminded Andrew of his grandmother's house.

"This really is a nice house," said Charlene as she studied the stainless refrigerator and stove and the crystal chandelier over the dinette set. "I remember you said my place had potential. I don't care how much might be done to it, it would never look this good."

"Don't give up on it so easily. Some time, some TLC, you never know." Andrew held up a bottle of Chateau Morrisette's Red Mountain Laurel. "This is wonderful, want to try? It's from a Virginia winery. Down the Blue Ridge a bit."

"Okay."

"Anyway," said Andrew as he took wineglasses from the rack by the window, turned them over, and proceeded to pop open the bottle. Rex plopped down on the small braided rug under the table. "I was lucky in that this place was in fairly good shape when I moved in. I had the floors refinished, and installed the appliances and light fixture. New curtains. But the rest was as is. Just needed some elbow grease."

"And a hefty amount of money, too, I bet." Charlene leaned against the sink and crossed her arms. Dressed as she was and with her hair loose and tousled, she looked for all the world like a young and tormented artist. Which, he guessed, she was.

"Well, some." He poured the wine, handed a glass to Charlene. "Here's to an evening a bit better than what you were having."

"Amen to that," said Charlene. She took a long drink, eyes closing for a moment, and then she put the half-emptied glass on the counter. "I like that. Thanks."

Andrew poured his own glass and took a sip. The awkwardness was growing. "How about we take the bottle to the living room? I could make a fire. We could pop some popcorn. I bought an antique popper, one you stick right in the coals. It burns some of the kernels but it's much more fun than the microwave."

Charlene nodded, her lips pressed tight.

Andrew stuck the bottle under his arm and reached on top of the fridge for the jar of popcorn. Then he pulled down a half-eaten pack of ginger snaps. "Cookies?"

Charlene nodded and looked at him with pinch-cornered eyes.

He put the popcorn jar and cookies under his arm with the bottle, then snatched yet another bag from the fridge top. "You like marshmallows?"

"Sure." Her chin began to quiver.

"Um..." Andrew dragged down another bag. "Peanuts?"

"Yeah."

Another bag. "Doggy rawhide chews?"

Her lips rolled in between her teeth, her head tipped down, and she burst into tears.

"I was kidding about the doggy chews."

Charlene put her hands over her eyes and turned toward the sink. She cried softly, her shoulders heaving up and down.

Rex clambered up from beneath the table and went to Andrew, his tail still.

"Charlene…" Andrew began. He moved to her, hesitated, and put his hand on her arm. "This has to be more than just a power outage."

She didn't nod, but she didn't shake her head.

"Let's go to the living room."

She nodded.

Charlene took the wineglasses and followed Andrew as he maneuvered back to the front of the house with the popcorn, cookies, marshmallows, peanuts, and two bottles of Red Mountain Laurel for good measure. He leaned his cane against the sofa, scooted the magazines on the coffee table aside, and placed everything down carefully. Then he sat and motioned for her to join him, but Charlene chose the recliner adjacent to the sofa.

Okay…

They sat in silence. On the mantel, the pendulum in the Seth Thomas moved back and forth, clicking off the moments, glinting softly in the light from the end table lamp. Rex lay on the floor across Andrew's feet. Outside, the wind knocked about, shaking the shutters. Charlene leaned over every once in a while to pick up her wineglass to drink. Andrew refilled it when it got low. Charlene didn't make eye contact with Andrew, but stared alternately at the dog, the red Oriental carpet, the bookshelves, the clock, and her glass. She was no longer crying, but her breathing was hitched and her eyes red-rimmed. She sat straight, feet beside each other, as if she were preparing to get up and leave.

At last Andrew said, "How's your hand? The splinter?"

Charlene wiped at her eyes and looked at her hand as if she'd forgotten about the injury. "Fine. It only hurts at certain times. I think it'll work its way out someday on its own. I didn't go to doctor." Her voice faded out.

"I'm glad it's better."

More silence.

Andrew leaned forward. "I'm a good listener, you know. I listen to all sorts of people share all sorts of troubles. And not all of them are legal issues."

"I'm really sorry to come here like this."

"It's okay." A pause. "Hey."

Charlene looked up.

"Tell me what's wrong. Maybe there's something I can do besides offer a place to stay for the night."

Her eyes welled again, and two drops slid down her cheeks. "You'll think I'm crazy."

Andrew smiled softly. "There's nothing wrong with crazy. I get crazy sometimes, too, and—"

"No, not funny crazy but losing-my-mind crazy."

Andrew scratched Rex between the ears. "Why would I think you're crazy like that?"

"The power didn't go off at my house. I lied."

"Okay."

"I called you because I couldn't stay there tonight. I think... Andrew, do you think a place can be haunted?"

"You mean really haunted? As in ghosts? Or do you mean it can hold bad feelings and bad memories?"

"I'm talking ghosts."

I don't want to say no yet. I don't think that'll do any good. "I don't know. There are lots of things in this world that are unexplained."

"But you don't think there are ghosts."

"Not really."

Charlene lifted her glass from the coffee table, looked at the remaining few drops of wine, and put it back down again. "There are stories that my ancestor was a witch. I told you that already. The stories also say she abused her children and her slaves, and hell, probably anybody else who challenged her. Word is that she still haunts Homeplace, doing her best to keep others from her land and house, and..."

"And what?"

"And to threaten any family member who plans on selling the land. Like it's never supposed to leave Alexander hands." Another tear trickled down to her chin, and she swiped at it fiercely, as if she'd had enough of crying, and tears were now an irritant.

Andrew had an urge to reach out for her hand but held back. "Tell me what happened?"

And she did. At first her words were hesitant, stumbling. She told of dead rabbits on her front porch, rabbits she burned but that then returned to the porch. She described a cabin called the Children's House, and how her flashlight rolled on its own across the attic floor. Then she told of the thumping in the room at the top of the stairs, and of an old journal written by a child terrified of "the hands." She said she'd gone into a trance and began painting a picture, but she wasn't in control. Something else was. And she painted an eye. An eye that winked at her.

Andrew took it in. He'd heard wild stories before. Legal clients' stories could be the most bizarre, especially when told by those who were in dire need of attention. But Charlene hadn't struck him as someone desperate for attention. Quite the opposite. She seemed to crave her solitude and independence. A very different kind of woman from Susan.

Don't think about Susan now.

"Charlene," Andrew asked, "have you been under any stress lately?" *Damn, you sound like the freakin' Rain Man. "Are you taking any prescription medication?"*

Charlene snorted. "That would be an understatement."

"Try me."

"Andrew." She sounded exasperated. "I hardly know you. It's all such personal crap. I shouldn't burden you like this."

Andrew spread out his hands. "You're here at my house and it's after eleven P.M. We're drinking my favorite wine together, and quite a bit at that. And don't forget, we did actually kiss each other last weekend. I don't know about you, but I liked the kiss. All that's personal, don't you think?"

"Yes."

"So."

"So." Charlene crossed her arms as if she were suddenly chilled. "So I left Norfolk because I had no career as a painter whatsoever. I was an instructor at a community college, teaching students to paint, and some of these kids were going off and making more money at their craft than I ever had. And I'm a good artist. I really am good. Most of my time was spent pouring over lesson books and deciding grades and doing pre-

cious few of my own paintings. Those I did were fluff,
though, an attempt to sell to beach tourists who are often as
happy with shells glued together to make a dog as a genuine
original painting. I wasn't making ends meet. Not by a long
shot. I got into debt. So I decided, screw it, I needed a new
start."

"I understand."

"I do what my best friend recommends I not do. I gave
away my sweet kitty, Reginald. I cashed in my retirement.
Stupid? You said it."

"I didn't say it."

"Whatever. I left everything behind and came here. My
check arrived and I finally had enough money to get some appliances but, of course, the appliances don't show up when
they're supposed to. I can't seem to paint, and when I do I get
a fucking winking eye! How am I supposed to make any
money if I can't paint? I need money." Her words picked up
speed, as if she were a car rolling downhill. "The house is
filled with mice. I can't afford an exterminator. It's really
drafty, too. There's no Internet access at the house, so I can't
get or send e-mails. I can't afford a real bed. The only working water aside from the toilet comes into the house through a
hand pump—a damned hand pump. Can you picture anybody
in this day and age using a damned hand pump? I can't afford
a bed because if I spend my money on that, what happens if
there are wiring troubles I wasn't expecting? Or I find termites? Or the roof leaks? Do you know I was thrilled when
you offered to pay for my lunch the other day at the Fox's
Den? I was praying you would, 'cause if you hadn't I'd have
been down to about three dollars to my name."

"Oh."

"Pathetic, right? You bet. And then," she paused, catching
her hair up in white-knuckled fingers. Her eyes were dark
now, raging with distress. "And then Maude, my next-door
neighbor, fills me in on all the family background. Oh, spec-
tacular stories, those! She tells me about the witch, a powerful fucking witch who used to live there, who was my
great-great-great some fucking or other grandmother. And

then the deer kills itself. And then the rabbits. And the noise upstairs and the flashlight rolling on its own and that awful journal and that fucking *eye...*"

She stopped. She looked down at her knees, frowned. Her fingers loosened from her hair. "Have you ever heard ravings of such lunacy?" She glanced up at Andrew.

He smiled sympathetically. "Well, that is pretty wild." *Oh, please see I'm kidding.*

"Tell me something I don't know."

"But it's not lunacy."

"Yeah, right."

"No, really. It's something else altogether."

There was a slight change of expression on her face. Hope, maybe?

"It sounds like you've been under enormous emotional and mental strain recently. Just half of what you've been through with the career struggle and the move and the lack of money would drive most people over the edge, at least for a while. I wouldn't be surprised if you didn't see or hear things..."

"That weren't really there?"

"I was going to say that were exaggerated, distorted."

"What about the deer?"

"It probably felt threatened. You haven't lived at Homeplace very long. The deer wasn't used to its territory being invaded."

"Maybe. But the rabbits?" But before Andrew could come up with an answer to that, Charlene said, "I know. Scavengers dragging around the carcasses. But the rest?"

Andrew held up his hand. "I've been where you are. Well, I don't have a relative who was declared a witch, but I know what I'm talking about." Andrew's pulse quickened. *Are you going to go there tonight? Andrew, do you really want to talk about this?*

"You've been insane, too?"

Andrew picked up the bag of cookies, tugged off the clothespin that held it shut, and dumped a couple out on the coffee table. One rolled off the table and bounced off Rex's head. Rex stirred and went back to sleep. Andrew left the cookie on the floor. He put another in his mouth and held the bag out to Charlene. Around the dry, sugary lump he said, "These are good. Especially if you're going to have to listen to me spill my guts."

Charlene stood and took the bag. Their fingertips touched and she didn't jerk away. Then she slowly sat back down. She pulled a cookie from the bag and held it before her mouth. "Tell me," she said.

He told her about Susan. The truth of how she was, how she'd been one person one day and another the next. How he had hoped for all good things with her, and how she'd pulled the emotional rug out from beneath him in short order.

"I was a normal, everyday person. Educated. Rational. But there she was, making me irrational, making me doubt myself, what I was doing, how I felt." He glanced down at Rex, peaceful, happy dog. He rubbed one socked foot on the dog's sleek side. "I never knew one person could drive another so crazy. At least not a rational person. As a lawyer I've seen what crazy people can do to others. But they had problems because, I believed, they weren't as steady or clear-headed or rational as I was. But I found out that it's very easy to get knocked off your balance."

Charlene tucked a strand of hair behind her ear. She kicked off her clogs then drew her feet up beneath her. It was a good sign.

"Susan made me..." He hesitated, but continued, feeling his blood heat up in his veins, his adrenaline prickle beneath his skin. "...hate her. I didn't want to hate her. I should have just divorced her. But I wanted to try to turn that hate around. Try to get her to care for me like I thought she did before we got married."

Charlene took a bite of cookie and nodded.

"The last week before, before she died, noises seemed way too loud to me. And I was seeing things out of the corner of my eye, things that when I turned around, nothing. I felt I was being watched, that Susan had hired someone to sneak around and watch me. I was so on edge, so uptight, I couldn't think straight. Paranoid, to put it mildly. I'm surprised I was able to do my work, though I know I didn't do my best. The day we bought the new car, the day we took it out for a drive, I was so angry, so furious at her, that I was picturing her..." He stopped. He couldn't say it.

But Charlene filled in the blank. "You were picturing her dead?"

Andrew said, "Yes. I didn't want her to die, I just was picturing her dead. It's different, can you see that? I was imagining her away from me, gone, with people feeling sorry for me but never really knowing how I had come to hate the way she was. And then she ran the car into the side of that truck and we crashed. And she died."

"Oh, my God." Charlene put a hand to her mouth. "I'm so sorry. That's awful."

"It is. But do you see what I'm saying? I imagined her wrecking, and she did. I believed I caused it to happen. I was devastated with guilt and grief. I took off work, stayed in my place with Rex, both of us with shattered legs. I heard her voice everywhere, echoing off the walls, the ceilings. Friends and family kept coming by—'Oh, Andrew, we're so sorry, what can we do, she was so sweet'—but I couldn't stand to hear their words. They were just blather, just nonsense in some other language that I understood but that made no sense. They tangled up with her voice to the point that I wanted to scream. I did, too, some late nights in the shower or with a pillow over my face."

Charlene put the pack of cookies back on the coffee table. It seemed she had lost her appetite.

Andrew's jaw was beginning to hurt. He had a sudden urge for a cigarette. He continued, "So what did I do when I finally got my legs, including the bad one, back under me? I did the sensible, rational thing. I quit my job. I up and quit a good job with a powerful, respected firm. My father was shocked. So was my best friend. I sold the townhouse, put the money in my account with Susan's life insurance, and came down here. I wanted to run somewhere where nobody knew me but where I had some slight connection so I didn't fall off the edge of the world totally. I didn't like it here at first, either. Everything was so different from back home. Of course, I wouldn't have liked any place. My mind had no space for liking things. But I managed. I took it a day at a time. The people here in Adams have been very accepting. Nobody's pushed to know the circumstances of me coming here, though I've seen the questions on their faces sometimes. It's been a year and I'm just now starting to feel like I may have a home in this place."

"I see."

Andrew swallowed against a dry throat. He was stunned that he had shared so much. "I think I am even starting to make some friends. At least two of them."

Charlene moved over to the sofa, taking care not to step on Rex's head. She sat beside Andrew and leaned against his shoulder. It wasn't a seductive move, it was a comforting gesture, and nothing could have felt better than that move at that moment. Andrew realized how much he'd needed to talk this out. And sharing with someone who was also struggling through her own loss and fear made it safe, made it mutual and intimate. It was the best he'd felt in a year. He wondered if he might fall in love with this disheveled artist.

She sighed heavily. "I guess I've got quite a vivid imagination. I guess I've been caught up in some wild and crazy mind crap."

Andrew smiled and put his chin on top of Charlene's head. "But you know, an artist without a big imagination would be an artist whose work I wouldn't find interesting."

"So I've got to suffer for my art?"

"Well, maybe not suffer as much as you have in the past couple of days, but yeah, a little bit of angst would be in order."

Charlene laughed then. A soft little laugh, but a laugh nonetheless. They sat side by side until well after midnight, and then quietly went off to their own rooms, to bed, to sleep.

22

~

She woke with a start, confused, uncertain where she was. It was dark, but there was enough faint light to see what was around her. The bed was soft and warm with tall spiraled posters, the walls a clean ivory, the drapes a deep blue. On the wall were prints of untamed mountains and rivers, very Hudson School–like. There was a cherry dresser and mirrored bureau, and a cedar chest beneath the windows.

I'm at Andrew's house. I wonder what time it is?

She sat up, still a big groggy, and glanced around for a clock and found none. She slipped from the bed to peek out the drapes. The morning was sunny, almost blindingly bright. Eight o'clock, maybe? Perhaps a little earlier?

Charlene was still dressed in her jeans and blouse, which were not much worse looking than they had been the night before. Her purse had somehow been kicked under the bed, and Charlene tugged it out with her bare toes. Then she stood before the bureau mirror, grimaced, and dragged her hairbrush through the tangle. There was a stick of cinnamon gum in her purse; a couple quick chews then she spit it out into the wrapper.

She hadn't gotten drunk last night, but the wine had relaxed her enough to tell Andrew her life story, at least the last few months' worth. He'd listened, shared his own difficult tale, and then had made simple sense of it all. The damned house wasn't haunted, she was. In a way. Her imagination and the stress she'd been under had brewed a noxious emotional cocktail that had knocked her on her ass. That wouldn't happen again. She was cured, thanks to Doctor/Lawyer Andrew. What a good guy. She wondered if she might be falling for him. It had been a long time since she'd even considered the possibility of finding someone she might want to be with.

"I feel so much better this morning," she told her reflection. "Last night was exactly what I needed."

On a whim, she dug through her purse to see if she had any makeup with her. Not that Andrew hadn't seen her at her worst, but today she felt better, a lot better, and thought that a little mascara, lip gloss, and blush might at least make her look less like a zombie than she had the night before. She found a broken eyeliner pencil, a compact of blush, and a tube of ChapStick. She scraped the ragged eyeliner across her upper lids, leaving faint brown streaks, then promptly rubbed most of the marks away. A quick touch-up with the blush and two streaks of ChapStick *(Well, at least my lips won't look like I've gone over them with sandpaper)* and she was ready to go.

With clogs in her hands and purse over her shoulder, she tiptoed to the door and opened it as quietly as she could. If it was really early, she didn't want to awaken Andrew or his dog. She'd rather just slip out and talk to him later. The upstairs hallway was carpeted in deep red, and the other rooms on the floor were closed.

There were voices downstairs. The television? No. Actual people. Someone was here, visiting Andrew. *Crap*. It had to be much later than she'd guessed.

Holding the banister, she eased down to the first floor and lifted her jacket from the coat tree. The door across from the living room was open, and she could hear men's voices clearly now.

"Mr. Marshall, how much do we owe you for your time?"

It was an elderly man speaking. "I ain't got much, and you can see Howard didn' leave much, neither."

"Don't worry about it." This was Andrew. "The matter was simple. Just consider it something I could do for my friend Yule, here. And again, my condolences on the loss of your son, Mr. Bryan. A tragedy, certainly. But the ceremony at the church was very moving, a nice tribute. I was glad to be able to attend."

"That it was, sir, a nice service."

Charlene peeked into the living room. The mantel clock read 10:27. *Oh, wow.*

"That's mighty nice." The old man again. "I appreciate it."

Then another man's voice, "Yep, thanks, Andy. Nice of you to take your time."

Chairs groaned; the men were standing up. Charlene looked back at the stairs. *Maybe I should run back up and wait until they're gone? But if they catch me running up the stairs then it looks worse than it is.* She almost laughed aloud at the ridiculous circumstances. But then the decision was made for her. The men came out into the hallway. Rex, the old black dog, hobbled after. He seemed to be feeling arthritis in his back leg.

Charlene stood, clutching her jacket and her shoes, offering a timid grin. "Good morning," was all she could think of saying.

"And good morning back," said Andrew with a broad smile.

"Mornin'," muttered the older man, bald and white-bearded, in baggy work pants with a crushed cap peeking out of his pocket. The younger man, someone Charlene had seen somewhere on the streets of Adams, a man with a thin face and bad teeth, nodded silently. He was dressed in overalls. His ball cap was stuffed into the bib.

"Charlene," said Andrew, tipping his head toward the two men. "I'd like you to meet Arnie Bryan and his nephew, Yule Lemons."

"Nice to meet you." Charlene extended her hand. Both men's handshakes were clammy, noncommittal.

"Arnie and Yule, this is Charlene Myers. She moved into the old Alexander place out of town. She's an artist, quite a talented one, as a matter of fact. She's going to be creating paintings of things around her home. I think our ladies of the Historical Society should arrange a display of her work when she has some ready. I'm sure it will be incredible."

Yule and Arnie drew back slightly and gave each other quick, uncertain glances. Yule wiped the hand he'd used to shake Charlene's on the side of his pants.

Charlene was startled, then immediately offended. *Well, fuck you if you don't like me. You don't even know me!*

"Well, gee, I see it's late. I really have to be running," she said. "Andrew, we'll talk later?"

Andrew had clearly noticed the men's reaction, too. "Wait, Charlene," said Andrew, "I thought that maybe—"

She slipped on her clogs and jacket and strode to the front door. "Later, okay?" Tugging the door open, she walked out into the bright sun and down the angled walkway to the wrought iron gate. She glanced back over her shoulder at the house on the hill, wondering what they were talking about now. Wondering if they were saying bad things to Andrew, whatever those bad things could even be.

Idiots.

But then she stopped, took in a long breath, and let it out. She felt good, in spite of those idiot men.

Relax. Don't let a couple goofballs ruin what started out to be a good day. Maybe they are some of those people Maude mentioned, who steer clear of Homeplace and anything that has to do with the place. That doesn't make them bad, just ignorant. Or maybe they think it's tempting luck to shake hands before noon with a woman, or an artist, or somebody in clogs, or somebody who is a woman artist in clogs. Who knows what crazy, old-fashioned customs still exist out here in the Southern wilderness?

She climbed into the car and turned it on. The radio immediately came to life with some song by Calf Mountain Jam about the sky falling.

Andrew doesn't believe in old-fashioned nonsense or superstitions. He's a good guy. And I really, really like him.

Charlene pushed her foot to the accelerator and revved the Cruiser as loudly as she could, hoping the men were in the house listening to her brazen exit. Then she dropped it into drive, made a squealing U-turn, and headed back to Homeplace.

23

~

Andrew couldn't hold back the question, in spite of the fact that he was still in the professional role of the Bryan/Lemons family attorney. "What was that, Yule? Why did you wipe your hand off after shaking Charlene's hand? Do you know how insulting that was?"

"Is she your girlfriend?"

"That has nothing to do with anything. You hurt her feelings."

"I don't like your tone, Mr. Marshall," said Arnie, who put his ball cap on his head and twisted it back and forth like he was screwing it on. "No need to lecture us on what we do or don't do. I appreciate your time and help but not your criticism." He yanked open the door and went outside to wait for his nephew.

Yule donned his own ball cap and stuck his hands in his pockets. "I tried to tell you the other day, Andy. When we cut up that deer what hit your car. That woman lives at that place, that no-good place. I don't want to be anywhere near somebody that lives there. Don't want to touch 'em or even see 'em."

"So she's, what, got some kind of infection? Some kind of disease?"

Yule sniffed. "You shoulda said before we shook hands who she was. It weren't right to spring that on us like that."

"You're kidding me."

"I ain't kiddin' you."

"Jesus, Yule."

"Lord's name."

"Then damn it, Yule. Don't be ridiculous. She's a regular, ordinary young woman. A very nice ordinary young woman who would like to fit in somehow but is having a difficult time so far."

"Ain't surprised. She's havin' trouble out at the house, ain't she?"

"I—" *Yes, she has, but it has nothing to do with your ghosts and witches. It's just anxiety and uncertainty.*

Yule looked at Rex, then leaned down to pet the dog. He was thinking it through, picking his words carefully. "Pardon me for askin', but you ain't," he leaned forward, almost whispering, "havin' relations with her, are you?"

Andrew was shocked. "That's personal."

"True, sir, but I don't want you messin' with something dangerous. She lives in a dangerous place. You know how if a dog walks into a puddle of oil on the street the oil gets sucked into his skin and he tracks it all over where he goes?"

"What does that have to do with anything?"

"She's trackin' the evil around—can't you feel it?"

"Can you? Can you truly tell me that when you shook her hand you felt something evil?"

"It ain't that obvious, not right away. But soon as you said who she was, I could feel that nastiness crawling up my skin. Like oil off a dog's paw."

"I'm really sorry you felt that way. I like Charlene, quite a bit."

"But I thought we was friends."

Andrew was mad enough to spit, but he tried to keep his voice in check. "This will make a difference, Yule? Really?"

"I can't be takin' chances. Howard, oh my God, Howard was stupid enough, was careless enough—" But then he stopped, looking as though he'd slipped up, badly.

"Howard was stupid enough to what?"

"Nothin'."

"Yule." There was something in Yule's eyes in that moment that actually frightened Andrew. He tried to soften his voice. "What was Howard stupid enough to do?"

Yule looked over his shoulder as if to make sure no one else was listening, no silent witness, no secret spy. No ghost. He licked his lips, his tongue reaching out past the bunched front teeth. Then he said, "I'm only tellin' you this 'cause knowin' the truth might save your life. We's buddies now. I ain't told nobody else, and don't plan on it."

"You're telling me this in confidence?"

"You're my lawyer now, well as my friend, right?"

"Right."

Yule spoke slowly, quietly, fearfully, as if the words were broken glass in his mouth. "Howard didn't fall drunk into the campfire. He got killed on that woman's land. On Homeplace. It weren't no accident."

Andrew's heart lurched. "What do you mean, it wasn't an accident?"

Yule's fingers began to play with each other. Andrew could smell a fresh outbreak from the man, a strong aroma of body odor, grease, and terror. "I told him not to go on that land, not to go in that old mill. People have died there in the past, bein' nosy, trespassin'. But then I said, oh, fuck it, Howard, go ahead, you always do what you want to do anyway."

"What happened?"

"It was that woman's land, that Homeplace. It was that old mill they used to run, back in the slavery days. It's empty now, a big old thing as dark and cold looking as the devil's gullet. He got out the boat, went up there to have a look around. I'd seen a light in there, and told him it weren't a good idea. I shoulda never told him about the light."

"Yule!" came Arnie's voice from out on the front porch. "What you doin' in there? I got to get back to work!"

"Comin'!" Yule called back, and then his voice went even softer, as if the old man were pressing his ear against the outside of the door. One of his hands reached out involuntarily and took Andrew's own, tightly, like a father preparing to give his son the direst of warnings. "Howard went in the mill. Then I didn' hear nothin' and next thing he comes out, all on fire like some damned stuntman that got it wrong, fallin' into the river and dyin' with his face half burned off. Was a ghost what did it. He told me, plain as day, there in the water. A ghost done it. Whole place is haunted, Andy. No two ways about it."

Andrew's body had gone cold, with the veins in his hands standing at attention. The anguish he saw in Yule's eyes held the purest honesty he'd ever seen, an honesty born of help-lessness, grief, and a desire to stop something awful from happening again.

Yule swiped at his lips with the sleeve of his jacket. Then his voice dropped even more, almost a whisper now. Andrew had to concentrate to hear him over Arnie stomping around outside on the porch. "I had to come up with the campfire story. I didn' know what else to do. I'da got blamed for lettin' Howard trespass, for givin' him beer, gettin' him drunk. If I didn' get arrested for that, then Arnie woulda had my hide, woulda done something bad to me. You ain't known him when he feels somebody betrayed him or stole somethin' from him." Yule let go of Andrew's hand. "Don't mess with that place. You hear me? Ghosts don't like people tellin' on them like I just did."

"I hear you."

Yule went to the front door. "I can't say it no more than I have."

"I know."

"All right." Then Yule was gone.

Andrew picked up the phone in his office and dialed Char-lene's cell. He had to at least warn her that there may be dere-licts or druggies hiding out in the mill, people who would as soon set a man on fire as shoot him in the head. No answer. More than likely she was driving in one of the county's dead zones. He'd give it another few minutes.

The next legal appointment was a pending divorce case at eleven thirty. He went into the living room, plopped down with the novel, and opened it. Rex snuggled up against his leg.

Andrew slammed the book shut and went upstairs to his computer. The dog, sound asleep, stayed put.

A click of the mouse and the manuscript appeared on the screen. Then he dialed Charlene's number again. Still, nothing. Damn dead zones.

He picked up where he left off with his novel. Chapter 3.

It took only two rings before a light went on inside the townhouse, showing through the window next to the front door. Moments later, the door was yanked open to the length of the chain, and a short woman in her early fifties was staring through the crack. "What do you want? Who are you?"

The officers held up their shields. "Detectives Chase and Alamong, Mrs. Huss."

"Oh, dear God. It's Jacob," the woman said. "We haven't heard from him in a couple of days. Is it Jacob?"

Hugh hated this part. "Yes, ma'am, it is. May we come in?"

The woman cried, "Tim, it's Jacob! Get up, oh, my God, something's happened to him!" Her voice was as ragged as her son's dead face had been, and cold with dread. Somehow, she was able to slide the chain away and let the detectives enter.

Andrew flexed his fingers and then leaned back over the keyboard.

Mr. and Mrs. Huss clung to each other in the hallway like children expecting to be beaten, shaking and wide-eyed. On the wall were framed family photos, showing beach trips, a Disney World vacation, a white-water rafting trip, a high school and a college graduation. Clearly, Jacob was an only child.

Andrew stopped typing. He picked up the phone by the computer and dialed Charlene again. Still no answer. It was insane, this day and age, to have any place in the United States where cell phone reception was unavailable.

Hugh said, "Mr. and Mrs. Huss, Jacob's body was found on a ferry in the harbor."

"His body!" squealed Mrs. Huss. Her knees buckled beneath her, and though her husband tried to hold on to her, she slid to the floor. "His body? No, that's not possible. He can't be dead!"

Andrew lifted his fingers from the keys. That was what Yule probably said to himself when he tried to save Howard in the river. *He can't be dead.*

The phone rang. Andrew saved the document and lifted the receiver. "Yes?"

"Andrew, it's me. Charlene."

Good! "Hi, yes, I was just trying to call you. Are you okay?"

"I'm so okay I just had to call and let you know." She sounded happy.

"But Arnie and Yule, the way they acted..."

"Forget them, they're just goofy guys. I wanted to say thank you for hearing me out last night in all my own silliness. You put up with a hell of a lot from me, and I appreciate it more than you could know. I'm almost home now and am ready to tackle what I can as I can without letting worries make me irrational."

"I'm glad to hear that. But..."

"But what?" There was a sudden edge to her voice.

"But you should be careful, regardless. It seems there may be people holed up in that old mill on your place, maybe people cooking crystal meth or something else they don't want people knowing about."

"Did Arnie and Yule tell you that?"

"I've just heard that there has been some activity spotted there, from the river. How about I call the sheriff's office and have them do a little look around to make sure the place is clean?"

"I've walked some of the land already. I went to the old mill. Everything seemed okay to me."

"That doesn't mean everything's all right."

"Now you're trying to scare me."

"No, not scare. Just alert. Do you have a gun, by any chance?"

"A gun? You're kidding. No. I don't have a gun. Do you really think I need one?"

"I just don't want you taking any chances. How are the locks on your doors?"

"They seem pretty sturdy to me."

"And your windows?"

"Okay, okay, Andrew. I get your point. I'll put in new locks on the windows and I'll call the cops, okay? Oh, hold on, I just got to my driveway. What a mess this thing is. As slow as I take it, I can just imagine the struts and tires and undercarriage begging me to stop and turn around."

"You take it easy there, on your car and on yourself. I want you to be able to crank out some of those beautiful paintings I have yet to see."

"I appreciate that. And I will. Whoa! I better slow down more. That was quite a bounce."

Andrew took a breath, rubbed his mouth, and blurted out, "I really like you, Charlene. I think you're a really nice person." *Oh, that sounded weak. Like some middle school kid with a crush.*

He could hear her smile across the wires. "Why, thank you, Mr. Marshall. I think you're a nice..."

Suddenly the reception started to fade. Charlene's words were choppy and indecipherable. "I'll talk to you later!" he shouted, as if speaking more loudly would clear the line. He thought he heard her say "good-bye" but wasn't sure. He hung up the phone.

The doorbell rang. Next appointment, coming up.

24

~

Charlene found no resurrected rabbits hopping about on her porch, no dead deer dancing in the yard, no witches peeking from the corners of the house, smokehouse, or cabin. The sky was a clear blue with thin streaks of white cloud, and the sunshine was warm and comforting. Andrew was so right. Everything was explainable. Everything was okay. As Charlene popped open the car door, she called out, "I'm home! And this is my place and everything's fine!"

Then she started singing the bouncy, upbeat "Don't Look Back" song that she'd heard time and again on her radio.

"You gave time to make things, make things right but I just didn't hear."

She knew she was a bit off-key, but it didn't matter. She sang louder to prove it didn't matter.

"You sent me sun, you sent me rain, it should have all been clear. I see the light now, shining through; now there's nothing to fear. I got my baby back with me, I got so much to cheer."

The tune made her smile and lightened her step as she went up the steps to the porch.

"Give a little hug, now, baby mine. Give a little kiss, it's so divine. Give a little dance and give a little whirl, never will be sad, now you're my girl."

Charlene spun about on the porch, holding her arms out and her head back. It felt good, so good, to be loose and free from the creeping mind-crud that had tried to stymie her and keep her from doing exactly what she'd been determined to do when she packed her bags back in Norfolk. If Andrew had been there that moment, she would have kissed him again.

"I see the light now, shining through; now there's nothing to fear!"

She stopped whirling and put her hands on her hips. "Yep," she said, "the Queen of the Amazon has returned!"

In the kitchen she scrubbed her teeth and took a quick sponge bath with cold water before changing into a fresh pair of jeans—her last—and a blue cotton knit sweater. Tomorrow, she'd need to take a trip to the Adams Laundromat and refresh everything she had. Maybe she would take her sketchpad with her and draw as she waited for the miracle of clean clothes to take place.

The painting with the eye was long reduced to ashes in the living room fireplace. Charlene swept the ash onto the dustpan and threw it out the back door. Yes, she had painted an eye, but no, it hadn't winked. She'd been expecting scary images and her mind had provided just that. She would start another painting and it would be exactly what Andrew had suggested, something fantastic, something beautiful.

But first, a call to the sheriff's office. "I promised Andrew I would, and it's not such a bad idea, anyway."

Having no phone book (*Note to self: Find a current phone book somewhere in town*), she dialed 411 for directory assistance. This put her through to the sheriff's department and a receptionist on the other end of the line who sounded as though she were chewing gum. Charlene asked to speak to someone in charge of checking out properties for trespassers, and the receptionist, who Charlene knew for a fact was chewing gum now, because she heard the pop of what sounded like a very big bubble, said she'd take the message.

"I'm concerned people might be trespassing on my

property," said Charlene. "It's possible that there is drug activity going on inside the remains of the old mill by the river."

"Have you seen the activity?"

"No, I've just heard tell."

"All right. And your name, ma'am?"

"Charlene Myers. The address is 238 Craig Road, Adams. It's out in the middle of nowhere, basically. But I'm sure you guys could find me."

"All right, ma'am. I'll get the word out to the appropriate persons."

"When?"

Wearied exasperation embedded in gum, "As soon as I can, ma'am."

Charlene then dialed Maude Boise. It was possible she'd heard tell of activity at the mill. After all, she had been a neighbor her entire life.

The phone rang four times and a man's voice answered. "Yeah?" It was Dennis, Charlene knew immediately. *Blech.* She made sure she sounded pleasant so as not to irritate the irritating man. "Dennis, this is Charlene Myers. I'd like to speak with your mother, please."

"I don't think so."

Charlene was taken aback. "Excuse me?"

"I said I don't think so. Are you hard of hearing?"

This had her pissed. She'd had her share of rude students back at the community college, kids who didn't really want to be in class and didn't care who knew it. She knew how to handle it, but the kids were always younger than she, and she had been an authority figure of sorts. It made her both angry and uncomfortable to be having a face-off, or a phone-off, with a man almost twice her age. "I have excellent hearing, Mr. Boise, which is why I found it surprising that you would be so discourteous to someone over the phone who was not discourteous to you. I was attempting to give you the chance to rectify that." *That's good, Charlene, pull out the teacher lingo.* Her heart was thumping loudly with tension and triumph.

There was a moment's hesitation, then Dennis said,

"There's no need for you to get uppity, Ms. Myers. We won't get anything accomplished that way, now will we?"

What a fucking asshole! She opened her mouth and the words almost slipped out, but then she heard a voice in the background, "Thank'ee, Dennis," then a mild thumping sound, and Maude was on the line.

"Charlene, honey. I was outside in the garden, pickin' grubs off the gourds. They's worse than the beetles was on the sunflowers this summer. Here, lemme put you down a second while I wipe off my hands." Clunk, clatter. Silence. And then, "All right, now. How are you doing out there all by yourself?"

"I'm doing all right."

"Any troubles with the house?"

"No. In fact, things seem very good right now."

"No troubles?" The old woman sounded surprised.

Not anymore, anyway. "Nope, no troubles. But I do have a question for you. Have you ever noticed vandals or transients hiding out in my woods or the mill? Or maybe druggies taking advantage of an isolated spot to make meth?"

"What's meth?"

"Crystal meth. Methamphetamine. Cheap, easy to make. But the process is volatile. Dangerous."

"No, I never seen nobody on your place 'cept for my own shadow at the graveyard," said Maude. "What makes you wonder?"

"There's word that some people boating on the river saw things that suggest there's something going on."

Maude's voice dropped. "There is something going on. I done told you that. You have to listen to me."

Yeah, okay, this was a mistake. "I'm sorry, I didn't mean to worry you. Really, I didn't. The people on the river probably just heard wild turkeys or deer, maybe saw a bear rummaging around the mill. I just wanted to know if you'd had any hobo encounters or had seen any evidence of people messing around here where they don't belong."

"No." Maude sounded as much irritated now as concerned. Charlene knew the old woman didn't appreciate her warnings being ignored.

"Thanks, then. And truly, things are great. The house is getting clean and I've made a good friend in town, Andrew Marshall."

"Don't know of him."

"Very nice. The town lawyer."

"You be careful. Lawyers, I don't know if I would trust one of 'em as far as I could heave 'em."

"I think Andrew's a fairly safe bet."

"All right, then. Now you let me know you need anything, honey. Any time of night, you give me a call."

"I will. Thanks."

"And if..." There was a man's low voice, and Maude said, "Yes, yes, I'm coming." And then back to the phone, "You take good care of yourself, Charlene. I got to go, stuff to do."

"You take care, too. Bye."

Charlene put the phone on the mantel. She placed a new piece of Bristol board on the easel and considered her options. Now that she had a handle on her anxiety, she could start fresh. Perhaps, though, instead of trying to do something from the photo printouts, it might be good to get some new perspectives, to do some preliminary sketches outside. Something to get her hands as well as her eyes back in the game. She'd thought the mill, but now she was leaning toward something showing the slave huts or the cemetery. The sky was clear and there was no wind, perfect weather to work en plein air. The day wouldn't have been more inviting to an artist if Mother Nature had written a "come hither, artist" sign in the sky with clouds.

Sketchbook under her arm, pouch of pencils and erasers at her side, and a new whacking stick in her hand, Charlene trudged across the yard and into the woods. This time, with the sun high through the tree branches and a sense of familiarity from having been there before, the trip through the forest was peaceful and easy. Her feet followed the rises and dips as if she'd been there many times instead of just once. She felt as though she could close her eyes and find her way; odd, but very comforting. It was only minutes before she found herself at the slave hut ruins.

The ground was cool beneath her folded jacket as she sat cross-legged on the path and did some quick preliminary sketches of the hut with the four crumbling walls—the vines crawling along the sides, fallen leaves snagged and dangling from craggy stone, the cooking pot outside what had once been the door, lying at a tilt as if inviting company, specks of sunlight, pools of shadow. With two sketches done to her satisfaction, Charlene got up, shook out her jacket, and got back onto the path. Time to find the cemetery.

The little cross was still in the path where she had last seen it, bobbing eerily with the encroaching nighttime. In the daylight, however, it was a benign bit of wood and paint directing passersby toward the narrow path that led to the Alexander burial spot. Charlene made a quick sketch of the cross. Maybe she could combine it with something else for a nice composition.

A breeze picked up on the narrow path, carrying with it scents of cedar and humus, and a mildewy odor of lichens. She broke branches as she went, snapping them back and away from her trail. *My trail. My trees. Bend them to my will.*

"Empress of the Forest!" The words echoed boldly deep in the trees.

The cemetery was sadder and smaller than it had appeared at night in the light of Maude's lantern. In the day, she could see it in its entirety. The headstones looked closer together, the etched names and dates more shallow except for Ellen's, whose marker still appeared more worn than it should have become in the time that had passed, though perhaps Maude's weekly cleaning had helped the wearing process along as much as mud or lichens might have. An iron fence lay in pieces around the small graveyard, claimed by the forest, tied up with verdant bows.

Charlene begged pardon from Julia then straddled her headstone, the most solid looking in the cemetery. She flipped open her sketchbook to a clean page, pulled a pencil out of the pouch, then scooted around to face the markers for Ginny and Mildred.

I wonder what these women were like, thought Charlene. *I know nothing except what Maude told me about Phoebe. Which can't be true. Maybe she was a cold woman, maybe even insane, but there is no such thing as a real witch.*

Then Charlene lifted her pencil and looked again at all the headstones. Where was Phoebe's grave? It wasn't here with the others.

"I bet she's buried somewhere else on the land. I bet nobody wanted the witch to be buried near anyone else."

Would you just shut up with the witch nonsense? Maybe she is buried here but her marker was destroyed over the years.

"Of course that's it. Or maybe she was buried somewhere else. I don't know how people figured those things out back then. And it doesn't really matter, now, does it?"

It does to Maude.

"Shut up, Charlene."

She wouldn't come here to take care of the graves if Phoebe were buried here. She's clearly afraid of Phoebe's spirit. She even said she built a protective stone perimeter out in the trees to keep the spirit away from her.

Charlene tossed her hair, throwing off the thoughts, and began to sketch, moving the pencil along at an angle, capturing the slope of the stones, the cracks, the moss, the counterpoints of shadow, tree branch, and cedar saplings just beyond the graveyard. Ginny's stone was an interesting shade of blue, appearing almost marble in the wavering shadows of the overhead limbs. Julia's stone tilted toward Ginny's, as if the two had been locked in eternity while sharing a deep secret.

"This will be a great piece. Maybe I'll do a series of studies, some in pencil and several in watercolor. Maybe the cemetery alone will make for a show. I'll call it, simply, 'The Women.'"

But where are the men?

The question came to her out of nowhere, as if a breeze had whispered in her ear. She paused with her pencil above the paper. "Well, damn. Where *are* the men?"

There were no gravestones for Alexander men in this cemetery. That was odd. Certainly the men of Homeplace had lived and died, but where were their remains? Was there another cemetery elsewhere, one she'd not yet found? If so, why were they segregated in death? Was this also an old-fashioned custom she'd never heard of?

Another question for Maude, Charlene thought. *Or maybe the Historical Society. They might have records of antiquated burial traditions.*

Charlene spent another two hours on Julia's stone, roughing out numerous drawings. Nothing strange happened. No odd noises from beyond. No animals striking themselves dead on trees. No pencil leaping from her hand to roll away along the ground. When her stomach began to growl and her mind turned to a deviled ham sandwich, she packed up her supplies and headed home.

25

She dreamed that night.

At first there was only sound, a soft pounding in the distance, the hammering of an old ghostly mill churning out cloth from the cogs of blood-oiled machinery.

Chunk-chunk-chunk-chunk-chunk.

Then there was a silvery light across the front yard, charging every thistle with electricity and causing the heads of the browned, brittle chicory to burr like tormented insects. Trees in the distance bowed back and forth, their leaves black, heavy tumors unable to fall. There was a scream, high-pitched and tortured. It came from within the board-covered well.

Charlene watched from the front porch, from the wide wooden swing on which she sat. Something held her there—straps, hands; she couldn't see because she had to look out at the yard, at the well in the weeds.

The scream came again, spiraling across the yard and onto the porch. Charlene wanted to cover her ears, but she could not. Her hands as well as her body were held tightly. A voice behind her whispered, "Listen. Hear it."

Then she was lifted by the forearms and elbows, and was

carried down the porch steps and through the grass toward the well.

"Don't make me look in there!" Her voice was a whisper.

"You must, my dear. You must see and you must hear."

The hands moved her across the matted thistles and grass. The soles of her bare feet were torn on the thorns and rigid stalks; she tried to lift her feet up but could not. The screams from inside the covered maw grew louder as Charlene got closer. Shrill, terrified. Agonized.

"I don't want to look in there! Don't make me look!"

"Shhh, now, dear. Trust me."

They reached the well, and Charlene was lowered so she could stand. Her feet were bleeding. She realized that her feet were not those of an adult, but were her child's feet, and her pants and shirt a child's outfit. The one she wore many years ago to a family reunion at Homeplace. She saw that her fingers were short and stained with dandelion juice. Her nubby toes dug into the soil of the ground, trying to root themselves in place.

So she would go no farther.

So she could not be thrown down that well, too.

"Look," said the voice at her side, and the bricks inched off the plywood, twisting and hunching like huge, red grubs. The plywood tore back with the sound of breaking bone, and the hole it exposed oozed blood around the edges.

The scream came again, louder, from that black pit. The sound was long, guttural, and it drove into Charlene's brain like a drill. The hands that held Charlene's arms forced her to kneel on the wet ground at the very lip of the well. Her toes dug-dug-dug at the dirt beneath her. Her fingers scrabbled at the weeds, seeking purchase so she would not tumble down to hell.

No, please, stop, let me go!

"Look there," said the voice. "Look down deep. See what is there." Charlene looked into the well. At first she could see nothing but the slimy, slippery stone walls leading into a bottomless, oil-black vortex. Then images began to take shape, spinning round and round slowly in the whirlpool. A pale blue child's shoe with a satin ribbon. A knot of wriggling, writhing earthworms. A man's broken pipe. And then the face emerged in the center. The face of a very young girl, her nose freckled with the sun, her blue eyes stretched wide in the purest expression of horror Charlene had ever seen. The mouth in the face opened, trickled thick, ruby blood like the edges of the well. And the girl screamed, again.

The hands holding Charlene shoved her forward.

"See the truth!" said the voice.

Charlene fell, her arms and legs flailing, toward that terrible, shrieking face. Her mouth opened wide to take in the worms, to kiss that screaming, twisted child's face.

She awoke to knocking on the door.

Her head hurt, the bottoms of her feet hurt, and she didn't want to open her eyes. The well and the screaming child and the worms spun away into nothingness. She took long breaths, glad to hear birds outside the window, relieved to glimpse the red hue of daylight on her inner eyelids.

The knock was persistent, and then a voice calling, "Charlene?"

She opened her eyes. She checked her watch, but it had stopped at two thirty A.M. *Now I need to buy a new watch. Crap.* Her mouth tasted like dirt, her eyes were crusted with dried...tears? Blood?

"What?" she called back, knowing as her brain came round that it was Andrew at the door. Why, she had no clue. She sat up, her head spinning. "What?"

"Is it better to come back another time?"

I wish you had called first, she thought. Following that thought was, *Oh, Lord, Charlene, that's how old hermits get started. A little time alone in the country and other people become an intrusion.* "No, wait. Give me a minute."

"Okay."

Eyes still pressed to slits, Charlene got up from her sleeping bag and stretched. Her back and neck popped. She pulled on her cleanest jeans and sweatshirt, then padded to the kitchen to wash her face and brush her hair. She didn't bother to look at herself in the compact mirror in her purse. Andrew had seen her worse, though her eyes felt puffy and raw.

At the front door she rubbed her cheeks, counted to three, and pulled the door open. Andrew stood on the porch, holding a box with a bulky paper bag on top.

"Good morning," he said. "Or is it not a good morning?"

"It's okay. Just some bad-ass dreams, is all."

"Not witches?"

"No, not witches," she lied. "Come on in."

Andrew moved past her into the front hall. "You look nice today," said Andrew.

"Oh, please don't make stuff up, I know I look like crap." It was Andrew who was looking good. He was dressed in gray slacks, a pullover sweater, his khaki jacket, and work boots. Charlene's hand went to her hair and smoothed it down.

"I don't know," said Andrew. "I like the country look. Casual. Free."

"That's a nice way to put it. But thanks." She stepped forward to give him a quick hug, and found herself caught in his warm and tight embrace. Against his jacket, in that moment, she could hear his breathing and his heartbeat. It dispelled all the awful sensations that the nightmare had dredged up. She stepped back and smiled.

"Listen. The reason I came over today was threefold. First, I brought you these." He held out the box and bag. On the side of both was stamped "Randy's Hardware."

"You brought me a new toilet bowl float and a plunger?"

"Did you need those? I could have picked them up."

"I'm kidding."

"Actually, they're a couple things I thought you really could use. Two deadbolt locks and a space heater." Then he rushed on, as if afraid she'd accuse him of interfering, "I know, it's none of my business, but I just want to make sure you're safe in your own home and that you don't freeze." Andrew put the boxed heater on the floor and opened the bag. "The locks are good, the best on the market. I can install them for you if you want."

Charlene said, "That's generous. But you don't have to clean up after me."

"I'm not. At least I hope you don't feel that way."

"No, I don't." Charlene realized she hadn't brushed her teeth. *Yuck.* "That's a nice gesture. If you're in the mood to install them, I promise not to get in your way."

Andrew pulled the locks from the bag as well as a hammer, drill, screwdriver, and screws. He put a lock on the back kitchen door then took the second lock to the front door. As he measured and drilled, he said, "The second reason I came over is because I want to invite you to a Harvest Barbecue next Friday night."

Charlene, watching with her arms crossed, said, "A barbecue?"

"I'm calling it a barbecue. I'm going to cook on the grill, but we'll eat inside. It should be fun. I hope it will be fun. I used to entertain a lot, before I got married. Then, well, it wasn't so pleasant anymore. But getting together with people is one thing I miss from the city. I've decided it's past time to break the ice, after a year, and invite my neighbors and acquaintances in Adams and thereabouts to my place. Plus, I called my best friend in Boston, and he's coming down for a few days. A sort of north meets south. Bring the two parts of my life together. Make this poor, fractured man whole again." He chuckled. "Well, it's worth a shot."

"That sounds like fun, Andrew." *But I don't know if I'm up to being social yet.*

"I tried to call you to ask if you could come, but I guess your phone is on the fritz."

"It is? That sucks."

"The barbecue will be casual. No evening gowns or tuxes or bowties. You don't need to bring anything. I'll have it all. Food. Drinks. Chairs. Good company. You like ribs? Are you a vegetarian? No, wait, you ate a crab cake."

"Ribs are good." *It would be nice if it was just Andrew, not a bunch of other people.*

"Can you come?"

"Will there be anyone there I know besides you?"

"Who else do you know around here?"

She pondered this. "Maude Boise is all, I guess."

"I can invite her, if you'd like, though I'll bet she'll turn me down." Andrew gave the lock bracket a final go with the screwdriver, then tested the bolt in the lock. "There. That's good. Now I'll feel better about you being out here alone."

"You're not my father, Andrew."

"I know that." He looked a little hurt, but Charlene added, "What I mean is you shouldn't have to worry about me so much."

"I don't mind. I like worrying about somebody besides myself."

"But about Maude," said Charlene. "Why did you say she'd probably turn down your invitation?"

Andrew put the tools back in the bag and rolled the top shut. "I was having supper at the Fox's Den last night, and talking to Dawn, one of the waitresses. She's going to help me do the food for the dinner, since I can't cook much beyond meat on a grill and burned cookies. I showed her the list. I had Maude on there since you seem to like her."

"Thanks."

"But Dawn said Maude never does any socializing. In fact, she rarely leaves her home. Dawn says she thinks Maude is, well, embarrassed."

"Of what? That sleazeball son of hers?"

Andrew shrugged. "Maybe that, too. But Dawn says it's because Maude's family lost their land years ago, and they've been dirt-poor tenants ever since, beholding to an absentee landholder who comes down once a year to make sure the house is in order."

"Oh, wow."

"Dawn suspects Maude's afraid she wouldn't fit in in social situations. Which is ridiculous, because I don't care about any of that stuff. But she seems to."

"She told me she owns Willow Vale."

"Like Dawn said, she's probably too embarrassed to tell the truth about that. I mean, you own this whole big estate."

"Oh, yeah, estate, that's what I'm calling it. So, this barbecue. How casual is casual? Rich lawyer casual or minimalist artist casual?"

"What's the difference?"

194   Beth Massie

"Loafers and cardigans versus clogs and sweatshirts."

"Whatever is comfortable. Sweatshirts, spike heels, you pick it."

"I donated my spikes to charity before I came to Nelson County."

"A shame." Andrew chuckled. He unlocked the deadbolt and opened the door. Charlene squinted over his shoulder to the yard. "Hey, what's that?" There was a bulldozer behind her Cruiser.

"Oh, yes, that was my third reason for coming out here this morning," said Andrew. "I rode over on that. I can't believe the noise didn't have you out on the porch, threatening me with your shotgun or whatever it is minimalist artists use to discourage noisy neighbors."

"You cleaned up my driveway? Wow. Thank you."

"Not a rut left. Well, maybe a few, but I got most of them. I borrowed the machine from Diamond Construction. The guy there owed me for some contract work, so I took partial payment by using that thing. It's fun to drive. I started early, around six o'clock. Wanted to surprise you, though I thought the noise would have dampened the surprise."

That was the screaming I heard, the screaming in my dream. It was Andrew on that dozer. That makes sense.

"My sleep patterns have been insane recently. I've been oversleeping more than usual. My body and brain still need to adjust to this new place. Though I am adjusting. I did some great sketches yesterday."

"So do you want to?"

Charlene focused back on Andrew. "Come to the barbecue?"

"You haven't said yes. I thought if I scraped your driveway you'd come. A little coercion."

"You're not giving me much of a choice, you conniving lawyer, you." She hoped it sounded lighthearted, and not like some witch. Make that bitch.

Andrew grinned. The grin was incredibly attractive.

Suddenly, there was a hot, passionate rush in the pit of Charlene's stomach. She took a quick breath against it, and another. A coil of desire sprang open, sending teasing tendrils swiftly toward her breasts and her privates. Her mouth went instantly dry, and the space between her legs went instantly wet. *What the hell? This can't be happening now!*

"You sure you're okay?"

Charlene managed to nod. She took another breath and held it, trying to fight back the exquisite urge that engulfed her.

"So, no, you don't have a choice unless you want to miss some great eats."

Why not, Charlene? It's just the two of you here. You've thought it before, he's good looking, he's got a great body. You like him. Don't you want to feel that body on you, in you?

It was all Charlene could do to keep from moaning aloud, from rubbing herself or rushing forward to rub against Andrew like some animal in heat. It felt at once glorious and terrifying.

"So?" pressed Andrew.

I can't just jump him!

Why not? You want it!

"So, can I put you down as a yes?"

Sweat popped out on her neck and arms, tickling the tender flesh. In her mind's eye she saw herself wrapping her legs around Andrew, clutching his hair with both hands, and Andrew taking her breast in one hand and shoving his other hand down the front of her jeans to probe the moist, anxious place there.

No, stop it! I can't do that to him. Not like this!

She braced herself against herself, locked her knees, and bit the inside of her lip until she felt the skin part and trickle blood. She said, "Okay, sure."

"Okay. Great." Andrew opened the door and then turned back around, as if waiting to see if a good-bye hug or kiss was in order. Charlene could only smile and nod.

She watched him cross the yard and then drive off in the squealing, groaning bulldozer. Very slowly her body began to relax, to let up on itself, and she found her legs trembling madly with the loss of adrenaline. Once the dozer was out of sight, she sat on the porch steps to catch her breath and her calm. Linking her arms around her knees, she stared out at the yard, wondering what had really happened back in the hallway. Was she that desperate for physical intimacy that her own body was starting to rebel against her mind?

"I mean, he's really good looking and really nice and all..." Her words on the air sounded silly, like a high school girl explaining to her best friend why she couldn't keep her pants on on prom night.

Damn, what a day so far. And she hadn't even brushed her teeth yet.

She put her head back, accepted the sun's rays, and sang softly, "Give a little hug, now, baby mine. Give a little kiss, it's so divine. Give a little dance and give a little whirl, never will be sad, now you're my girl."

It was mid-morning. She had phoning and painting to do.

26

~

Charlene taped two of her cemetery sketches up on the side of the easel and picked up the paintbrush. She took a long, cleansing breath, then dipped the brush into the water and then against the Paynes gray on the palette. She held the brush against the Bristol board, waiting for the splinter to flare hot, and made a stroke. Her hand did not fight her and the splinter's sting was minor.

She felt her shoulders relax a bit. "Good. Okay. I'm back to my wonderful, talented self. Let the paintings flow!"

She stroked gray, then several shades of blue across the paper, then added strips of green and some dabs of red. And she stopped. It looked like shit. She tore up the paper, threw it in the fireplace, and tried again. Broad strokes of green, some angled browns and blacks. A dab of gray where the first tombstone lay. And she stopped. It looked like something done by a ten-year-old.

"No, damn it. This isn't working at all."

Maybe I can't paint anymore. Maybe that part of me was left behind in Norfolk.

"That's stress talking. You're strong stock. Mom said you

came from it, and damn it, you are strong. Now, cut it out and do it right."

She studied her drawings, and then on a new piece of paper she sketched out a nice-looking composition. Brush in hand, she dabbed on browns and blacks, the shadows on the ground. And it looked like more shit.

"This is stupid!"

Then she put the brush in her left hand.

Don't do that, Charlene.

Her left hand immediately put the brush to the paper, as if it had been waiting for its turn. Her breath caught. Her heart hesitated.

This is where you got in trouble last time.

The pain of the splinter disappeared completely. Charlene's left hand moved the brush in a competent upstroke.

There was a truck on the driveway. Charlene dropped the brush into the easel tray and went to the front door. It was a delivery truck from Sieber Appliances.

"Oh, good, good, good!" she said. "This is a major step in the right direction."

Charlene had phoned the store, assuring them that no, she had not called the day before to cancel her order, there had to have been some mistake. The Sieber man swore someone had phoned and said forget the appliances. Charlene made it clear it had to have been someone else's appliances canceled. "There can't be anyone in the whole of Nelson County more in need of a refrigerator and stove than I am," she'd said, trying to keep her voice pleasant. "I'd appreciate it if you could get them out to me as soon as possible."

With a smile on her face and her hands on her hips, Charlene watched as the two delivery guys wrangled the boxed appliances onto a wheeled dolly and up the front porch steps. When Charlene held the door open, the men shook their heads and went back to the truck. One said, "You're lucky we came this far, lady, what with what you put out there on the driveway."

"What's wrong with the driveway?" Charlene ran after the men. "My driveway got plowed, it's driveable now, so what's wrong with the driveway?"

"We know witchcraft when we see it," said the man.

"Witchcraft?" Charlene called.

The second mumbled, "Well, I don't know if it's witchcraft exactly but..."

"But what? What are you talking about?" said Charlene.

The men climbed into the truck.

"You have to take those in for me!" she said, in tears and enraged that she couldn't be angry without crying. "Take a good look at me! You think I can move those? There's no way!"

The men rolled their windows up as she reached the truck. She smacked on the glass. "You can't leave that junk on the porch!"

"Yeah, we can," said the driver. "It's your junk now." He backed the truck around and they sped across the yard and into the trees.

"You can't expect me to move them!" Charlene screamed to the dust the truck had left behind.

But obviously they did.

Furious, she stalked down the driveway in her clogs, tripping over occasional lumps of freshly turned dirt and rock and not caring if she broke her ankle at that point, and found a groundhog hanging from a tree branch directly over the drive, swinging in the breeze, its neck slit and the blood drained out, with little sticks tied to its claws and a bell around its neck. After she heaved into the roadside weeds, she knocked the groundhog down with a large stick and kicked the carcass under a pile of leaves.

Who did that? Teenagers who found out I'm living here, who think I'm the descendant of a witch? Kids who have heard the same stories Maude has heard? Kids who are too afraid to party at Homeplace? A groundhog doesn't gut itself and hang itself up from a tree! This isn't witchcraft; this is harassment!

"Who did this?" she shouted to the trees. "Who came onto my land, *my* land, and killed this poor animal to try to scare me? What's wrong with you?"

Her brain began to buzz again, fear, anger, and determination battling it out. The frightening experiences she'd had at the farmhouse had been exaggerations of her imagination. But this was real, this was in-the-flesh, this was nothing to shrug off.

Her mother would have said, "Do something, Charlene. Take charge of things."

I will. I know I can. I'm finally starting to figure that out.

Time to quit pretending to be a bold, brave, free-spirited woman, and act like one. Time to find out just what was known about her family, from someone other than Maude Boise. It was time to clear the cobwebs of superstitions away from Homeplace. And away from herself.

The Adams Historical Society was located on the second floor of what had been the old Adams School, a boxy 1920s-era brick building behind Randy's Hardware on Hewitt Road. The entire first floor was home to Mountain View Antiques, so advertised on a stenciled sign affixed to the side of the building. Charlene entered the front door, setting a large brass bell clanging above and bringing a shop employee trapping out from the rear right room into the antique-cluttered hall to see who was visiting.

"Hello, there," the woman said with a broad, commercial smile on her face, her curly white hair bobbing. A little hand-painted ceramic pin on her blouse indicated that her name was Mary Tettle, and she was the shop's owner. "Is there something I can help you with?" Mary Tettle tipped back and forth, indicating the first two rooms. "We have lots of fine items, and I'm sure you can find what you're looking for!"

Through the open doorways, Charlene could see shelves crawling with old soda bottles, musty books, Nippon ware, tarnished silver, dolls, clocks, and myriad housewares and tools from times gone by.

"Actually, I was on my way to the Historical Society." Charlene nodded toward the stairs at the back of the hall.

Mary's cheerful face instantly went down a notch. "Oh, dear, I'm sorry, but it's not open today, except by appointment. Are you sure you wouldn't like to have a look around here, though? I've got lots of nice things, a whole table at half price."

"No, thanks. Do you have a phone number? So I can call the person in charge of the Society and make an appointment?"

"For this afternoon?"

"Yes."

"Hmm. Just a moment." The woman went into the back room again and emerged with a slip of paper. On it she had written the number for a woman named Denise DeBoer. "She's a sweetheart. She'll probably come right down to open up. While you're waiting, you could have a little look around. I've got some wonderful old LPs. You do know what LPs are, don't you? Records?"

"Yes." Charlene flipped open her phone and tapped in the numbers.

"I'm sure you could find something."

The phone began to ring. Once, twice. "Thanks, but I have laundry to do, so I'll..."

A woman's voice answered. "Hello?"

"Ms. DeBoer?" Charlene turned away from Mary's hopeful gaze toward a bronze dragon lamp on a narrow hall table. Price tag, $250. *Good luck with that, Mary.* "I'm calling because I'd like to have a look through the Adams Historical Society archives. Is there any chance I could get in this afternoon?"

"Ah, I'm in the middle of something right now. Could this wait until tomorrow? I could meet you at the office at nine."

Crap. "Well, I suppose I could do that."

"Is it important?"

"To me it is, but..."

"Hold on." There were some children's voices in the background, and then, "Can you give me an hour?"

"Sure. Thanks."

As Charlene put her phone in her purse, Mary said sweetly, "She's probably hoping you'll buy a T-shirt. They have them for sale, you know. A whole bunch that they ordered two years ago for the Adams bicentennial. All sizes. White and navy."

"I'm sure I could spring for a T-shirt for her time and trouble."

"While you're shopping for something new to wear, then, I have some vintage outfits in the back room. Very nice stuff, things that the young people in the big cities are just clamoring for."

Charlene thanked Mary for her own time and trouble, then drove to the Laundromat to toss in a trash bag full of her filthy clothes. As she forced her clothes into one load, popped a small box of detergent from the vending machine, and plugged quarters into the washing machine slot, she wondered how many of the women and men who were seated on the plastic chairs scattered about the humid room knew anything about the Alexander family history. If they did, did they believe the witch story?

Finding her own cracked plastic chair by the plate glass window looking out on Main Street, she dialed Andrew's number. The phone rang four times and then his voice mail kicked in. She didn't leave a message. She'd try to call him again after visiting the Historical Society.

When the clothes were washed, Charlene tossed them into a dryer. She checked the clock on the wall. She was to meet Denise DeBoer in just five minutes.

"Excuse me," she asked a dark-haired young woman in a nearby green chair. The woman looked up from the sleeping baby she held on her lap. "I have to run out for just a short bit. Is there any chance you would be willing to take my clothes out of dryer number three when it's finished and just throw the clothes in the plastic bag I have on the top of the dryer? It should be done in about an hour. Just put it in the bag and leave it on a chair. If you'll be here that long?"

"Sure," said the woman.

"Thanks."

The woman nodded. Charlene wondered if the woman would be so accommodating if she knew Charlene's ancestral name.

Charlene pulled into the parking lot of the old Adams School behind Denise DeBoer in her green sedan. The woman

was as Mary Tettle had said, pleasant and happy to help out,
an energetic woman in her forties with a graying brown braid
and wire-rimmed glasses. She led Charlene to the second
floor, where one room housed the Society and its artifacts in
glass cases, on bookshelves, and in numerous metal filing
cabinets along two of the walls. Black-and-white photos of
old town parades and Little Miss Adams pageants hung at
slight tilts on the walls, along with a couple color shots showing the fire that burned down the Blue Ridge Bar and Grill.
There was a framed letter to the town mayor, dated 1946,
signed by President Harry Truman, thanking the town for the
brave young men who had fought in Europe and the Pacific
and had "given their lives for the cause of peace."

"And what specifically can I do for you, Ms. Myers?"
asked Denise as she shrugged off her windbreaker and
dropped it on the back of the chair behind a cluttered desk.
"Are you thinking of moving here? Do you have relatives in
the area?"

"I have. I did," said Charlene. "I moved to the old Alexander homestead two weeks ago. My great-grandmother was
Ellen Alexander, the last person to live there. I inherited the
land and house from my mother in the spring, when she died."

"I'm sorry about your mother." Denise sat on the edge of
the desk next to a lidded cardboard box with "Historic Adams
T-shirts" scrawled on it with black marker. She adjusted the
box so Charlene could see the label.

Charlene nodded. "I know virtually nothing other than what
my neighbor, Maude Boise, has told me. I figured if there would
be anyone to know the facts, it would be you guys."

"Okay."

"Here at the Historical Society."

"I see."

"So?

"I'm afraid I won't be much help finding information
about your family. To keep things manageable with only two
volunteers, our Society follows families who are specific to
the town limits of Adams, which hasn't changed in about one
hundred fifty years. No need to annex any more land. The

town hasn't grown or shrunk in all that time. I've lived here all my life, grew up on the north side, and though I've heard of your grandmother, I never met Mrs. Alexander. I mean Miss Alexander."

"Miss?"

"Well, she never did marry."

"She didn't?"

"You didn't know that?"

"No." Charlene slipped out of her jacket and hung it on a hook on the back of the door. "I know so little. I do know my grandmother, Sissy, was born at Homeplace but moved to Richmond when she was in her twenties. My mother never lived here at all. Until two weeks ago, I didn't care to know about the family. I didn't feel much of a connection. But now..." *Now I need to know as much as I can about my family so I can prove that the matriarch wasn't a witch.* "I would like to find out all I can."

"I understand."

Not really you don't.

Charlene sat in a chair next to a filing cabinet. "I know there are the ruins of slave quarters in the woods by the house. And there's a family cemetery, too, with Alexander women but none of the men. I haven't explored the whole property, so the guys could be there somewhere. It's quite a bit of land, and I don't like wandering around where there aren't any pathways. But I know that Phoebe Alexander, if she really existed, isn't in the cemetery."

"Phoebe, yes."

"Yes, what?"

"I remember that name."

Charlene sat up straighter. "Really? You do?"

Denise nodded. "I've seen it somewhere in our files, though I can't remember exactly where. You want to find out where she is buried?"

"If it's recorded. Or anything else."

"Do you know when she was alive?"

"I was told she moved to Nelson County in 1809, somewhere around there. But that's it."

Denise stood in front of one wall of cabinets, her eyes studying the labels on the drawers. Then she yanked open one near the bottom. "We've filed everything by decades. The oldest piece we have is a wonderful map of this region of Virginia, drawn in 1702. You can see it on the wall there." She nodded at a small inked map in a frame between the two office windows. "Of course, we have much more material about Adams from the twentieth century and on. You'd be surprised at how little people hold on to, not knowing that in another hundred or two hundred years, people will want to read and see what they had."

"I'm not surprised."

"My specialty is the war years. The Civil War, the Spanish American War, the World Wars. It's an interest of mine, finding and cataloging the connection between Adams and the world at large during conflicts. Udenia, on the other hand, is more into the economic and cultural aspects of our history. Apples. Cattle and horse farming. Tourism. And now wineries. We were never able to afford microfilm or microfiche. But someday we'll get these records scanned into a computer for easier access by the greater public." Denise pulled a thin manila folder from the drawer and handed it to Charlene, who eased herself down to the floor by the cabinet. "Here are the few items from the 1810 to 1820 time period. Maybe you'll find something helpful?"

Charlene flipped through what was there. There were photocopies of wrinkled maps of the county indicating townships, rivers, and hills. There were copies of pages from the *Adams Reporter*, a newspaper that was clearly the word of the day. There were several letters written to and from Adams citizens, tucked into plastic sleeves. Charlene skimmed one. It was from a Samuel Blackburn to his brother in Philadelphia, dated 1815. It was filled with trivia about the weather, health, church, and crops.

"Anything?" asked Denise.

Charlene shook her head. She skimmed another letter, dated 1819. Nothing that caught her eye. There was likewise nothing in the other letters or newspaper articles.

"Maybe the next decade up?" Charlene suggested.

Denise took out another manila folder and passed it over: 1820–1830. Other maps, showing newly surveyed farm property lines. A clipped advertisement seeking return of a slave who ran away from a blacksmith in Adams. More photocopied newspapers sheets. Another runaway slave. Corn for sale. A new dress shop opened by a Leslie Ingersoll. Nothing mentioning the Alexanders. Nothing about the witch ancestor.

Charlene then checked the file for 1830–1840. This was a thicker folder than the earlier ones, with more clippings, more photocopies of news articles, deeds, bills of sale, wills, and more letters.

Charlene skimmed one letter, then a second. And she stopped, blinked, and read again, much more slowly.

November 2, 1839

My dearest sister June,

How nice to receive your letter of last month, keeping me appraised of the condition of our father and the matters of your husband's company. I don't doubt you and Lawrence are managing well, assuring that each carriage that is constructed is the finest possible product. Were you but to move the business south, I could help secure labor of Negroes for free as opposed to hired hands. But you have made clear your husband's view on slavery, and as he is the head of the household and head of the company, I can do nothing but make suggestions at this time. As long as you and he are happy, and as long as you are able to provide for Father, I shall keep silent.

My shop is doing well, keeping the residents of Adams warm and fashionable with the array of leather goods we provide. We spent little Abby's birthday with the Coffeys, and it was quite pleasant. We took a ride in our buggy to the countryside to partake of the view and to purchase apples. The only marring of the day was the incident concerning the lady Phoebe Alexander, who, as I've

*mentioned in earlier missives, is an odd soul, behaving
more a man than woman in her manners and speech, and
rarely leaving her land. Our carriage came upon Mrs.
Alexander's own wagon in the middle of the road, over-
turned, with the lady Phoebe gone and her near-grown
daughter Sarah standing by, injured but silent. Abby was
disturbed at such a sight, but I stopped to ask Miss Alexander what had occurred. She said only that several boys had
found them on the road, had flipped the wagon for sport,
and had beat her mother and dragged her off. I did not
offer assistance, for there was nothing I could have done,
and my wife begged we have nothing to do with that family. The whole woman was not found, only small parts of
her—the rest, as the constable has told, devoured by wild
animals. I do not mean to upset you, dear June, but only to
tell you that which Abby will likely relay when she comes
to visit you next month.*

The letter went on a bit longer, chatting about a sick horse
and a new healthy child born to their only slave, Yennie.

"You found something?" asked Denise. Charlene handed
the letter to Denise. Denise looked at the paper then said,
"Yes, now, that's it. That's where I saw the woman's name.
But honestly, that's all I know that we have. The Alexanders,
it seemed, preferred to stay out of the spotlight. Or maybe the
community just didn't find them interesting enough to report
on."

"Or they were afraid to report," said Charlene.

"Why so?"

"Rumors have it Phoebe was a witch. Don't tell me that
you, as one of the main historians in Adams, hadn't heard that
somewhere along the line. Surely you know that some people
around here believe the old witch stories."

Denise's lip twitched and she let out a sigh. "Well, all
right. I've heard tell there was witchcraft going on at Homeplace long ago. And I might have heard the name Phoebe in
connection with that. But I never paid half a mind to it. Why
would I? It's nonsense."

"Why didn't you say something to me when I first mentioned her?"

Denise's shoulders fell. "I don't know you. I didn't want to offend you."

"Some people around here clearly believe the stories," said Charlene. "Do you know what I found hanging from a tree over my driveway today?" The moment she said that she realized she didn't want to tell Denise. She wanted to tell Andrew.

"What?" Denise asked. She looked as if she didn't really want to hear the answer.

"It was some kind of...oh, it was a magic charm, a bad charm. I don't appreciate it, and I'm going to get the word out that I won't tolerate that kind of thing. Not if I'm going to stay in the area for any time."

"Was this any help?"

Charlene stood up and stretched her legs. "It was. Thank you."

"You're welcome." Denise stood and walked to the desk, where she adjusted the box of shirts again.

"Oh, by the way," Charlene asked, "how much is a T-shirt?"

27

~

Chapter One

Hugh Chase hadn't planned on leaving the city, but sometimes life had a way of throwing you in a direction you didn't anticipate. And Hugh hadn't known for certain until he was packing to leave that he would be going south to solve a mystery.

But he had to. Because it was a mystery no one else cared about.

She was pretty in a plain way. Reddish-brown hair, brown eyes, and baggy clothes that suggested a beautiful body beneath, a body she was not keen on showing the world because she had other worries on her mind. Her name was...

Andrew rubbed his beard.

Her name was Carol Miller.

She lived alone in a large old house on an isolated farm where she...

She what?

...she worked as a composer, creating beautiful tunes on her baby grand piano.

No. She couldn't afford a baby grand.

...she worked as a composer, creating beautiful tunes on her flute as the rest of the world passed by. But she had started to suspect something dangerous was lurking in the old barn at the corner of her land. She had called the police, who had investigated and found nothing. She had hired a private investigator...

No, she didn't have enough money for that.

She had told a reporter with the town newspaper that it might be worth checking it out, seeing what was happening, because she was hearing noises in the barn at night, soft but unearthly noises that had her frightened. The reporter had humored her, had done an article, and had left Carol a laughingstock of the county—the elusive flautist who imagined demons in her barn. The reporter, Hugh's brother, had sent him the clipping. The accompanying photo, showing Carol standing in the field, with the barn in the distance, looking as though she were ready to bolt at any minute, caught Hugh's attention. She had an expression of intelligence and vulnerability. And Hugh had four weeks of vacation coming.

Rex, under the desk, pawed at a rabbit hole in his sleep. Andrew took a sip from the cup of coffee next to the computer. It was getting cold. He hopped up and stuck it in the microwave he kept on a wheeled cart by the door, and punched in one minute.

The clock on the wall read 5:47. Almost dinnertime. He thought he'd cook something himself instead of going to the Fox's Den. There were a couple frozen pizzas in the fridge, some smoked sausage in the meat drawer. And if he remembered correctly, some still-fresh salad makings in the crisper.

The microwave beeped; he removed the coffee and sat back down in front of the monitor, flexed his fingers.

He saw her first from the window of the Horsefeathers Café, sitting at the stoplight in her white convertible, wearing sunglasses, with the top pulled down and the radio on.

"I can tell you, my love for you will still be strong, after the boys of summer are gone," Andrew sang. Then he deleted the last paragraph.

He'd scrapped his novel about the dead bodies in the ferry bathroom. After a running start, it had fizzled like a helium balloon with a big old puncture wound. He'd lost all interest in Hugh and Deb and their squabbles. So, he'd started over. He wasn't sure where it would go. Unlike the other book, he'd not made a mental outline on this one. It would happen as it happened. He'd been inspired by Charlene, her curious life circumstances, and the feelings he had for her. Who knew how that, or this book, would turn out?

And if the novel sucks, I'll take the hint. I wasn't supposed to be a writer in the first place. Maybe I should take up woodworking. Or skydiving.

As he took a tentative sip of the steaming java, the phone rang. It was Charlene.

He lifted the phone, feeling almost guilty, as if she knew somehow that he'd been fictionalizing her story, inspired by her troubles. Maybe she would think it was creepy. Maybe it was creepy.

No, writers do that all the time, taking bits from real life. Don't they? "Hello?"

"Andrew, it's Charlene."

"Hey, good to hear from you."

"I just left the Adams Historical Society. Seems my great-great-great and so on grandmother was a witch, after all."

"She...what? Really?"

"Well, not exactly, but listen to what I found out." There was an air of confidence in Charlene's voice. "There was a letter suggesting some people of her time didn't trust her, thought she was peculiar. Enough to drag her out of her wagon one day and kill her."

"Wow. That's awful."

"No wonder she wasn't buried in the family plot. Most of her body was never recovered. Now I know that what Maude said was true, to a point. It wasn't just her own fears she was sharing with me, but the long-standing fears of some people who live in and around Adams."

Like Yule Lemons.

"Knowing this is good. It helps put even more things into perspective."

"I'm really glad that you found out, then."

"Yeah, me, too. Knowledge is power, right? Oh, and thanks again for the locks. I don't think a hurricane would get those things to give way." She sounded chirpy. Andrew found himself smiling for her.

"I hope not."

"Listen, hate to cut this short, but I've got work to do. But I want to thank you for everything...well, you know."

"You're welcome."

There was a pause, as if Charlene wanted to say more but was hesitant to. Andrew hoped she would. But then she only said, "I'll see you Friday evening?"

"Yep."

"Bye!" She hung up.

Andrew typed a few more sentences of his new novel, saved the file, and then called the Fox's Den to speak with Dawn. There were a few more catering details to iron out before Friday's barbecue. Then he had to start cleaning, because Tom was flying in to the Charlottesville Airport the next morning and Andrew had to have everything in order before going to pick him up.

If nothing else, Susan had been good with details when it came to having guests, had never missed a beat. Susan was an incredible hostess. The condo would sparkle with candles and silver, and every inch would be decorated with flowers and ribbon and new pieces of artwork. But it had always been Susan entertaining, Susan's friends, Susan's choice of music and food and conversation. It had never been Andrew's.

Andrew was genuinely looking forward to Friday night. It was the first thing he'd really looked forward to for over a year. He hoped Charlene would have a good time, too. She deserved it as much as he did. And he was very much looking forward to seeing her again.

2 8

~~

Come Friday, the appliances were still sitting on the porch, the boxes getting soft with the weather. Charlene called the store at nine A.M. to lodge a complaint, and finally got through to the owner of the store. He didn't apologize for the behavior of his employees ("You were told about the ground-hog, weren't you?" Charlene almost asked but didn't), but said he'd get someone out there the first of the week.

"First of the week?" pressed Charlene.

"It's the best we can do, miss."

"But that's not good enough. They're just sitting on my porch—"

"It's the best we can do. I'm sorry for any inconvenience."

She slapped the phone shut and gritted her teeth. *I should get a discount for all this inconvenience!* Then she went out to the backyard to try to calm herself.

The mountains to the west were slate blue and the sky that hung above them the color of sun-bleached periwinkles. The trees of the forest surrounding the yard offered up, amid their early autumn greens, samplings of the crimsons, burgundies, burnt oranges, and golds that would soon dominate the land-scape. Charlene shook her arms to loosen them and rolled her head back and forth, but the tension remained, digging its claws into her muscles and nerves. "Let it go," she told herself, but for some reason, her body was having none of it. The backs of her hands grew cold and a hot knot lodged at the base of her neck. Twisted energy cut through her arms and legs, making it impossible to stand still.

She went back inside and paced up and down the hallway, from kitchen to front door and back again. It felt like an engine had been turned on inside and she didn't know how to turn it off.

Slow down! Don't let a freaking appliance store get you so worked up, she thought. But she could not slow down, and something deep in her mind whispered that it wasn't just the appliance store. It was something else.

"What is it, then? Am I sick?"

In the living room she sat on the sleeping bag. She closed her eyes and tried to meditate, to clear her mind. *Calm down, Charlene. Deep breath. Let it go. Think a good thought. Think of all you're going to accomplish here. Let your fears go, they are only chains holding you down, holding you back.*

The floor beneath her shifted, almost imperceptibly, like a monster taking a slow breath. Her eyes snapped open. She jumped to her feet.

There was something moving through the house, and moving through her.

There is nothing in the house, and only you control you. Nothing else does.

She went out to the front porch and did some clumsy jumping jacks to shake off the tension, then jogged down the driveway to the line of trees and back. It didn't work.

Okay, don't just flop around, do something worthwhile and maybe you'll feel better.

She went into the kitchen, and, on her knees, proceeded to pull piece after piece of the tattered linoleum from the bare wood floor and throw the pieces into trash bags. Pieces she couldn't get up with her bare hands she carved away with a steak knife. When she was done it was just after noon. The floor looked worse—bare wood gone white and black with mold and water stains. Charlene's heart beat unusually fast, but not from exertion.

There's something in the house, and it's toying with me!

"No, there's not."

She began to wander the downstairs again, stopping on occasion to glance up the stairs where the silver tarp hung, unmoving, like a magician's cloth hiding dark secrets.

She picked up her phone to call...*who? Who are you going to call, Charlene? And why? To tell them you're sick? That you're falling apart again? Or to tell them there is something here that is having its way with you?*

She put the phone on the mantel, clenched her fists, and moved across the floor to stand before the easel. Since coming to Homeplace she had done no paintings at all. She'd had artist's block before, but this was way beyond that. The splinter in her right hand began to sting. She picked up the paintbrush in her left hand. The stinging stopped. She put the brush down again.

Back in the kitchen, she opened a can of SpaghettiOs, but it smelled funny, off a bit. She dumped it into the pan and put it atop the hot plate, but as she stirred, the slimy appearance made her stomach lurch. She tossed the pan, pasta, and spoon into the backyard. She tried to consciously slow her breathing, but the moment she stopped focusing on her lungs, the rhythm picked up again.

And the Harvest barbecue was in just a few hours. *I don't feel like going.*

"Maybe I could read. That might help." There were several old art magazines she'd brought in her suitcase, but the moment she sat down on the sleeping bag to flip through them, she had to stand up again.

There's something else you can read.

She took Opal's journal out of the icebox, looked at the last few pages, and then closed it up. She could not read what was there. It made her gut twist. Charlene returned it to the icebox.

And then she painted, though the results were worthless. She used her splintered right hand, forcing it with all her might to slap paint on new paper in spite of the pain that flared each time she held the brush. She pushed on, her teeth clenched, sweating and cursing. The pictures she created were pathetic, cartoonish renderings of the mill, the slave quarters, the rear of the house. Her left hand trembled as she worked, as if anxious to hold the brush again.

She wondered what she would paint this time if she gave her left hand the chance. That thought made the buzz in her brain more intense, so she went to the back porch to sweep log bark into the yard.

At three o'clock, Charlene decided she had to get ready for the damned barbecue. She wanted to call and decline. But she liked Andrew and didn't want him to think otherwise.

But fuck it all, I can't fathom being social tonight.

Retrieving the pan from the weeds outside, Charlene scooped out the last of the sticky pasta. Then she heated several gallons of water over her hot plate, her fists clenching every time she recalled the brand new stove on the front porch, and poured the water into the tub, creating a lukewarm bath.

The scent of coconut shampoo, which used to be soothing, was sickeningly sweet. As the water cooled around her, she listened to the mice digging and scurrying in the floor and the walls. She had set the snap-traps a few days ago, and had rigged them with peanut butter. But with the first dead mouse she had felt guilty at what she had done, and had thrown the traps out on the junk pile. As long as they weren't in her sleeping bag or pooping on her clothes, she figured she would let them have their space.

At least these little guys weren't breaking their own necks against her front door.

Not yet.

"Shut up."

Charlene tipped back to rinse out her hair, then closed her eyes. She wanted to think about things, to grasp them, to figure them out—her house and the bizarre occurrences, Opal's journal writings in the icebox, the Children's House and what might have happened there; she wanted to figure out what she was doing at Homeplace and what she was supposed to do, whether she would ever paint something worthwhile again, if she would slowly go crazy, if she should just leave the place to the mice and spiders. But she could not focus on any one thought. Her mind stumbled over itself in search of clarity. She latched on to an idea only to have every idea whirl away into a tangled, heavy cloud at the back of her head. And behind her eyes, the buzzing continued like the crackle of radio static.

Her left hand moved through the water and paused on her abdomen. She stretched her neck and waited, her eyes opening and closing slowly. The hand moved up and down on the smooth flesh, bringing warmth out in spite of the cool water. The fingers, on their own, strummed the rim of her navel, moved upward and stroked the alert nipples. Charlene was shocked yet pleased that in the midst of this dreadful day there could be pleasure. She sighed into the touch, and then held still, afraid to move, waiting to see how it would unfold, not wanting to lose the solitary passion that gripped her body.

Downward the hand slid, toward the patch of pubic hair, where it caressed the folds of skin and the most delicate spot of flesh. She imagined her hand was Andrew's, gentle, insistent, passionate. Her body writhed slowly in the tub. The warmth grew around her and within her. Her fingers continued to probe, to tease, and to enter. Charlene took a breath, let it out, took it in, keeping in rhythm with the buzzing in her skull. Her lower torso went hot, caught in the rising tension of impending orgasm. Charlene clamped her jaws and panted through her nostrils.

There was a splash in the water next to Charlene's head. Her eyes snapped open. Several inches from her face, a mouse with a chewed ear treaded water and stared at her.

"Damn vermin!" she shouted, and slapped the mouse up and out of the water. It hit the floor on its side, then righted itself and fled beneath the icebox. Charlene was on her feet, her arms wrapped around her body. "See if I won't set those traps up again—just watch me!"

She dried herself off and stomped, naked, to the living room. She hoped a mouse would race across the hall, because she would crush it to mouse-grease beneath her bare heel.

Upstairs, behind the tarp, there was a rustling, a creak. Charlene grabbed the banister at the base of the stairs, stared up, and yelled, "Goddamn this whole place! I hate it! I hate *me*! I hate everything I am and everything I'm not! Fuck this, fuck me! I have to get out of this stinking house and get a fucking ass shithole teaching job again!" Furious tears cut her cheeks and she dug them away angrily. She stormed into the living room. Her left hand reached for the paintbrush.

"Yeah, fuck you, too," she said to the brush.

The hand picked up the brush. She stared at it for a moment.

Then she let her hand have its way.

Charlene flew away as her hand painted, her senses wrapped in a cottony cocoon of oblivion. The world rocked her back and forth, back and forth. Nothingness stretched upward and downward, outward and inward, holding her thoughts at bay, for there was nothing to think, no need to think.

Ahhhh... this is good, this is peaceful.

Back and forth. Forth and back.

No light. No darkness.

No sound. Only the comfortable void.

There was a soft click beneath her and the oblivion pulled away like a heavy drape drawn from a window. Light filtered into her consciousness and she blinked at the painful intrusion. Her body was drenched in sweat, and her left arm was cramped. "Ow, that hurts!" She flexed her muscles to ease the tightness.

On the living room floor beside her foot was the paintbrush she had dropped. It had made the little click. She looked up at the painting on the easel.

29

~

The house had never looked better. The floors had been polished by professionals, the drapes and rugs steam cleaned, and even the lightbulbs had been dusted. Vases of asters and mums sat on tables in the hall, living room, and dining room, and the centerpiece on the dining table held colorful leaves and sprigs of pine that Andrew had collected over the last two days. Soft background music played on the stereo as the guests began to arrive. Sallie had been hired to collect coats and purses and retire them to an upstairs bedroom, and to help Dawn out in the kitchen. Dawn was on hand to prepare and serve the appetizers and side dishes—Swedish meatballs, pepper cheese spread, garlic-seasoned toast points, spinach salad with raspberry dressing, homemade biscuits, spoon bread, sweet potato casserole, green beans almondine, and of course, several of the pies for which she was so well-known at the Fox's Den.

Andrew hadn't planned on the dinner becoming quite as fancy an affair as it seemed to have turned into, but so far, everyone seemed to be having a good time. Yule and his uncle Arnie had shown up first, a good half hour early, each toting big coolers filled with beer, which they situated in the back near the grill, and two 'pounds of deer jerky, which they handed over in plastic freezer bags. Both men were dressed as they usually were, in overalls and denim shirts, though it was clear the clothes had been recently laundered and the men had shaved and showered. Yule's normal oil scent was greatly reduced by the washings. Yule and Arnie had stood with beers in hand and yammered with Andrew and Tom in the backyard as they flipped the marinated ribs and chicken halves over on the grill and jabbed them to check their doneness. Arriving on the dot were the DeBoers and Rick Evans and his wife Perri, followed by the fashionably late Martins, owners of a local winery, dressed in the heels and pearls Andrew had promised Charlene would not be required. An eclectic gathering, but by the time Andrew and Tom, with help from Yule and Arnie, brought in the platter of meats and everyone had gathered around the dining room table set for thirteen, no one had as yet brought up politics, hunting, or religion, so all was well.

It had been nice having some quality time with Tom again. Though they communicated frequently via e-mail and occasionally by phone, this was the first time they'd seen each other since Andrew had cut and run. Tom hadn't mentioned Susan, or Susan's father, since Andrew had picked him up at the airport yesterday. And, happily, talk of work didn't center on Andrew's old firm, since Tom no longer worked there, either. He'd taken on a better position at another firm in Cambridge—had moved to an apartment just a block from Harvard Square. Tom was happy. Tom was busy. Tom had a new girlfriend named Ella, and they'd been seeing each other since June, though Tom doubted she was "the one."

"How can anybody tell that, really?" Tom had said earlier as he'd knocked the meat around in the marinade pan with the barbecue fork. He was a short man with scruffy black hair and cool blue eyes, and this evening was dressed in new jeans and a blazer. The air out back was pleasantly cool, and the breeze light. On the other side of the brick wall that separated the patio from the yard was a flower garden and behind that, the apple trees. The trees had dropped most of their apples and were beginning to lose their leaves. Andrew had gathered a small basket of the nicest apples for Charlene and they were waiting in the kitchen; he would give them to her tonight.

"And you're asking me that question?" Andrew said. He lifted the pan from the card table and held it in front of the grill so Tom, who had been known for occasional clumsiness, wouldn't drop any of the meat onto the flagstone as he made the transfer. Rex held close by, tail wagging enthusiastically, hoping for the very mishap that Andrew wanted to avoid.

"It's rhetorical, dude," said Tom. "Nobody can know. It's luck. Luck enhanced by research and a clear head. Ella's smart and cute, but there are little differences that are problematic."

"Like?"

"Like she hates the Three Stooges and she never read comic books as a kid."

"Ouch."

"She can't eat spicy foods."

"That's rough."

"Plus, her family hates lawyers. Her brother was found guilty of a robbery he didn't commit because of some piss poor representation, though he's okay now, he's out. Only in a year and a half."

"Well, then just enjoy it while it lasts, my brother."

"I intend to. And how about you, Andrew?"

"How about me?"

"Any nice ladies down here catch your fancy? Any blushing Virginia peaches charming your pants off with their soft little accents and naughty lifts of their hoop skirts?"

"That would be Georgia peaches."

"Virginia what, then? Hams?"

"Ha."

"Well?"

Andrew shrugged.

"Oh, really?" Tom's interest was immediately piqued. He paused with barbecue fork and half-chicken in hand. "I was kidding. But now, do tell."

"Nothing to tell, really."

"That was not an empty shrug, my friend." Tom put the last slab of meat on the grill. It sizzled as it hit the hot metal.

Andrew looked at his watch. His guests would start appearing in less than an hour. Dawn and Sallie were in the house, finishing up their preparations of the side dishes. The kitchen windows facing the back of the house were open, and he could see movement inside. Andrew lowered his voice. "Her name's Charlene. She's an artist who moved here recently. Has an old farmhouse outside of town."

"Wow, an artist. Artists are kinky. Ride it, Andrew, my man! Whoo hoo! You tell her you're writing a novel?"

Andrew laughed lightly. "No, that hasn't come up in the conversation. I'm not even sure if I'm writing a novel yet. My attempts are pretty sad."

"How's the sex?"

"No sex yet."

"What's the holdup?"

"I haven't known her very long. She's pretty, she's nice. She's a bit of a loner. I'm still trying to figure her out, though I really like her."

"Oh."

"Oh, what?"

"I was hoping you'd meet someone lighthearted and fun. Someone to make you laugh, to screw your brains out, to go with to movies, bars, take spur-of-the-moment weekend trips somewhere. You need some fun with the ladies for a while, not another—"

"Another what?"

Tom tried to regroup. He rubbed his chin. "I just think you'd be smart not to get serious with anybody. You need time."

"Time to what?"

"You know exactly what I'm talking about. I could see on your face when you mentioned Charlene that you were hoping for a relationship with this woman. You don't need a relationship."

Andrew took a deep breath. He thought he heard someone around the front of the house, talking loudly, men. *Yule and Arnie?* "Tom, I'm not rushing into anything, don't worry."

"I do worry. And I have good instincts about things, you know that."

"You're going to say 'I told you so' about Susan?"

"God, no."

"You don't think I learned something from that?"

"Of course. Jesus. But I'm afraid you're still drawn to women who seem to need something from you."

"I think it's fine to need and be needed."

"To a degree, Andrew, sure, but..."

Two men ambled into the backyard, huffing and grunting, each bending over a large cooler.

"Andy!" said Yule.

"Andy?" whispered Tom. "Now you're Andy?"

The coolers were placed on the flagstone near the back door; handshakes and introductions were exchanged. Then Yule opened one of the coolers and retrieved bags of deer jerky. He held them out with pride. "Good stuff from that deer you give me. Got two flavors, too. Barbecue and plain."

"That's great, Yule. You want to take it in to Dawn? She can put it out with the rest of the food."

"You want to taste it first?"

Andrew and Tom each reached for a piece of the barbecue jerky, though Tom hesitated before putting it in his mouth. Andrew could read his friend's expression: *Holy crap, this is from the deer that ran into your truck?* But after a couple chews, Tom's brows went up and he nodded. "You know, this stuff is really quite good."

"Course it is," said Arnie. "What'd you think, we'd bring something that tasted bad?"

An hour and a half later, the guests were there and gathered around the dining room table. Dawn and Sallie had put out a fine-looking spread, and after Andrew thanked everyone for coming, the plates were filled and the conversation picked up. The beer coolers had been brought inside and set by the French doors, so those who were so inclined could hop up at will and grab a cool one to top off the wine and bottled water Andrew had ordered for the occasion. Easy topics drifted around the room, talks on grape crops and the weather, the price of gasoline, the roadwork out on Route 29, the hopes for the Nelson County High School football team to go all the way to the finals this year, and the best place to get a Volkswagen Beetle repaired, which, according to Merle Martin, who owned several of the classic vehicles himself, was C.J. Buggs over the mountain in Fishersville.

The room was filled with the sounds of laughter, chatter, clinking glasses and silverware, and the popping of wine corks and the cracking of beer tabs. Even Sallie, who had hesitated to eat with the regular guests—"Mr. Marshall, these are all old people. There's nothing for me to talk about."—found herself enjoying the ribs and offering advice to the Martins when they said they were conflicted about their teenaged son's new slew of tattoos.

Everyone seemed relaxed. Everyone seemed to be having a good time.

Except that two guests weren't there. One was Maude Boise, who had said she "might make it," but hadn't. This hadn't surprised Andrew. The other missing guest was Charlene. This had surprised Andrew.

A half hour into the dinner he wasn't too concerned, but when that time had stretched to an hour, he whispered to Tom that he needed to make a quick phone call.

Rex, who had been relegated to the downstairs office, was thrilled when Andrew came in. Andrew scratched his head, then punched Charlene's number into the phone. After a moment's pause, the phone rang. And rang. And rang.

Damn.

He hung up and dialed again. It rang. And rang. And then, over the ringing, or beneath it, or woven into it, he heard a soft, hissing giggle. It drew a chill down Andrew's back.

"Hello?" he demanded. "Is anyone there?"

The giggling quieted and the ringing continued.

Andrew hung up. He went back into the dining room and sat down.

Tom leaned over and said, "Charlene's not coming?"

"She said she was. She as much as promised. I think something's wrong."

"Maybe she just changed her mind. She's an artist, remember. And a woman."

"That's tacky."

"No, my friend, that's facts."

"She said she was coming, and that she was looking forward to it."

"Things can change. Just let it go."

Andrew picked up his fork and stabbed at the sauce-covered rib, but his appetite had waned.

The conversation as well as the supply of ribs, chicken, jerky, and casseroles wound down. Sallie and Dawn then brought out slices of pecan, apple, cherry, and mince pie. Yule and Arnie claimed two slices each, but there was plenty for everyone, and compliments to the chefs abounded. When dessert was done, some of the guests retired to the living room while others went out back to smoke stogies Merle Martin had bought at a cigar shop in Charlottesville. Yule and Arnie were first to light up, leaning on the brick wall that separated the flagstone patio from the rest of the yard.

Andrew sat at the patio table while the other men stood about with their cigars, but soon the desire for a smoke got to be too much, and his leg was starting to ache mightily. He went back inside, dry swallowed three ibuprofens in the kitchen, and then limped to the living room, where Tom was entertaining Kitty Martin, Dawn, and the DeBoers with tales of Boston traffic. Sallie had left, off to meet her old boyfriend, Steve.

"You just close your eyes, hang on to the steering wheel, and hope for the best," Tom was saying. "It's worked for me for a number of years. I always get where I'm going."

"I can't imagine," said Denise with a grimace. "I get heart palpitations just driving the Lynchburg bypass."

"It's even more fun in the snow," said Tom. "And the last few years we've had our share as early as the first week in December. We Northerners love a good challenge behind the wheel." He glanced up to where Andrew stood in the hall at the doorway, arms crossed. "Hey, buddy, nice get-together."

"Thank you." Andrew didn't enter. He nodded slightly at his friend.

"Excuse me," Tom said to the others, then joined Andrew at the base of the stairs. "What's up?"

"I think I should go check on Charlene. I really do think something's wrong."

"Come on, Andrew. Let it go. Let her go. Talk to her tomorrow."

"No. She may have had car trouble, or something might have happened to her at home." *Those deadbolt locks were good, but how were her windows? I should have checked her windows.*

"Did you call her?"

"I tried a while ago. I got…" *weird, creepy giggling that made my skin crawl* "…no answer. But her reception isn't very good much of the time."

"How far away is she?"

"I could be there and back in half an hour, forty-five minutes tops."

"You know, it's not polite to leave your guests for the sake of another guest."

"Fuck you and polite, Tom."

"I mean, she's not dying or anything."

"I don't know anything for sure."

"Here you go again, not picking up on the clues. A no-show speaks volumes."

"I want to check on her, Tom."

"Jesus, Andrew. What kind of trouble could she be in?"

"I don't know."

"It's probably nothing."

"Probably. But I'm going. Keep the party rolling as best you can, all right?"

"Andrew…"

Andrew grabbed his cane from the umbrella stand and left Tom in the hall. In the kitchen, he collected the basket of apples then went out the back to his truck, crossing the patio where Yule, now seated on one of the lawn chairs between Arnie and Rick, dabbed at the air with the glowing cigar. Someone had lit the tiki torches against the settling night, and the flames bobbed and dipped. "Hey, Andy. Where you off to?"

"To check on Charlene Myers. She was supposed to be here tonight."

Yule frowned and lowered the cigar. "You invited her?"

"Yep."

"And you didn't tell me?"

"That's right."

"You're going over to her place?"

"Yep." Andrew climbed into his truck, tossed his cane and the basket of apples on the seat, and slammed the door shut. He turned on the engine. Through the windshield he could read the warning on Yule's face. *Don't go there, Andy! Don't you remember me telling you not to go to that haunted place?*

Andrew stomped on the gas, throwing the truck backward down the driveway. The basket flipped over and the apples rolled to the floor. *Yule, you're so damned superstitious. Just sit there and have another beer with the boys.*

He steered his truck down to Main Street, turned left, and then gunned it out of town. *Either she can't make it or won't,* he thought. *Either way, I have to find out.*

30

~

Yule told Arnie to catch a ride home with the DeBoers. "I got to check on something," he said as he stubbed out his smoke in the antique wolf's head–shaped ashtray Merle had brought for the occasion. "I don't know how long I'll be, so don't wait on me."

Arnie was into his sixth beer, and so didn't care much who drove him home. He and the wealthy Merle Martin, as unlikely as it seemed, had a lively and agreeable conversation going on about the finer points of cabin-building—Arnie because he'd done it, and Merle because he'd read a Foxfire book. Yule was glad Arnie hadn't asked where he was going or why. It would have been too hard to explain.

Though in his mind it was a simple matter. Terrifying, but simple. Andy was in a shitload of trouble.

His old Chevy Nova didn't have much horsepower anymore. He often laughed to friends that most of the horses had up and died, and if you took a little sniff beneath the hood you could smell them decaying. Tonight it wasn't funny, though. He couldn't get the car past forty, and he wanted to get to Homeplace before something bad happened to his buddy. He hadn't been able to save Howard, but damn if he wasn't going to try to protect Andy. Terror had a cold hand around his throat and spooks were breathing down his neck.

He reached the town limits and gritted his teeth as the road narrowed and grew more uneven and potholed. His headlights carved a small niche in the night, showing what was ahead thirty feet or so. He couldn't use the high beams as they hadn't worked since July. Come inspection time in October, he'd have to shell out even more cash to keep this bucket of junk street-worthy.

It had been a while since Yule had driven this stretch of country road. There was no reason to. He wasn't the mailman. He wasn't a newspaper delivery guy. Besides, the road ended just another half mile past Homeplace, with no other homes or farms off it, so there was no one to visit. Just that old bit of land that the witch had lived on so long ago, an old lady who, according to stories passed down through his family, had wielded her magic on anyone who dared to cross her.

And now Andy was obviously falling in love with one of the witch's descendants, and he refused to see the truth. Yule had no doubt that his friend was heading for disaster, a fate that could be worse than what Howard had endured. Though Howard hadn't endured it at all. He'd died, and in more agony than Yule had ever witnessed in all his years of life.

"C'mon!" he urged his Nova as they took another gravelly curve. "Get the lead out!" His hands on the wheel were ice cold. His knees began to shake up and down and he couldn't make them stop.

He had no idea what he would do once he got to the farm-house, but he'd do something. He'd pleaded with Andy before to let well enough alone, but obviously pleading was worth-less. Should he fight with the man, try to make him leave? Should he threaten him? But what could he use as a threat? He didn't know any secrets Andy might want to keep silent. Yule did have his shotgun in the trunk. Would he resort to armed intimidation? And if so, would Andy have him thrown in jail for brandishing a weapon, even if it meant he'd been saved?

Yule raised one fist to the ceiling and growled at the rushing night surrounding him.

The road grew even more narrow and rough. Yule slowed the car so he wouldn't snap a shock. Trees hung over the road on both sides, huge black splashes against a near-black sky, holding there as if any moment they would let go, crash down, and swallow up intruders. Through the closed windows Yule could hear night creatures chigging and chirring, warning him to go back.

Chigga-chig-chig-chigga-chig.

Homeplace property was on his left now, a dark and tangled mass of forest. Soon he would reach the mailbox and the driveway.

"God help me," he whispered.

Chig-chig-chigga-chigga-chig.

And then there was a resounding crack, and an enormous oak fell directly in front of Yule's car, striking the road and bouncing up toward the Nova's windshield. Yule shrieked and jerked the wheel to the left, realizing he'd made a mistake even as it was too late. The car crashed through the undergrowth and down a steep incline, branches slapping the sides like angry hands, the window glass cracking. Yule stomped on the brake, but the line had ruptured. He screamed, letting go of the steering wheel and covering his face with his hands. "God!"

The car bucked over logs and rocks that punched out the bottom of the car. It felt as though the earth itself was undulating and rolling, a black-green ocean throwing the Nova like a rubber raft. Yule sucked air and waited for the end. He was on Homeplace, and he was doomed.

The car slid to a halt. The engine died. Slowly, Yule pulled his fingers away from his eyes and looked. The car was at the rim of a deep ravine, the front half straddling the edge, balanced precariously, with the front tipping just slightly downward. Yule gasped, then drew himself up slowly in the seat. The insects and tree frogs seemed closer now.

Chig-chigga-chigga-CHIGGA-CHIGGA-CHIG.

Help me, Jesus!

His heart thundered; sweat broke out and rolled down to his lip. "I can get to the backseat," he told himself, trying to pace his words evenly so as to convince his mind and body that things would be all right. "Ease on over and back and I'll be okay. You ain't so big as some guys; you can do it, no problem. Once I'm back there, the car will be rear-heavy and'll hold still while I crawl out a window. They's all broke out already. Piece o' cake. I'll be okay."

Okay.

He licked his lips and pulled his right leg up onto the seat. The car creaked slightly but held still. Out in the forest, the tree frogs and cicadas suddenly softened their chatter, as if they'd paused to watch. Yule hoisted his ass up and got his second leg up and folded under him. Then, he eased his right leg over the back of the seat. So far so good. Sliding his right elbow over and grabbing the torn fabric behind, he prepared to inch over to the rear of the car.

Easy, boy, easy. You'll make it. You'll be all right. Dear God, I'll be all right.

But then something slammed down onto the car's hood, something invisible and powerful that knocked the car forward and over as Yule, straddling the seat and holding the ripped upholstery, screamed. The car struck the bottom of the ravine on its top, driving a stout, broken tree branch into the windshield and into Yule's skull.

31

~

Charlene stared at the painting her left hand had created. It was a face, the eyes huge, gray-green, shadowed with heavy brows. The cheeks were gaunt, the lips thin and pale. Her hair was wild and long and auburn. Her expression was one of cool, calculated power.

It's the witch.

There she is.

Phoebe.

Charlene's heart beat in her ears, rushing like waves up and back against her temples.

There was noise in the front yard, but she could not move from the painting to see what it was. As the sound grew louder, she recognized it. Andrew's truck.

Andrew? What are you doing here?

She squinted at the clock radio on the mantel. The digital numerals read 10:12.

The truck door slammed. Andrew's feet pounded up the porch steps and he hammered on the door. "Charlene, are you there?"

She opened her mouth, but could not speak.

"Charlene! I see a light on in there. Open the door, please."

What's happened to me? Andrew, I don't know what's wrong with me!

"I tried to call and it rang, but you didn't answer. I was worried about you. Are you in there?"

Yes!

She heard him cuss, then throw open the door. She could not turn to see him in the hall, but felt his shock at finding her there, nude, sweating, and silent.

"Charlene? What the hell is going on?" he whispered.

She could not answer.

She heard him put something down against the wall—his cane? Then he walked up behind her and spun her around. She saw the anger and fear in his gaze. "Are you sick?"

Yes!

"You didn't come. You didn't call. I called but you didn't answer. I was so...I just didn't know what to think."

He seemed to be trying hard not to stare at her naked body, but his gaze flicked up and down from her face to her breasts. There was anguished concern in his eyes. She wanted to reach for him, to hold him and thank him and beg him to help her, but she couldn't.

"I was afraid you were ill," he said, "or had had a wreck, so I excused myself from the party and drove over here. But there's your car in the yard. And here you are, ignoring me, refusing to say anything, and naked, and painting, what is that, a witch?"

Yes!

"Won't you speak to me, Charlene?"

I can't! And then she did something she had not planned on doing and did not want to do. She felt her lips pull up in a cool, emotionless smile. And then, she heard herself chuckle. A deep, taunting, throaty sound that was not her own.

Andrew looked startled. "What's so funny?"

Andrew, I don't know what's happening to me!

"I thought..." Andrew began. He stepped back into the hallway, shaking his head. "No, I guess I wasn't thinking at all, was I? I was only hoping." She could see him grasping for words. His eyes were narrowed in frustration and confusion.

"Shhh," Charlene heard herself say through her hideously grinning lips.

"Why should I be quiet? I thought we had an understanding, a friendship. Something. I thought you might even care for me. But it's clear I'm a fool again. Story of my life."

She felt her body loosen. She stepped to him, and her hands reached up and took his face. "Shhh," she said. "Shhh, now, this is for the best."

"What are you doing?" He shook her off, but she grabbed his face again with a force that stunned her.

"Shhh, my dear." She kissed him fully, deeply, and then slid one bare leg between his, drawing her knee up slowly until it touched the soft flesh of his groin. *What am I doing? I don't want this, not this way!*

"Charlene! Cut it out!" Andrew pulled away, but Charlene's arms locked around his back, drawing him to her. Strength and desire surged, consumed her. *This feels so good! Ah, yes!* She kissed him again, hard, and he resisted.

"Charlene . . . !"

"Shhh." She pressed her breasts against his chest and pulled his face down to her shoulder. "I'll take you now, Andrew." His breath was hot on her skin, but he did not do as she commanded. Her leg hooked around his, and in an instant she had him on the floor on his back. He tried to push her off, but she forced his hands to his chest and pressed her knee on them. He tried to roll but she held him still. Incredible power surged through her body and she knew there was no one who could resist her. No one could stop her.

"Damn it, Charlene!" It was more of a plea now than a command. She liked that. In his huge brown eyes she could see his astonishment, his panic.

Up the stairs, behind the silver tarp, the locked and boarded door began to rattle on its hinges. Charlene began to laugh, a sound that at once startled and pleased her, a voice that was as much another voice as hers. What was that upstairs, all in a frenzy? Was it hot and bothered, too? Was it enraged? Was it delighted? It didn't matter. *Let it rip itself to pieces!*

Charlene opened Andrew's pants. "You must let me, my dearest, my darling. Hold still." She put her mouth on his penis and licked in long, wet strokes, up the front of the shaft and down the back. Her fingers kneaded the balls, gently, persistently. The shaft stiffened quickly and held up straight, ready, waiting.

"Ahhh," groaned Andrew. She glanced up to see that he was on his elbow, watching. His eyes were glazing. He would not resist anymore. "There, you see?" she said. She rolled her tongue over the soft tip, then took the head in her mouth and sucked lightly while her hand squeezed the base. Her mouth came away with a loud, wet, popping sound. "Shhh, now. It's time."

Charlene straddled Andrew and lowered herself onto him. She sucked air through clamped teeth and then began moving up and down, up and down, pressing on the hairy patch of his lower stomach as she moved. Andrew groaned, snarled. His breathing became shallow and rapid, matching the shaking of the door upstairs. Charlene met his breathing with her own rising and falling. The delicate, sensitive internal walls of her body spun madly and then with a wail, her lower body exploded with a torrent of pulses and throbs.

Andrew climaxed at the same time, crying out, arching his back so as to drive himself in her more deeply.

Then he collapsed and put his hands over his face. Charlene stood up, wiped the insides of her legs.

She heard herself say, "So there, Andrew. That's all now."

The rattling of the door at the top of the stairs slowed, stopped.

Andrew lay panting, and then slowly pushed himself to his feet. He turned away from Charlerne, zipped and buckled his pants, and without saying a word, went out to his truck. Charlene pulled a blanket from her sleeping bag and wrapped herself. She went out to the porch in time to see the wake of dust rise to the night sky as the truck drove off.

With Andrew gone, Charlene's sense of power drained from her body immediately, and a deep, toxic despair washed over her.

Oh, my God.

What the hell happened? What had she done?

She grasped the porch railing to keep from dropping. Her arms shook madly. Her head spun. She was wrong, she was terrible, for having forced him into sex. Her body had betrayed her into acting as she had never acted before.

Shit. Shit. Shit!

But how had she been so strong? How did she overcome a man so much larger than she was?

Out in the woods, a distant whacking sound began. Her heart picked up the heavy beat. She crushed her fists against her chest to slow it down. "Be quiet!" she called out to the trees. "Shut up!"

The phone rang. Charlene staggered inside. The painting she had made of the witch woman did not wink, but only looked out at the room with bright eyes. Charlene reached for the phone.

Andrew, is it you? God, I'm so sorry! I don't know what happened! Please listen to me, I don't know why I did that to you!

She flipped the phone open. "Hello?"

"Judy? Hey, this is Chuck. I never did get to tell you what I want for my birthday so I wanted to—"

"Wrong number," Charlene said, and she slowly closed the phone.

32

~~

"There is no one else I can turn to," Charlene said softly into the phone. Not that whispering would do any good. If there were spirits, they could hear you no matter how quiet you were, so it wouldn't make a difference. "No one else could understand what's been happening."

There was a patient, sad sigh on the other end of the line. "I tried to tell you. Livin' there's madness. She's after you. She won't let you be."

Charlene stood on her front porch, staring out through the morning sunlight at the weeds and the well. It sounded like Maude was talking from inside a rain barrel. Some old-fashioned piece-of-crap phone she must have. It was all Charlene could do to keep her voice steady and low. Out in the grass, it looked as if the bricks over the well were moving, but then she saw it was only a squirrel rummaging on the cover. "This is my place, at least for now. But I'm scared, and I'm angry..."

"You should be scared."

"I have to do something. Tell me what I can do. You know the history here. You know about Phoebe. You must know something I can do to protect myself."

"I said it before. Burn the house. Burn the mill. That will destroy Phoebe's spirit. S'only choice you have."

Charlene's teeth came together with an audible click. She had been up all night pacing, cursing, fighting back tears, slamming in and out of the house, shaking her fists at nothing, and then cowering on her sleeping bag with a towel draped over the painting of the witch and a balled-up blanket at her chest. She was frightened of the power that had consumed her, that wanted to control her, terrify her, and drive her away. Yet she was equally furious at it. "This is my place. I'm an Alexander, too."

"You ain't been hurt much yet, but Phoebe's toying with you. She was more clever than you can imagine, more cruel, more heartless. Don't give her no more time."

"Do you know how to exorcise a house?"

"Do I know what?"

"How to rid a house of spirits, of ghosts? Short of burning the place down. There must be some kind of formula, some kind of rituals. People can't just be at the mercy of things like spirits, can they? People can't just be the victims. There has to be something to level the playing field."

"Only thing that'll do it is to burn it all. Then leave and don't never come back."

"I can't, Maude. I'm afraid but I'm also completely and totally pissed! I don't want to give up without a fight!"

"Fightin' will only lead to more trouble than you ever seen in your life, sweetie. How can I convince you o' that? Hear me out: You gotta burn it all."

"Sorry. But thanks, anyway." Charlene pushed end on the phone, then put her hand over her face. Maude was worthless, the old bitch.

Don't get like this. She's afraid. She knows the truth about the past. She's trying to help you and has nothing else to offer.

The house behind Charlene was quiet except for the music playing on WBAM's Saturday morning radio show. The phone had rung several times that morning, and twice it had been Chuck looking for Judy and once Ryan saying he'd try to get down to visit her next weekend, if that was all right? He would take her out to dinner and they'd have a good time. Charlene had only told him she was deep into painting and a visit wouldn't work out yet because she needed to focus, to concentrate. Reluctantly he'd said, "Then let me know a good time, will you? I do want to see the digs and see the new art." She had said she would.

Then, "I love you, Charlene."

Her heart clenched. "I love you, too, Ryan." She closed the phone.

The door to the mysterious room at the top of the stairs had remained silent throughout the morning. Her splintered hand had not burned and she had not felt dizzy. The painting witch-woman had not flown off the easel nor winked. Charlene had seen no animals with broken necks today, and last night had not dreamed of wells and earthworms, but only of stars and moons.

Anyone else would have said she had imagined the fearful occurrences. That's what Andrew had said. He had convinced her of that. But now she was certain that she hadn't imagined any of it. It was all real. And this was just the calm before a storm.

And what kind of storm, she could not even imagine.

She sat on a porch step and picked at the splinter with a ragged fingernail. It seemed to be working its way to the surface of her palm. In another few days, she would be able to get it out with a pin. Her crotch was sore from the sex (*The rape, Charlene*) with Andrew last night. The details were vague, as if she had been watching it from a distance, as if it had not been her, but someone else overpowering him. Though she clearly recalled the expression on his face as he lay on the floor and the satisfaction she had in driving him down.

"I was possessed to do that. Possessed by Phoebe Alexander. I was taken over by the spirit of a witch. Why, I have no idea."

She had tried to call Andrew, but he had not answered. It seemed he'd even disabled his voice mail, and she was not able to leave a message. She didn't know what she would have said, but she was ready to try. *It was a witch, Andrew.*

He would have probably hung up on her. In a way, she knew he had hung up on her already.

"How powerful are you, witch?" she asked aloud, catching her hair up in her fingers and twisting until it stung. "How can I fight something I don't know anything about?" She recalled the witches she'd feared as a child. They could cast spells, fly on broomsticks, command flying monkeys, disappear in puffs of smoke, and make brews out of bits of animals and bones. She looked at the Cruiser and rubbed her hands on her jeans.

It was time to do more research.

The Adams Branch of the Jefferson-Madison Public Library was a four-room doublewide trailer permanently parked at the south edge of town, surrounded by little ball-shaped barberry bushes, and with a narrow set of steel steps leading to the front door. There were two computers in two tiny cubicles at the rear of the library beside the bathrooms. One was being used by a woman who, from a glance over her shoulder as Charlene moved past, seemed to be researching garden pests. Charlene slid into the chair at the second computer, draped her purse over the back of the seat, and typed "witch" on the search bar. She hit return. A message appeared: "This term has been blocked by the Adams Library. We are sorry for any inconvenience. Please try again."

You've got to be kidding.

She typed in "occult." Hit return.

"This term has been blocked by the Adams Library. We are sorry for any inconvenience. Please try again."

Charlene went to the checkout desk. The woman explained, "We have impressionable young children who like to play with the computer, so we decided it was best to keep them safe from things that could be harmful."

"But what about adults who have genuine interest in, say, the occult?"

There was a moment's hesitation, and the woman said, "I can't imagine that could be a genuine interest. But there may be some books that touch on the subject. In the adult section, of course."

"Of course."

One room was designated for children, so noted by colorful construction paper cutouts of monkeys and cats that were taped around the doorframe. The other two rooms were for adults. Charlene went to the room with the sign that read NON-FICTION FOR ADULTS. Inside were tall shelves and narrow aisles, with Dewey Decimal System numbers tacked to the end of each aisle.

"I bet there's nothing in here I can use," Charlene said to herself, and someone she didn't know on the other side of the room said, "What?"

"Nothing. Sorry."

There was a collection of volumes on the paranormal, but it was minuscule, old titles such as *The Complete Charles Fort, An Encyclopedia of Witches and the Occult, The Witches of Eastwick. (Who shelved these things, anyway?)* Charlene sat on a little wheeled footstool in the aisle, flipping through the occult encyclopedia until a young library assistant found her and said the stools were for standing only. Charlene opened her mouth to ask why there was such a needless policy, but then let it go. It would be enough of a shock to the staff when the Alexander woman was caught checking out a witch book. Certainly the news of the hanging groundhog had made it around Adams's tiny social circles.

And what of the rape of Andrew Marshall? Had Andrew told anybody what had happened?

The librarian did give her a sidelong stare as Charlene filled out her library card application, and again as she swiped the occult encyclopedia across the scanner.

Driving back through town, Charlene braced the book open in her lap. Every few seconds she glanced down at a new page showing a listing and a drawing of a demon, or a vampire, or poltergeist or werewolf or evil sprite. So many terrible things people had believed in throughout history. So many frightening beings had been birthed in the human mind, beings that kept one in line or drove one mad. Imaginary creatures that terrorized, oppressed, and even killed.

But not all are imaginary. Not all spring from the primitive brain. Some birth themselves and then reach over into our world to stir things up and make our lives hell.

The light at Main and Maple was red. Charlene slowed and stopped behind a white Toyota. She closed the book and put it on the seat beside her. Then she glanced up. Andrew was on the sidewalk outside the Fox's Den. Her heart flipped. She rolled down her window.

What am I supposed to say? Do I apologize here and now? Should I pull over and see if we can talk now?

But when he looked up, his eyes narrowed and his jaw tightened. He locked gazes with her for the barest second, shook his head, and retreated into the diner.

Tears stung Charlene's eyes. *What was that? So he does hate me now. He's not even willing to hear me out.* The light went green. Charlene floored the car through the intersection. *Fine, then. I really don't care. What an idiot I was to give him my time.*

On the porch steps at home, Charlene flipped through the illustrations of witches in their elements. There were a few photos of contemporary, motherly Wiccans paying homage to the spirits of wind and earth and water, but most were engravings and paintings showing power-deranged witches devouring babies from fireplace spits, flying through night skies with bloodied hands, casting spells of death on entire villages.

"The magical art of witchcraft exists universally," Charlene read aloud. "It is a type of sorcery involving casting spells and divination. In most cultures, witchcraft is considered to be malevolent, though some distinctions exist between white and black witchcraft."

Phoebe was a cruel witch, the coldest of the cold.

"Witches are proficient in foretelling the future, sorcery, and astral projection. They can kill at a distance, can make themselves invisible, or can shapeshift. They can fly, and they have the gift of clairvoyance. Witches are known for the ability to create potions for any circumstance they deem fit. Spells are a witch's blueprint through which she can create chaos, change persons internally or externally, fold time, project visions, or kill or heal."

Charlene slammed the book shut and threw it onto the porch. How could someone fight all that? What was there that a witch couldn't do? Could she be defeated? If not defeated, could she be appeased?

"What would it mean to appease you, Phoebe Alexander?"

The thought made her shudder. If only Andrew was there to help her get through this. He was practical, he was sensible. He was strong and caring.

And you raped him, Charlene.

But Phoebe made me. Why, I have no idea. To prove her strength? To show me she can make me do anything she wants?

Charlene went inside, took a long breath, and then stared at the painting. "Are you Phoebe?" she asked the image. "Do you really want to destroy me?" She waited, expecting the picture to wink, but it did not. "If you do..."

Shut up, Charlene, this will only make things worse!

"...then you must know the land will be sold anyway. Or do you plan to drive me mad, to reduce me to some sort of babbling imbecile who will stay here until I die? Is that why Ellen stayed? But I have no heir, Phoebe. Nobody to carry on the Alexander line. What do you think of that?"

The eyes stared off the paper, emotionless.

"If you want to kill me, at least let me first know about you."

Charlene! Would you fucking shut up?

"Do you want me to beg you? To promise I won't sell the land? Is that your demand?"

Light flickered over the surface of the painting, and it looked as though the witch smiled slightly.

There was thumping in the room at the top of the stairs. Charlene's head whipped about and she stared at the steps. *There is an answer up there. In that locked, dark room.*

She walked into the hall and took the first step. The banging grew louder now. The tarp flapped up at her and then dropped back down.

"I don't want to look in there."

You have to. There's truth to be learned in there.

"Dear God, this is not good."

Charlene, slowly walked up the stairs. When she reached the tarp, she pulled it off the nails then tossed it down behind her. Her breath on the air was suddenly frosty and white.

She stood before the sealed door, relieved on one hand that she did not have the key to open that door, terrified on the other hand because there was a rusted sledgehammer in the trash pile out back that could open that door.

I should leave this alone. Go back to Norfolk. Stop by Andrew's house to apologize in person and then retreat to what is familiar, what I know, what is safe.

"No! I can't! I've been a worthless wimp for too long. I have to do at least this if nothing else. If nothing else, the souls of those tormented, murdered children need to have their fates unveiled by hands of a kinder family member, someone who cares what happened!"

Listen to yourself. You sound as insane as Andrew thinks you are. Let it go!

I won't. I can't.

She got the sledgehammer and returned to the door.

Help me, God, help me. She caught her breath and braced her feet apart. Arms over her head, she held the sledgehammer behind her, ready to swing. "One, two, three..."

The head-heavy hammer coursed up, around, then down with an airy whoosh. As it reached the surface, the door flew open of its own accord, nails and wood blowing apart. The hammer struck the floor.

Charlene gasped and wiped scraps of wood from her hair and off her shoulders. She let go of the handle. The hammer dropped to its side with a clatter. She stared inside the dark room, clutching her chest. Faint light filtered in from the hall, and slowly her vision adjusted.

It was a parlor, furnished in mid-nineteenth-century fashion. A bricked-over fireplace sat on the far wall. A brocade divan held the middle of the floor, with a bearskin rug before it. Small, wall-side tables held hurricane lanterns and lace doilies. Mounted over the fireplace was a painted portrait of a family in long-ago clothing, standing by a gate—a mother, father, several children, and a little spotted dog. Someone had slashed the painting in several places and had made round cuts to remove all the faces.

Charlene stepped into the room, her eyes flicking back and forth. As the house had smelled like the thing it was, this room also smelled like the place it was—a room of torment. The scents of blood and decay, fear and rage were cloying. Charlene's eyes stung. She took breaths through her teeth.

I'm in here. I've found your private room, Phoebe. Is this where you tortured your children before you bound them and threw them into the well?

A tall, glass-fronted display case was on the wall by the door. It was filled with a man's things: a rack of pipes, cans of tobacco, deer antlers, pistols, hunting knives, dark leather riding gloves.

Where are your books of curses, Phoebe? Where is your sack of birds' feet and animal skulls, raven feathers and crow eyes?

The floor began to shake. Charlene grappled the edge of the display case. "Are you mad because I came in here?" she shouted to the ceiling. "Are you pissed I dared to cross this threshold?" The shaking increased. The glass on the case cracked top to bottom, then side to side with a bright and tingling sound. Charlene dropped to her knees and braced her palms on the floor. "Stop it!"

Lanterns crashed from the tables. The tables followed. The painting over the fireplace rocked back and forth violently. The divan shimmied up and down on the floor, and then moved toward Charlene on its wooden feet.

Get out, Charlene, get out get out!

Charlene scrabbled at the floor with hands and feet, forcing herself toward the door. The glass front of the display case blew open. Pistols and knives were hurled across the room. The case wobbled, tipped, and then fell. Charlene looked up in time to see the cracked glass and flapping door rushing down at her. She didn't have time to scream before the case hit her and drove her down.

Down...

Down...

She was floating downward, round and round, as if falling
into a...

...lightless well.

No!

No...not a well...

She landed on something soft—a mattress. A bed. She was
on her back in a bed in the dark. She could hear nothing other
than her own labored breaths, her own pulse raging through
her temples. All about her was the earthen, bloody odor of
earthworms. Hands came up from under the bed and took her
arms and legs, held them firmly in place. *Not this again, no!*
She could not struggle, nor speak. Behind her came the familiar voice, whispering, "Shhh, it's for the best." Faces rose
up on both sides of the bed, the faces that belonged to the
hands that held her down. Faces she'd never seen before. And
she knew them, and was afraid. They were the Alexander
women, generations of them, their hair the same dark red,
though fashioned from their own peculiar times, their faces
gaunt and stern, their lips pressed into expressions of stern in-
tent. Their eyes glowed with unearthly fires.

*You're all witches, aren't you? Not just Phoebe, but all of
you!*

"Eat," whispered the voice behind Charlene. The Alexander women shook their voluminous hair free of pins and caps.
Earthworms dangled from the oily strands. The women leaned
over Charlene and forced her to eat.

No!

She gasped, chewed, swallowed. Her stomach hitched with
nausea, but more worms were presented to her lips and she
opened her mouth to let them in.

No, I won't!

Her mouth did not obey her, but obeyed the Alexander
women. They began to smile then, pleased with her obedi-
ence. She ate until her belly was full.

Then the woman tossed back their hair. The voice behind
Charlene whispered, "Look, and see..."

The blackness over the foot of the bed opened. Like a

nightmare movie for an audience of one, red, swirling clouds and flashes of light hurtled across the spectral screen like formless witches on brooms. Then the clouds and light vanished, sucked backward into the void, leaving in their place a little girl. She stood alone in an old-fashioned petticoat and tiny leather shoes, head down, hands folded.

Opal?

The girl slowly lifted her head. Charlene watched, stared, as the girl opened her eyes. But the eyes were gone, leaving gaping crimson holes. Opal opened her mouth to speak, but she could not. Blood oozed from the corners of her mouth. The girl's hands reached out for Charlene. Her fingers strummed the air.

no no NO!!!

"NO!"

Charlene heard her own voice, and she shuddered and blinked.

She blinked again.

She was not on the bed. She was in the parlor on the floor. The display case lay across her legs, spatterings of glass lay on her stomach and on her face. One hand was pressed against the floor. The other hand was on her chest, holding...

...holding a hunting knife.

The knife blade was poised at her throat.

Charlene heaved the knife across the room. She screamed, "I won't let you do this to me! You fucking bitches!"

She scrambled from under the display case and stumbled into the hallway, her legs cut and bleeding. She slammed the parlor door shut then stumbled down the stairs and into the living room, hissing, snarling.

"I won't let you do this!"

She took the painting of the witch, ripped it into tiny pieces, and flushed the pieces down the toilet.

33

~

The phone rang and she did not answer.

It rang again a minute later and she did not answer. She lay in the yard in the weeds, curled up with her arm over her head, unable to move. Her body was exhausted, her mind drained. She thought of Reginald and Mary Jane, of Denise and Maude. Of Ryan. Of Andrew. Normal lives they lived. Normal lives for normal people. But Charlene was not normal, not now, maybe never.

Perhaps fate was real, like Maude said. Maybe Charlene had not come to Homeplace to regain her footing as a painter, but by some inescapable fate. Maybe it was her destiny to face these terrors, to confront these spirits. What would be the consequences? To go down in flames trying to avenge the deaths of children she didn't even know?

I'm so fucking tired.

Beside her on the grass was Opal's journal, retrieved from the icebox.

She reached out her hand and placed it on the journal. It radiated heat. The only way to deal with everything, she knew now, was to embrace the horrors instead of struggling, to see what they had in store for her.

"I give up," she said, feeling like a condemned prisoner baring her neck for the noose, feeling a dreadful, resigned peace. "I give in. You hear me?" She looked at the sky. There was a tiny beetle on a nearby chicory stem, crawling about as it sought food. It stepped into the white fibers of a small spider's web. It struggled once, then stopped. She had stepped into a huge web. What would happen within its tangles?

Okay now. I won't struggle.

Okay.

She sat up with effort and opened Opal's journal. She forced herself to read.

Each page revealed the details of Opal's final days, Opal's own fate, a fate that, Charlene knew, was the same for every child who had intentionally or accidentally offended their mother. Opal banished to the cabin. Opal made to stand in the center of the cabin floor for three days straight while her siblings were marched to the cabin window to look in at her and her shame. Opal bound and put into the attic on a stinking, bug-infested mattress, blindfolded until the hands came to take her out again.

The hands that took her into the parlor and forced her to strip in front of the fire. The hand that tapped tobacco residue out of a smoldering pipe, put it into its stand, then reached for her body. To pinch it. To caress it. To slap and fondle it.

Pipe? Charlene drew back from the page a bit. *A tobacco pipe?*

"Did Phoebe smoke a pipe?"

The hands that made Opal cry with pain and embarrassment. The hands that forced her to kneel and beg forgiveness for sins she had and had not committed, hands that were shoved deep into the pockets of smelly wool trousers while listening to the girl's confessions, and fumbled deep within those pockets as if fighting a snake.

Wait... what?

The hands that then patted her head reassuringly, but then whipped her, tied her with twine, and put her back into the cabin with the warning that soon, she would kiss worms in the bottom of the well.

*Phoebe, it wasn't you? You didn't harm Opal, it was...
who?*

Charlene slammed the journal closed. She went inside, put
fresh paper on the easel, and took up the brush in her left
hand. "Okay, if there is something I should know, show me
now." Her hand trembled with the brush. "Show me now!"

Tell me!

The fire welled up inside her, taking her over completely,
and she painted. The brush dipping in and out of the water jar,
smearing watercolors onto page after page of Bristol board.
Her eyes could not focus on what she was painting but she did
not care; she was given up to the spirits, whatever that might
mean. Energy surged, pouring through her mind, her body.
Faster, faster the paints flew, the pages turned. She thought
she heard the phone ring, she thought she heard the crackling
of thunder and the whistling of wind, but thoughts were vague
and worthless as her hand painted, painted. At some point she
felt a pencil in her hand and she was writing like a mad thing.

Then her hand went still. The pencil, paintbrush, palette,
and water jar fell to the floor. Charlene pressed the heel of her
hand against her forehead, then collected the stack of papers
and spread them out in front of the fireplace. She had no idea
of the time except that it was night. Her watch had stopped.
Her clock radio had gone blank. At some time a thunderstorm
had blown through, killing the electricity. Was it ten? Eleven?
Midnight?

In the beam of her flashlight she studied the sheets of
paper on which the pencil had scribbled. It was a collection of
recipes. Brews. For sterility: click beetles, acorns, and pep-
pers. To paralyze an enemy: spiders' legs, vinegar, and hair-
cap moss. For traveling outside one's body: blood from
bloodroot, river water, ash, and earthworms.

These are directions for a witch's potions!

Then Charlene examined the pictures, one by one. They
were crude but clear. One revealed a young auburn-haired
Phoebe Alexander in a long dress, holding a baby on a porch.
Another showed Phoebe, now gaunt and thin, in the kitchen,
two small girls clutching her skirts, an infant in her arms. A

tall man with black hair pointed a pistol at one of the children. The successive paintings continued the horrific story: A dark-haired girl staring out of the cabin window, hands over her eyes, blood on her cheeks. Another girl being beaten by the bearded man as Phoebe grabbed desperately for the whip. A third girl on the floor of the parlor as the man penetrated her with a hideous grin on his face. A fourth girl clutching a torn blanket in the attic of the Children's House. A fifth girl, pale-haired, bound and lifted over the open well by the bearded man. In the background, wild-haired Phoebe struggled as a second man held her back. Thirteen pictures in all, showing thirteen different children terrified, abused, and killed.

By their father, not their mother.

34

~

Chapter One

Hugh Chase stood on the corner, waving for a taxi, in the twilight shadow of the Custom House Tower. The day had been a long one, a bad one all around, and the only impending bright spot was getting together with his friends at the Wharf Bistro on the Harbor to celebrate Hugh's birthday. Not that Hugh was keen on birthdays; who needed to get older in this world, when staying in your twenties was the ideal? But after today, the idea of getting smashed on someone else's tab gave him a sense of relief.

Dead bodies rarely affected the seasoned detective. Smashed, bloodied, burned, he'd seen it all. It was his job to study, consider, and determine, based on the old journalism standards. Who was the victim? What was the cause of death? When had it happened? Where had it occurred? Why had this person died? How had this person met his or her fate? Of course, the Big Final Question that would be answered by answering all the former ones was yet another who. Who, if anybody, killed this person?

This person in this case was a young woman who was raped and then dismembered. Nasty, brutal stuff. The who and when had been established. Her name was Sherry Franklin. She was a high school student who had gone to Faneuil Hall Marketplace with her friends to do some shopping. According to forensics, she'd been killed at 12:34 A.M., and though she'd disappeared from Faneuil Hall, no one knew yet where she was raped and where she was dismembered. Her body was found in the bathroom of a Boston Harbor ferry. The rest of the questions, the bigger ones, still hung over Hugh like a toxic cloud. Yes, it was his job to solve these crimes, but this dead girl was his...

"Who should it be, Rex?"
No answer from under the desk.

...his niece. His sister's eldest daughter.
Hugh's superiors didn't want him on the case. It was too close to him, they said. He wouldn't have the objectivity needed. But Hugh didn't care; he'd work it secretly if he had to. Yes, it was personal. How the fuck could it not be?

Andrew stopped typing, then read the first page of the book aloud. "What do you think, Rex? Possibilities here? I still like the idea of bodies in the ferry bathroom."
Rex turned his head back and chewed at his hip.

Hugh Chase was thirty-six, twice divorced, and father of none, thank God. He was an angry man for the most part, wounded...

"Wounded how?"

...wounded in the war...

"What war? Has he had time to be a soldier as well as a seasoned detective?"

...wounded in a gunfight between a kidnapper and the police four years earlier, and betrayed by every woman he'd ever known.

"He sounds pathetic."

...wounded in a gunfight between a kidnapper and the police four years earlier, and distrustful of all things that had to do with women. Since his divorces he never opened himself to relationships, and avoided any contact with the feminine species except for the occasional fling or call girl.

"Now he sounds like an asshole."

Life was too damned complex to muddy the waters even further.

"Further or farther? I think farther."
Rex didn't know.

Andrew rubbed his fist against the pain in his leg and stretched it out over the top of the dog. As had Hugh's, Andrew's had been a long day, indeed. Last night, when he arrived back home from his visit to Charlene's place, some of the guests were gone and the rest ready to leave. He'd managed a civil exterior, thanking everyone for coming and bidding them all a friendly farewell. Then Andrew had cleaned the apples from the inside of his truck and had thrown them out in the backyard for the birds.

Tom sensed something was wrong, though he didn't press it. Clearly he thought Andrew and Charlene had had a bad scene, a breaking up of sorts. Which, of course, it was, though not of any sort Andrew had ever experienced. This morning he and Tom had chilled with some pre-noon beers left behind by Arnie and Yule, listened to music, watched a Three Stooges DVD, and had a late lunch at the Fox's Den. Tom hadn't seen Charlene drive by the restaurant; he'd been inside trying to get a stuck gumball out of the machine. It was clear that Charlene wanted to get Andrew's attention, but he'd turned away. What the hell was there to say?

He'd been attacked, she'd forced him to have sex, and it was one of the most frightening, intense, pleasurable, and confusing moments of his life.

Andrew had driven Tom to the airport after lunch, then had returned home to do the after-party crap that Sallie and Dawn hadn't been hired to do—cleaning up beer bottles and cigar stubs in the backyard, taking bags of trash out to the barrel, running loads of dishes through the washer. But it was impossible to stop thinking about the night before, replaying everything from his discovery of the naked Charlene, looking at once beautiful and terrifying at her easel, to her knocking him to the floor, to her climbing off and snarling, "So there, Andrew."

What the fuck happened? It was as though something had taken her over, as if there was someone else inside her, controlling her.

But that's insane. That's what crazy people believe.

The doorbell rang. Rex clambered from beneath the desk and barked.

Charlene thought her place might be haunted. That was why she spent the night here. But it can't possibly be true. There is no such thing as the supernatural.

Rex went to the door and looked back impatiently. Andrew saved the document and went down the stairs, dragging one set of fingers through his hair while the other trailed the banister. Rex clattered after. Through the glass semi-circle over the door he recognized the top of the ball-capped head. It was Arnie Bryan.

"It's Saturday night. Why isn't he out drinking or playing cards or whatever he does on weekends?" Andrew said to Rex, who sat down on the hall rug as Andrew reached for the knob. He pulled the door open.

"Mr. Marshall?" Arnie held his hands in front of him in a knot. He looked nervous and small in the porch light.

"Arnie. What can I do for you?"

"You heard from Yule?"

"You mean today?"

"Or since the party last night?"

"No, sorry."

"Well, I ain't, neither."

"He was gone when I got back, and you were, too. I figured you'd left together."

"No. He went after you."

Andrew felt a cold fist clench in the pit of his stomach. "What do you mean?"

"You tole him you were goin' to see about that Alexander woman. He didn't want you goin' out there on your own. He was scared for you. I could see his face, so I knew what he was up to, but I was too drunk to care too much. Now, though . . ." Arnie's shoulders hitched.

"Doesn't he sometimes just stay out for a night or two? Get a little drunk, off somewhere by himself?"

"Hell, no. His wife'd kill him, he do that. She told me I had to go find him. I called Rick Evans, but he said he'd give it 'til tomorrow. He thinks Yule just hidin' out somewhere since his mother-in-law's taken to the Witnesses and he don' want to be around her come Sunday mornin'. Since you and Yule's friends, I thought I'd ask you if you'd help me look for him."

"I have no idea where he is, Arnie."

"You sure you didn' see him out at Homeplace last night? Comin' or goin'?"

"No."

"Didn' see nothin' unusual there or along the road, maybe?"

"I didn't see anything out of the ordinary, no." *Oh, yes you did. You saw Charlene act like some kind of woman in a trance, with more strength than most men I've ever known.*

"You sure?"

Could she have possibly attacked Yule after I left?

Of course not.

"I'm sure."

My God, did she?

"All right, then," said Arnie. He seemed to slump even further, his head down, his hat slipping sadly to one side. Moths hummed around his ears. How hard must it be to have one son burn to death and then a nephew vanish?

Andrew touched the old man on the arm. "Tell you what, I'll help you look. I'll go back out to Homeplace right now. Just give me a minute to get the keys and my jacket."

I don't want to see Charlene. I hope we find Yule, but I don't want to see her again.

"Oh," said Arnie, his head shaking. "I best stay in town, keep lookin' around here."

"Why won't you come with me?" Arnie's eyes flicked about, but he said nothing, and it was clear. Arnie was as afraid of Homeplace as Yule. "Listen, don't worry about it. I'll check out the Alexander place and you keep asking around Adams."

"Good idea," said Arnie.

"We'll find him."

"Okay."

"You have a cell phone? I can call you if I find out anything."

"No. Just call over to Yule's house you find him."

"All right."

"And thank you, Mr. Marshall."

"Please. Call me Andy."

35

~

Maude didn't want to let Charlene in. "You're scaring me, child. I don' wanna see what you got there."

As she stood on the porch in the glow that pooled from Maude's front hall, Charlene knew she looked like a she-devil herself, with her hair wild, clothes wrinkled, and eyes blazing with clarity. She had banged on Maude's door, knowing from the clock on her Cruiser's dash that it was nearing eleven thirty, but knowing this couldn't wait. Maude needed to be told. Together, they could rid Homeplace of its evil.

But Maude would not open the screen, and from behind the old woman, Charlene could hear Dennis complaining and Polly crying.

"Chase that bitch out of here! I've got my shotgun. I can say she startled us, that we thought she was a burglar!"

"Maude, please look at what I have." Charlene pulled the rolled-up papers from her jacket pocket. "Here, see?" She dropped the rolls on a porch chair, quickly opened one, and held it to the porch light. "I didn't know what I was drawing. I was in a trance. You see? It's not Phoebe who was so cruel, it was her husband, William."

"Get out of here, you witch's spawn!" called Dennis.

"Shut the fuck up, you oily asshole!" Charlene shouted back, and then raised her hand and talked even faster so Maude would not slam the door shut. "Maude! I nearly slit my own throat today. But it wasn't Phoebe who tried to force me, it was something or someone else. Phoebe painted through me so I would see the truth. She's frightened me, but has never really harmed me. I think William's spirit is trying to kill me because Phoebe helped me discover what a cruel man he was in life!"

Maude pressed her face to the screen. "No! William was a stern man, but not cruel. I don' know what you've heard, but ain't no men who is witches. They might play at it, but they ain't for real."

"Aren't there warlocks?"

Maude spit, hard. "Warlocks? Warlocks is made-up boys' play, all silliness and toys. Witchin' is a woman's evil, pure and simple. There weren't no power with William then and there ain't now. I'm tellin' you God's truth. It's always been Phoebe. She's deluding you, tryin' to run you in the wrong direction like a chicken with its head cut off. Then, she can have her way just easy as can be."

Maude's insistence made Charlene hesitate for an instant, but then she said, "Maude, you're wrong."

"Get out of here, witch girl!" shouted Dennis from behind his mother.

"Ooo!" cried Polly from deeper inside the house.

Maude came outside, pushed the screen door closed, and gathered the sweaty, crumpled Charlene in her arms. She held her tightly. Charlene could hear her crying softly.

"I'm afraid for you, for my family, for my son and my granddaughter and her baby to be! Do you know what you're getting into, lettin' spirits come into you willingly? You're openin' a door what can't be closed. You'll never have power to defeat that sly, wicked woman. And as she uses you, her own power'll grow 'til it can't be held back no more. It'll pour out like poison sludge 'til it covers everything." Maude backed away. "It's been Phoebe all along. Hasn' she done things around you to scare you? To threaten you? Give me them pictures, honey, and them spells."

What if she's right?

"Honey, please." The woman held out her hand.

Couldn't a witch twist the truth to her own purposes? Couldn't she make lies of truths and truths of lies?

Charlene hesitated, then handed her the rolls of paper.

"Thank you, Jesus," breathed Maude. She let out a long breath. "I'll burn these now. Fire'll get rid of some of the trouble."

"Yes. I suppose." Charlene felt completely drained. *Now what?*

"Burn it all," said Maude. "It's the only way." She went inside. The door closed.

Charlene drove on Craig Road toward Homeplace, the headlights cutting the gloom, insects rising like cinders from a campfire and dashing themselves to death on the windshield.

I could keep on driving, she thought. *I could turn around and head back to Adams and keep on. I tried to fight. I thought I could do it, I thought I had it figured out. I thought I could rid my home of the evil and redeem the children from their lasting torment. I'm weak and so easily defeated.*

I always have been.

The Cruiser took the dirt road around the last curve before she reached her driveway, and it was then she saw the cracked, flattened brush to the left off the road, and a large, broken tree on the ground on the right side of the road. She slowed the car and stared. It looked as though someone had missed the curve at a high speed and had crashed through the trees. Skid marks had torn up the weeds, chewed up the ground. She could not see beyond the lightless dip where the rogue car had gone. When had this happened? Who ever came this far up Craig Road besides the mailman? Deliverymen who swore to never return? Kids who wanted to hang up dead groundhogs?

She thought at first of letting it go, of going on to her driveway, turning around, and doing what she had decided was best—leaving Nelson County. But then something clenched in her gut and she thought, *What if someone's hurt in there?*

"Shut up, Charlene."

No, what if someone's hurt? This is part of my land. I'll call for help if there's a need.

Checking her cell phone, she noted three bars.

She steered the Cruiser onto the broken patch of brush. She clambered out, taking the emergency flashlight from the glove compartment. Flicking the switch, she trained the light on the ground and moved down the first few yards of the incline. Then she stopped and stared at the track. The tracks.

Two cars have made this mess. There are two sets of tire marks here.

She opened her phone to dial 911. The three bars were gone. "No service" showed on the readout.

"Damn it!"

Charlene went into the middle of the road. Still no service. Back beside the Cruiser, she shone the light down into the dark maw of the sloping forest. A cicada hummed past her ear; she grunted and slapped the air. It would be best just to drive into Adams and get help. She waved the flashlight about the trees. Then she saw it, down about sixty feet, sitting slightly sideways, bumped up against the trunk of a large sycamore. It was a truck, beat up, with a dented tailgate. The engine was off. Charlene took several steps closer. It was Andrew's truck.

"Oh, my God. Andrew?"

The land was steep and the ground slippery. Her breath coming in rapid gasps, Charlene worked her way down, clutching tiny branches with her free hand, waving the flashlight in front of her to keep from tripping...and to hold back the witches.

You can't hold back witches!

"Andrew!"

Past the truck a good hundred yards, at the end of the track of torn grass, earth, and saplings, was the lip of a wide, deep ravine. Charlene skidded to a halt. Carefully, and with a lump of dread pressing from behind her ribs, stepped up to the edge. She did not want to look.

She bit her lip. She shined the flashlight down.

An old car was upside down in the ravine, a good forty feet down. There were clots of vegetation caught up in the undercarriage. An arm hung out the shattered driver's side window.

Oh shit oh shit! "Hello?" *I don't want to go down there! I don't want to see who that is!*

"Who's down there? Are you okay?"

There was no answer.

"Andrew?"

There was no answer.

Oh, God.

Charlene knelt on the wet, uneven ground, the knees of her jeans immediately soaking up the damp. Her hands were held before her mouth and her body shook. "Who is down there? Say something! Please be okay!"

The arm didn't move. But something in the darkness shifted, something in the thick pile of leaves beside the car. Charlene angled the light. It was Andrew, lying on his side, his jacket pulled up and torn, his arm over his head.

"No!" cried Charlene. Clamping the flashlight in her teeth, she climbed over the edge of the ravine and lowered herself down the muddy side, her hands digging deep into the muck and between the exposed roots. *Please be all right!*

She reached the bottom of the ditch and dropped beside Andrew. She lay the flashlight on the ground and with a trembling hand, reached out to touch his back. "Please," she said, and the word caught and turned in her throat. "Please."

His back was warm. She leaned closer. His breathing was raspy but strong.

"Andrew?"

Charlene glanced over at the car. The trail of light that cut alongside the broken window let her see that it was Yule Lemons at the wheel. Dead, with a tree branch smashed into his face. Charlene cried out, and bent over Andrew protectively, her arms wrapping the man, her face pressed against his body.

"Wake up, Andrew. Don't die."

Charlene's chest folded in on itself and she sobbed. "Please stay with me. I'm sorry for everything. I tried to fight the witch but I'm failing, and now she's come after you. I don't know what else to do!"

In the forest above and around were the sounds of owls and foxes, howling and barking. A frosty breeze cut through the ravine, rattling bone-bare branches and stirring dead leaves.

Andrew moaned, then coughed. Charlene sat bolt upright. "Andrew!"

His arm fell away from his head and he rolled onto his back. Slowly his eyes opened, blinked, then closed again.

"Andrew!" Charlene dug tears from her cheeks and then reached for Andrew's face. There were welts along his forehead and his nose was bleeding. Holding his face gently, she whispered, "Please."

Andrew opened his eyes and looked at Charlene. His cracked lips opened and he whispered, "What are you doing here?"

"This is my crappy land, that's what I'm doing here. What are you doing here?"

"Looking for Yule." Andrew's face drew up. "Damn, that hurts."

"We have to get you out of here."

"Yeah." Another cough, softer this time. Then, "Yule was afraid for me, afraid of me coming to find you. Afraid of you."

"I know. I remember how he acted back at your house, how he didn't want to shake my hand. But Andrew, we have to—"

"He was right, wasn't he?" Andrew's brows pulled together and he studied Charlene with an expression that at once frightened and awed her. "It was dangerous to come here, to spend time with you here."

Charlene put her hands to her heart. "I am so, so sorry for everything that has happened, and I know you won't believe this but it wasn't me. Say I'm insane, I won't disagree. I tried to tell you that last week. Tell me I've lost my senses. But I didn't lose them, they were stolen from me."

Andrew sat up, grimacing, sucking air.

"Have you broken anything?"

"I don't think so. But I'm pretty banged up."

"Andrew..."

"Charlene." He looked at her fully, and his eyes showed

something she had not dared to hope for—compassion, sympathy. "I believe you now."

"What? What do you believe?"

"This place is haunted."

"You believe that?"

Andrew nodded, wincing with the effort.

"You don't think it's just mental and emotional strain?"

"I saw it."

Charlene froze. "Saw what?"

Andrew looked around, as if making sure no one was eavesdropping. "I followed Yule's car tracks down here. I thought he'd just lost control and flipped the car. He'd had a few beers, after all. But then," he lowered his voice, "it came after me."

"Oh, God, what did?"

"I don't know exactly. I was looking down at Yule's car when it appeared overhead. I heard the laughter—shrieking, piercing. I glanced up. There was a dark spot, darker than the night, hovering over me." Andrew put his hand to his nose. "Hell of a punch. Is that your witch?"

"I think so."

"I ended up down here."

"I'm so sorry."

"It wasn't you."

"No, it wasn't." Charlene stood and reached her hand out. Andrew took it.

"Does she hate all men," he asked, "or just some of us?"

"I'm not sure." *There are no men buried in the cemetery, Charlene.* "Maybe all of them."

Charlene helped Andrew to his feet. He drew a sharp breath. "Where's your cane?"

Andrew nodded at the ground, where the cane lay, snapped in half.

They hobbled the length of the ravine to a flatter stretch of ground, then climbed up and around through the deep leaves. Andrew leaned heavily on Charlene, and she could feel his breathing, his heartbeat, his fear, his courage. She clenched her teeth. *Damn you, Phoebe! I won't let you do this to him!*

At last they reached Andrew's truck. Andrew tried the key. The engine wouldn't start. He and Charlene continued up to the road. At the Cruiser, Andrew placed his hands on the roof, panting, while Charlene unlocked the car and eased him into the passenger's seat.

"Andrew," she said, holding his hand through the open door. "Friday night. I didn't…it wasn't me." Tears welled again and she brushed them away.

"I know." He squeezed her hand tenderly. "I know. It's all right. And listen, can you take me to the hospital instead of home? I don't…feel so good. Charlottesville. We can make it in half an hour."

"All right. Hold on, sweetie."

"You don't have a cigarette, do you?"

"What?"

"I'm just kidding."

"Okay."

"And Charlene, you don't need to go back to your house. Enough is enough."

"You're right." *Enough is enough.*

Charlene got into the car and stabbed the key into the ignition. The car refused to start.

36

~

Charlene could not drive into Adams for help. She could not help Andrew as far as Adams on foot. Her cell phone was dead. She would not leave Andrew here alone. They would have to return to her house.

There, she would take a stand. Though she had no idea what that might mean, and it drove cold spears through her heart. But as Andrew had said, "Enough is enough."

Enough, Phoebe.

By the time they reached the front porch, the moon high in the black sky like a stone scythe waiting to fall, Andrew was barely able to move. His feet shuffled like a dying man's, his breathing was labored. When he realized where they were headed, he hesitated, and struggled, then Charlene had said simply, "I have no choice. This will be over soon. Trust me."

And for some reason, he seemed to. He must have been able to read her mind, to sense the searing fury and resolve in her, and gave in to her direction. As she helped Andrew up onto the porch, around the boxed appliances, and through the front door, she knew what she would do. She had no choice anymore.

Yes, I do have a choice. And this is it.

She heard doom in the thought, but knew that if she went down, she would try her fucking damndest to bring down the murdering spirit, too, so it could never frighten another, wound another, kill another.

With Andrew on the sleeping bag, his cuts cleaned and dressed, and wrapped in the wool blanket, Charlene went to work. It took the rest of the night to collect the river water from the Tye, bloodroot from the forest floor, earthworms from the soft soil by the well, and ash from the spot where she'd burned the rabbits. All these, she recalled, made up a powerful recipe. She marched about in the darkness, waving her flashlight like a snake-smacking stick, almost daring Phoebe to come after her. In the woods a barred owl flew toward her with outstretched talons, but she slapped at it and it had veered off and disappeared. By the well a timber rattlesnake crept toward her from the weeds, its head bobbing, but she stomped on it with her boot, and it convulsed, twisted, and died.

Don't mess with me now! I have work to do!

Sunlight was an orange glow through the woods as she checked on the sleeping Andrew, then sat cross-legged on the front porch to mash the last of the ingredients into a pulp inside her teacup. It was a dreadful mixture, with bits of worm still wriggling amid the ashy water and the red juice from the bloodroot.

My nightmare is coming true. I'm going to eat earthworms.

"No, your nightmare has already come true."

She pinched her nose, then let it go. She held the cup to her lips and drank the foul potion.

She did not have to close her eyes to feel the spinning of the world beneath her. She lay back on the porch and watched the wooden slats in the ceiling whirl like paper in a spin art machine. If this worked, she would be able to see things she could not see from her own, limited vantage point in her own, limited flesh. She would be in another form, a spirit herself, and in that way she could encounter Phoebe, could see the witch in the witch's realm.

Then and only then, face-to-face, could she stake her claim. Only then could she—

Charlene was suddenly and violently projected from her body and hurled up toward the porch ceiling and through the ceiling, into the air above the house. It took her breath away, and then she realized she had no breath to take away.

Help me!

She scrambled to fly, to glide, to hold in the air so she would not fall, but she looked and saw she had no legs to scramble, no arms to fly, no body to fall and die. She was mind only, spirit only, hovering like a spectral hummingbird above the tin shingles and the square black mouth of the southern chimney.

It was thought that allowed her to swing down and see herself, prone on the porch, looking like a woman who'd had way too much to drink.

And that I did. Earthworms, river water.

Where are you, Phoebe? Meet me now!

She willed herself toward the river. Low over the trees she moved, casting no shadow, disturbing not even the smallest sparrows perched on high pine branches. Threadings of pathways were visible through the branches, and the ruins of the slave cabins in their small clearing. And then, a pattern of gray stones below the tree branches—the family cemetery—and a dark perimeter around it. Not the broken iron fence, but something else. Charlene moved down, closer. This was the hex sign, the protection Maude had laid in stone around the graveyard, to protect herself from the spirit of the vengeful Phoebe Alexander.

But why is Maude afraid of Phoebe?

The thought caught Charlene off guard. Why would the long-dead witch care if a next-door neighbor came to care for long-forgotten gravestones?

That doesn't make sense.

Charlene moved upward again, and could see the tips of brick smokestacks in the distance.

Rhythmic whacking and whining sounds rose up from the direction of the mill. The blood that no longer coursed her veins chilled with the sounds. Were there truly ghosts of slaves in the mills, working day and night into infinity, the machines banging and thumping, creating substanceless fabric out of thin air and time, fueled by a fear that could not be eased even in death?

Witch! Show yourself!

She moved closer to the river, circling to the south of the mill, and then saw what was making the noise.

It was not a gathering of ghosts, struggling with an eternal fate. It was Dennis Boise with several other men in a huge bald patch in the forest, a place of stumps and fallen timber.

37

~

Andrew awoke to sunlight, silence, and a sense of dread. His head throbbed and his face was hot. He rolled over on the floor—*What am I doing on a floor?*—and touched his nose. There was a large bandage there; beneath it, the sensation that he'd been whacked with a machete. His leg was stiff and sore, as was his back.

I'm at Charlene's. I'm at Homeplace.

He reached around and found a pillow he'd knocked away sometime during his sleep. It smelled faintly of dust and coconut. He held still, letting thoughts arrange themselves into memories.

He'd gone looking for Yule last night. Arnie had been afraid, and Andrew had gone. He'd driven to Homeplace and spotted the tracks off the side of the road. Then he'd gotten out of his truck to see if he could find his friend.

"Shit."

The memory drove the pain in his head up another notch. Yule's car had fallen, flipped over onto its top. Yule was dead. And then some laughing, disembodied hand had struck Andrew down, as well.

Andrew pushed himself up onto his knees. Vomit threatened

to rise; he forced it down. "Charlene?" She didn't answer. He stood shakily and pressed his hand to his skull. Where the hell were his ibuprofens? In the fucking truck, of course, back down the road.

"Charlene?" His mouth dry, his chest tight, Andrew limped to the hall. Then, holding to the wall, he made his way into the kitchen. She was not there. No sign she'd made any breakfast, or had been there recently. He looked out the back screened door. There was a large pile of junk, but Charlene was not in sight.

"Hugh Chase had a mystery to solve," Andrew said bitterly to the crap in the yard. "Where was the woman who had saved his life?"

He moved back through the hall and glanced up the stairs. The motion of tilting his head back stirred the nausea again, and the hammering in his brain grew stronger. In the shadows at the top of the steps he saw a smashed door and a dark hole beyond it. What had happened there? Had some entity blown it out? No, in? When did it happen? Was Charlene there? "Charlene?"

No answer. *Dear God, let her be all right!*

He pulled himself up the stairs with effort. "Charlene, answer me!" There was no answer. The dark room seemed to have been trashed by vandals. Or an angry witch? Charlene was not there. Neither was she elsewhere upstairs. He made his way back down.

"Charlene!" Andrew pulled on the front door. It was heavy, almost too heavy. But then it gave way, and he stumbled backward as it swung open. He regained his footing then saw her, lying on the porch next to the refrigerator box, her hair blown back, an empty teacup in her hand.

Andrew went outside and fell beside Charlene. He stared at the cup. Was this poison? Had she been forced to drink some deadly mixture? *Christ, no.* He pressed her wrist; she had a pulse, though it was very weak. He shook her, shook her again, then drove his fist against the warped wood of the porch floor.

"Charlene." He lifted her head and held it close. "What happened? What can I do? Come back to me. I love you."

3 8

~

A large flatbed truck sat in the center of the clearing. Dennis and another man were at work on one downed tree,
Dennis burring into the center of the trunk with a chainsaw,
the other man whacking smaller braches off with rhythmic
strokes of an axe. Several other men worked on other fallen
trees, chopping off small branches and feeding them into a
chipper. In the back of the flatbed was a good load of wood,
ready to take away. The trees were on her land. Dennis Boise
and his hired help were stealing lumber from Charlene's
land.

Charlene moved on to Maude's house, over open ground
and dense thickets, tall willows and stubby dogwoods. Did
Maude know of her son's theft? Surely she did. She did and
she didn't care. The Boises were in financial trouble, and
Charlene knew that could drive you to many things. She
would be angry about it later.

She reached Willow Vale in an instant, and drifted down to
the porch. Maude was not there. Charlene moved around the
house to the back, where from an open window she could
smell food cooking—a breakfast of bacon and toast. Charlene
paused at the window, unable to see through the screen, and

then with little thought, found herself inside the kitchen itself, holding at the ceiling beside a naked lightbulb.

There was bacon in a frying pan on the eye of a coal-burning stove. Beside it, a pan of water boiled. There was toast, cooked and ready, peeking up from a toaster. On a kitchen table were papers on which were written names of clients, types of wood, dates for delivery, cash paid for timber. Dennis's business records. The stealing son-of-a-bitch. Strapped in a chair at the table was Polly, one hand flailing, the other shaking atop her pregnant belly. The girl winced and glanced up, as if she sensed something was different in the room. But then she looked down again and, clumsily, grabbed a slice of toast from a plate, put it to her mouth, and pulled away a chunk.

Charlene did not see Maude right away. But she heard the woman, her voice a low whisper and then rising into a bizarre growl. It came from the corner of the kitchen, where a garbage can and a pile of old, black rags lay. Charlene watched, mesmerized, as the pile of rags raised up, straightened, and revealed itself to be Maude in a long black dress. Her glazed eyes were ringed with black soot. Streaks of soot patterned her forehead, cheeks, and chin, as if she were ready for tribal warfare. Her upper lip hitched up and down like that of a mad dog. She was chanting.

The only words Charlene recognized in the chant were her own name. "Charlene Myers...Charlene Alexander."

Oh, my God.

"Repeat with me, Polly," said Maude, moving to her granddaughter and poking her in the shoulder. "You got to learn this. You got to know how to do this before I'm gone, before your baby comes. You ain't stupid, you's stubborn!"

Polly opened her mouth, revealing the partially chewed toast, then closed it. She frowned, shook her head, and banged the table.

"Don't you disobey me!" demanded the old woman.

Polly seemed to sigh, heavily. She forced the toast down. "Shhhhhh...leeen."

The old woman went to the boiling pot and stirred it, then

reached into a bowl for crushed plant matter and dropped it into the steaming liquid. She closed her eyes and continued her chant. Then, she flung open her arms and spoke clearly, "Knife to hand, hand to throat, crush the air, slash the vein! Let the last one die at last! At her own hand, take her life!"

Polly's head bobbed, then bowed.

Maude then went back to her corner and huddled against the wall beside the trash. She smiled as if she had done something wonderful, as if she was tired and needed a rest. She said softly, "Perhaps you could not be frightened away, stupid child, but you can be tricked. Soon you will join the others in their earthy beds. It shall be done. The prize shall be mine."

Maude is the witch!

Charlene's spirit railed against the truth she'd just discovered.

It's been Maude all along, trying to get me off my land!

A hot fury rose up in Charlene's soul, then slammed her back down, hard. She could not breathe. Her mouth gulped open, closed. She panicked. *Help, help me!*

Then a rush of air filled her lungs. She gulped air, and then more. It was cold and welcomed. She opened her eyes to find herself back on the porch, back in her own flesh and bones, furious tears on her face.

And Andrew was cradling her in his arms.

39

~

Andrew stood on the porch, holding the post, his forehead pressed to the wood. "Charlene, don't face them alone."

Charlene stopped beside the well and looked back. Her hair was caught up in a ponytail, and her face was newly scrubbed. In her jeans was a piece of paper, folded neatly in her pocket, ready for the right time to pull it out if need be. "I'll be all right. For the first time in weeks—no, the first time in years—I know I'll be all right."

"Wait until I can come with you. I'm healing. Give it a day. Tomorrow."

"I have what I need to do this."

"I'm afraid for you, and for me."

Charlene smiled. She looked strong, powerful. Beautiful. "Don't be. Not anymore. I'll be back soon, I promise. Then we can start over."

Andrew lowered himself onto the top step. His head spun and his nose ached. So this was what it felt like to be a heavyweight loser. "I used to think that the supernatural was bunk. Ghosts, witches, mystical powers? You had to be kidding."

"I thought so, too."

"But now I know that whatever is, is. Something is either

real or it isn't. And if it's real, it's natural, no matter how terrifying or unfamiliar or incredible it may seem to ordinary
guys like me."

"Yep."

Andrew took one step down. "Is there anything I should do
to help while you're gone?"

"Not that I know of."

"Should I pray?"

"Couldn't hurt."

"Maybe I should make lunch? I saw a can of Spam in the
kitchen." He didn't feel like joking but didn't know what else
to say.

Charlene chuckled softly. "Okay."

"So you'll be back, safe and sound? You aren't going to get
yourself killed. I think I'd have a lot of trouble with another
death."

"No, I'm not. I promise."

Suddenly, behind Andrew, the front door slammed shut.
Andrew looked at Charlene. "Maybe you're protected. But
I'm not so sure I am."

"Can you keep up? With your bad leg and all?"

"I'll find a stick. I'll keep up."

Charlene waited as Andrew limped over to her, then together they cut across the yard, and entered the dense growth
of trees.

40

~

"What the hell are you doing here? This is dangerous work," demanded Dennis as he placed his chainsaw in the front seat of his flatbed truck and slammed the door shut. His partner, some mute redneck, stood idly by in the clearing, watching, listening. The other men, wearing heavy gloves and holding armloads of jagged branches, stopped their work to watch.

"This is the corner of my land," said Charlene. "You're stealing from me. Though," she added with a smile, "in the greater scheme of things, it's pretty much the least of my concerns."

"Who the hell is that?" Dennis nodded at the edge of the trees, where Andrew held to his makeshift oak branch crutch. Andrew stood as straight and defiantly as he could, legs apart like a gunslinger, head up. His nose had been smacked with a low, thorny limb, cutting open the wound beneath the bandage, and it was seeping bright red. But he had not complained and he had kept up. And he was ready to come out swinging if need be.

Charlene said, "You best be asking yourself who I am, Dennis."

"I know who you are."

"No, you really don't."

"Get away from the front of my truck. I'm moving it. You'll get run over."

Charlene placed her foot on the front bumper and tossed her ponytail. "You won't run me over."

"You know I will. What's wrong with you?"

"You know I found Phoebe Alexander's spells."

Dennis pushed back his ball cap. His mouth opened and then snapped closed. Rage played across the sun-wrinkled skin on his face. He said, "I don't know what you're talking about."

"Yes, you do."

"My mother burned them. Burned them all when you gave them to her the other night."

"She didn't burn my memory."

"Roy," said Dennis, snapping his head in the direction of the redneck, "move this bitch out of the way so we can get this wood out of here."

Roy held up his hands and said, "Nope, sorry." The other three workers were already trotting away, getting the hell out of Dodge.

"Roy!" snarled Dennis.

Roy shook his head. "I know 'bout them Alexanders. You hardly pay me 'nough to cut wood on her land, let 'lone touch one of 'em."

"She's nothing, she can do nothing!"

"Oh, really?" said Charlene. "Then why do you look like you're ready to pee your pants?"

"Go get my mother, Roy," said Dennis. His voice was faltering. It was a beautiful sound. "She'll talk some sense into this little girl."

Roy ran off through the trees. Dennis and Charlene stood in the sun, staring at each other, gazes locked as if in a standoff. In Charlene's jeans pocket was her spell, in case she might forget the words. It was a spell she had written, on her own. She was not absolutely certain it would work, but she had to try. For her sake. For Andrew's.

When she had come back into her body at Homeplace, Charlene had been terrified with the knowledge that Maude was a witch, *the* witch. It was the old woman who had caused the animals to break their necks. She had caused the phone interference, had made dead rabbits squirm and return to the porch after they were burned. She had given Charlene the dreadful visions and had put the knife in her hand so she would kill herself. Her magic had thrown Yule Lemons's car into the ravine.

Phoebe was long dead. William was long dead. The other Alexander women were dead. None of them haunted Homeplace. All were tucked in graves or absorbed by elements of nature. Gone and almost forgotten. The hauntings were all Maude's doing. She wanted Charlene frightened off the land or dead.

But then Charlene had thought, *What of the hand that knocked me down the steps in the Children's House? It gave me a splinter that forced me to use my left hand to paint. My untrained left hand was free to make paintings and write out the potions. It showed me that terrible parlor. It wanted me to know, to see, to understand. Surely some insightful spirit did this to me, a kinder spirit, not Maude.*

There was something else at work, something other than Maude's sorcery. It wasn't a ruse to trick Charlene, as Maude had suggested.

And now Charlene stood near Dennis Boise as Maude came tapping out from the trees, her dirty shoes puffing along the dust of the clearing, her clothes changed back to flowered skirt, yellow blouse, and pink sweater.

"Charlene, what's the matter, honey?" she said. "What are you doing here? Roy says there's trouble, but that's all he'd say. Has something bad happened?"

Charlene was silent. She wanted to see how Maude would try to shape things.

Maude reached Dennis's side and gave him an exasperated glance. Then she looked at Charlene. "Ah, I see. You're upset 'cause Dennis been taking your trees. Oh, if I could make that better I would. You see, truth be known we don't have as much money as we needed this month, and it's jus' a few trees, an' I didn't think it would matter much if..."

Charlene abruptly lifted her chin and raised her index finger. Maude went quiet, her mouth holding open slightly. *Maybe she's afraid I might have power. That's good, very good.*

"I don't care about the trees he's taken, though he'll never take another one from me."

"No?" said Maude. "Why, thank you, honey, you're mighty understanding."

"I'm more understanding than you even know..."

"I'm sure you are."

"...you fucking witch."

From the edge of the trees, she heard Andrew clear his throat.

Maude froze and blinked twice. Then her expression changed in a heart's beat, melting into another form—from that of kind old woman to enraged sorceress. Her voice dropped nearly an octave, her body drew up, and her eyes flashed. "So, you think you know something about something? Don't fool yourself."

Charlene was startled by the old woman's transformation. Sweat broke out under her arms. It was an effort to keep her voice even and cool. "You know, you were right in one respect. Phoebe was, and is, a powerful spirit. And she did frighten me with some things she did. Frightened the hell out of me, actually. But nothing she did was to harm me, only to get my attention. To show me the truth and teach me about my family. It was you who tried to scare me, and then, to kill me."

Dennis backed away behind the truck, sensing the rising tide. *Fucking baby.*

"Silly, stupid child," hissed Maude.

Charlene felt Andrew watching the scene. She felt the equal measure of angst and anger that radiated from him.

"Phoebe shared her recipes with me," said Charlene with a toss of her head. "I wanted to show them to you, but you talked me into giving them to you to burn. That was silly, yes."

Maude chuckled, a deep sound like that of an animal preparing for the kill.

"But I remembered several," Charlene continued. "One was a recipe that let me fly out of myself, let me travel over the forest and right down to Willow Vale. To your house. Into your kitchen, where I saw you casting a spell that was supposed to make me kill myself. But I'm protected. I didn't kill myself and I won't."

Maude flinched, then snarled.

The woman's second of unease gave Charlene more confidence. "You wanted to frighten me off at first, but when I wouldn't leave you wanted me dead. I don't understand why, though. That's my big question. You killed Yule and tried to kill Andrew. Why all this violence?"

"She killed Howard, too," said Andrew. "Yule's cousin. Burned him to death in the old mill."

Charlene didn't turn around. Someone else had died? *God damn this woman!*

Maude nodded, proudly. "Folks around here know better than to snoop on Homeplace. Howard knew better."

"But why go to all that trouble? To keep people away, to be rid of me? Are a few acres of logs worth such effort?"

"Logs! Them's just Dennis's way o' bringin' in some cash. Got nothing to do with you or your kind, Miss Alexander."

Charlene moved from the front of the truck. She wanted a clear shot when the time came. "Answer my question, or I will kill you. You're on my land now, and I have a witch's advantage with that."

Maude's eyes went blue to near black, a horrifying alteration, and Charlene struggled to keep her stare. "You can't hurt me, Alexander," Maude said. "You ain' no witch!"

"I wasn't yesterday."

Maude's body trembled with anger, but then a pitiless smile spread across her lips. "What harm can it do, to tell you now, now you got so little time to live? You hear this, too, Mr. Marshall. You got roots 'round Adams, don' you, boy? I know about you, your family. The Pinkertons was nothin' but a footnote in Adams history."

"Now that's just being petty," said Andrew.

Charlene burst out laughing.

Maude sneered. "There's always been rivalry 'tween the Boises and the Alexanders. The Alexander men what built Homeplace were brutish, cruel, like mos' men. When Phoebe Black married into the Alexander family, she was a docile wife, pretty but weak, worthless 'cept for breedin'. She bore her husband thirteen children in thirteen years. William Alexander and his brother Sean cleared much of the land and tried to raise tobacco, forcing their slaves to work in the fields, sixteen hours a day, more sometimes. If a slave died in the sun, William left 'em to rot, to fertilize the soil. William weren' no better with his own children. He hated their whinin' and their cryin'. He'd go in a fit o' rage in an instant, lockin' them in that cabin, then throwin' them into the well to die. Sean was harsh like his brother. He killed his wife, Ada, for spillin' soup. She was carryin' his third son and he didn' hardly care."

Charlene sensed Andrew coming up behind her, but didn't want to turn to tell him to stop. It was not safe to turn her back on Maude.

Maude pursed her lips. "Phoebe, well, she couldn' take no more. She trained herself in witchcraft, took control from William and Sean. She made brews, potions. She let herself to get pregnant once more, and after her daughter was born she sterilized her husband. But she kept him there under her thumb to do the heavy labor, makin' him build a textile mill for the cotton crops she wanted to raise. Sean she drove away with visions o' hell. She set the slaves free, let 'em to stay on if they wanted. An' they did, workin' that mill. But Phoebe weren't no angel, she weren't no saint. She used devilment to lure slaves from neighboring farms, and made 'em a safe haven in the old mill. Was that her business to steal from others? No, ma'am!

"Phoebe raised her child, Sarah, and Ada's boys, but once the boys was grown she sent them off. Didn' want no men around. Didn' trust 'em. Course, men around Nelson County didn' trust her or her family, neither. Some point she got beat to death by some young boys from Adams. Her body got ate up by wild animals, an' you'd think good riddance, wouldn't you?"

"It wasn't riddance, though, was it?" said Charlene. "Her body might have been gone, but her spirit stayed at Homeplace."

Maude ignored this. "Phoebe'd taught her magic tricks to her daughter, Sarah. Then, each new generation o' Alexander women practiced the craft. Each produced only one child, a girl, by couplin' with unsuspecting travelin' salesmen or preachers. This way, the family'd go on forever."

Charlene's breath caught. *Was it really Phoebe, then, who had me overpower Andrew, and not one of Maude's cold tricks?*

"Phoebe'd swore the family would never give up their land. T'was as much a part of the family as the mothers and the daughters."

My mother was the first to marry. The first of the line to never live at Homeplace, to ignore the legacy. The first to have more than one child.

But no. She had only one. Me. Ryan is my stepfather's child. My stepbrother.

"I see the confusion in your face, Miss Alexander," said Maude.

"But why do you want me gone?" Charlene repeated.

"The Boise family was rich in them days. But the Alexanders made my family poor, lured our slaves away so we couldn't farm our land! When the constables came lookin' for the slaves at Homeplace, they was scared off by witchcraft. Alexander women charmed the deer and other game to their land, and then punished our men when they come on Homeplace property looking for somethin' to hunt! We tried to farm, but the rain favored Homeplace and the insects favored Willow Vale. Boise women found out 'bout the Alexanders' witchery. Decided to fight them on their own terms. We learned the craft ourselves to battle Phoebe and her kind. No matter how hard we struggled, we got more in debt. We lost our land some forty years ago."

Maude lifted a clenched fist and shook it 'at the sky. A cloud drifted across the sun, casting a cold shadow on the two women in the clearing.

"Maude," said Charlene, "I didn't do any of this to you."

"You's my long-standing enemy. I'll have your land, I'll see you dead, and I'll spit in Phoebe's eye!"

"That's insane."

Maude laughed. "Oh, I tried to scare Ellen away, but she knew witchcraft. So did your grandma, who kept her spell on the place even though she didn' live there no more. But when your mama took over, I knew the end of our battle was comin' soon. I met your mama at Ellen's ninetieth birthday party. Shook her hand, knew in that minute she had cancer startin' to grow and she'd be dead before I was. She had one daughter. And a sterile child at that."

"What are you saying, sterile?"

"Puh, I knew it when we first met in the cemetery. Makes my life easier. No more Alexanders once you all died out. I'll have got my family redeemed, won out over all the ills you done to us, will have outlived you all! I'll have got done what my mother said I had to do, lest she come for me in my sleep. And Polly, she gonna have a baby. Paid a boy in town twenty dollars to do her, since I don' think Polly'll ever be married, never have a boyfriend. But the boy didn' care, he wanted that twenty dollars, and Polly didn' fight. That baby will be in my stead. Our family will live on. Yours won't."

Is she wrong? Can she know if I'm barren? "Why didn't you just kill me, Maude? Why all the games, the tricks? Why all this wasted energy on me?"

Maude hesitated, her smile faltering.

Then Charlene knew. "You can't kill an Alexander, can you? You're not only poor in money, you're poor in power. You could kill other people to keep them out of the way, but not me. You can only chase me away or cause me to kill myself!"

Maude pointed her bony finger at Charlene. Charlene could see a flicker of fire dancing on its tip. She stepped closer to Charlene, eyes narrowed. "You've seen my power! Don' doubt I can do what I want."

"And," said Charlene, "don't doubt I can do what *I* want!"

With her hand in her pocket, should she need to draw it out, Charlene recited her spell, shouting as loudly as she could, raising her own hands and waving them toward Maude Boise.

"From now 'til ever, be here, but gone, well before the next red dawn. From now 'til ever, be here, but gone, the wrath of all, your head to be on."

Dennis put his hands over his ears and cried out, "Stop! Stop it!"

"From now 'til ever, be here, but gone, well before the next red dawn. From now 'til ever, be here, but gone, the wrath of all, your head to be on!"

Maude began to chant in her own slurring, mysterious language. *"Adu-conlo-randi-jenida-scifay!"* Fire crackled and popped from all her fingers now, dancing like tiny, freakish fairies. Charlene could feel the ground heat up like a brasier beneath her.

"From now 'til ever, be here, but gone!"

The air now hummed, rippling, feverish. Charlene's skin prickled and the hairs on her arms danced in protest. She closed her eyes to focus. Maude's chants grew louder, stronger. *"Adu-conlo-randi-jenida-scifay!"*

"Well before the next red dawn!" Charlene shouted. And then she heard it, a slight echo following her own voice. Other voices that were chanting along with her. Not Andrew's voice, but female voices. "From now 'til ever, be here, but gone!" They rose up around her, chanting powerfully, forcefully, in a melodic blend of intonations and key. Charlene could feel them around her, invisible hands reaching for her, holding her, supporting her. They were the Alexander women, come to help her, their last chance to survive. "The wrath of all, your head to be on!"

Charlene opened her eyes and faced the witch. Maude stood directly in front of Charlene, just an arm's length away, her eyes solid black, her face contorted, her teeth flashing like razors, her fingers ablaze. "You'll kill yourself now!" Maude screamed, and raised her hand for one last incantation.

But Charlene and the spirits of the Alexander women shouted, together, "From now 'til ever, be here, but gone!"

A brilliant, orgasmic energy blew from Charlene's hands and coiled around Maude's neck like a phantom noose. Dennis, behind the truck, cried out. Andrew shouted something Charlene could not understand above the screams. Maude grabbed at her throat and clawed, but the energy expanded, moved across her face and down her body, wrapping her in a glowing shroud. Maude gasped, unable to breathe, until Charlene chanted one last time, "Be here but gone be here but gone be here but gone be here but gone!"

In an instant, the energy did what Charlene's spell had been created to do. Maude was transformed into a tiny, hideous, twisted creature that squealed, pig-like, and scrambled away into the forest on its six spindly legs.

Charlene gasped a breath. And another. Another. She leaned down to catch her knees and her equilibrium. When she looked up, Dennis and his truck were gone. He would stay gone, she was certain.

"I didn't want to kill her," she said to Andrew, to herself, to the spirits of the Alexander women whom she knew had already gone. "I don't even like to kill mice."

"I know." Charlene turned around. Andrew was holding out his arms, his branch cane on the ground, his face full of awe, understanding, and love. She moved to him and he encircled her.

"I didn't want to kill anybody." She was surprised to find herself crying.

"You didn't."

"I just wanted her to leave me the hell alone."

"I know."

41

~

Chapter One

Hugh Chase had no idea what he was going to face when he first went out to the ranch house on the far side of the canyon. He was the new sheriff in town, a reluctant recruit who had spent most of his adult life herding cattle across the Great Plain. He'd heard there'd been trouble brewing at the ranch house, but didn't know what he would be riding into.

"You like westerns?" Andrew asked.

Charlene flipped the slices of Spam over in the frying pan. Damn, but that new stove was nice. "I don't think I ever read one."

"No Louis L'Amour?"

"Nope."

Andrew leaned back in the kitchen chair and put his foot up on the chair across from him. He stared at the laptop screen. Under the table, Rex snored softly. "Hey, I could make it science fiction. Hugh Chase could be a brilliant alien who comes to Earth to solve mysteries no one else can solve, using his unique powers."

"Oh, I don't think so."

"No?"

"No. Stick with the human detective."

"Yeah?"

"Yeah."

Late afternoon sunlight filtered low and warm through the kitchen windows. The screened porch off the kitchen was gone; Andrew had discovered termites in the flooring and had dismantled it and hauled the wood away and rolled the screen up for some future use that he couldn't really think of. At the far side of the backyard, the trees of the forest were in full late-October regalia, fireworks of reds and oranges and golds. Beyond the forest, the mountains lay a silvered lavender against the sky.

Charlene's stepbrother and his wife were coming the first weekend in November. Andrew had spent his free afternoons helping her get the house into more livable condition. Wobbly front porch slats had been repaired and a brand new white porch swing with a blue and green plaid cushion had been installed just outside the living room window. All the broken windows in the house had been replaced, and vinyl flooring had been ordered for the kitchen. The bathroom cubicle had a new toilet, shower stall, and mirrored vanity and sink. The new appliances from Siebers were in place. One of Charlene's favorite improvements was the addition of a genuine spigot in the kitchen and a water heater large enough to provide hot water for an hour-long shower. The upstairs bedrooms had been scoured and furnished with beds, dressers, and chairs. The windowless parlor at the top of the stairs had been cleaned out and boarded up again, the shattered, broken, and tainted furnishings burned in a silent ceremony in the driveway.

Charlene had briefly protested that all Andrew had done and was doing was too expensive, that she feared never being able to reciprocate. Andrew had said, "If this helps you get back to painting, then it's worth it." Charlene had hesitated, but Andrew had added, "When you make your first million, you can get on a repayment plan. How's that?" She said that worked for her.

Charlene scooped up the meat, one piece at a time, and slid it onto hamburger buns. She brought the sandwiches to the table and sat next to Andrew. Andrew pushed the laptop back. Charlene reached for his hand.

"How you doing?" he asked.

"Okay." She looked at him, the sun's glow dancing on her auburn hair.

"Yeah? Want me to hang around here tonight?"

"I think I'm going to bed early, so only if you want to." Charlene tapped his thumb.

"You sure you're okay?"

She shrugged. "I don't have much energy right now. I'd like to paint. I feel really good about the cemetery scene I've got going on the easel. But I just feel...funny."

"Why don't you eat? That might help."

Charlene picked up the sandwich, grimaced, and put it back. "I don't know. Just looking at that Spam, just smelling it makes me feel woozy."

"Are you coming down with something?"

"I better not."

"You feel like going to bed now?"

"Ha."

"No, I mean going to bed bed. To sleep."

"That might be a good idea." Charlene stood up. She seemed a little wobbly. Andrew and Rex helped her upstairs. Andrew tucked her in and gave her a careful kiss on the forehead. "Love you," he whispered.

"Love you, too," she whispered back.

Back downstairs, Andrew stood in the living room, arms crossed, and looked at Charlene's painting-in-progress as Rex found a sleeping spot on the new braided rug. The painting was stunning—a poignant portrait of headstones, marble and granite etched with time and shadowed in the past, tangled and forgotten, yet poised as though waiting for the rays of sun, which appear in the tree branches overhead, to touch them, to affirm their existence.

"This one's going to knock them on their asses," Andrew said. "This one is going to put Charlene's name in lights. If artists put their names in lights, that is."

He glanced about the room, at the fireplace, the window, the ceiling, the front hall. There had been no more visits from Phoebe or any of the other Alexander women. The few weeks since Maude's "change" and Dennis's disappearance had been peaceful and productive. Andrew had suggested that Phoebe might be upset that a man was now spending so much time at Homeplace, but Charlene countered, "I don't think Phoebe knew, or ever allowed herself to know, that a man could be as caring as you."

Andrew returned to the kitchen, happy that at least for today, his leg wasn't aching. He ate his sandwich, wiped off his hands, and began typing.

The woman who owned the ranch house had long been labeled peculiar by all the folks in town, from the saloon keeper to the schoolmarm to the ranch hands who came in and out of town on business to the children who played cowboy in the streets. Some feared the woman because there were rumors she could cast spells on anyone who crossed her path. Others thought she was a gunslinger who could kill with ease at two hundred paces. And so when Hugh rode his...

"Is a palomino too stereotypical?" Rex was still back in the living room on the rug. "Probably."

...his pinto across the dusty stretch leading to the log structure, he wondered what the hell he was getting into. And when she stepped out onto the wide front porch, one hand on her hip and the other shading her eyes, her loose hair and full skirt flapping in a hot Arizona wind, he knew there would be trouble in more ways than one. But it could be good trouble. And he was willing to give it a go.

Andrew heard a soft, irregular clicking moving toward the kitchen. It was Rex. The dog snuggled up under the table against Andrew's leg.

"I guess I can't use bodies in a ferry bathroom in this one, can I?" asked Andrew.

Rex grunted, rolled over, sighed.

"You're right, buddy. Thanks."

Epilogue

December came with snow and ice and a rash of new watercolor paintings completed in the Homeplace living room. Andrew sold his Victorian and moved in with Charlene, creating a tidy law office in one of the bedrooms overlooking the front yard. Polly Boise, who was discovered living alone at Willow Vale by Charlene and a Nelson County social service worker, went into labor and delivered a healthy, five-pound baby boy at the hospital in Charlottesville. Andrew and Charlene visited her in the maternity ward, and on hearing that Polly and her baby would become wards of the state, signed the papers to let them live at Homeplace.

"Maude, wherever she is now, would hate the idea of a Boise at Homeplace," Charlene told Andrew. "And I think Phoebe, wherever she is now, would approve. The only thing she really wanted was to protect the innocents."

Come February, Charlene's own condition was obvious. Maude may have been right when she detected sterility, but if she was, Phoebe had exerted her own powers to correct the problem.

Polly proved to be a surprisingly helpful addition around the house. Not only did she care for her child tenderly and determinedly, but two of her favorite activities were running the vacuum cleaner and doing laundry. For fun, Charlene gave Polly a set of paints, and she created wild and glorious modern expressionistic pieces, several of which Charlene framed and hung in Polly's room.

In May, Charlene sent the first slides of her watercolors to Norfolk galleries. All of the gallery heads phoned her immediately, begging her to solo with them first. "Incredible work!" they cooed. "Masterpieces!"

Late June arrived with the completion of Andrew's first novel, *Mystery on the Boston Harbor*, and the birth of Opal Marshall-Alexander Myers.

At Homeplace, spiders still spun their webs in the corners, mice continued to scurry in the walls. Baby rabbits were born under the smokehouse. A new generation of birds nested in the Children's House.

And the screams in the well were never heard again.